THE SECRET

THE TUESDAY CLUB BOOK ONE

LULU MOORE

Cover Art by Lori Jackson

Photography by Michelle Lancaster @lanefotograph

Model Chad Hurst

Editing by Katy Nielsen

To all parents everywhere. Single or otherwise.
You are superheroes.

PROLOGUE

We all know Mondays have a bad rep as the worst day of the week, but Tuesday, Tuesday sneaks up on you. Tuesday is the day that the serious shit goes down because you're lulled into the false sense of security that the worst day of the week is over.

Because you're not ready for it.

Because you're not looking over your shoulder.

Case in point…

Tuesday was the day Penn found out he'd flunked his mid-terms.

Tuesday was the day Rafe got dumped by Bronwyn Chambers, his high-school sweetheart, the girl he lost his virginity to and the one who decided in the first week of college she'd rather be with a future pro-athlete than a future lawyer. He cried for a while after that one.

And Tuesday was the day Murray missed out on the finals of the Ivy League Swimming Conference, the one he was about to sweep gold on, because of a freak ice storm that caused him to slip outside the pool house and break his leg.

So they did the only sensible thing they could do; they took a stance, and The Tuesday Club was born with three rules - no girls, no drama, no injuries. Tuesday was the new boys' night in at the Beacon Hill brownstone.

And it continues to this day. With the same three members.

Who aren't paying close enough attention...

1

MURRAY

There's a pivotal moment in everyone's life that fundamentally changes who they are. Everyone has it. You don't know when it'll happen, but you know when it does. And in order to survive it, in order to get through the lung-crushing, heart-stopping, neck-breaking speed at which it occurs, you need your friends with you.

Let me introduce myself. My name is Murray Williams, and the two bozos standing behind me arguing about the Yankees new relief pitcher are my best friends in the world, Rafe Latham and Penn Shepherd. Friends for over a decade, we met on the first day of college where the three of us had been assigned the same dorm, and I was the Brit who'd flown in to have his higher education experience in the good ol' U.S. of A. We sized each other up for thirty seconds, then cracked open some beers and bonded for life.

I know what you're thinking… Why's he telling me this? Who cares? Why should I give a shit?

And I'm almost in agreement. Except for one thing. Because that pivotal moment I mentioned?

I was about to have mine.

The doors to the elevator opened and Barclay let out a loud single bark, running forward down the long corridor, causing Rafe and Penn to momentarily pause their heated discussion about Ace Watson.

That was odd. My black Labrador wasn't known for barking much.

"Huh."

Rafe resumed his bouncing of the basketball he'd carried back from our weekly game as we followed Barclay in the direction he ran, toward my apartment door at the very end, where he was sniffing a large package. Or box.

I squinted down the darkened hallway.

Was that a baby car seat?

Barclay stopped sniffing and was now whining softly, lying down as we reached him.

Turns out, the most obvious question to ask isn't always the one asked. I probably would have wanted to know why there was a baby in a car seat outside my apartment, but actually, Penn was more on the money.

"Everyone else is seeing a baby, right?"

Rafe and I both looked at him before we all peered back down at the tiny infant sleeping soundly, wrapped in a blanket and wearing a little pink striped hat.

"Yes. I am."

I looked up and down the corridor to see if there was someone standing there, waiting to claim this infant… But no. And I couldn't hear anyone trying to hold in their laughter as they pissed themselves at what they thought was the most hilarious prank they'd ever played. Although this was a stretch, even for my friends.

I didn't know anyone who'd just had a baby, and I also didn't know anyone who'd be willing to part with their child even to make one of my very real nightmares come true. I had one other neighbor on this floor, an actor, each of us taking one side of the building, and as far as I knew, he didn't have a child. He was also currently out of the country filming his latest movie.

Rafe bent down and lifted out something I hadn't noticed - a thick brown envelope tucked into the side between the baby and the car seat; an envelope with my name on it.

"Okay, this isn't fucking funny anymore. Which one of you two is responsible?"

But I could tell by the looks on their faces that they were just as horrified as I was. And the ball-shriveling, New York February cold we'd just walked in from had nothing on the icy chill spreading through my chest and rattling my bones.

We stood there, all three of us, in a state of shock; the type of shock you only experienced when you find an abandoned baby on your doorstep.

"Barclay, stay here," I ordered, running to the elevator, pressing the buttons as fast as I could, hoping it would sense the emergency and arrive in seconds - which it did.

The elevator dropped, following my stomach which was currently located somewhere in the Pits of Hell. This had to be a joke, it had to be. And yet, even as I willed it, the tiny voice in my head was saying it wasn't. That baby had been left for a reason.

Fuck. Who leaves a fucking baby?

And how long had it been there? I'd been gone all day.

I raced out of the elevator doors before they'd had a chance to fully open, and over to the concierge desk where the evening porter was on duty.

"Kevin, did someone come and ask for me today?"

He stopped typing into the computer he was using. "Yes, sir, about an hour ago. She said she was a friend of yours and had to drop a package off. I remember because she had a baby with her."

My eyes widened in horror. "And you let her up?"

The apartments in this building started at the low tens of millions, bought by the wealthy to ensure not only privacy, but the utmost security which they needed in their lives, and allowing someone up without permission would cause a major uproar among the residents. Aside from my movie star neighbor, I knew of at least ten more A-list Hollywood types who owned apartments in this building, as well as many of my colleagues from the world of finance. I was probably one of the youngest residents, but I bought it for its old-world English charm and incredible views over Central Park. And no one socialized in this building anyway, so it didn't really matter.

"No, sir, of course not. You weren't home. I asked her if she wanted to wait or leave it with me, but she said she'd come back. My apologies, I forgot to tell you when you walked in."

"Well she fucking got up somehow! Her package was a baby. She left her fucking baby. How could you not notice?" My voice bounced off the cavernous vestibule of the building, making my anger seem even more pronounced than it was which was saying something, because I was on the verge of breathing fire and summoning a cloud of brimstone to rain down on their heads.

The blood drained from his face so quickly I was genuinely worried he might collapse.

"Wh... What?"

"There's a baby on my doorstep," I repeated slowly, so he didn't miss a single word.

A hidden door opened behind him and out walked Graham, a second porter, and the one who was usually in charge, having clearly heard my shouting. To be fair, my current volume levels could probably raise the dead.

"Evening, Murray. Is everything okay?"

"No, everything is not okay. I want to know how a

woman with a baby got up to my apartment and left it outside."

"Left her baby?" His reaction mirrored Kevin's. "Are you sure?"

The expression of incredulity my face was currently sporting told him *yes, I was fucking sure.*

My phone had been buzzing in my pocket the entire time I'd been shouting, and I reached in to turn it off only to notice Penn's name.

"Hey, man, where did you go? You need to get back here."

"I'm in the lobby, trying to find out how the fuck someone got up to my apartment without a pass and left a baby outside my door." I was answering Penn, but all my animosity was directed straight at Graham and Kevin. "But it's clearly because the security here is as efficient as a chocolate fucking tea pot."

"Get them to bring you the security tapes, it'll be on there. But you need to come back."

"Okay." I hung up and pointed to the cameras discretely placed around the building. "I want that footage. Now. Bring it up to me."

I stormed back the way I came, back to the epicenter of the explosion that was currently my life.

Penn and Rafe had let themselves in and I found them in the kitchen, the baby still in the car seat and currently parked on the island counter. I gave it a wide berth, like I would anything that had the potential to detonate, and perched on the kitchen table instead. Penn took one look at me and disappeared.

Rafe had opened the letter and was reading through it, pages and pages of something I knew instinctively was about to blow my life apart. His expert eyes flickered as they scanned across the words. He was an excellent lawyer, even if he did look like he belonged in a biker gang most of the time.

When he wasn't dressed like a choirboy in a suit and tie, he was usually seen with full sleeves of tats, riding about on one of his vintage Harleys, or in any number of his sports cars, especially the Bugatti.

"Do I want to know what that letter says?"

I mean, I didn't. I really, *really* didn't.

He kept reading, his eyes still moving. "Well, apparently she's yours."

The rest of my stomach bottomed out as he finally looked up and I gripped onto the edges of the table to stop myself from falling over, because the room was spinning worse than anything any hangover could produce.

"How?" I managed to croak.

"Do you remember last Memorial Day when we were up at the house?"

I nodded, because even without specifics, I knew we'd been there. Every Memorial Day weekend since we'd been at college had been spent at the summer house Rafe's family owned in Bridgehampton.

"Yes, what about it?"

"That was when it happened."

"Allegedly." Penn returned carrying a bottle of twenty-five-year-old Glenfiddich single malt scotch and three glasses. "And anyway, that weekend is always boys, so there's no fucking way it happened then."

Rafe shook his head. "I thought that, but remember Rory and the boys turned up with that group of girls they'd met on the way and decided to bring them along too?"

Penn's paused in the pouring of the bottle as his memory came back. "Fucking Rory."

Rory was Rafe's youngest brother. He'd taken the weekend off from Harvard and brought his housemates. And while Rafe had never played Varsity, Rory was the king; Quarterback and Captain of the football team. He was a legend among his peers, and a magnet for all women. His whole house was, because they all played together and sport was currency. He'd turned up explaining to Rafe that a weekend of just guys was a wasted weekend, and the girls would join us for twenty four hours, then leave.

Which they did, but not before making it clear what they were up for.

We'd all got very drunk, and I'd ended up wrapped around a beautiful brunette several times over the course of the evening, all night and the next morning. We never exchanged numbers and afterwards went our separate ways, or rather, she'd left with the girls as Rory had agreed.

And the most I could say about it was… it was fun.

"Annabel? Lizzie? Fuck. I can't remember what she was called. And I don't think I ever knew her last name."

"Reagan…" he shook one of the pages at me. "She clearly knew who you were."

That wasn't hard. I was in the financial pages more often than not, not to mention that the three of us were regularly featured in any number of fucking stupid lists of Most Eligible Bachelors or whatever. As much as Rafe tried to stay under the radar with his do-good, not-for-profit legal aid firm, his family name got him noticed, and even if Penn wasn't currently on a one-man mission to fuck every single actress/model/singer between the ages of eighteen and forty in a massive but totally unnecessary act of rebellion, he was practically American aristocracy, and anything he did garnered headline news. Couple that with the fact my two brothers-in-law were part of New York's sporting elite…

Bottom line, people knew who we were. We liked to party, but we also worked fucking hard and had no plans to apologize for it, unless legally required to - which Penn had been - on more than one occasion.

"I want a paternity test. I have never had sex without suiting up."

"I agree, and I'll sort one out, but I have to say, I don't

think this is financial. She's signed over everything. There's not even a birth certificate, so we have to sort that immediately. She doesn't want this baby."

My head fell in my hands. What the fuck was happening? Was I in some kind of alternate universe that I was about to return from at any second?

"Why didn't she have an abortion? Or put it up for adoption?" Penn handed me a glass of scotch, which went straight down my throat.

Women could do whatever they wanted with their bodies, I was not one to judge, but if you didn't want a kid then don't have one to just give it away. My sister, Freddie, had been adopted, and there was no shame in that either. But he had a point, because however you looked at it, this situation was fucked up and I'd been left to pick up the pieces.

"She said she found out too late and couldn't go through with adoption; she said she tried. She also said her family doesn't know; she's kept it a secret. She was still on her parents' insurance."

Penn looked at my ashen face and asked the question I didn't want to. "Fuck, how old was she?"

"Twenty-five."

I sighed in relief and pushed off the table, needing to pace.

"Fuck. Fuck's sake. A secret? Why didn't she come to me sooner? I could have helped her."

"Dude, don't shout too loudly." Penn's eyes shot over to the baby.

"How long have we been here?"

Rafe looked at his watch. "An hour?"

"Fuuuuck," I hissed, pulling on the ends of my hair. If I knew anything about babies it was that they didn't sleep for long, and this bomb was ticking on borrowed time. "What the fuck do I do? Was there anything else in the car seat?"

"Like a return policy?"

Penn's lip was quivering, and at any other time I would have found it funny, likely something I would have said myself. But not right now. Right now my teeth were grinding hard to distract myself from the bile churning inside me.

"No," I seethed through my teeth. "Like diapers, milk. We need something for when she wakes up."

Penn peered around the car seat as gingerly as an explosives' expert would a tripwire, patting gently before lifting the blanket, but came up empty.

"Nothing? Seriously?"

He shook his head with a grimace. He had sisters, he was also aware of the consequences of a screaming, hungry baby, and promptly snatched my key card up and took off. "I'll be back."

Barclay got up and followed him, his tail wagging.

"Hello?" A voice called, getting nearer.

My head shot up from where it was resting on the table, to see Graham hovering in the kitchen doorway, looking nervously at the car seat. Barclay returned with him, glued to his side, sniffing excitedly around his pockets, hoping to be given one of the biscuits Graham usually carried with him.

Traitor.

"Penn told me to come in."

"Tell me someone has come to claim 'the package'." Even though deep down, I knew there was no way of that ever happening.

"No." He held out his hand. "I have the security footage."

Rafe raised an eyebrow, walking over and taking it from him. "Thanks, Graham."

"Have you watched it?"

He nodded, his eyes holding mine but filling with remorse. "I let her up. I'm sorry, Murray. I didn't even… I could never have imagined…"

I wanted to see what was on the USB before I decided whether I was feeling forgiving or not, seeing as either way there was still a baby asleep in my kitchen that someone was claiming to be mine. I leaned across the table and pulled my Macbook over, holding my hand in the air for Rafe to chuck me the footage.

It fired up in black and white. She was wearing a bobble hat and a thick winter coat, the car seat down by her side. I watched her speak to Kevin and start to walk away, but then Kevin turned his back. She snuck around the side at the same time Graham had exited the third elevator and he'd swiped his card, letting her straight up.

Everyone wanted to help a woman struggling with a baby. No one doubted that there would ever be an ulterior motive.

My head dropped in my hands. I was going to be sick.

"I'm sorry, Murray." Graham's face was still ashen.

"It wasn't your fault. Anyone would have done the same."

"Let me know if there's anything you need. Or anything we can do."

"Thanks."

He didn't hang around for any longer than he had to, and I heard the door shut behind him as he made a swift exit.

I looked back over at Rafe. "Do we need to call the police? Do we have to tell anyone? When can we get this paternity test?"

"I'll try and get someone here tonight. I can call in some favors. I suggest we don't go down the route of social services until we get the results. But if you are her father, and as nothing is filled out, we need to get it done immediately and get round the issue of the birth certificate. I'll see if I can get an extension, but if I do it'll be one of days, not weeks. And you'll need to name her."

Oh Jesus.

I could hear his words, understand them as they made

their way into my brain… but the pressure of everything he was saying was bearing down on me like a thundercloud and finally my body caught up.

She really wasn't coming back. Who doesn't name their kid?

I barely made it to the kitchen sink before I threw up everything I had in my stomach and more, until there was nothing left and my internal organs were hanging on for dear life.

"Oh my God." My knuckles gripping the counter were as white as the fresh snow we'd been skiing on during our New Year trip to Jackson Hole.

How had our regular Tuesday night game of basketball turned into a checklist of tasks I had to accomplish for a kid that may or may not be mine? Fucking bastard Tuesday.

Penn arrived back and dumped several giant grocery bags from CVS on the counter. I heard him rummaging around in one before handing me a bottle of electrolytes.

Rafe walked out with a phone to his ear.

"Thanks." I twisted the cap and swigged it, trying to rid myself of the acid burning my throat.

I looked around at the haul; he must have bought the entire store out of diapers and formula. I was momentarily raised out of my haze to find Penn staring at me.

"I didn't know what to get, so I got everything I could find for a newborn. But, I know my sister had this because I fed Romy with it once when I was babysitting." He ripped open a box and pulled out what appeared to be a pre-made bottle of formula, shaking it at me. "The lady in the store was also very helpful, she offered to show me how to put on a diaper but I said we knew. We do know, right?"

"How many diapers have you changed?"

His shoulder lifted in a lopsided shrug. "None, I always hand them back. What about you?"

"Same. But it can't be that hard."

He opened a packet and took one out, examining it, ripping the sticky tabs on the side before getting stuck to them himself as he tried to figure out which way round it went. And there didn't seem to be any instructions.

We all stopped dead when a single piercing cry emitted from the car seat. Neither of us moved a muscle. We may have stopped breathing. Barclay started growling low.

A minute later we were still frozen to the spot.

"Can we move yet?"

The answer came from the baby as another garbled cry rang through the room. Penn stood there staring at me until I realized one of us needed to stop it, and by the look on his face, he'd designated that one to be me. I made my way over. Her little face was screwed up, her gummy mouth wide open, her lips quivering as she bawled.

I took the blankets off her and unstrapped the buckle holding her in place. I had several nieces and nephews and I'd held them all, the most recent not much older than she was. But the weight of her, the sudden weight I could feel deep in my marrow was heavier than a ton of bricks. Her crying didn't stop though, the shock of a stranger lifting her into his arms doing nothing to soothe her. Because that's what I was. A total stranger.

Penn removed the lid from the bottle he was still holding, only to reveal nothing on the top that would help her drink. And I'd seen enough babies feeding to know I couldn't pour it down her throat.

"Mate, hurry up."

He tipped the box upside down and the rest of the bottles fell out, along with a packet of teats, turning into a race against time to fit them together and save our hearing before we were deafened forever.

I snatched the bottle from his hand. "Here goes nothing. Milk is milk right?"

"I dunno, dude. Let's hope so, because this noise is going to make my ears bleed soon."

I moved it to her lips, like I'd done so many times before with my siblings' kids. But her eyes were still screwed shut, the crying going strong, and my panic shifted up another notch.

"She doesn't want it."

"She will, just hold it there."

I tried again, but nothing happened. "What if she needs it warm? Should we warm it? How do we do that?"

He read the label on another bottle, his voice rising in agitation. "I don't know. It doesn't say. Why doesn't it say?"

Barclay started whining.

Rafe came back, removed the bottle from my hand, calmly adjusted the teat then turned it upside down, shaking it until the milk appeared.

"Now try." He passed it back to me.

Her lips clamped down and we were surrounded by crushing silence, the type of silence you could only hear after a car alarm stops from incessantly ringing - or when a baby finally stops crying.

Rafe, Penn, and I let out simultaneous sighs.

"Penn, can you get Laurie over? We need someone tonight, and better to keep this as quiet as possible for now, especially as we need an official medical sign-off on the birth certificate."

"Yeah, probably." Penn's youngest sister, Laurie, was a pediatrician. He reached for his phone, dialing a number then handed the phone to Rafe, who walked out again.

Penn and I watched as this tiny baby ate like her life depended on it, and I realized I had no idea when she last ate. I had no idea about anything. I was completely clueless.

And then she opened her eyes... Eyes the exact same shade of green as my sister, Wolfie's. Which were the exact same shade as my mother's. And her mother's. The paternity test would be a formality. This little girl was mine.

My daughter.

Forty-eight hours ago I'd been at my sister's house for Sunday lunch, watching my two year old niece, Florence, smear pudding all over her face. And my niece is cute. But she's cute when she's clean and not covered in chocolate pudding.

Forty-eight hours ago I'd said *Nope. I'm not ready for kids. No thanks.*

Forty-eight hours ago I was perfectly happy sewing my metaphorical wild oats.

But apparently, one of my wild oats had stuck.

My legs started to buckle under me and I sank to the floor, propped against the side of the counter.

Rafe returned and the two of them sat down next to me.

"Fuck. What the fuck am I going to do?"

"Laurie's coming over to take your DNA. We'll get the results back in twenty four hours, so let's just wait until we hear back before we panic."

"No, she's mine. She looks just like Wolf did."

They peered down at her.

"Her eyes are the same color. What am I going to do? How am I going to look after a kid? Raise a daughter? I have no fucking clue! Jesus Christ, we were only supposed to be playing basketball."

I watched her still suckling at the bottle and the enormity of how massively my life had changed in a matter of seconds punched me hard in the face. The pressure and anxiety reached boiling point in my gut and pushed up through my chest, into my throat until I couldn't hold it in any longer.

Penn put his arm around me as I sobbed on his shoulder. "It'll be okay, you're not going to do this on your own."

Rafe stood up. "I'm ordering us burgers before Laurie

arrives, then I'm going to shower and will be borrowing some clean sweats."

I peered up at him. "You guys are staying?"

We might not live under the same roof anymore, but we all treated each of our places like we all lived there, all with keys and instructions to the doormen they were allowed entry without a pass. There normally wouldn't be any question about them staying, but given a screaming baby had just been thrown into the equation, I was half expecting them to cut and run.

"Buddy, we're not leaving you here tonight. This would be a nightmare for any one of us." He grinned. "I'm just thankful it's you, not me."

I laughed as tears of gratitude prickled the backs of my eyes. "Oh thank God. I don't think I've ever loved you more."

I looked back down at her tiny face as the bottle stopped moving; she'd stopped eating. "Do you think she's had enough?"

Penn's face told me he knew about as much as I did. "Dunno, maybe move her around a bit. That's what my sisters do. Put her on your chest and pat her back."

I moved her about, gently jostling her tiny body against my chest. I'd watched my sisters and brothers-in-law do this so many times, but it never occurred to me how delicate their kids were when patting them on the back. Jasper and Cooper were not small guys either.

I patted as softly as possible. "Now what?"

He shrugged. "Just hold her there I guess."

"No, I mean, now what? She has nothing here. I have nothing here for a kid. What's she going to sleep in tonight? That car seat? I don't even know what to buy."

"Do we even know how old she is? She's new, but what's her date of birth?" Penn peered up and reached onto the counter for the paperwork which Rafe had been going through.

I gave out a silent prayer to whomever was listening that she'd at least left that. Because not knowing my daughter's birthday would probably be the most depressing part of it all.

His eyes scanned the page as Rafe's had. "It was February fourteenth."

"It's the twenty fifth today, right?"

He nodded.

"She's eleven days old?"

"Yep."

I nodded to one of the papers he was currently holding. "Is that it?"

He passed it over to me, the bubbly round penmanship far too frivolous for the gravity of its contents.

Murray,

This is not a letter I ever expected to have to write, so I'll just go ahead and say it. She is your daughter. You probably won't remember me, but we met last Memorial Day in the Hamptons, and she is the result.

I have plans for my life and that doesn't include a kid. I was five months pregnant when I found out so I couldn't have an abortion. She was born at home because I couldn't let it show on my parents' insurance. I haven't told my family, but she was checked out and she's healthy. I've looked after her as long as I could, but I don't want this responsibility.

You can give her a good life, and I know she's better off with you than with me.

Please don't try to find me, this is what I want.

Reagan

I tried not to hate this woman I barely remembered. What about what I wanted?

I knew I'd always wanted kids, but not like this. Not by default. This wasn't how I pictured ever becoming a father.

My throat grew tight again. My heart was pounding in

my chest, the air had thinned out and I was struggling to breathe. Then my ears began ringing.

I couldn't do this. I couldn't do this by myself.

At that moment a loud burp let out from the smallest member of the group, and I felt warm liquid run down the collar of my shirt.

I needed to call in the cavalry.

2

MURRAY

The intercom sounded, which meant my sisters were on the way up. Graham was under instruction to warn me when they'd arrived and let them straight in. Laurie had left an hour ago with the promise of getting the results back as swiftly as possible, and we knew she'd keep her word.

I took a deep breath as Barclay ran out of the kitchen because he could hear them getting out of the elevator, and I could hear his tail thudding against the wall as he waited for them with excitement.

I was less excited.

Since I'd moved to New York two years ago, my older sisters had taken it upon themselves to try and get me to settle down. They'd decided that since they, along with my eldest brother, Jamie, were all married with kids, then I should be too, and that it was *time to stop dicking about, Murray.* It was one of the reasons I had Barclay; he'd been a birthday present from them last year, because in their opinion, if I met someone who loved dogs, then that would be a good start.

And the best place to do that would be the park.

Their logic wasn't far off; Barclay was the best wing man

I'd ever had, not only for me but for Rafe and Penn too, because a cute puppy was the number one generator of a hot woman's contact details. A one hundred percent certified pussy magnet. But the girls had failed to take into account that we were all more than content with our lives as they were, and Barclay had simply expanded our dating pool.

However, this baby would no doubt add some fuel to their relationship rocket chat. The thud of Barclay's tail got louder at the click of the door opening.

"Murray?" That was Wolfie, the eldest of my sisters.

"Murray, what's going on? There better be a good reason why you dragged my pregnant ass over here just as I was going to bed." And that was Freddie – or Franks - as only I called her - slightly younger than Wolf, but still six years older than me.

I did have a good reason. Even though I'd sent them a message telling them to get to mine ASAP due to a life and death situation, it wasn't far off. I was also pretty impressed at how quickly they'd arrived. I wasn't known for panicking, so they'd clearly taken my 911 alert seriously.

They marched into the kitchen, Wolfie's blonde hair flying around her like a whirlwind, while Freddie's jet black hair stayed poker straight, as though not daring to move out of place.

Wolfie pulled me into a big hug, then gave me a thorough once over, the type that only big sisters do, which was then followed by Freddie's.

I just about stopped myself from bawling again, from the emotions tearing around like a hurricane inside me. "Thank you for coming."

The look of worry deepened on Freddie's face. "Jesus, Murray, what's happened? Have you been crying? You're scaring us."

"He has been."

Their heads snapped around to Rafe and Penn who were

sitting at the long kitchen table against the wall, and whom they hadn't noticed until now.

"Oh, hey, how are you guys?" Wolfie gave Rafe a hug, before rolling her eyes so hard I thought they might actually get stuck. "Should have known you two'd be here, given it's Tuesday."

Freddie snorted. "Oh my God, is that what this is about? What trouble have you got into this time?! Please tell me I didn't get out of bed because of your idiotic superstitions." She stopped dead as she focused on Penn, holding the baby who'd fallen asleep again. "Whoa, when did you have a baby? And who the fuck managed to get you to settle down? Also, congratulations, I guess."

He looked over to me as he answered. "I didn't, she's not mine."

The pair of them followed his line of sight and I was pinned with two confused faces, which soon filled with concern.

I moved over to the table and pulled a chair out, sitting down. "She's mine."

"Allegedly," Rafe added.

Their heads flicked back and forth between the baby and me, and then on the baby paraphernalia which was still spread all over the counter.

"Sorry, what?" Freddie's ice blue eyes bore through me. "What's going on?"

I swallowed thickly, gesturing to the empty chairs, willing them to sit down before the world's hardest conversation began.

"She was on the doorstep when we got home tonight, along with a note saying she's mine."

I wasn't sure what the etiquette was on how long you needed to wait on someone in a state of shock, but I think it lasted two or three minutes before either one of them said anything, their heads moving back and forth between the baby and me.

Finally, Freddie broke the silence.

"Oh God, Murray." She moved over into my lap, her swollen belly pressing against me as she held me in a giant hug, which, considering she was one of the smallest people I knew, was pretty giant. She was actual proof that size didn't always equal strength. "Are you okay? How did this happen?"

"Apparently it happened last Memorial Day when we were up at the house." Rafe passed the letter over to Wolfie to read, her hand flying to her mouth, her bright green eyes widening with shock as she moved through the words.

"You need a paternity test." She passed the letter to Freddie's outstretched hand.

"Laurie just left. We'll get the results back in the morning, but if she wakes up you'll see how similar she is to you and mum, and granny."

Freddie gave a loud sniff and her chest heaved as tears starting pouring down her face. "I'm sorry, these are pregnancy hormones, but she must have been so scared if she didn't want to tell her family. I can't even imagine what she must have been going through to see this as a solution, to leave you with a baby."

"You mean to clear up her mess," I replied bitterly.

Wolfie stayed silent, eyeing me.

"What?"

Her lips rolled, she had something she wanted to say but didn't want to say it. "Nothing."

"Wolf, spit it out!"

She took a deep breath. "When you have a baby, hormones are all over the place. Mine are still pretty strong from when Macauley was born, and that was three months ago. She can't have been thinking clearly."

The snort I let out dripped in cynicism. "No, I think she knew exactly what she was doing. She's left everything."

"What d'you mean?"

"All the paperwork, her name, everything."

Freddie's face filled with a combination of shock, horror, and disbelief, her lip quivering. "She doesn't have a name?"

I shook my head slowly. "Nope. I need to name her."

That set Wolfie off, her eyes watering until they spilled over and she wiped the tears away with her fingers. "Oh, Murray."

"Yeah." Because I knew what she was saying, and there weren't any words in existence which allowed me to adequately articulate how I was feeling.

"Can I hold her?"

She stood up, moving over to Penn who gently handed her over; trying hard to make sure she didn't wake. Of the three of us, he seemed to be the one she liked the most so far; at least he was the one who could get her to stop crying. Or the two of us, because Rafe had been too busy working to make sense of the shitstorm I'd found myself in to hold her yet.

She looked down, her tears making an appearance again. "She's so beautiful. You're right, she does look like mum. She looks like Florence, too."

"Did Laurie check her?"

I nodded. "Yes. She said she seems healthy, but a bit underweight."

Freddie got up and stood next to Wolf, looking down at the baby. "Have you fed her?"

I nodded again.

"When did you last feed her?"

"Um, about two hours ago, just before I called you."

She walked over toward the counter and the piles of baby stuff. "And where did all this come from?"

"I got it." Penn's voice held more than a little pride at his achievement.

She looked over at him in surprise. "Impressive. Did you buy the whole store?"

"Pretty much."

She picked up one of several different cans of formula. "And what did you feed her with?"

"We gave her a bottle?" His answer turned into a question.

Her eyebrows shot up. "You made it?"

Penn's brows dropped slightly. "Um, no. There was this pre-made stuff I found that Dylan uses."

"And did you sterilize it?"

"Um… She was crying, so I just opened the bottle and put the nipple thing on it."

Her eyes were flicking between Penn and me. "And she drank it?"

I nodded.

"How much?"

"I dunno, until she stopped?" Frustration started to lace my tone at the twenty questions she was firing out, because they were only making it abundantly clear I didn't have a fucking clue what I was doing. "How am I supposed to know?"

Wolfie put her hand over mine. "It's okay, we can help. What do you need?"

"Everything. I need help with everything. I don't know what to do."

"We can go through what you've bought and then order anything else so it's here in the morning."

That made me feel slightly calmer, although only very slightly. "But what about tonight? Where's she going to sleep?" It was safe to say that it was unlikely I'd be getting any.

"She'll be okay in there tonight," Freddie pointed to the car seat, "but I can get Coop to bring over our spare bassinet now if you'd like."

"Franks, I don't know anything. I don't know whether I'd like a bassinet. I'm not even entirely sure what a bassinet is."

She rolled her lips as she thought. "Let's leave her in there tonight as she's used to it, then we can transfer her tomorrow. Have you changed her diaper?"

Both mine and Penn's chests puffed slightly and we sat up straighter, because we had actually accomplished a successful diaper change. I wasn't about to tell her it'd taken us half an hour. "Yes."

I didn't miss the look of surprise which passed between my sisters.

Wolfie glanced back down at the baby, who'd not even stirred in her arms. "How long has she been asleep?"

I checked the clock on the kitchen wall, because the concept of time seemed to have taken a hiatus - along with my reality. "An hour."

She chewed on her lip as she thought. "Okay, so she should be feeding every three hours at the most and then sleeping in between."

My eyes almost popped out of their sockets as I looked between her and Freddie. "I have to feed her every three hours? Even at night?"

Freddie nodded. "Yes, while she's this little. But we can get her sleeping through the night… eventually, so then at least you'll have a rest."

"Just be thankful you don't need to get up to pump in the night, even when she sleeps through."

I didn't want to tell Wolf that there were several points at the top of my list I had to be thankful for, and none of it was to do with this current situation.

"When will she sleep through?" I tried to keep the panic out of my voice as the thought of my own beloved sleep swiftly vanished - along with my sanity.

"We'll write it all down for you, and we'll help you get through the next few days. In the morning I'll call our nanny agency so we can get you some permanent help, get her on a schedule, and sleeping through the night. But with a night nurse, you'll be able to sleep as she'll do the feeding."

Freddie sat back down at the table and pulled the Macbook over, opening it up. "There's some good stuff on the counter and we'll show you what you need, but I'll order everything else to help you."

I slumped back in my chair, taking a full breath for what felt like the first time since we'd arrived home. "Thank you."

"You're welcome. Do you want us to stay with you tonight?"

I was flooded with gratitude again because my sisters were the best, even if I didn't always appreciate their interference. But they had their own families and children to worry about, not to mention Freddie was pregnant. And Wolfie had a little one at home who needed just as much attention as the one she was currently holding.

"No, thank you, the boys are here with me. But could you come back tomorrow to make sure we've survived?"

Wolfie laughed. "Yes, of course we can. Have you told mum and dad?"

I shook my head. "No, it's the middle of the night for them."

"Okay, I'll call them in the morning too. You know they'll be on the next flight, right?"

I groaned. "Yes, I'll send the jet, but can they stay with you?"

She laughed hard, but stopped herself in case the baby woke. "Good one."

If I thought my sisters laid it on thick, my mother literally brought the motherlode when it came to discussions about my sex life, or 'relationship status' as she liked to call it. It wasn't enough that between my brother and two sisters she had nearly seven grandchildren already, so there was no way she'd be staying anywhere except here.

But sometimes you just needed your mum.

"Okay." Wolfie stood up and gently placed the baby back in her car seat, tucking her in. "Let's get to work. Is there another laptop here? I'll get started on a 'What To Do' list."

I had no doubt that my two sisters could have ruled the world if they put their minds to it, which was good, because I needed all the help I could get. And more.

Freddie looked up from typing away, smiling softly. "Don't worry, we'll be here. You're not on your own."

True. I now had an eleven-day old baby to care for. I was a team of two.

And yet I don't think I'd ever felt more alone.

3

KIT

"Eviction?! I've just signed the lease!" I fumed at the woman on the end of the line, emphatically waving around the notice I'd been served as I'd walked out of my apartment an hour ago. "The ink can barely be dry."

"As I said, the building was sold to a private cash buyer last week and they have plans for it." Her voice was so annoying and nasally and calm that it only made me rage more. "But they've given all tenants six weeks' notice, as well as double their deposit back for any inconvenience caused."

My deep breath buoyed every shred of self-control I was currently using to not explode at her, only managing to speak through gritted teeth. "I don't want double my deposit! I want to have to not move all my things again."

I paced up and down the floor of my best friend, Payton's, apartment, where I'd stormed over to as soon as I'd opened the envelope. If there was carpet on the floor, I'd have worn it out approximately twenty minutes ago, while I was getting nowhere on the phone to this irritating representative for my landlords.

"Yes, Ma'am, I understand that." There was some shuffling down the line. "Could you please hold?"

Musak began playing through the phone before I had an opportunity to object, then it went dead.

"Hello? Hello?"

Cut off.

Ahhhrrrrrghhhhh. My phone found itself launched across the room into the couch cushions, because even though I was angry, I wasn't about to smash it. I didn't need the hassle of sorting out a new phone as well as finding somewhere else to live.

Payton appeared with a margarita, handing it to me in silence. I gagged at the strength of it and overzealous salt edge but downed it in one, thrusting the glass back out to her for a refill from the enormous jug she was holding.

She obliged, filling it to the rim once again. "So, evicted huh?"

"Can you goddamn believe it?! I only moved in two months ago! I'm just getting used to the neighborhood; I've even found a favorite coffee shop! I've worked out the quickest route to the subway! And now I have to start all over!"

I threw myself down on the couch. Trying to find a decent, affordable apartment in New York City, which didn't require you signing the soul of your first born child over, was as easy as trying to figure out Quantum Theory or Jet Propulsion... or something else which was really hard to figure out.

Payton perched at the end of the couch opposite me, tucking her long legs underneath her. Most of her thick dark hair was twisted up in a knot on top of her head, but as always, there were still some long tendrils which had escaped, falling down the side of her face and framing her perfect cheekbones. She was one of those people who looked put together no matter if she'd just woken up and thrown on whatever she'd found on her floor – which she usually had –

or if she'd spent four hours getting ready, which she'd rather die than do.

We'd met on our first day of college, where we shared the same dorm, and courses. Both studying English Literature, we'd become best friends by the end of our first class after Professor Higgins spent the entire session talking about the cleanliness of pigs, having drastically veered off the topic of George Orwell's Animal Farm, and we'd struggled to hold in the giggling.

"You can stay here for as long as you need." She sipped on her own margarita, wincing. "Oooh, I think I put too much tequila in this."

I chuckled at her reaction, and sighed. "Thank you, but hopefully I'll find somewhere else. I have six weeks. I just really, *really* didn't want to be traipsing around in the cold to find another place to live. I had plans the next few weeks; we were going to go out, I was going to start dating again, seeing as I don't have to study all hours of the day and night anymore, and now I have to change them. I love you for offering though."

"You're welcome. You know the couch always has your name on it when you need it."

"I know. You can always come apartment hunting with me again," I added, with more than a little hope in my voice. It would make it more bearable if I wasn't on my own.

"Of course," she scoffed. "I need to make sure we're closer together this time. Maybe I can persuade Mrs. Kellerman upstairs to finally move into her son's house, and then you can have her place." Her eyes lit up and she clapped her hands together. "Ohmygod, that would be amazing! Like college, but better."

"Think we can start on her today? Take her one of these," I waved my empty glass around at her, "you'd only need to give her half before she signed it over."

She leaned forward with the jug and refilled my glass

with no objections from me. I'd decided it was acceptable to get drunk before noon under extenuating circumstances, and eviction certainly qualified as that.

"Yeah. We'll finish this and I'll make a fresh one," she grinned.

I took another large gulp.

"Urghhhhhh." My head fell back against the back of the couch, still smarting at the situation I was in. Reaching underneath me I discovered the culprit of what was digging into my shoulder – a well-thumbed copy of a mafia romance with a naked, tattooed torso - Payton's current literary obsession - and dropped it on the floor. "This is so frustrating. I was supposed to be looking for a job, not an apartment."

Payton and I had graduated together six years ago, and while she'd gone straight into work for a publishing house to begin her dream of becoming a book editor, I had stayed on, earning my doctorate in Early Childhood Education. I hadn't quite figured out what I wanted to do with it yet, but I did know I wanted a career where I'd be shaping the minds of the next generations. During those six years, I'd spent time teaching in an elementary school in Brooklyn and then moved on to become a part-time nanny to save more money while I studied. And I'd saved enough so that when I graduated I had some time for a few months while I figured out the path I wanted to take - as well as catching up on sleep.

Except that had all gone to shit at approximately ten thirty-two this morning.

"Still haven't changed your mind about the Columbia position?"

I shook my head slowly. My old professor at Columbia had offered me a place as a research fellow on her program, and though it was a great opportunity and an honor in itself, I didn't want it. Or, more accurately, I didn't want to take the first job I'd been offered because I'd been her favorite student. I wanted to prove to myself all the years of study I'd put in had been worth it, which is why I'd worked so hard to save some money.

"No. Although now I'm thinking it's good I have it to fall back on." I slurped my drink. "But I probably shouldn't be making this decision until I'm sober."

A ringing stopped Payton from saying whatever she was about to, as I felt around underneath me trying to find my phone which was still wedged into the side of the couch where I'd thrown it.

"Hello?" I answered, without checking the caller ID.

"Hi, Kit, it's Marcia. How are you?"

I immediately sat up straight, my drink sloshing over the side and down my top, and tried hard to make sure my tone didn't convey the three very strong margaritas I'd just drunk on an almost empty stomach. Marcia was the owner of the nanny agency I'd been working for part-time while I studied. She ran a tight ship, like a stern English matron, and even though she couldn't see me, she had a sixth sense for when someone was misbehaving. Not that I was misbehaving. I was twenty-eight and well within my right to drink a pitcher of margaritas on a Wednesday morning if I chose to. But still, I would never slouch in Marcia's presence.

"Hey, Marcia, I'm good thanks. How are you?"

"Good, good. I've had an urgent request come in for you, for an interview this afternoon. It's a brand new assignment. Can you do a call in an hour?"

I slumped back down slightly, though not enough that she'd notice through the phone. "Not really, no. I've graduated now and you know I'm taking a break from work before I make any more decisions. Can't you offer them one of the plenty of other very qualified nannies you already have?"

"Kit, they've requested you. Just you," she reiterated firmly, as though that explained everything, and making it clear she hadn't listened to a word I'd said.

My lips pursed, because I knew I was on the losing end of a battle. This morning wasn't going to plan, at all.

"How do they even know me?"

"It's one of our current families. They remembered your résumé from when they were looking."

I sighed. "Marcia, thank you, but I really don't have time. I just got evicted and I need to look for a place to live."

"This is live-in, so it's perfect." I could have sworn I heard her clap. "And they've doubled your salary for the short notice."

Payton's eyebrows rose; she could hear everything Marcia was saying, given that Marcia didn't talk quietly. She took the silence as a reason to continue on her pitch in her trademark sing-song voice, like she was trying to give Mary Poppins a run for her money.

"It's a single father, in need of a lot of help by all accounts, not sure of the exact details. It's a brand new baby so you'll be doing nights to get a sleeping routine, which is why it's live-in. His sisters are our clients and the interview will be with them. I suggest you take it and see. They're lovely employees, they've had really good feedback, and both our nannies have extended their time twice. There are plenty of extras, including a car, expense account, travel, full membership to a gym called…" I heard a shuffle of paper, "Body by Luck." Payton's jaw dropped, mainly because she had more than a small obsession with that place. "And it's much nearer the college than where you live now, so you're closer to the city and any interviews you may have. They've also said you can have time off for interviews, plus your weekends free..."

Payton began vigorously gesturing her hands while nodding her head in a way that was both confusing and distracting.

"Sorry, Marcia, can you hold please?" I held the phone away and looked at Payton, mouthing to her. "What?"

"Take the interview," she mouthed back.

I shouldn't have picked up the phone. I'd never been able to say no to her, so I wasn't clear why I thought I could now, especially with Payton still flailing around. Damn margaritas. It was no wonder Marcia ran a business as successful as it was. She could persuade anyone to do anything.

I brought the phone to my ear again. "Okay, fine. One interview."

"Great! Well done, Kit. I'll send the details through."

"Wait, how long is it for?" I stopped her before she hung up.

"Sixteen weeks… initially."

"And when does it start?"

"They want you immediately, but I'm sure we can arrange for something to be done about moving your things out of your current place."

"Okay, I'll take the call," I replied, thoroughly defeated. "But only sixteen weeks, Marcia. I mean it."

"Wonderful. How serendipitous."

She hung up.

Payton took a large swig of her drink. "Jesus. She could sell oil to the Texans."

I nodded. Marcia didn't take no for an answer.

"Still, she's not wrong. This sounds awesome. Plus, a Body by Luck membership! There's a huge wait list on that place. You do remember how long it took me to get that through, don't you? And now you've just been handed one! I'd take the job just for the membership! But at least now we can go together. And you never know - this single dad might be hot…" She winked with a loud guffaw as she tried to fill my glass.

I held my hand over it. "No, I need to sober up."

"I don't." She topped her own glass up. "I'm so glad I decided to work from home today, makes life so much more interesting."

I stood up. "I'm going to get some water."

"What time are they calling?"

"In five minutes."

"Here." Payton barged into the bathroom while I was sitting on the toilet, throwing a brush at me with no warning. I ducked just in time or it would have smacked me in the face. "Maybe run that through your hair."

I'd spent thirty minutes trying to drink as much water as possible in order to sober up, and then another twenty-five preventing my bladder from bursting. Not sure why I even cared. I didn't want this job, and I'd pretty much been bullied into taking the interview.

I flushed the toilet, pulled up my jeans, and stood at the sink staring at myself as I washed my hands. Payton was right; I did need to brush my hair. It was the least I could do. My hair was so thick that if I wasn't careful I could quickly take on the appearance of someone who'd been dragged through a bush.

I checked my watch.

Two minutes.

I poured a glass of water and sat down at the kitchen counter, propping my phone up on the flowerpot Payton kept there. I turned to her as she took the stool next to me.

"You're not sitting there while I'm doing this! You're distracting enough."

"I'm giving you moral support."

I pointed through to the living room. "Support me from the couch, where I can't see you."

She smirked as she moved away. "You're very uptight about a job you don't want."

The phone started ringing before I could respond to her. I answered the video chat to see two women staring back at me; one blonde, one brunette, both smiling widely. At any other time I'd have probably thought it was weird, but they seemed so genuinely happy to see me that it immediately put me at ease.

"Hello."

"Hiiii," they replied in unison.

"Thank you so much for meeting with us at such short notice. We really appreciate you making the time. I'm Wolfie," said the blonde one, in an accent that wasn't American. English? Australian, maybe? "And this is my sister, Freddie."

"I'm Kit," I smiled. "It's nice to meet you."

Freddie's bright blue eyes lit up with more enthusiasm than a kid in a candy store. "How much did Marcia explain to you? Shall we tell you a little bit about ourselves and the situation, and then we can go through questions?"

I smiled, finding it hard to hold one in against their eagerness. "Yes, thank you. That would be good. She mentioned it's a new baby and that was about it."

"Did she say it's not our baby?" Wolfie asked.

"Yes, she did actually. Your brother's?"

She nodded. "Yes, that's right. We do both have children though. I have a two-and-a-half-year-old daughter and a three-month-old son, and Freddie has a two-year-old son, with another one due soon."

I chuckled. "Sounds like a handful."

"You're not wrong, and that's how we know Marcia. She's been brilliant for us with our nannies. We love them. And when we were originally looking, we remembered your résumé, but you weren't available long-term. However, you were the first thought we had when the new baby arrived, and we contacted Marcia straight away."

"And thankfully you're available."

It didn't surprise me that Marcia hadn't told them that I wasn't actually planning to go back to nannying. But the way these two were going, it sounded like Marcia would have had as hard a time saying no to them as I did to her.

"Anyway," Wolfie continued, "this would be working for our brother, Murray. It's a bit of an unusual situation. He's recently found himself to be the father of a newborn."

I frowned, because how does one suddenly find themselves to be a parent of a brand new baby?

Freddie rolled her eyes at her sister. "Stop being diplomatic; she needs to know the truth." She looked back at me through the screen. "The baby was left with him yesterday, with a note saying she was his."

I heard Payton gasp loudly from the other room as my eyes opened wide, and I had to remind myself to blink. "What..?!"

"He didn't know," Wolfie interrupted defensively before I could say anything else, although I was struggling to figure out what else there was to say. "He wouldn't have ever let the mother of his child feel she couldn't ask for help. He came home and found the baby on the doorstep."

I'd been rendered speechless. Never, in all my years of child education or nannying, had I heard of this. I knew of Safe Haven laws, but not on the doorstep of a stranger. Or maybe not *exactly* a stranger.

But either way, that must have been the biggest shock of his life.

Freddie's laughed pulled me out of my stunned silence. "This was our reaction too."

"Is your brother okay?"

Wolfie's face softened slightly. "Yes, he is; thank you for asking. He's in shock, but our parents are coming over to help him. He just needs something permanent for the next few months to help him find a routine and adjust. He really is great with kids; he's brilliant with our three, and we have another brother in England who also has three kids. We have a big family."

I was right with the English accent thing.

"And the baby?"

"She's twelve days old."

"Her birthday is February fourteenth?"

Freddie's eyebrows shot up. "Wow, that's quick math. Yes. Valentine's Day."

I laughed. "I'd like to take credit for that, but not really. It's my birthday, too."

She tried to hold back a smile. "Interesting."

"Now that's out of the way, hopefully it explains why Murray isn't on the call and it's us interviewing." Wolfie gestured between the two of them.

I nodded.

"Your résumé is very impressive, as are your recommendations, and like I said, we remembered you from when we were looking. Do you have any questions for us?"

Considering I only found out about this an hour ago and was still slightly stunned by the baby on the doorstep revelation, my brain had frozen. I dug deep into my old list of interview questions.

"Yes, let's start with what are your expectations? Do you already have parenting methods?"

"We do, but Murray doesn't. He's great with our kids, but he's never looked after a baby properly. He needs to be shown everything and taught everything. He needs help with creating a routine so he can get back to work."

"What does he do?"

I wasn't so interested in his job but more his schedule. If he was a doctor, he'd work erratic hours which were hard for routine, but if he was a teacher, he'd work a more sociable nine to five.

"He works in finance, and he runs a company with our brother."

"Okay. And where's he based?"

"He lives up near Lincoln Square. He's not far from Columbia, which would work for you, right? Marcia told us about your college course."

I clearly hadn't been very good at hiding the surprise at them knowing that because Wolfie started talking really quickly.

"Marcia mentioned that you'd finished your degree and were taking a break to look for jobs, and we'll make sure you still have the time to do that. She also called to explain the situation with your apartment but we can help with all that, too. Freddie knows loads of good moving companies, and we can organize getting everything into storage for you, and even help with finding somewhere new for you too. If you want some of your things to come with you, that's no problem. Whatever you want."

Freddie grinned broadly. "Can you tell we really want you to take the job?"

That got me and I started giggling. "I can, and I'm flattered, really."

"We can arrange for you to speak to our current nannies, if that would help, so you can see we aren't total nut jobs. Murray is very kind and funny too, everyone loves him, and we just want to find him the best help."

I laughed again. These two were very amusing, or maybe it was the Englishness, but they were certainly incredibly easy and likeable. I guessed it wouldn't hurt me to postpone my plans for four months. Plus the prospect of having someone help with the moving was more than enough to sway me.

"We totally understand this has been sprung on you, so take some time to think about it. However, we'd really like you to say yes. We'll get Marcia to connect you with our nannies so you can get the proper low-down."

"Sure, thank you. That would be good. Marcia mentioned you wanted a start ASAP, but what exactly does that mean?"

Wolfie winced slightly. "How about this weekend?"

Wow, it really was ASAP.

I nodded, my face neutral, because while I was probably going to say yes, I still needed to think about it.

"Okay. Is there anything else you wanted to ask?"

"Do you like dogs? Murray has a Labrador, but he's very gentle."

I grinned. "I love them. I used to have Labradors growing up, so it won't be a problem."

"And do you have a boyfriend?"

Freddie jerked sideways from the force of Wolfie's nudge following her question, but they both stared at me waiting for an answer.

"No, no I don't. But don't worry; my personal life and professional lives aren't mixed. I don't invite my friends over, even when I'm live-in."

"Oh, that's not…" Freddie earned herself another nudge.

"That's good to know, we appreciate your honesty," Wolfie interrupted. "Anyway, we'll let you go and get Marcia to connect you with our nannies. We'd really love for you to come and join our families, and we'll help get you whatever you need for your moving situation."

I smiled gratefully. "That's very kind, thank you."

They hung up and I was left staring at the phone, wondering how I'd managed to get railroaded into looking after a newborn and a single dad, when an hour ago I was worrying about sorting out my eviction.

Payton sauntered into the kitchen, perching on the stool next to me. "Wow, baby on the doorstep."

I glanced up at her. "I know, right? That's heavy shit."

Her head bobbed slowly in agreement. "You're taking it, aren't you?"

"Honestly?" I held her gaze. "They had me at movers. Plus, it's sixteen weeks with a newborn, it'll be easy, and then I can search for a proper job."

She jumped off the stool.

"Great, now that's settled, we can start drinking again."

4

MURRAY

"Has she got a name yet?" Penn slunk into the kitchen, sitting down at the breakfast counter next to me, sunglasses still on, and considering it was raining outside only meant he was hungover.

I wished I was hungover. I wished I had a hangover so bad my brain felt like it would never be whole again; that I could only manage to function when I had sunglasses and a bottle of electrolytes.

Because anything would be better than this.

Better than the zombie state of semi-conscious limbo I was currently living in; the foggy, grey area between asleep and awake.

For the past five days, my mornings had all started the same - with an ear-piercing, shrieking cry that wrenched me out of wherever I'd managed to find a place to close my eyes for the briefest of moments since the last time she'd been awake. In fact, in the past five days, I think I'd slept a total of seven hours.

I wasn't sure how much longer I could manage. Right now, if sleeping were an Olympic sport, I'd bring home gold for England. Or America.

No wonder they used sleep deprivation as a form of torture. My blood pressure must have shot through the roof, and I was so hopped up on caffeine that I could almost feel my heartbeat in the very ends of all my extremities.

My body couldn't decide what temperature to be.

I shook my head. "No, not yet."

I could barely think in any direction, let alone straight, and definitely not enough to come up with a suitable name for my daughter, because the results were in. They'd come back three days ago, making it official.

I was a father.

My mum walked into the kitchen with a loud tut, having heard our brief conversation, before hugging Penn.

As Wolfie predicted, they were on the next plane out as soon as she'd spoken to them. They'd arrived less than thirty-six hours after the baby had made an appearance, and as all parents do when faced with a crisis of any magnitude involving one of their children, they'd jumped into action and I couldn't be more grateful. But I was determined to do the heavy lifting, which meant the baby was sleeping in my room – in a bassinet – so I could give her a bottle during the night when she woke up. She'd already been abandoned by her mother, I wasn't about to start palming her off on other people.

I'd live up to my responsibility, even if I did need all the help I could get.

My apartment was now filled with every baby contraption under the sun. One half of my kitchen was covered in baby bottles, formula, sterilizing machines, teats, burping cloths, and bibs. And more things that I didn't even know existed until five days ago.

They'd taken to her immediately, owning her as another grandchild to add to their already growing brood, even before the results of the test made it official. But the flip side had been trying to organize me, which included my need to come up with a name, something I hadn't wanted to do until the results came back.

"No, she doesn't have a name," she repeated. "Penn, darling, did you have a late night? Would you like breakfast?"

He looked longingly at her as she started taking eggs and bacon from the fridge. "I'm never going to say no to one of your bacon sandwiches, Diane."

She placed two glasses of fresh orange juice down in front of us. "Murray, you need to make a decision, darling."

"Mum, normal people get nine months to decide. Stop fucking pressuring me to do it in three days! It's been three days since the results came back," I snapped.

She pursed her lips at my swearing, and I would have felt guilty about snapping at her if I had the energy.

But I didn't.

Penn knocked back the orange juice, placing his empty glass on the counter. "Dude, you need a name. Raf has to get her forms in tomorrow."

"I know that, Pennington," I grumbled, "but this name is with her for life. She needs to carry it when she's head of a Fortune 500 company, or Chief Justice of the Supreme Court. Surgeon General. Or President."

He took off his sunglasses, staring at me with bloodshot eyes. "President? Jeez, this kid isn't going to be under any pressure at all."

"She can be whatever she wants to be. Point is, I'm not going to fuck up her name because you all pressured me into calling her something shit."

Barclay groaned loudly in agreement from his bed.

My mum started laying the bacon into a hot pan, filling the air with the sound of sizzling, the smell causing my mouth to fill with saliva.

"What about Granny Ottilie?" she asked, turning the rashers over.

"What about her?"

"Well, that would be a pretty name for her, and Granny would have loved that."

I grunted.

"Still got something against Olivia?" The innocence coating Penn's tone was not about to fool me in the slightest because he was almost a bigger shit-stirrer than I was. He knew full well I fucking did, smirking at me as my body spasmed, like someone had poured ice water over me.

"Fuck yes. I'm not naming my daughter after the most horrifying sexual experience of my life."

When I'd been a very horny sixteen year old, walking around with a constant boner and jacking off every spare minute, I'd had a massive crush on one of Wolfie and Freddie's school friends. Her name was Olivia, and to me she'd been utter perfection; the star of nearly all my wanking sessions and every wet dream. One summer, my sisters had their friends over, including Olivia, and they were spending their time by the pool in my parents' garden. I'd spent most of my day watching them rub sunscreen over each other, all of them wearing miniscule bikinis, while drinking a bottle of vodka I'd swiped from my dad's liquor cabinet. When I'd bumped into her later that afternoon, in my inebriated state I'd mistaken her friendliness as being into me and leaned in to kiss her, which is when all the vodka made an appearance. As any girl would when puked on by the younger brother of her friends, she ran away. And it naturally put me off anyone named Olivia, for life.

A huge plate of bacon sandwiches was placed in front of us, Penn diving in like he was about to die from his hangover and this was the only cure.

"These are epic," he mumbled through his massive mouthfuls. "Thank you, Diane."

"You're welcome," she laughed, bumping into Rafe on her way out of the kitchen, giving him a kiss on the cheek. "Just in time for breakfast."

He slapped me on the back before reaching for a sandwich and sitting down. "Hey, man, how are you today?"

"Same as yesterday, but more exhausted."

He got back up and started making coffee, handing me one when he was done.

"Thank you." I sipped it. "I don't know how new parents do this and there's two of them. Single parents are literally superheroes."

"Got that right." Rafe sipped his own coffee, before putting it down to stare at Penn as if noticing his hungover state for the first time. "What's wrong with you?"

He smirked. "Hooked up with that girl I met the other day when I took Barclay for a walk, and I haven't been to sleep yet."

My face fell into my hands. "Oh my God, I'm never going to go out and have sex again, am I? I'm going to be too tired to function. How do parents even make a second kid? If I'd known what was about to happen, I would have made more of my last weekend of freedom."

"Of course you will!" Penn laughed. "What about Dasha?"

"Dasha?"

The evil glint in his eye told me he knew what he was suggesting, because he liked to remind me of any occasion when I hadn't made the best decisions. "Yeah, maybe you should rethink that situation. She wanted to settle down, remember?"

I scoffed. *Dasha.*

Even though she'd graced more than a few magazine covers, Dasha wasn't so much a model, more one of those girls where you never really knew what they did. But because she was so extraordinarily beautiful - on the outside - it was never questioned. We'd crossed paths a few times at the end of last summer, bumping into each other at events as we moved in similar circles, briefly flirting but never going beyond that. It also hadn't been immediately obvious how vapid and narcissistic she was, because when conversations take place after enough alcohol to sink the U.S. Navy, it's not that easy to tell.

Then, on one more very drunken night at the New York Rangers' legendary Halloween party, it happened. She'd looked smoking hot in a masquerade mask and a dress that left nothing to the imagination. One night had led into a few weeks – not quite dating, because you can't really call it that when the time spent together is confined to the hours between eleven p.m. and five a.m. - which was about all I could manage before I became concerned for my life.

And the very legitimate worry I might be skinned alive.

"Absolutely not. First off, you know she wanted to settle down with my money. Second, I've never met anyone with less maternal instinct. Third, she would always pick fights with me, which, admittedly, would then end with fucking insanely explosive sex, but," I held my finger for a pause, "and I hate myself for saying this, it was too much. The pay-off wasn't worth it. My back got totally scratched up from those talons she had, and I had to get some antibiotic cream from the doctors. It was like having sex with a velociraptor. Plus, she hated Barclay, especially when he tried to sleep on the bed. And after the final fight about fuck knows what, I had enough and threw her out."

Rafe started laughing hard.

"Fuck, I bet that was funny. I wish I'd seen how angry she'd been. I told you not to go near her. She's always been an evil bitch, and this is a classic example of you letting your dick control your decisions," he added, as though he'd never done the same thing. He peered over to where Barclay was sleeping. "Poor Barc, you're a good boy, aren't you?"

Barclay lifted his head up to look at Rafe, his tail thudding once before he went back to sleep. He was also very tired, having been up almost as much as me. He still wasn't entirely sure about what was going on, or who this new creature was taking up all my attention.

"When's the nanny coming?"

"Today, after lunch. The car's going to collect her."

"What's she like?"

I shrugged. "I don't know; Mum and the girls organized her. Wolf and Franks really like her, and Mum met her and started talking about her as though she was the fucking Messiah. But honestly, if she can give me some time to sleep, then I really don't care."

My eyelids started feeling heavy again so I walked over to the patio doors off the kitchen and opened them, blasting myself with the fresh March air.

"Once I can sleep, then I can think." I stood in the doorway, allowing the cold wind to hit me. "Raferty, I'll give you a name for her tomorrow."

"One fit for a president, apparently," muttered Penn.

"Who's the president?" asked my brother-in-law, Jasper, as he walked into the kitchen carrying my two-year-old niece, Flossie, in one arm, and a baby car seat holding my three month old nephew, Macauley, in the other, which he placed on the kitchen table.

"The newest member of your family, by all accounts," replied Rafe as he hugged Jasper. "Hey, man, how're you doing? Good game last night. Sands is making a good captain."

Jasper, married to Wolfie, was a retired NHL player, having captained the New York Rangers for a long time, and where he'd spent his entire career. Following retirement a few years ago, he then rejoined the staff as an assistant coach, and was having a lot of success. The Rangers were currently top of the league tables and heading for the playoffs.

"Thanks. Yeah, he's doing a good job now that he finally started taking things seriously." He placed Flossie on the floor and she promptly ran over to me, her arms lifted high for me to pick her up.

"Hi, Floss." I kissed her cheek. "I like your dress. How are you?"

"Good." She kissed me back then wriggled in my arms until I put her down on the floor, and ran off.

I called after her, "Granny is in the playroom."

"How are things here?" Jasper hugged me and walked over to what I'd named The Bottle Station, which was essentially the baby equivalent of a cocktail bar. He examined everything that was laid out. "Girls do this?"

I nodded.

He looked toward the door, before back at me, lowering his voice. "When the girls are out one day, I'll come over and go through what you actually need. I've found some good baby hacks they don't know about, but have saved my ass on more than one occasion."

I laughed. "Mate, I'll take anything."

He started making up a bottle. "Where is my new niece anyway?"

"Asleep right now." I looked at my watch. "She'll be awake soon though."

"And are you doing okay? Got a name yet?"

I shrugged, wondering how many more times I was going to be asked that question. I should have put an ad out in the New York Times saying *No Fucking Name Yet.*

"I'm okay, or I will be once I sleep. And no name yet."

"But he'll have one tomorrow," Penn offered up.

"Really?" Jasper raised his eyebrow.

"Yeah, once I get some sleep tonight. The nanny is starting today so I'll actually be able to think."

He rolled his lips, nodding his head. "Fair enough. You'll get used to the tiredness."

"I doubt it."

"Don't worry, once you've got the nanny here and she's settled you'll find a routine. What's her name?"

I hesitated, searching my brain, I should probably know. I did know, I'd been told, I just couldn't remember. Oh.

"Kit, I think." I nodded to myself. "Yes, it's Kit."

"We'll get her together with Sylvia and they can take the kids out, make sure they're spending time together as cousins," he said, mentioning the nanny who'd been with them since Florence had been born. She was like a slightly older Mary Poppins and always seemed to have something in her bag designed to keep Floss clean and out of most trouble, which was a feat in itself.

"Yeah, that would be good. Thanks, buddy."

"Sylvia and Greta get together a couple of times a week, so Kit can join in," he continued. Greta, Freddie and Cooper's nanny, looked after their son, Samson. He'd just turned two, and even though he was a couple of months younger than Florence, he was easily twice her size. However, Florence had no issue asserting her authority over her cousin, and Sammy, at any family get together, was usually seen following her about, doing her bidding without question.

"Speaking of, what time are they getting here?" At that moment there was a loud clatter from down the hall. "Never mind, that sounds like them."

Thirty seconds later, Sammy waddled into the kitchen, ignoring all of us standing around and went straight over to Barclay's bed, sitting down almost on top of him. Barclay shuffled back slightly then positioned his head so it rested against Sam. None of us could remember when this relationship started up. It was a move that happened every time they were together, and Sam was easily Barclay's second favorite human after me, probably because he always had some sort of food on him, and Barc was usually seen closely on his heels hoovering up the trail of breadcrumbs. The only reason Sam ever wanted to come over here was to see Barclay.

"Hey, Sammy, do we all get hugs too?"

Sam looked up at us, as though noticing for the first time there were other people in the kitchen. He silently got to his feet and waddled over to me, his hands in the air for me to lift him, just as Florence had done. I picked him up, blowing a raspberry on his cheek which caused him to erupt in a fit of giggles.

"Throw, throw."

"You want to go to Uncle Jasper? Or Uncle Rafe? Or Uncle Penn?" I turned him toward the guys so he could choose.

This was a game we like to play, where he'd be thrown between people for hugs instead of walking. He was the sweetest kid in the world, and I'd always hoped that if I ever had kids, they would be half as amazing.

And now that time had come, so I needed to concentrate on not fucking it up.

"Raf!" he requested.

Rafe stood up from the stool and held his hands out. "Whoa, aren't I lucky to be chosen first?"

I looked down at Sam. "Ready?"

He nodded, then I threw him through the air to Rafe, who caught him, turning up the volume of his giggling.

"Who's next?"

"Penn!" He was launched across the room again, his hysterics getting louder each time.

It was a good job we all worked out regularly because it was like throwing the heaviest medicine ball. A minute later, Cooper moseyed into the kitchen, just as Jasper had finished blowing raspberries on Sam's neck.

"Thought I could hear you causing havoc already," he said to his son.

"Papa!" His arms reached out toward Cooper who took him, positioning him on his hip so they both faced the room.

"Hey, man, how're you doing?"

"Yeah, alright." I looked around the kitchen of guys. "Where are the girls? They came, right?"

Cooper nodded. "They're helping your mom with the nanny's room, and getting the baby's room ready."

"Oh, cool."

My daughter – a term still sounding so alien - had been sleeping in my room with me, so it was easier for when she needed feeding in the night, but that was something the nanny would be doing now, until she slept through the night. And the baby's room was connected to hers, a feature in my apartment that I'd never understood before my mum had explained it. Because while I didn't need six bedrooms, I hadn't been able to find a smaller apartment in the area and building I'd wanted to live. And since Wednesday, the room had been transformed into a baby nursery, thanks to Freddie's skills as an interior designer. The nanny's room had also been transformed. While it had already contained a separate space off the main bedroom, Freddie had turned it into a small kitchen, with a fridge and microwave, along with a sitting area filled with books and a flat screen television.

"Heard she still hasn't got a name."

I snorted, unsurprised. "Oh yeah?"

"Yeah, I left them talking about it." He walked over to the coffee machine, flicking it on. "Who's this nanny that's coming? Is she special or something?"

"What d'you mean?"

He shrugged. "They just seem to be making a really big deal about it. We had to stop and pick up fresh flowers for her room. It's why we only just got here."

I held my arms out in an expression of cluelessness. "I've had nothing to do with it. They've sorted it all. I just assumed this was what always happened when someone came over to look after your kid."

"Grandpa!" shrieked Sam, deafening us all momentarily as my dad walked into the kitchen carrying my daughter.

"Hey, Sammy boy," he replied to Sam's wide open arms, the universal signal that he wanted to move onto someone else. "Give me a second. I'm just holding your new baby cousin. Let me give her to Uncle Murray."

"Can I see?"

"Sure, bud." Cooper carried him over to where my dad was standing, the baby in his arms.

Samson peered down, his face taking on an expression of reverence.

"She's little, like baby Mac," Sam whispered, looking up at Cooper for confirmation.

"She sure is. And just like you were." Cooper tickled him, making him laugh.

"Not quite like he was," muttered Jasper.

And that very was true. Samson had never been small, he'd clearly taken after his father.

"Here, let me." I gently took the baby from my dad, her green eyes open but not quite managing to focus on what was going on.

"Your mother said there's a bottle in the fridge for her. It needs warming."

"I'll sort it; I'm doing Mac's anyway." Jasper took the bottle out and got to work.

I sat down at the kitchen table and stared at my daughter, as I'd done every time I'd had her in my arms, felt the weight of her body, watched her tiny chest rising and falling with each breath. I'd tried to find the similarities between us, but beyond how much she looked like Florence when she'd been born, there'd been none.

Nothing I could call mine.

"Here." Jasper thrust her warm bottle of formula at me before he took Mac out of the car seat and sat down next to me.

"Thank you."

She took it immediately, so much better than the first

time I'd fed her, latching on instinctively and gulping it down noisily. I could probably claim she ate like me, and I'd even say she'd grown since Wednesday because of how well she'd been eating. And she definitely didn't like being hungry, also like me, making it known to everyone when she was ready for her bottle.

Jasper was watching her drink while Mac was guzzling down his own bottle. "She looks good."

"You think?"

"Yeah, she really does." He glanced up at me. "You're doing a good job, really. I know this is life changing, but it's going to be the best thing that's ever happened to you."

I could feel my eyes prickling. I was too tired to have any handle on my emotions. "Thanks, Jas."

"You, me, and Coop will have a little dads' club. We've been waiting for this day for a long time."

I frowned. "What day?"

"The day you're brought down by a woman." He laughed hard at his own joke.

I shook my head, laughing myself. "You're a dick."

"Hey, gang." Wolfie walked in and straight over to Jasper, kissing him as she smiled down at Mac. Even though I was used to their constant and nausea inducing displays of love, I didn't have a good enough grasp on my emotions right now to handle it, so I looked away.

Fuck.

I'd now be dating as a single dad - if I ever managed to date again.

"We're going to order in from the Italian place on Eleventh."

My stomach rumbled along with the general agreement of everyone else in the kitchen that ordering in was a good idea. My eating patterns had gone out of the window with my sleep, but I could always fit something in from the Italian place on Eleventh.

“She’s doing so well, Murray,” Wolf said as she gently stroked the baby’s head. “And she’s going to love her new room.”

“Thank you. Thank you for everything you’ve done for me.”

“My pleasure.” She picked up a phone from the table. “Okay, I’m ordering. We can eat, and Kit arrives in a few hours.”

If I was less tired I’d be questioning Wolfie’s unadulterated glee which had reached the levels of a kid before bedtime on Christmas Eve.

5

MURRAY

"Again, again!" demanded Florence for the seventeenth time as she bounced up and down on my knee.

I groaned. "One more time, or I won't have any knees left."

For a two-and-a-half-year-old she'd perfected the eye roll, something she'd definitely picked up from her mother. "Uncle Murray, you will."

"I won't," I argued. "Ready?"

"YES!" she squealed.

I held onto her hands and bounced her, lifting her high into the air and then dropped her, catching her at the last minute before she fell onto the floor in fits of giggles.

I placed her back down on the carpet, straightening her dress. "There you go.'

She ran over to where Samson was quietly playing with the train set which ran around the room, next to Cooper and my dad who were building a train station. I might not have had kids before five days ago, but once my sisters had started growing their families, I made sure that my place was always filled with plenty to occupy them, a place of fun and games that they wanted to visit. I had enough rooms in my apartment that I turned one into a playroom for when they visited, and we were all currently sitting on giant beanbags in the middle of the floor. Wolfie was feeding Mac, my daughter was asleep, Jasper, Penn, and Rafe were talking about the upcoming playoffs, Freddie was having a nap, and I had no idea where my mum was.

I could feel my eyes getting heavy again and blinked them hard to keep them open.

"What do you guys think about Elizabeth? Betty for short. That's a strong name, right?"

Everyone stopped what they were doing and looked at me.

"For the baby?" asked Wolfie.

I was too tired have the mental ingenuity to come up with a sarcastic and witty retort to her stupid question.

"Yes, for the baby."

She smiled. "Betty is cute, I like it."

"Right, but when she has a serious job…"

"Like when she's president," Penn grinned.

I pointed at him. "Exactly, then she can choose Elizabeth if she wants."

There wasn't as much enthusiasm in the room as I'd have liked. "Well, anyway, that's the type of name I'd like for her. Optional fun or serious, classic, and ages well."

"And has great leadership skills," added Rafe.

"Correct."

"What about a middle name?"

I'd already decided this. "Valentine, because that's when she was born. I want her to know how much I'd loved her even if I didn't know her so well."

Because I did. I couldn't explain it, but this baby was a part of me, intrinsically owning a piece of my heart from the second she opened her eyes. Jasper hadn't been wrong about a woman taking me down. She had. I knew without question she would have me wrapped around her finger.

"Betty Valentine sounds like a stripper," smirked Rafe, eliciting a snort of amusement from Penn, Cooper, and Jasper. "In fact, I'm sure she used to work at that Hooters in Cambridge; the one we used to go to for wings every Monday."

"Fuck off."

"Language," warned Wolfie, her eyebrow raised, although Floss and Sammy were too engrossed in the trains to be paying attention.

Penn's grin widened. "Hey, you said she could be whatever she wanted to be."

"She's not going to be a stripper!" I grumbled.

Maybe I needed to rethink my plan. This is why people needed more than double digit hours to decide. Fuck! Single parenting was hard, and I'd only been doing it for five days.

"Graham just buzzed; Kit is on the way up," my mother announced as she walked into the playroom, a sleepy looking Freddie behind her.

"Okay, great." I pushed off the beanbag and stood up. "Should I wake the baby?"

The adults in the room shook their heads hard, eyes filled with horror.

"No, darling," Mum smiled kindly. "Kit can meet her when she wakes up. We'll get her settled in properly first."

We walked to the front door just as the doorbell rang, and my mum opened it. I wasn't sure what I'd been expecting, but based on Sylvia and Greta - who looked like she'd be more at home at a German beer festival than looking after kids - I thought Kit might be older. But she was definitely younger than me.

"Hello, I'm Murray." I held my hand out and she shook it. "Thank you for coming. Good to meet you finally."

Before she could answer I was pushed aside by my mother who enveloped her in a hug. "Welcome, welcome! It's wonderful to meet you in person."

Kit laughed. "And you, I'm glad I was available to help."

"Oh, so are we, darling. So are we." She looked at Kit's empty hands. "Is Graham bringing your things up?"

Kit nodded.

"Good, come and meet the rest of the family. The baby is sleeping right now but we'll get you settled, and then we can go through all your questions."

"Sounds good."

I followed them back into the playroom where my mother introduced her to everyone. Freddie got up to hug her, followed by Wolfie, who still had Mac in her arms.

"Okay, I'll take Kit round and show her where her room is, and the baby's things. You can stay here."

"Sure." I looked at Kit and couldn't decide if she was amused or slightly horrified. "Welcome to the chaos. As you can see, my mother is in charge right now, but thank you for coming. I'll wait until you guys are done, and hopefully you won't change your mind when you see how much help I need."

"Don't worry; it's nothing I can't handle. You'll be a pro by the time I leave." She smiled at me before allowing my mother to drag her off.

I flopped back down on the chair, my head resting on the back, my eyelids heavy again, but the thought of finally being able to sleep was currently giving me more joy than I'd ever felt in my life. I jerked, opening my eyes wide, halting them from closing permanently, only to find Cooper and Jas staring at me.

"What?"

Cooper tilted his head. "She's going to be living here?"

I nodded.

"And you hadn't met her before today? Had you seen a picture?"

I shook my head. "No, she seems alright though I guess. I saw her résumé and that was solid. Thought she'd probably be a bit older. Do you think she should be? Yours are much older, right? She seemed experienced though and had good references, but I don't know what to look for in a nanny apart from 'Keep Child Alive'," I air-quoted.

Cooper looked at Jasper, then got up and closed the door, moving to stand in front of the girls.

"What do you two think you're doing?" Wolf and Freddie halted the deep, whispered conversation they were in.

"What do you mean?" Wolfie's tone exuded innocence in a way that made me pay more attention than I normally would have.

"Cub..." Jasper warned.

I frowned, my head moving between the four of them. "What's going on?"

Cooper's glare stayed trained on the girls. "They're meddling."

"In what? I said it was okay for them to hire the nanny, they know better than I do for what I need."

Jasper scowled at Wolfie. "Yeah, that's not what they're doing. Is it?"

The pair of them stayed silent, holding the boys' stare with dogged determination.

"Mate, I'm not following. What are you talking about?"

I think even if I wasn't surviving on an hour's sleep a night I'd still be having trouble following this line of conversation.

Jasper turned to me. "They haven't hired Mrs. Doubtfire; they've hired a Jude Law fiasco waiting to happen."

My frown deepened. "What?"

"Darling, I don't know what that means." Wolfie's voice held strong, but I could tell by the way she wasn't quite meeting his eyes that she knew exactly what he meant, even if I didn't have a clue.

Jasper's arms crossed over his chest. "You know exactly what that means. He's got enough to deal with, without this."

"She came highly recommended; she has an excellent résumé. She's just got her PhD in early childhood education," she argued back, listing the points off on her fingers. "And she's got the same birthday as the baby."

What the fuck did that have to do with anything?

"Victoria Jacobs!" He dropped his head, shaking it as he first named her. I still had no idea what he was talking about, but it must have been serious if he first named her. She was rarely called Victoria, even though that was her given name, having been known as Wolfie since she was little.

My patience, already thin from my lack of sleeping, was currently so stretched from my inability to follow this conversation, it was see-through.

"Can one of you please explain what the…" I looked over at Floss and Sam, still occupied by the train set, "EFF you're talking about?"

Cooper sat back down on a beanbag. "They're setting you up."

"For what?"

He raised his eyebrow at me. And suddenly, all the enthusiasm, insistency to manage the interviews, and assurance they knew best, became crystal clear. It was more than simply trying to be helpful. Bloody matchmaking, nosy sisters, with my scheming mother as the ringleader!

"Seriously?!" I glared at the girls who wouldn't look at me, and I knew I was right. They were trying to set me up. "You two are fucking unbelievable! Unbelievable. Anyway, she's not my type."

Although in my tiredness I hadn't really noticed what she looked like, beyond short and blonde, but neither of those were attributes I usually went for, so I was pretty confident in my assessment.

"Why? Because she's not six feet tall and eastern European, with razor sharp cheek bones and a stick up her arse?" snapped Freddie.

I ignored the jab, and Rafe's low chuckle.

"Whatever. But even if she was, I'm still not interested. I've got bigger things to worry about, like how to raise a daughter. Not to mention she's now my employee."

Jasper dropped his head. "Just you wait man, just you wait. She's going to be living here and you are in for a world of trouble."

I let out a deep sigh of irritation at their lack of faith in me.

"Mate, you're overeacting. I am capable of keeping it in my pants, you know." I rolled my eyes, turning to Penn and Rafe, who were sitting quietly in the corner drinking wine and watching everything unfold. "What do you two think?"

Penn propped his chin in his hand pensively, tapping his finger against his cheek, taking a second as he gave it some serious thought. "I think… if she was a teacher, I'd definitely be giving her my apples."

He snorted as Cooper high-fived him. Don't know why I bothered fucking asking, of course that would have been his answer. Even my dad started laughing, and I could feel my annoyance at all of them swiftly rising.

"Seriously, I'm not about to sleep with the nanny!" I protested, not really sure why I was bothering to entertain their stupidity.

"Fine. But I'm going to re-read the NDA she signed," Rafe said as he sipped his wine.

"Why?" I frowned, not realizing I'd played right into his hands.

"Need to make sure you're covered for when you finally admit we're right; and because of your track record."

Everyone started laughing hard again at my expense, but my sense of humor had long since disappeared a few days ago, along with my sleep.

"Fuck off, the lot of you. That was one secretary, and it wasn't my fault she became a level five clinger." I stood up, pointing to the girls, aiming all my annoyance and tiredness at them. "Seeing as you two think you know best, you can deal with the rest of today. I'm going to bed and I don't want to be woken up under any circumstances."

Even if the building caught fire, I'd likely sleep through it.

I stormed off up the stairs to my bedroom, not bothering to say goodbye to anyone, their laughter still ringing around my head. I would have gone to see the baby but as I walked past her room I could hear my mother and Kit talking, and I was too pissed to make polite small talk.

I stripped and jumped into the shower, soothing my tense muscles and washing away my irritation. Grabbing a towel from the hot rail, I dried myself off before standing in front of the mirror, staring hard. I might not look different, but I felt it. I was a father now, I had actual and real responsibilities beyond taking care of myself, and I wasn't going to fall at the first hurdle, no matter how much my stupid friends and idiot family expected me to.

I looked at my watch - three-forty five p.m. If I was lucky, I'd sleep through until tomorrow morning and emerge feeling more human. I opened my bathroom drawer and rummaged around until I found the bottle of Valium I kept in there for emergencies, popped one and crawled into bed.

I was asleep before my head hit the pillow.

It was still dark outside when Barclay's soft snoring woke me up from the middle of my bed. Even though it had been custom-made to not only allow me to stretch out my six-foot-three frame and take Barclay into account, he still somehow managed to spread across seventy-five percent of the space, until I was squashed on the edge.

I gently shoved him over and uncurled my body, lengthening it out on the mattress, already feeling a million times better than I had all week. I looked at the clock; I'd slept for nearly fifteen hours and could probably go for another fifteen.

Instead, I got up and padded through to my dressing room, pulling some pajama bottoms and a hoodie from my drawers, throwing them on. The apartment was silent as I walked downstairs to the kitchen, clearly far too early for anyone else to be up, although the baby would be awake soon for her first bottle of the day.

The baby. *The baby*. I needed to decide on her name, and today was the deadline. I flicked on the coffee machine while I mulled it over. I still liked Betty, although maybe I needed to change it so no one else made one of Rafe's asinine comments.

Betty Grace Valentine Williams.

Hmmmm.

Arabella had been next up on the baby name list I kept in my head.

Arabella Grace Valentine Williams.

Bell?

The coffee finished dripping and I picked up the cup while I continued debating with myself.

"Good morning, did you sleep well? Feeling more human? Look, baby, Daddy is awake. Would you like to hold her while I make her bottle?"

The coffee cup stopped halfway to my lips and I fought the urge to rub my eyes to make sure I wasn't hallucinating.

Kit smiled wide, her body almost pressed to mine as she gently placed the baby in my arms, the scent of sandalwood fighting the coffee aroma, not detecting I'd been rendered speechless.

This was not the nanny I met yesterday. I would have noticed.

Definitely.

I would have noticed if the woman I'd met yesterday had

hair the color of melted caramel, hair that was tied up in a long, thick ponytail on top of her head, swishing as she reached into the cupboard for the tub of formula. I'd have noticed if she been all soft golden curves, perfectly proportioned with full, pert boobs and an ass so round and tight in the yoga pants she was wearing that you could bounce a quarter off it.

I would have noticed.

No, this was not the woman I'd met yesterday.

The woman currently in my kitchen, staring up at me with deep chocolate eyes, rosy pink cheeks, and a mouth whose sole purpose was to be kissed, looked like she'd just fallen out of the Teachers' Edition of Sports Illustrated. Like she always had snacks in her bag, a rainbow variety of crayons, and finger painted without worrying she'd get dirty.

"Murray?" she waved at me, breaking my gaze.

"Sorry, what did you say?"

She laughed. A throaty laugh that was both innocent and dirty all at the same time, whether she meant it to sound like that or not, and it licked across my body as though it was her own tongue, making my dick stir instantly.

"Where are the spoons?"

I pointed to the drawer and she took one out.

"Maybe you need to go back to sleep for a bit. Your mom said you haven't slept this week." Her gentle smile was more beautiful than the sunrise slowly creeping up the horizon and leaking through the kitchen windows, and hit me with just as much might. "It's really hard with a newborn, but we'll get her on a proper schedule soon and it'll be much easier for you. Just a few more nights and you'll be all caught up."

I forced myself to look away from her; from the freckles that dotted across her creamy shoulders, visible due to the tank top she had on.

I coughed through my spiraling thoughts and thrust the baby back at her. "Yes, good idea."

I practically ran out of the room, and back up the stairs two at a time, desperately needing to create distance between us and get my shit together.

Jas and Cooper had been correct. I was in for a world of trouble, because for the next sixteen weeks, I'd be living with the hottest nanny in existence.

Penn had also been correct. But I didn't just want to give her one; I wanted to give her an entire orchard full of apples.

They'd all been fucking correct, and I cursed my sisters again for their meddling; for putting me into a path more tempting than anything Eve ever had to deal with.

I reached my bedroom and shut the door. Taking a deep breath I stood tall, pulling my shoulders back. I might be on the precipice of my own personal hell, but I wasn't going to cave.

I was a fucking father now. And that was the most important thing.

I was responsible.

I was her employer.

My head fell back against the door and all I could see was her smile as I'd handed the baby back. See her full, peachy lips as she took the baby from me. Lips I wanted to feel against mine.

Fuck.

This was going to be harder than I thought.

6

KIT

I squeezed the water out of my hair as much as I could before blasting it with the dryer until it reached an acceptable level of dryness - acceptable because no one had the amount of spare time required to dry my hair to actual dryness - then braided it into a crown, got dressed, and went to find Bell. I could hear the financial analysts discussing the day's predictions on the stock market performance as I walked down the stairs to the kitchen, carefully pulling a sweater over my head.

In the five days I'd been living here, I'd learned the only channels the televisions were tuned to were the financials ones. And the latest count on televisions was seven, not including the one in my bedroom. Not that I could really call it a bedroom when it was bigger than my entire, soon to-be-ex, apartment. A wave of annoyance washed through me, still smarting over the inconvenience of the eviction, even though Wolfie and Freddie had stayed true to their word and organized the big move for next weekend, plus storage. Despite my irritation, I was now sleeping on very-fucking-sleepable twelve hundred thread count sheets, and despite the fact I was getting up three times a night with Bell, I'd never slept better.

I peered into Murray's study, where four of said seven televisions were playing on the wall, all but one on mute. But that's all that was happening. I found what I was looking for when I reached the kitchen, entering as quietly as possible so as not to disturb the scene playing out in front of me.

Goodbye ovaries. It was nice knowing you before you exploded.

I held back the sigh I wanted to let out, a sigh I would have felt deep in my bones.

I don't think a sexier man had ever existed.

I was living with a walking, talking, Gillette ad.

A poster child for Girl Dads everywhere.

And that English accent? I didn't know accents could set a pulse racing, but his did. And right now… well, my heart was about to go the way of my ovaries.

Murray was feeding Bell, Barclay lying on the floor underneath them, and I would never get enough of watching it.

Since my second morning, we'd begun a routine. I would get up at six thirty a.m. and prepare her bottle, Murray would wake her at seven, change and feed her while I had a shower and got dressed. Given that my room connected onto Bell's, if I timed it correctly, I'd hear him talking to her. More adorable conversations had never occurred, I was certain.

But this morning?

Murray was sitting at the kitchen table, still in pajama bottoms, his bare feet propped up on the chair next to him, Bell in his arms, snuggled up against the huge bicep flexing underneath the soft crimson cotton of an aged Harvard Varsity shirt. I didn't know finance guys had muscles to put pro-athletes to shame, but this one did.

He held the bottle under his chin and turned the page on the newspaper he was reading. One of many, given the amount scattered over the table, because along with the TV, Murray seemed to devour the print news like it was a ritual.

"Oohh, Bell, listen to this." He was using the soft, lilting voice he always did whenever he spoke to her. "*Stock on MerryTown Drinks Incorporated is up four hundred and thirty-five percent following the holiday season.* Your daddy was clever investing in that pre-IPO, and that's what we call a long position, because we know it's not going to make money straight away. We need to be patient. Uncle Jamie will be pleased. And actually, so will Uncle Penn and Uncle Rafe because I've made them a lot of money."

I pushed off the kitchen counter I'd been leaning against. "Teaching her young?"

He looked up at me, his eyes lingering with a level of intensity that made my breath catch before his gaze dropped back down to Bell. My body reacted in the same way it always did when Murray was around, hot shivers breaking out in waves across my skin, and even though I'd checked the thermostat several times to confirm it wasn't broken, I still wasn't convinced. Because every single day so far, I'd felt like I was on the verge of a hormonal flush, originating from the very center of my core.

"Of course. She needs to learn early if she'd going to run the FED one day."

I smiled to myself at the ever-expanding list of companies she'd be running, took a burp cloth from one of the drawers and placed it over his shoulder. "Here you go."

"Thank you."

"How's she doing?"

His eyes stayed trained on hers, watching her little hands as they curled and uncurled, trying to touch the bottle he was holding. Like always when he talked about her, his voice overflowed with pride. "She's doing so well. She's nearly finished this."

"You can probably burp her, and then give her the rest of it."

I busied myself organizing Bell's things, stopping myself from staring as he pulled the bottle from her lips and shuffled her around, laying her over his shoulder as I'd shown him to. He rubbed her back until she let out a loud burp and resumed her position, snuggling in his arms.

I'd been here five days and my fascination with this new family hadn't yet waned. It hadn't merged into all the other families and babies I'd looked after, the way it usually did. I'd also never felt so aware of being; of standing in one place; of watching. Because I wouldn't just watch to make sure he was okay, I'd watch *him*. The way his lips parted oh-so-slightly as he fed his daughter; how the heaviness of his brow softened as he watched her, mesmerizing himself, losing himself in her, watching her the way one might watch their first snow fall after a lifetime of living in the desert.

"What are you going to do today?" He glanced at me with an expression I couldn't read. In fact, I'd been finding it hard to read any of his expressions.

I ran through the mental checklist I made myself. I tried to check it all off every day, although usually by eleven a.m. something would have happened and then everything else would get pushed to the next day. So far, we were still on track, but it was only seven forty-six a.m.

"There are a lot of clothes that keep arriving, so I need to wash them and sort her wardrobe."

I ignored the flutter of my heartbeat as he laughed loud. I'd heard him laugh before, I just hadn't seen it yet, because when I was around, he was more the concentrating, silent type, focused on the baby. And now I didn't ever want to miss it, because when he laughed, he wasn't just sexy, he was easily one of the most beautiful men I'd ever seen. His inviting, full mouth was wide open, showing off perfect white teeth as he threw his head back, his bright green eyes sparkling with relaxed amusement. His beard had grown thicker since I'd arrived, and I was suddenly desperate to discover if he had a dimple under all the scruff covering his chiseled jaw.

"Yeah, I think between my mum and sisters they bought Manhattan out of newborn stuff. I liked this one today." He glanced back down at Bell.

Today's outfit choice was a tiny white onesie, covered in ice-creams and cones. So, *so* cute, and one he'd chosen, because he wanted to do everything he could. Mornings, bath time, bedtime bottle, and story. The only thing he willingly handed over was the middle of the night feeds. And I'd quickly started to look forward to seeing what he chose for her to wear each morning.

"That'll explain it then." His laughter was contagious. "And your parents have gone out so I think I'll take her out to the park after her first nap, if that's okay?"

All week, the apartment had been a thoroughfare of Murray's friends and family, and his parents especially had been filling the grandparent's role perfectly; bonding with Bell, taking her out every day, and playing with her when Murray was busy. Because even though I was here to look after her and put her on a schedule, it was a novelty to me having so many other adults around that wanted to help. But there was still plenty to do, and it meant I could spend my days organizing the dozens of deliveries which arrived daily for Bell – bouncers, a bath seat, diapers, clothes, bottles, more furniture, more clothes, baby everything - and sending back anything which wasn't needed.

"Do whatever you want. You're in charge." He paused, frowning, like he was waging an internal battle with himself. "In fact, I'll come and bring Barclay. She can sleep in her stroller, right?"

I nodded in surprise. We hadn't actually spent much time alone together, or any really, mostly because of everyone else being around, but I'd also had the distinct feeling he didn't want to be alone with me, more than simply wanting to bond with his new baby daughter. I'd never worked with a single dad before, always the moms. Usually, new dads didn't want to be alone with their baby; too worried about doing something wrong or breaking them. But with Murray, he'd rather be with her or with his family, always staying slightly apart from me, moving away as soon as I'd placed Bell in his arms.

"Yes, she can, unless you want to have a go at strapping her to you. A baby sling arrived yesterday."

He ran his thumbnail over his lower lip, hesitating.

"I'll show you how."

"Yes, okay." He nodded slowly. "Yeah, let's do that."

"Cool, okay." I tried to hide the surprise I was still feeling, and ignore the desperate churning in my belly at the prospect of spending time alone together. "I unpacked another snowsuit yesterday too so you can put her in that. I'll leave it out for you, unless you want me to do it."

He nodded again. "Yes, thank you. I have some calls to make and need to shower. I'll be done in a couple of hours, and then we can go."

He stood up. I was unprepared for the power of the electric shock which ran through me as his fingers brushed against my arm when I took Bell back. I was even less prepared for the power of Murray's gaze as it held mine for a second longer than was appropriate for an employer/employee relationship. I was still standing there two minutes later, trying to make sense of my very confused thoughts.

I zipped up the bear shaped snowsuit and pulled a cream cashmere beanie, with little bear ears, onto Bell's head. Her long black lashes fluttered as she tried to focus on what I was doing.

"Oh, Bells, you look so cute in this. Daddy's very lucky to have such a beautiful girl to walk to the park with."

"I am."

I startled, turning around, immediately biting down on the inside of my cheek to stop the blush which was rapidly rising up from my chest.

What the *fuck* was wrong with me this week?

He was standing in the doorway, dressed in jeans and a thick cable-knit sweater, impressively emphasizing his biceps until my mind could think of nothing else, and I had to force myself to blink. The navy sleeveless body warmer and navy ball cap pulled down low over his dark blonde hair, was equally appealing, bringing out the jade green in his eyes, and along with his low slung jeans, firmly cemented my earlier assessment that he was the best-looking man I'd ever seen in my life.

My *entire* life.

As I got closer, I noticed his cap and body warmer both featured the logo of the gym Payton loved, the one I'd been given a membership for – Body by Luck. And then I was enveloped with the most delicious scent of moss and oak, combined with a rich smoky amber, all of which seeped into my pores and under my skin. I wasn't sure what was happening to me, but I was losing all sense of myself, my head in a spin.

I handed Bell over, at the same time hoping he hadn't noticed my growing awkwardness, clenching my fists to stop them shaking. "Good, you're ready. I'll get my coat and we can head out."

I grabbed the baby sling and held it in front of him, showing him how to wear it.

"This way you know how to do it when I'm not here. Slip it over your head, pull on the toggles to make sure everything is secure and tight, then you put Bell in and secure it again."

As with nearly every time before, he remained silent,

listening to me and doing what I'd said, but offering nothing back except a slight raise of his eyebrow which flared my pulse until every inch of my body hummed. Then the kiss he gave Bell before he slipped her into the harness made my heart thud erratically, just like it had done earlier, and I tried to rub away the spinning feeling again.

There was definitely something wrong with me. Maybe I should grab a cereal bar on the way out. Or stop drinking caffeine. Forever.

I added a blanket to her, tucking her in tight, all while very consciously trying not to touch Murray in any way, which was much harder than it sounded. Virtually impossible.

"We're all good. Ready?"

His low chuckle did nothing to ease the tightness building in my chest at the sight of them together. "Ready."

Five minutes later, we walked out of the building doors into the crisp, bright sunshine that was counteracting the cold bite of the New York air, and across the road straight into Central Park, Murray carrying Bell, and me holding Barclay on his leash. I hadn't been out to explore the neighborhood yet, managing only a couple of runs during my breaks, but even in the two days since I'd last been, the spring flowers had emerged properly; the bright yellow daffodils confirming that winter was finally over.

We started down the path which led to the lake. "You can let Barc off."

I unclipped his leash and he bounded off to the nearest tree.

"I like that you like Barclay," he said quietly.

I looked up at him curiously. "Who wouldn't like him? He's beautiful."

He shrugged, not offering any more of an explanation, his concentration on Bell, and we continued walking in silence. I soon found myself almost jogging to keep up with Murray's long strides until he realized what was happening, trying to hold back the amusement creeping up the corner of his mouth.

"Sorry. I always forget to slow down. Franks always shouts at me for it, and she's even shorter than you."

As if to illustrate how tall he really was, he ducked under a looming branch.

"Who's Franks?"

"Freddie," he clarified. "Her first name is Francesca. Her initials used to spell Fred before she married Coop, but I always called her Franks because I couldn't pronounce Francesca when I was little."

My heart squeezed again.

"You English love a good name change. Wolf, Freddie, Bell…" I grinned at him.

"Yeah, I guess we do." A smile twisted his lips, as he gently stroked Bell's head. "But are you telling me Kit isn't short for Katherine?"

"Yep."

"Wait, that's your *whole* name?" He blinked in surprise, almost shocking himself out of the quiet brooding I'd only known up to now. "Kit?"

His clipped British accent, and the way he emphasized the T at the end, commanding and final, licked along my spine, transporting me straight back to my sixteen-year-old self discovering that Jake Torre, star wide receiver of Oakbay High Football team, and Number One Crush, knew her name. It was the greatest day of my young life.

"Kit Isobel Hawkes, yes."

Barclay ran back to us with a loud woof, bouncing around on his paws in front of Murray, until he pulled a ball from his pocket and threw it.

"Huh, can't really shorten that. Where does Kit come from?"

I rolled my lips, pausing before I told him, unsure I

wanted to share. He noticed, even as we both watched Barclay sprint after the ball.

"Okay, now you have to tell me. There's a story there."

I gave him a wry smile. "My dad collects classic cars, and his favorite is his Fifty-Seven Chevy, which he restored before I was born. And it was called Kit. So, yes, I've been named after a car."

He laughed loudly. "That's brilliant. What does your dad do?"

I wasn't sure what I'd expected from this walk. I still hadn't quite got a grasp on how different he'd been this morning compared to every other day, but I was finding him surprisingly easy to talk to for someone who'd got by using as few words as possible up to this point. This wasn't a stilted, polite conversation; he seemed genuinely interested in finding out the answers to his questions.

"He works for Nike. I grew up in Oregon, and he's worked there since I was a kid."

"That's cool, what does he do there?"

"He's part of the research and innovation teams."

His head turned so he could look at me directly, his bright green eyes wide and curious. "Seriously?"

I nodded. "Yes."

"Wow, that's… what does he do for them?"

"Actually, he coaches track there, but works on the innovation in all elements of women's sport clothing. Aerodynamics… that sort of thing."

His eyebrows rose and we continued walking in silence for another minute.

"Has he ever thought of leaving?"

He wasn't the first person I'd met who thought my dad's job was cool, but it was the first time anyone had asked me that. "Nike?"

"Yes."

I shook my head, picturing my dad's face of horror if

anyone asked him to leave. "Nooooo. My parents were born and raised in Oregon, as was Nike."

He laughed at my tone, the air relaxing around us. "Fair enough. So you're from Oregon? Have you got a big family?"

"I have two sisters, both younger than me."

He picked up Barclay's ball again and threw it. "Are they as noisy and chaotic and interfering as my family?"

If I'd thought that first call with Wolfie and Freddie was intense, the past week had nothing on it. His family was full-on loud, boisterous, demanding… but so filled with love for one another that it was heartwarming and endearing. And I'd been brought into it with the same level of enthusiasm they gave everything else.

"Almost."

His low chuckle hit me again, a thick heat coiling my veins. "Yeah, I'm yet to meet anyone who can beat them out for noise. What do your sisters do?"

"My middle sister just had a baby, and my youngest sister is still in college."

Barclay's ball sailed through the air once more. "Did they both leave Oregon?"

"Yes, but they stayed on the west coast."

"What made you leave Oregon?"

I dodged a sprinting Barclay as he bounded back, followed by another dog looking to play. "I always wanted to go to Columbia to read English."

His tongue ran along his top lip as he shook his head and tutted.

"Madness. Why Columbia when Harvard is clearly the best?" he teased.

I grinned at his tone. "Because Columbia is better for research, and I always liked that it was founded by a King. Sounds more romantic." I side-eyed him, noticing him smile. "If it makes you feel better, Harvard was my backup."

His loud snort erased the final vestiges of any awkwardness I'd been feeling between us. "Wow, way to make a guy feel inferior."

"New York is a better city too, there's so much to do as a student. I worked my way through the Met and I couldn't have done that in Boston."

He raised his eyebrow at me. "What? Like a room a day?"

"Something like that, but the special exhibits took precedence. It took me a few years, but I did it. Now I go for the new exhibitions," I shrugged. "I like learning."

"I'm very impressed."

"Thank you." My cheeks warmed slightly at his compliment, enhanced by the cold March air.

"You know," he picked up the ball and threw it, "you don't look like an English major."

"Oh yeah? And what does an English major look like?"

His teasing, confident tone returned. "Lots of black, maybe an ironic beret, going around quoting Shakespeare and shit like that."

I just about stopped a very unladylike snort from destroying any good impression I'd made this week. "I'm an equal opportunist English major. I can quote most of the greats... Wordsworth would have had a ball with all the daffodils out today."

He laughed loudly.

I side eyed him. "Shakespeare is my favorite though. You can't beat him."

"I knew it." He nudged me lightly.

A faux gasp escaped my lips. "This coming from the least geeky looking math geek I've ever met," I shot back before I could stop myself, earning another eyebrow raise which pinked my cheeks again because it was very clear I was aware of how he looked. Who was I kidding? Even blind people could tell he looked good, along with the entire population of New York City – which was evident by more than a few of the head turns I'd noticed since we'd entered the park, and I don't think Bell added much to that. I had a feeling he always turned heads, because he had a face that everyone wanted a second and third glimpse of.

The difference between him and every other guy I knew was that he either hadn't noticed or didn't care. His attention was focused entirely on Bell.

And me.

I coughed my awkwardness away. "What about you? Why did you come to New York?"

He gave Bell a kiss, straightening her hat, before he answered. "Work and family. My brother and I own a company, and we've always wanted to set up an office in New York, especially as I was in college here. Then Wolfie and Franks got married and stayed here, which made it easier." He turned to me, his grin setting my heart racing once more. "Plus, I have the boys. They might seem independent, but they fall apart without me."

Rafe and Penn had been over at the apartment every day, and the times I'd heard him laugh were because of them. I still didn't know the full story of what happened, but they had both been glued to his side, giving him more than a little confidence that he could raise a daughter. They did it all while constantly making fun of him, and he could give as good as he got, which again made me wonder why I'd only ever seen the quiet, brooding Murray. That was until this morning. Because right now, we were well into the longest conversation we'd ever had.

It was a turn of events I was almost grateful not knowing about, because if he'd been like this on my first day, this charming and this funny and sweet instead of the aloof and reserved father he had been, I'd have probably turned around and left because alongside his huge muscles and Godlike levels of beauty, it was a deadly combination.

I had a job with a very clear line, which wasn't to be crossed under my own or any semblance of professional standards. And having a crush on your boss was bordering on way too close. It was reaching out to grasp the live wire when you knew it would do nothing but shock you to within an inch of your life.

Not to mention a goddamn motherfucking cliché.

"I think I should get one of those." He pointed to a woman powering along with a running stroller, who very obviously slowed down as she passed. "You like running, don't you? You could run with Bell and then you could use your breaks for something else."

"I do, thank you, but she's a bit young for it right now. The summer will be good, once she's bigger. I can find you one to use for when I'm gone though."

"Right, right, because you're only here four months," he murmured, almost under his breath.

We reached another part of the park, Murray holding the gate open for me to walk in ahead of him which was another thing I'd noticed about him this week: his impeccable manners. And even though we were only on a walk, it felt more like a date than any other actual date I'd ever been on.

I *really* needed to get a grip.

"Oooh, hot chocolate," he announced excitedly, and I followed his line of sight to the wooden booth selling drinks. "Come on, let's get one."

Barclay sat down next to him as we joined the line. I shifted the blanket around a now fast asleep Bell, making sure she was warm and comfortable, ignoring my Amtrak sized train of thoughts that anyone would be warm and comfortable against Murray's huge chest. My movements earned the attention of an older lady standing ahead of us in the line.

"Ah, how sweet. First outing?"

I shook my head, smiling. "No, but she's getting used to it."

"How old is she?" The lady looked up at Murray through spidery, mascara coated lashes.

"Three weeks today."

"How sweet," she repeated, her eyes moving between us. "And you're a beautiful couple."

I nearly choked on my own saliva. "Oh no..."

Murray put his arm around my shoulders before I had a chance to correct her. "Thank you."

"I suspect your baby is beautiful."

She tried to shift around to see, but I'd placed the blanket over Bell like a hood to shield her from the wind, so her face wasn't visible.

"Yes, she is," replied Murray, and even though he was smiling back, I could tell he was beginning to get annoyed, his spare hand moving to protect Bell's face as the lady peered in. I should have made more of an effort to get rid of her, except I was finding it hard to concentrate, still very aware of his arm over my shoulders, which was pulling me closer into him. "She's sleeping right now."

The lady's smile held strong, in the way that made you wonder if her face was stuck. "So precious."

"Next!" shouted the guy at the cart, forcing the woman to halt her continued efforts to have a glimpse of Bell.

Murray looked down at me, his eyes flaring wide open with amusement, and I hid my smile before she turned back around and caught me. My shoulders felt instantly cooler as he dropped his arm, while surprise replaced the amusement in his eyes. "Sorry, don't know why I did that."

We stepped into the second line as it became available and ordered two hot chocolates, waiting at the side for them to be made after Murray handed over some cash.

"Goodbye." The old lady made one last failed attempt to see Bell, and we watched her walk off.

I burst into laughter. "Wow, I think you have a fan there."

He shook his head in amusement. "No, Bell does."

We took our drinks as they were placed on the side and found a nearby log to sit on, Murray checking on a still sleeping Bell, his long legs stretched out in front of him.

"The lady had a point though, she is beautiful."

"Yes, she really is isn't she?" His smile was so wide and genuine it made my heart swell.

"She looks like you, you know."

"You think?" Surprise flashed across his face. "I can't see it."

"Definitely. She has your mouth and your eyes, long lashes like you…" I trailed off before it started to get weird that I'd reeled off a list of his flawless features without blinking - or that he noticed I could.

He sipped his hot chocolate, his pink tongue darting out to lick the foam from his lip. "Thank you."

"What did her mom look like?"

His playful mood vanished instantly. His throat began working hard as his jaw tensed from his teeth grinding together, making me wish I'd kept my big mouth shut. We'd been getting on so well, and now I'd overstepped.

"I'm sorry, I shouldn't have asked. I didn't mean to offend you."

His eyes met mine and I could see more than a little pain swimming around; pain and guilt. "You didn't." He took a deep breath. "Truth is, I don't remember what she looked like, except that she was brunette. How shit is that? This tiny little thing I've known a week and a half, one who's become the love of my life, and I can't remember anything about where she came from, or how she was made. What kind of father is that? What am I going to do when she's older and asks? This wasn't how it was supposed to happen."

His shoulders dropped in defeat, weighed down with the considerable worry he was carrying, as he rubbed his fingers over his temples. I fought all my impulses to hug him.

"You tell her that. That she's the love of your life; that

even though you hadn't known about her existence until you met, you wouldn't have it any other way, that her mom was fun and spirited and beautiful, because otherwise you wouldn't have spent time together. And you don't regret a single second, because you were chosen to be her daddy."

He stayed silent, his gaze trained in the distance, with another one of those expressions I couldn't read. When he finally looked up again his eyes found mine, flashing with so much emotion we may as well have been sitting by a furnace with the way my body heated. "Come on, let's get back. Bell will wake up soon and she'll need feeding."

Forty-five minutes later we stepped into the elevator and pressed the button for his floor.

"Hold the door!" a voice called just before a man slinked between the closing gap. He noticed Murray, tipping his head to him. "Hey, man, how're you doing?"

Then I forgot how to breathe. Holy fucking *actual* shit.

Jackson Foggerty.

The Hollywood bad boy. Recipient of the most recent Best Actor Oscar. Sexiest Man Alive according to, off the top of my head, People, Vogue, Gucci, Patek Philippe, and the newest issue of the New York Times Magazine, where he was interviewed about his latest film.

And now he was here.

In the elevator.

With me.

My fingers twitched, desperate to get my phone and immediately text Payton, because she was going to *freak.* He'd been her number one crush at college, and unbeknownst to every single boyfriend she'd had, they'd all been compared to him. Yet he looked smaller in person, especially standing next to Murray, although his blue eyes were still as piercing.

"Yeah, not bad, mate. You know how it is. How about you?"

"Yeah, same." He stroked Barclay's head. "How's parenthood going?"

I was standing there, my head moving between them, fascinated. Then, I saw the only expression of Murray's I could read, the one which appeared whenever he spoke about Bell. Love. Pride. Happiness.

"Good, getting the hang of it I think."

I sighed at the cuteness, earning myself the attention of the two gentlemen I was sharing the elevator with.

Jackson Foggerty's gaze slowly scanned up and down the length of my body in a way that made me instinctively step back, even though I was already pressed against the wall.

"And who, are you?"

He didn't notice Murray stiffen next to me. He also didn't notice his green eyes narrow and darken to a color almost imperceptible from black. The door pinged before I could respond, sliding open on our floor. But then we *all* got out. Barclay bounded down the corridor.

I'd already taken five paces before I realized Murray wasn't next to me, and turned to find him blocking Jackson Foggerty's way.

"Off limits, Foggerty," he snarled, but not quietly enough for me not to hear. "Don't even fucking think about it or you can get the stairs from now on."

"Whoa, calm down." His hands went up defensively. "Message received."

Murray stood there staring at him until he turned and headed in the opposite direction, and then spun around to me.

"Stay away from him," he snapped, overtaking me before I could say a word or even have a second to consider his bizarre behavior.

I followed him silently back into the apartment, just as Bell opened her eyes and started grumbling as she always did when she was getting hungry. Murray was too focused on getting her out of the sling, while I was still wondering what the fuck just happened, to notice the suitcases by the door until Diane came into the entrance hall.

She took Bell out of Murray's arms, giving her a kiss, which was when he saw them.

He motioned to all the bags. "What's going on?"

"We're going to get out of your way, let you all settle in together. We're going to be staying with Jasper and Wolf for a little while."

I didn't miss the look of panic crossing Murray's face. "You're leaving?!"

"Yes," she replied firmly, as she deftly removed Bell from her snowsuit with the skill of a woman who had four children and seven grandchildren.

Murray's eyes shot over to me and whatever was going through his head, he didn't look happy about it.

I coughed awkwardly, needing to get away from him and his weird mood swing, not wanting to be part of whatever conversation they were about to have. "Diane, can I take her for her bottle before she starts crying?"

She turned to me, smiling, spinning around so her back was to Murray and pulled me in for a tight hug, her voice low. "Thank you for everything you're doing for my son."

The ever-familiar blush rose up my cheeks again. "It's just my job."

I took Bell from her, walking toward the kitchen to make her bottle.

"Kit?" Murray called after me.

I glanced back before turning the corner, catching Murray's eye as Diane whispered to him and immediately wished I hadn't. The color hadn't changed back from when he'd been glaring at Jackson Foggerty, but instead of anger, his eyes flared with a level of heat that could put molten lava to shame, melting us together.

Consider me on fire and in dire need of an entire station full of hoses.

I tore my gaze away from his, almost running to the kitchen. Putting Bell in her bouncer, I leaned against the counter and attempted to make sense of the reams and reams of questions shooting through my brain while trying to still a succession of mini cyclones using my insides as practice for their destruction, whirling around my bones until my entire body was shaking.

I was in trouble. *Big* trouble.

I needed to pretend this wasn't happening.

Because maybe this week the apartment had been too chaotic for me to notice; and maybe I should have paid better attention to how my belly did a little churning flip thing every time Murray walked into a room, which had nothing to do with a faulty thermostat. And maybe, if I hadn't been so busy, I would have recognized sooner than ten seconds ago that I'd developed a Herculean sized crush on my boss.

But I hadn't, and now it was only the three of us. Alone.

And as huge as the apartment was, I didn't think there was anywhere I could hide.

7

MURRAY

A soft, tuneless singing was coming from the connecting bathroom between Bell and Kit's rooms as I walked into the nursery to wake the baby. The shower was doing a good job of trying to drown it out, but not quite good enough. Barclay was managing to sleep through the noise however, already lying on his bed in the corner of the nursery where he'd seemed to take permanent residence whenever Bell was in here.

I chuckled to myself, leaning over Bell's crib to see her staring up at me with wide open eyes. It had been three weeks, and I knew I would never get enough of this, of gazing at my daughter.

"Looks like we've found something that Kit isn't perfect at eh, Bells?" I lifted her gently, kissing her cheek and smelling her sweet baby scent as I held her for a little cuddle before putting her down on her changing table.

I congratulated myself on discovering that little nugget, because in the two weeks she'd been here, I had yet to find something that Kit couldn't do. Every day there was something new that she revealed - another tantalizing part of herself - and I found myself impatiently sitting on the edge, drawn to her, jittery and impatient until the next piece of her was disclosed. It was like discovering a new and highly addictive TV show, only to find out the network was making you wait a week for the next episode. Or desperately needing to start the next chapter of a book you couldn't put down, even though you should be sleeping.

But all it really did was serve the very necessary requirement for me to actively remind myself on the regular that she was off limits and I had to fucking behave. Couple that with the raging jealousy that surged through my veins the second that fuck, Foggerty, laid his eyes on her, or anyone laid their eyes on her, and I was a step away from writing it on my hand like I was still studying for finals. And I was struggling to come up with more excuses to stay away from her because my brain was actively defying me. It didn't help that Penn and Rafe were in my ear all hours of the day and night, trying to make me crack.

Trying to make me admit they'd all been fucking right.

Something I was absolutely loath to do, because admitting out loud that I liked her, that I desperately wanted to touch her, taste her, smell her, wouldn't just be a highway to Hell. No, that would be powering along the *Autobahn* in Rafe's SCC Tuatara with no seatbelt.

But if I thought the first five days of not being around her was difficult, avoiding being alone with her as much as possible, distracting myself with work and spending obscene amounts of money on the most volatile investments just to replace the constant anxiety she put in my head with another, after we'd walked to the park it was nigh-on impossible.

Then my interfering family decided to desert me for a reason that had fuck-all to do with us settling in together, and everything to do with them pushing me further toward Kit.

They may as well have fed me to the wolves.

Except, I think - scratch that - I *knew* I was the wolf in this scenario, because every day my mouth watered with longing for her. It didn't matter what she was doing or wearing, I wanted her more every day, like I'd lived in a cave for the entirety of my almost thirty-two years on this earth and never seen a woman before. I was a wank away from ordering her to wear a burlap sack, not that it would make any difference. She'd still look like an autumnal angel with her honey blonde hair and dark *café-con-leche* eyes, peering at me through long thick lashes.

But that was nothing compared to her kindness and understanding; the way she played with Bell for hours on end, reading to her, talking, teaching – all of which was her job, but I hadn't expected her to be quite so good at it, because, let's face it, there's no riveting two-way chat with a baby. Even the non-judgmental way she'd reassured me when I'd opened up to her when I'd almost lost it and bawled like Bell in front of her. Not to mention her sense of humor, her patience, her ability to make anything seem easy. Barclay was besotted with her. The doormen and building concierge were besotted with her, everyone was besotted.

Fuck, and she'd started baking.

Even the terrible singing was adorable. Terrible shower singing, where she currently was. Naked.

Wet.

Fuck's sake.

I shook my head, hard, before my dick and my brain ganged up on me with a torrent of inappropriate thoughts. All before my heart got in on the action too; a piece of me I'd been ignoring, mostly because it now belonged to Bell. My heart had never been owned before. I'd never given it away freely, but Bell had carved her name into it the second she'd opened her eyes. And I'd almost succeeded in convincing myself that the tight squeezes and heavy thudding it gave out when Kit was with Bell was because of Bell, and nothing else.

As if to reinforce that theory, Bell let out a little gurgle, blinking up at me with her incredible eyes. The baby books I'd been reading said they would change color, but the pale shamrock green hadn't disappeared. The only difference was the appearance of a delicate ring of navy around the outside, the one just like mine. She continued gurgling and staring up at me as I unwrapped her from the duck-covered swaddle she slept in, put her in a fresh diaper and opened the drawer underneath for her first outfit for the day. I'd very quickly learned that nothing stayed clean for long. I'd also learned how to properly fit a diaper, because if you didn't, those things fucking leaked and that was something no one enjoyed.

I glanced down, seeing that Kit had organized her clothes by night and day, then color coded them all; a level of organization that I both appreciated and was secretly impressed by, and could probably do with in my life. I picked out a tiny navy blue cashmere onesie, made to look like a boiler suit, which Rafe had bought her, with Bell's name embroidered on the front pocket underneath a little bunny. And I gave zero shits about how much I enjoyed dressing her, because my daughter was fucking cute. And beautiful.

I was a bona-fide girl dad and proud of it.

I froze as the shower stopped. While I didn't expect Kit to walk into Bell's room, the thought of her dripping wet, wearing only a towel, was absolutely too much for my brain, and dick, to cope with so early in the morning. I scooped Bell up and carried her downstairs as quickly as possible, Barclay hot on my heels.

I laid Bell in her bouncer sitting on the table, and turned the coffee machine on just as Rafe and Penn walked into the kitchen.

"I'll take one of those, thanks." Rafe sat down at the table and lifted Bell from her chair, the sleeve of his sweatshirt rising up as he did, revealing an inch of the tattoo which crept up his arm, wrapping around him and decorating his body like a mural. "Look how beautiful you are in this. Clever Uncle Rafe."

"Me too." Penn took Bell's bottle from the warmer and threw it to Rafe. "Heads up!"

He caught it mid-air, removing the lid and giving it to Bell. "Breakfast time, Bells."

They had the synchronicity of a well-oiled machine, which was even more impressive considering I had no idea they were coming over. But that was how we'd always rolled.

Penn started opening and closing the cupboards, walking into the pantry and coming back empty handed. "Where are the muffins?"

It then became clear why they were here, because I wasn't the only one enamored with my new nanny, although they were more interested in the daily baked goods than I was. I pointed to the oven.

He opened it, pulling out a tray of warm raspberry muffins. "Holy shit, she's already been baking this morning? Dude, you really need to marry her."

I rolled my eyes, not wanting to engage in an argument I wasn't going to win. "Is that why you're here before eight a.m. on a Saturday? Muffins?"

"No," replied Rafe. "We're here because you're on your own today and we're taking Bell and Barclay to the park, and then to brunch. Muffins are an added bonus."

I placed coffees in front of them and joined them at the table, putting a burp cloth over Rafe's shoulder, just as Kit did to me, then watched Penn take a massive bite of a muffin.

"Fuck, our weekends have changed."

An overwhelming surge of gratitude and emotion that they were here rolled through me for the trillionth time, although it would have been more shocking if they hadn't been. We'd always done everything together, even when I was living back in London I still spent a long weekend here every month.

"I know, three weeks ago I was suffering from the worst fucking hangover of my life after I'd spent the night fucking that Swedish girl and drinking all the vodka we could find, so consider me happy with the current state of our weekends."

I raised an eyebrow at Rafe in silent question as I sipped my coffee.

"I mean the no hangover part, obviously."

Penn picked up another muffin. "I think we can all do with a few hangover free weekends."

My stomach churned to the point of vomiting at the thought of being hungover and up early with a baby, almost as though I had an actual hangover. And neither was fun.

"I don't think I'll ever be hungover again."

"Don't be so dramatic. Of course you will." Rafe put Bell's bottle down and moved her to his chest, patting her on the back.

"Raferty, move her higher," ordered Penn, like he'd done it a million times, which he hadn't. Between the three of us we'd had less than a month of learning how to parent a new baby and we were all on the same chapter of the baby book we were reading in sync. "She can't burp like that."

Bell proved him wrong by burping loudly.

"Nice job, Bell, well done." Rafe threw him a smug grin.

The air suddenly thinned to the point where I couldn't breathe. We all turned around to see Kit as she walked into the kitchen, her hair falling in thick waves around her shoulders, her perfectly innocent jeans and sweater combination doing nothing to hide her curves which filled my mind with thoughts that were far from innocent, that were so deep into the gutter my mind needed a good scrub with Clorox. Her eyes widened to a perfect almond shape as she smiled at Bell, her lips soft and glossy and so fucking kissable that I was almost weeping with sorrow that I would never get to experience the feel of them on mine.

Jesus Christ, I'd become a sentimental knobhead.

"Hi, Kiiiit," Rafe and Penn greeted her in unison, far too eagerly in my opinion, like they were in fucking high school and she was their favorite teacher.

Her cheeks glowed pink with a blush, making my cock ache. Fuck, fuck, *fuck* she was beautiful. Even from where I was sitting, far across the kitchen from her, I could almost taste her scent, like soap and springtime and freshly mowed lawns, making my head spin and my tongue practically vibrate.

"Hey, guys." Her eyes landed on Penn. "Found the muffins then?"

"Sure did. They're perfect, as always. Can you give me the recipe?" Penn swallowed his current mouthful, winking at me deviously while simultaneously flashing her one of his million dollar smiles, which usually had a girl on her back in less than sixty seconds. "In fact, when you're done with Murray, you can come and work for me. I'll pay you to make muffins all day instead of dealing with shitty diapers."

She laughed loudly and I shot Penn the darkest scowl I could muster while pushing away all irrational thoughts of banning him from my apartment while Kit was here. I was the funny one of the group, and I wanted her laughs all to myself, especially as that was the only thing I'd ever get.

He responded with a smirk. Dick.

Rafe picked up Bell's bottle and started feeding her again while shaking his head at how easily I'd fallen for Penn's deliberate attempt to bait me when I'd ignored his earlier comment, but I didn't care. If I needed to behave around her, so did everyone else.

"I'm good, but thanks for the offer."

Then my annoyance grew ten-fold at the tidal wave of relief I felt as Kit looked away from him, unfazed by his stupidly perfect face, impervious to the charm he was deliberately exuding simply to piss me off. Because the thing about Penn is that while he might look like a cherub with a face that had people of all sexes falling at his feet fighting to do his bidding, he actually gave zero shits about any of it. And while everyone desperately wanted to be friends with him, connected to him in some way, he very much did not want to be friends with anyone outside our little group. So when he did turn on his superpower, he usually got whatever he wanted.

Therefore, it was always a surprise when he didn't.

"Losing your touch, sunshine," I grumbled into my coffee cup.

"You wish."

I knocked his hand away before he could slap my cheek, and before Kit noticed us behaving like we were on the playground.

"Murray, there's a new tub of formula for her in the cupboard, and I've left everything out you'll need for today."

"Thank you." I tried to smile at her in a way that wouldn't provide more ammunition for Penn. "We'll be fine though. You go and enjoy your day off."

She scoffed. "I'll try, although packing up my apartment won't exactly be wild."

"Do you need some help?" Penn grinned widely, clearly having no desire to give up on his new game of *Annoy the Fuck Out of Murray.*

"No, my best friend, Payton, is coming over, and I'll just make her do all the heavy lifting." Her light giggle made my chest tight. "Call me if you need anything though."

"It's all good, don't worry."

"Okay, cool. See you later." She walked over to Bell, who'd almost finished her bottle, and stroked her head. "Bye, cutie."

"Bye, Kit," mouthed Penn to me as she left the kitchen.

"Pennington, I will knock your fucking head off." I

pushed out of my chair to make another coffee. "Did you take extra strength dickhead pills this morning?"

He started laughing so hard tears were soon pouring. "Dude, your face! You're literally boiling with rage. Sure you don't want to admit we're all right and you have the hots for your hot nanny? Might save you from an early heart attack."

I sipped my coffee to stop my jaw from snapping with the tension I was holding in it. "Don't call her that. Her name's Kit."

He stretched out in his chair. A magazine article had once called him *'effortlessly leonine'* and he was exactly that right at this second in my kitchen, his arms lengthening over his head with a smarmy twat grin spread across his face. "I know full well her name's Kit, jackass. I literally just said 'Bye, Kit', but until you admit that you have the hots for her then I'm going to be calling her Hot Nanny."

"How are you being such a fucking pain so early in the morning? Fine! I have the hots for her!" I blurted out before I could stop myself. "Fucking happy now?"

He looked like he'd just been handed the secrets of the universe and it took him a second to get over his shock before he answered. "Yes, I am."

"Well I'm not because I can't do anything about it! It's irrelevant anyway. Bell is my priority, and that's all there is to it."

I looked over to Bell, content in Rafe's arms having had her entire bottle. She'd grown so much in the past three weeks, and I was certain she was about to start smiling. Her little face was so engaged and inquisitive as she gurgled, unlike Rafe's, which was filled with ill-concealed amusement at my plight. I ignored him and picked up one of Kit's muffins, breaking off a chunk and throwing it in my mouth, just managing to stop a sigh from escaping as the sweet raspberry sugar hit my taste buds. Christ, this was good.

I slumped down in my chair, suddenly feeling lighter; the

pressure in my chest easing slightly like a weight had been lifted at my admission. "It's torture."

And I meant it. Because for the first time I realized it was *actual* torture. A situation I'd never been in before; confounding, and perplexing, and slowly driving me to madness. Because this wasn't the intense heat and attraction between two people, no matter how much I wanted to believe the quick, furtive glances I'd catch from her were exactly that. And it was nothing like the lingering dance of flirtation I'd had with other women either. We weren't prolonging the inevitable, we weren't edging closer. This wasn't the enforced wait of building up to an explosive, dirty weekend of intense fucking before going our separate ways.

No, there was none of that. There was only my fucked up head and no escape.

It was punishment for something I hadn't yet worked out.

It was hell.

It was me knowing this would never be more than simply wanting what I couldn't have. Because there was something greater at stake, stopping me from taking what I wanted.

Bell.

Case closed.

I reached over to a brown envelope on the table, which I hadn't noticed until now. "What's this?"

"That is your revised will and the trust fund set up for Bell. You need to go through the changes and sign it with witnesses," Rafe replied.

"Amazing. Thanks, buddy. Can I sign it now?"

"No, do it later. I can't be one of the witnesses and you need two. Come on, let's go out." He stood up, Bell still in his arms. "I rarely see Saturday this early and I'm keen to discover what it's like. Then we can decide what you're going to do."

"I'll carry Bells. I want to test the theory that babies are better at getting pussy than dogs." Penn looked over to Barclay. "No offense, Barc."

"You're not using my baby as an alternative to Raya," I snapped.

"Fine, you carry her then. I'll take Barclay, and we'll test it that way," he reasoned, giving zero shits about the point I was trying to make.

Two hours later, we walked through to our regular table at our favorite brunch spot, situated on a secluded street off Central Park, following the waitress and ignoring the heads that turned as we passed the diners already seated. We were here at some point most weekends, although not quite so early, so while our presence wasn't unusual, we hadn't been here for a month, and our party had now expanded to include Bell, currently strapped to my chest.

"Here you are, gentlemen. I'll bring your usual bottle over and some water for Barc." She bent to stroke his head from where he was already laying under the table.

"Thanks, Ally." Rafe sat down, watching her ass sway as she walked off.

Penn took a seat, putting down the enormous bag which contained all of Bell's things. I passed her over to him before removing the sling and my jacket, as Penn removed Bell's snow suit and sat down. I'd never realized how much longer everything took with a baby. Or how much stuff they came with. I'd discovered I had to add a bare minimum of thirty minutes onto any plans just to be on time.

I looked up to find the pair of them staring at me. "What?"

"Are you wearing a cardigan?" Penn blinked through his question, shuffling Bell so she was comfortable.

I looked down as if needing to confirm that yes, I was

indeed wearing a cardigan. "I'm a dad now. This is what dads wear."

Rafe failed to hold back his glee. "It's to hide his dad bod."

I leaned back in my chair, stretching out. "If by 'dad bod' you mean a better six pack than yours, then you would be correct."

"Better six pack," he scoffed, patting his stomach to check it was still there. "No fucking chance."

Ally returned with a bottle of champagne, pouring out three glasses. "I've put an order in for Eggs Benedict too."

"Good girl." Rafe picked up his glass, glancing up at her but her eyes were fixed on Penn who was still holding Bell.

"Who's this beauty? Is she yours?"

"She's mine, Penn's just practicing, so get the word around he's looking for someone to help him with that." I could feel my smile reaching from ear to ear, knowing he was currently wishing me a slow death at the prospect. Pennington Cabot James Shepherd the Third was never short of women wanting to bear his children, and a rumor spreading like that would be a battle cry for all his fans.

She jolted very slightly in surprise, before she composed herself. "Wow, Murray, she's beautiful. What's her name?"

"Bell."

"Congratulations." Her voice carried an edge that hadn't been present before.

I tipped my head with a smile. "Thank you."

"I didn't know you were seeing anyone." She stood there waiting for me to respond, which I didn't, until it bordered on awkward. "Right, I'll go and check on your breakfast."

"Is that how it's going to be now? Women on the verge of tears when they find out Murray's already got a woman in his life?" Penn scoffed.

"Yeah, did you hear that?" Rafe cupped his hand around his ear.

I couldn't hear anything beyond the chatter of other

diners. "Hear what?"

"Hearts all over the city starting to break now The Tuesday Club has lost a member."

"Oh, fuck off," I grinned, shaking my head and nodding to Bell. "We haven't lost a member, we've gained one."

Penn started opening up Bell's bag one handed, pulling out a burp cloth, wipes, and her bottle of milk. "Dude, even if Bell wasn't around, you are so far off the market and you don't even realize it."

"I assume you're talking about Kit, in your not-so-subtle way. And no, I'm not off the market, I'm on hold. I'm not doing anything about Kit. She's not mine, she's Bell's. I'm not fucking this up for Bell. I'm not."

I was fully aware of the fact that I sounded like I was trying to convince myself more than anything else. Penn rolled his eyes while he started laying Bell's things on the table.

"I don't see what the big deal is. So what if you have the hots for her?"

I sighed heavily, admitting what was really bothering me. "We bumped into Foggerty the other day. He was his usual obnoxious self, and she looked like a deer caught in the headlights. She has this bright-eyed, innocent teacher thing about her, and I don't want to sully it. Even if Bell wasn't around, I'm not going near her."

Penn pointed the bottle of milk at me. "I don't like that guy. He's a dick. You'd better not be comparing yourself to him."

"I concur, also," Rafe scoffed hard. "Is this because she bakes? No teacher I've ever known was that innocent. They act like it, but you know once the school day is over they all have stockings and suspenders on under those fucking tight skirts, because it's easy access."

"No, it's not because she bakes, idiot. She looks after my daughter. She's sweet and kind and gentle." I crossed my arms over my chest, just before I told him she sang in the shower too, which would open up this conversation to further scrutiny about her being in the shower. I had no intention of conjuring up that visual for anyone besides me. "And you've watched too much porn."

"No such thing. And *I'm* speaking from experience."

"You always say I shouldn't let my dick make my decisions. I'm simply trying to take your advice," I replied pointedly.

He lifted his glass up to me. "Touché."

Ally returned with three portions of Eggs Benedict and a huge plate of crispy bacon, placing them down in front of us, the tangy, vinegary smell of the Hollandaise causing saliva to pool in my mouth. "Can I get you anything else?"

Penn shook his head. "No thanks, sweetheart. We're all good."

She smiled at him, glanced down at the baby and walked off.

"Do you want me to take her?" I nodded to Bell, still in his arms, eyes wide and watching everything he was doing.

"Nah, I like having her." He smiled, reaching for the hot sauce and smothering his eggs in it. "Plus, I'm getting my time in now. I need to shoot off after this."

"Why?" I cut into my own breakfast, the bright orange yolk spilling all over my plate, and forked a big mouthful in.

"Need to go over to my grandparents' place."

I looked at the date on my watch. "Are they back already?"

Penn's grandparents owned several houses around the world, but the winter months were always spent on their island in the Bahamas, and, according to his grandmother, winter didn't stop in New York until April first. It was only March seventeenth, and Penn's grandmother was nothing if not a stickler for a schedule.

"No, but there's a new Picasso exhibit coming to the Met next month which the family is sponsoring, and Gramps is loaning out three of their collection. Apparently I'm the only one available to supervise the museum curator removing them from the wall or something. Only fucking dumbass to answer the phone is more like." he grumbled.

I reached over and grabbed a slice of bacon, crunching down on it. "Kit's been all round the Met. She told me she's seen everything."

"Everything? All of it?" Rafe's eyes widened as he picked up his own piece. "Even the boring stuff?"

I nodded. "Yep. Impressive, huh? She did it while she was at Columbia, took a couple of years she said."

His eyebrows rose in confirmation that he was correctly impressed. "What else do you know?"

I dug through the memory of what she'd shared, and what I'd noticed, because those nuggets I wanted to keep all to myself. Like the way she added Half 'n' Half to her coffee until it was to the brim and nearly always spilled when she lifted it to drink; or that she only seemed to braid her hair on Tuesdays and Thursdays; that I'd deduced her favorite color was green because it was what she wore the most...

"Oh my God! Stop!" Penn hissed, picking up Bell's bottle.

I frowned. "What?"

"You look like a Taylor Swift song."

"What?"

"You're in deep shit."

I groaned. "Tell me something I don't know."

"How long until she leaves and you grow your balls back?"

"Thirteen weeks and three days." I was both counting down the days until she was leaving and counting down the days I had left with her, living with me, seeping into my life and under my skin.

Penn's fork stopped in mid-air.

"Oh fuuuck. Heads up at six o'clock," he mumbled with an exaggerated shudder, and before Rafe and I had the chance to turn around, we were asphyxiated by a sickly sweet, cloying scent so suffocating that Mustard Gas would have been a preferable alternative. Barclay stood up, his hackles rising.

"Christ, if that isn't a sign I don't know what is." Rafe nodded at Barclay, before his eyes narrowed at the woman heading for our table. "Dasha."

"Rafe," she replied, matching his level of animosity with a raised eyebrow so sharp it could have drawn blood. "Penn. I see you're all still incapable of doing anything alone."

"And I see you're still an evil bitch."

Lesser death glares had brought thousands of men to their demise, but Rafe merely sipped his champagne exuding a coolness that would have kept the lake in Central Park frozen year round.

I held my breath as she leaned down and kissed me on the cheek. Barclay growled, loudly.

"I never understand why they let dogs in here."

"They let you in," drawled Penn, forking up the remainder of his Eggs Benedict.

She ignored him, her eyes still trained on me. "How are you, Murray? You look good."

I put down my glass. "Thank you."

"What have you been doing with yourself? I haven't seen you around recently. I've missed you."

In the sober, cold light of day, she was even more vapid and narcissistic than I remembered; shallower than a puddle. Dressed like a Bond villain in all black, her leather pants gave the appearance of having been painted on her mile-long legs, and a fur trimmed sweater wrapped around her neck as though she'd arrived at brunch via Siberia. Such was the contrast between her and Kit that I couldn't, for the life of me, fathom how I'd ever found her attractive, even with several units of alcohol. They were the antithesis of each other. Kit was warm where Dasha was ice cold, soft where she was razor sharp, light versus dark. I'd question how she hadn't noticed Bell yet, but you don't become vapid and narcissistic by noticing things that aren't about you.

I looked over at Bell, who was now guzzling her bottle in Penn's arms. "Well, I became a father."

Dasha's previously immovable face moved slightly, such was the shock that it broke through her barricade of Botox. "This," she pointed at Bell, her haughty face filling with horror - or maybe not filling, seeing as she could still barely move it - but if she had been able to, it would have had horror written all over it. "This is your child. How? Who with? You mentioned nothing to me."

I'd rather have my fingernails pulled out through medieval torture means than share Bell's history with Dasha. "I'm a single dad."

Her face contorted into something I assumed she thought was kind and empathetic, but the actual result was more terrifying and horrific, and again made me wonder if I'd actually just been insanely drunk the entire time I'd spent with her. Or just insane. Her severe cheekbones and wide, slanted, feline eyes were not made for smiling.

"Murray," she purred, "you can't do this on your own. I will come and help you."

My jaw clenched, not willing to rise to her veiled insult. Or maybe it wasn't even veiled because this was how the fights started. "Thanks, but I'm all set. I have all the help I need."

Penn and Rafe snorted in stereo, making it very clear how I was all set with a lot of help, earning themselves another glare.

"Murraaayyy," she elongated my name and reached out to touch me, but I moved away before she could, grabbing Barclay's collar as his teeth bared. "You don't have to be a single dad."

"I want to be one."

"Why would you want that?" Her voice hardened as the volume increased, and I half expected a colony of bats to rise up from the floor and attack me on her command.

"Dasha, he's not a single dad. Now will you fuck off and stop ruining our brunch?" Penn snapped. "Go and find a new victim to sink your claws into. My boy is off the market."

I stayed silent, while she waited for me to respond. When it became clear I wasn't about to, the snarl on her lip would have made any Doberman proud as she turned on her heel and stalked off.

"Ker-ist. She'd probably murder you in your bed if you're not careful." Penn shook his head. "You should up security, or you'll find she's removed your balls in the night without anesthetic so she can wear them for earrings."

Rafe laughed. "Yeah, she'd definitely do that. The guy she dated before you was into nasty shit, so she's bound to have picked up some bad habits. I had to dig up some stuff on him last year for a case."

I threw my hands in the air. "We didn't date; we slept together until the novelty wore off. You can't blame me, she looked fucking hot and she wasn't walking around with a psycho warning strapped to her. You remember what that night was like? We were all wasted and if I recall, you went off with the Truman twins." I pointed to Rafe, who shrugged with no shame, a smile slowly slanting on the left corner of his lip in memory. "Anyway, what's done is done. It's over and I made that very clear to her after she tried to throw a plate at me."

Rafe scratched his fingers through his hair. "You know, I always thought Beulah Holmes was the most evil woman to walk the planet, but Dasha would wipe the floor with her."

"Fuck, Beulah Holmes. Not heard her name in a while," Penn whispered. Bell had fallen asleep in his arms. "There never used to be a day where you didn't complain about her."

"Yeah, I swear she'd drink the blood of the freshmen just

so she could stay up all night to study and fuck with my grades."

Beulah Holmes was a girl on Rafe's law course, the only person who'd ever been able to raise him from his permanent insouciance. His favorite present we'd ever given him was a dart board made with her face printed on it. Every day he'd come back to the house, complaining about how much he hated her and throw some darts at her until he felt better. And the feeling was mutual. They made each other's lives hell, but she was also why he graduated first in their class, because Hell would have *actually* frozen over before he'd let her beat him. Penn and I had a secret bet going that they'd fuck it out, but they just went their separate ways, hating each other from afar.

"Wonder what she's up to now."

"She's out in Chicago reigning terror at a big firm, or was last time I checked." He knocked back the last of his champagne. "But as long as she's far away from me, I couldn't give a fuck."

I caught Penn's eye, the glint matching mine, grinning at him.

"Can I get you gentlemen anything else?" asked Ally, as another server cleared our table of empty plates.

I looked at my watch. "No, I'm good thanks, Ally. I need to head off."

"Shall I bring the check?"

"Yes, please, sweetheart. That would be good," Rafe nodded, and looked at me. "What're you doing now?"

"I've got some work to do this afternoon and I want to get Bell home for her next bottle, so she can sleep in her bed."

Right on cue, Bell woke up and started crying, the universal signal for needing to get the fuck out. I took her from Penn, kissing her cheek as she grumbled.

"Come on, little one, time to go home." I looked back over at Rafe. "What are you doing? You want to come with us?"

"Nah, I think I should go and supervise Pennington's supervision. Especially as I'm his legal counsel, and the likelihood he'll fuck it up somehow."

Penn responded by flipping him off.

"Yeah, okay." I stood up, loading myself up with Bell's things and threw some cash on the table. "Right, fellas, we're heading off."

"What time is Kit home?"

"Seven, just before bedtime."

"Your bedtime?" The idiots in front of me high fived as they laughed. "Is she going to tuck you in too?"

I ignored them as was standard. "Are you going to say goodbye to your goddaughter?"

They both got up and gave her a kiss.

"Gym in the morning?" Penn asked.

"Yeah, see you there at ten."

"It's only a matter of time..." Rafe called after me as I walked off, causing the entire restaurant to stare more than they already were.

I grabbed a beer from the fridge, picked up today's New York Times and headed back into the playroom where Bell was on her mat, gurgling up at the little ducks flying above her on the mobile. I sat down next to Barclay, who was on the floor as close as he could possibly get to the baby, relishing in the fact I'd survived my first afternoon of just the two of us.

I hadn't needed to call anyone for help.

And I'd kept to Bell's schedule. She'd had two naps and two bottles, and we were both still alive to tell the tale.

I'd graduated *Summa Cum Laude* from Harvard; ran a very successful investment fund making enormous amounts of money for people, and was, miraculously, still on speaking terms with my family.

But surviving the day as a single father? That felt like a real achievement.

For the first time it dawned on me that maybe, *maybe,* I could actually do this without fucking things up.

I opened up the paper until I found the crossword, scanning through the clues, writing the answers to the ones I knew instinctively.

"Okay, Bells, what's this one?" I looked down at her. "'*Of Mans First Disobedience, and the Fruit Of That Forbidden Tree.' Poet.* Six letters."

She didn't answer, but someone else did.

"Milton, Paradise Lost."

I glanced over to Kit, standing in the doorway of the playroom, then back down to the paper. Of course she had it right, but I wasn't about to let her see how amused I was, making a show of checking if the boxes matched the letters, which it did.

I filled it in, turning to Bell. "Listen to Columbia over there… she's got it," I grinned. "Let's try another shall we?"

I scanned down the clues until I found one I definitely didn't know the answer to.

"1998 Faith Hill song that describes perpetual bliss." I picked up my beer and sipped it, watching Kit.

She started humming a tune that I would've had an almost one hundred percent certainty I'd never heard before, although given that Kit was practically tone deaf it was quite possible she'd got the tune wrong anyway. Her lips pursed as she hummed to herself, and I tried not to focus on them, or focus on where I wanted them to be right now.

I shifted my sweatpants before I started getting uncomfortable.

"This Kiss."

"What?" I coughed away the beer that stuck in my throat, momentarily concerned she may have had mind reading abilities.

"The Faith Hill song, it's called This Kiss."

I filled in the gap. "Correct again."

She grinned at me in challenge, as if she'd get any of them wrong.

"Okay," I found another one I knew, but would be seriously impressed if she did. "Reciprocal in trigonometry."

"How many letters?"

I counted out. "Eight."

She bit down on her lip, holding back a smirk. "Pass."

She walked over to the mat, crouching down and tickling Bell's tummy. "Hi, Bells. Did you have a good day?"

My eyes narrowed as she glanced back up at me.

"You know the answer don't you?"

"Maybe." She peered down at the crossword, her fingers moving over the boxes. "Cosecant."

I raised my eyebrow. "Just to be clear, I hadn't got to that one yet, but I knew the answer."

"Uh huh. Sure." Her eyes flared in amusement, sparkling brighter than any diamond. My grip on the paper squeezed tighter to stop myself from grabbing her face and kissing her until neither of us could stand. "I'll take Bell for her bath now. If you need more help with that, you know where we'll be."

I'd managed to not kiss her, but I couldn't stop myself from staring at her ass as she walked off.

She wasn't simply the sexiest nanny I'd ever seen, she was the sexiest woman I'd ever known or laid eyes on. She wasn't just beautiful; she was funny, striking, and fucking smart. Maybe even smarter than me.

The whole goddamn package.

Thirteen weeks and three days to go. It was only a matter of time. It may as well have been the Doomsday Clock, because my crush was growing to an earth-destroying meteor size.

And it was anyone's guess if I'd even survive that long.

8

KIT

I bent down nearer the kitchen counter and slurped my coffee, which I'd filled to the brim. Again. It was one of life's mysteries how I was so incapable of judging the volume of liquid in a mug, but there we go. I had other strengths like never being late, baking, the ability to get up without hitting *snooze,* and managing to keep a plant alive longer than a month. One of those ones that didn't need water, but I was still taking that as an achievement.

I put a cup under the machine for Murray, unloading the dishwasher while I waited, and placed all of Bell's bottles in the sterilizer.

"Murray!" I yelled seconds before he appeared in the kitchen, Bell in his arms, his eyebrow raised.

"Yes?"

I laughed, picking up my coffee and finishing it. "Sorry, I thought it would save time over searching all the rooms for you.

"All the rooms?"

"Yes, all the rooms."

He pulled the stool out at the counter and sat down. "There aren't that many rooms."

"There are enough that warranted me shouting when I'm stretched for time," I shot back with a smirk, placing his mug in front of him. "Here you go."

It had been gradual over the past month or so, but we'd got to a place where we were comfortable with each other, united by a common and very cute goal. Also helped, in no small part, by the fact that we were the only two people in the apartment who could speak in coherent sentences, aside from the housekeeper who came a couple of times a week. We weren't exactly best friends, but we were miles away from the first week I'd arrived when he did everything he could to avoid being in my presence.

It was easy, almost.

What wasn't easy was the only, yet wildly glaring issue I had with this development - the effort I had to make on a minute-by-minute basis to push my crush down as deep into a trench as I could possibly get it, something that was becoming harder by the day, especially when he walked around in... well, anything really.

There was the sweatpants and t-shirts Murray.

There was pajamas and hoodie in the morning Murray.

Then shorts and hoodie in the evening Murray.

Murray at the weekend in jeans and a sweater.

Murray after the gym. Or after basketball with the guys; sweaty, raw, and smelling like a locker room; like pure testosterone which had me clenching hard the moment it wafted through the air.

Then, *then,* one day last week, he'd had a meeting, and he'd walked into the kitchen in a suit. A custom fitted, Italian merino wool bespoke suit in deepest Prussian Blue, and my mouth dried up on the spot.

He was a life size Ken doll, except better. Each one different, each one exceptional.

"Bye, cutie. See you later." I kissed Bell on the cheek,

trying not to look Murray in the eyes, or breathe him in while I was so close. "Have fun with Daddy."

"What are you doing today?" He followed me out of the kitchen to the front door, holding it open for me.

"Payton and I are going to a spin class at the gym, then brunch, then…" I shrugged, "who knows? Shopping, maybe, if Payton has anything to do with it. I'll see you at seven."

He leaned against the doorframe, one of his enormous biceps flexing as he held onto the top of the jamb, Bell nestled against the other. "Have fun. Enjoy spinning."

"Thanks. What are your plans?"

"Standard Saturday; boys and brunch, and we might watch a game here later." He shrugged, scratching his stubble pensively. "I know you probably want to get away from here at the weekends, but you can always bring Payton over too. Or if she wants to come over in the week, that's okay. I don't want you to feel like you're imprisoned here, even with the 'all the rooms'."

Although his final point was delivered with a massively exaggerated eye roll, the sweetness and concern wrapped around me like a cozy cashmere blanket, not to mention his trust in me beyond my job and the very comprehensive NDA I'd signed. Because I'd learned that Murray was extremely protective about his private life and not many people were part of his inner circle.

I hoped the smile I gave him conveyed how grateful I was. "Thank you, I appreciate the offer, but I don't feel like that. I love being here and looking after Bell."

And the rest…

"The offer's open whenever you want it."

"Thank you. Have fun with the guys, and tell Penn there's a chocolate and apricot loaf in the pantry for him."

His eyes flashed a darker green than normal.

"I can't believe you're baking for my friends. You don't have to do that," he growled.

"I made something for you too; there are waffles in the oven."

His groan of approval set off a deep throbbing at the apex of my thighs that dampened my panties.

"Okay, I'll see you tonight." I walked down the corridor before he could say anything else likely to set off an involuntary reaction which would result in me throwing myself at him.

I'd been so distracted I'd gone six blocks before I realized I'd forgotten my gym bag, including my change of clothing, and I didn't relish the thought of spending the day in sweaty gym gear.

Fuck's sake.

I pulled my phone from my pocket.

Kit: *Forgot my bag and need to run back. Meet you at the gym x*

Payton: *Cool, I'm running late anyway. See you there x*

Fifteen minutes later, I was back in the apartment.

"Hey, I forgot my bag," I called out, running up the stairs two at a time to my bedroom, not hearing any response. Maybe they'd already gone out.

I grabbed my stuff from where I'd left it and ran back out of my room into the corridor, stopping dead just before I reached the stairs. My breath caught in my throat, and I only just managed to stop my mouth dropping open. The throbbing I'd experienced earlier started up again, intensely and swiftly travelling over my entire body until I was shaking. Hot arousal seeped between my legs, giving me no doubt I needed to change my panties immediately.

Murray was walking out of his bedroom, his eyes focused on Bell, wrapped up in her little bunny towel, cuddled to his chest; his wide, *bare* chest, because Bell wasn't the only one in a towel.

Holy. Fuck.

I now had another one to add to my list of Murrays.

I'd known he had an impressive body from the thick arms and broad back I'd glimpsed under his shirts. I thought I'd been able to imagine the rest of him when I'd allowed my mind to wander that far… but I'd never imagined this.

I didn't even know *this* existed beyond pages of fitness magazines and a good photo editing program.

He was definitely *not* edited.

Beads of water were still clinging to him, causing his skin to glisten from the sun pouring through the windows. My eyes followed a droplet as it travelled from his damp hair, along the sinews of his neck and onto wide shoulders, before running down a heavily defined left pec to his torso, and across the many, *many* abs that he'd clearly dedicated his lifetime to building, before hitting the towel sitting snug on his hips. The white towel, which made his skin look like it was permanently golden, was so low-slung it wrapped around a V-line as sharply impressive as the rest of him.

Actually, impressive was doing him an injustice. He wasn't impressive. He looked like he'd been carved from a slab of golden marble. Magnificent. Spectacular. Hedonistic.

He was hedonism personified, and I wanted to derive all my pleasure from him. *All* of it. Every. Last. Drop.

His throat cleared waking me from my trance, and I looked up to find him staring with what I could swear was a tiny leer, his emerald eyes sparkling brighter than anything I'd seen in the jewelry store windows on Fifth. "Kit..? You okay there?"

"I… er… I forgot my bag… I called when I… I…" I trailed off, totally unable to focus on anything while he was standing in front of me.

"Bell threw up her bottle all over both of us, so it was easier to clean off together," he explained, like it was perfectly normal to be standing in front of me, a small stretch of thick, soft cotton away from being naked… *in front of me.*

"Is she okay?" I wanted to step forward to touch her but that meant I'd be right up against his nakedness, which was far too close not to be affected by the scent of him already intoxicating me to the point of inebriation. I could smell him from here; smell his fresh, clean, woodsy scent, like a forest at twilight and April rain showers. My eyes widened as he kept walking, until I realized he needed to pass me to get to Bell's room.

"Yes, she's fine. Drank too quickly probably, it was a big burp."

I swallowed thickly, trying to moisten my cottonmouth. "Okay, well, I need to go. I'll see you later, have a good day."

I dodged to the side as he stepped forward, running back down the stairs as quickly as I could, focused solely on getting out and away, putting as much distance between us as possible. I didn't stop running until I hit the sidewalk again, sucking in the fresh air the second I was out of the building.

Jesus.

Unfair. That's what this was. Holy, *wildly* unfair.

I was living with a walking fantasy come to life, twenty-four hours a day.

I'd never been in this position before. Couldn't remember the last time I'd had the hots for someone so unattainable, and *so* inescapable.

Not to mention so inappropriate.

This wasn't a celebrity crush situation with the poster on the dorm wall where I'd stare at it wondering *what if* and *I wonder what he's like in real life*, or one which saw me lusting after the Varsity quarterback from across the quad, both of which I had experience with.

No.

I knew.

I knew what he was like.

Sweet, smart, kind, protective, assertive, masculine. Oh, so masculine.

Pulling it out of my pocket, I answered my phone as it rang.

"Where are you? You're so late! We've missed the class, so I managed to get us into the next one, as someone cancelled."

I shook my head, focusing. "Crap, sorry, I got tied up. I'm on my way. See you in twenty."

I slung my backpack over my shoulders and took off at a brisk running pace.

I needed this workout.

I needed something so hard and sweaty it would melt my brain and all thoughts of what I'd witnessed this morning, along with the visual branded into my retinas.

"I've never done one of Mikey's classes before; I didn't think they'd be so hard. Now I've sat down, I'm really starting to doubt I'm going to be able to stand back up..."

I was holding my coffee in my hands, just holding it halfway to my lips, not moving. I could see her talking, I could hear her talking, but I wasn't really listening. I wasn't even really sitting across from her in this busy, noisy, popular brunch spot with a line round the block. No, I was still in the apartment with Murray and his towel.

And his muscles.

When you're a nanny, you see stuff. You're in the thick of a family during one of the most personal times of their lives. You stand in the middle of blazing rows. You hear things you shouldn't. You walk in on things you shouldn't. Not once had I ever dwelled on any of it again, because the second the doors closed, my focus would be taken elsewhere, normally by a hungry, crying infant.

But this morning... this morning was different.

And I knew instinctively that his wet, ripped, naked torso

would be all I'd be able to see when I closed my eyes to sleep, tonight and every other night.

That's if I could sleep.

Payton's fingers snapped in front of my face, bringing me back to the present.

"Sorry. What?"

"Were you even listening to me?"

I gave her a sheepish grin. "Nope."

"Do you want to tell me what you were doing instead?"

I rolled my lips. "Nope. Not really."

"Too bad, spill it."

I sucked on the inside of my cheek. "It's Murray."

The waitress placed two giant stacks of pancakes and eggs in front of us, ones I had no memory ordering. Payton reached out before the waitress could walk away. "Thank you, and could we get two more coffees please?"

She nodded and walked off.

"What about Murray? I thought you were getting on better."

I forked in a mouthful of eggs, suddenly famished. "We are."

"Is he still being weird?" She tucked into her breakfast, drowning everything in maple syrup.

My brow furrowed at her. "Weird?"

"Yeah, after you saw Jackson Foggerty…" Her big brown eyes widened dramatically, "Fuck, have you seen him again? I'm so jealous. I need to come over, you know."

"Yeah, come. Murray said today that you could come over. And no, he's not being weird anymore, we're getting on well. It's good."

I hadn't seen Jackson Foggerty again, but I also hadn't forgotten about the way Murray reacted to him, growly and possessive. Because when it came to Bell, he didn't want anyone near her.

Because that's what he'd meant.

Because the alternative was absurd.

"Then… it's what?" She forked a portion of pancake into her mouth so massive I was amazed it fit, chewed it and washed it all down with coffee while I watched on in silence. "Ooh, did he figure out you've got a crush on him?"

"God I hope not…" My face dropped in horror. "Actually, probably, given what happened this morning."

"Okay… what does that mean? I assume this is why you were late." She loaded up her fork again and bit into it.

I sipped my coffee, and placed it back on the table. "Yeah. I ran back to get my bag and when I was leaving the house again, I bumped into Murray and Bell. They'd just got out of the shower, and he was only in a towel." My voice dropped with dramatic effect, but also to stop the table next to us from overhearing my plight. "You should have seen him! He was like a Grecian statue with all the…" I started gesturing around my body, "you know…"

"Muscles?" Her eyebrows rose at me.

I pointed at her. "Yes! Muscles! Obscene muscles everywhere. I couldn't stop staring. And he noticed."

She started cackling hard. "What did he do?"

"Nothing really, kind of grinned at me…"

Yes, he definitely grinned, the type of grin that had deep dimples; the type of grin that could get me in a lot of trouble.

"Course he did, he knows he's hot. You don't look like that and not know."

"Yeah I guess. I just wasn't expecting it, ya know? I think I'm in shock. It's so embarrassing and unprofessional. You could have literally wiped the drool." I laughed through my mortification. "It was like that time I saw Hudson Forrester across Van Am when he was coming back from practice. Only better, much, *much* better. His body…"

In our first year of college, Payton and I were walking across Van Am Quad on the way back from class, when Hudson Forrester jogged out of the shadows of the rotunda.

He was a sophomore and already star quarterback of the football team, having had the best freshman season on record. He'd been sweaty and muddy, and sporting the beginnings of a black eye. And when he'd lifted up the bottom of his jersey to wipe his face, I'd gotten so distracted by his abs I'd walked into one of the lampposts, giving myself a very visible bump on the head. It had taken over a week for it to disappear.

But Hudson had nothing on Murray. Even if it had been equal footing, with a college aged Murray, I knew that had I seen him, no one else would have existed for me.

"I've never had the hots for a client before." I shook my head hard and slapped my cheek. "Ugh. Okay, I need to give myself another five minutes then it goes in the vault."

"But what if he's got the hots for you too? OhEmGee, this would be perfect. Like that movie..." She snapped her fingers, thinking.

I smacked her on the arm, stopping her train of thought before her imagination got too carried away and I was swept along with it like a rip tide. "Shut up. He doesn't have the hots for me."

She smirked into her coffee. "Hudson had the hots for you, you know."

My forked stopped halfway to my mouth. "What? No he didn't."

"Um, yeah, he did." She would have made a good Blair Waldorf impersonator with the smug, pursed smile she was wearing right now.

My face scrunched as I looked at her with a lot of skepticism, and more than a little disbelief. "He never ever said one word to me."

"That's because you intimidated him." She casually popped a piece of pancake in her mouth like she hadn't just delivered a Hiroshima sized bombshell of information.

"Okay, have you smoked something? He was Captain of

the Football Team," I replied, as if that explained everything, which it should. Even before he'd been drafted, Hudson was always surrounded by girls. Any type of girl. Sometimes you couldn't even see him through the gaggle. We hadn't lived in the same area; we hadn't shared the same classes. The only day we ever crossed paths was Tuesday mornings between eleven and eleven o' five a.m. Payton and I would be leaving our class on Romanticism and the Victorian poets, and he would be walking toward the Fairchild Building for whatever class he had, again surrounded by girls.

"Exactly. He was all brawn and you were the brains. He didn't know how to have a conversation with you. To be fair, he didn't know how to have a conversation with most people, which is why he was always stuck to the *Gamma Phi* girls. They didn't care."

"Okay, now you're being ridiculous," I scoffed, "and he wasn't all brawn. He was a biology major."

She held the Girl Scout salute. "I'm not, I swear. Deacon told me once. It was after that time we were at O'Malley's, when they'd beat Harvard."

Deacon Hills had been Payton's boyfriend through our sophomore year. He was the year below Hudson, but they'd played together on the football team and hung out after games. We'd joined them sometimes, although, usually by the time we arrived, they were too drunk to form coherent sentences and Hudson was nowhere to be seen. So I was still very unclear about how this had taken place.

"We graduated six years ago, how have you never told me this?"

"I forgot for a while," she shrugged. "At the time I didn't think it would matter. Plus, I wanted to keep your secret intact."

"What secret?"

Her eyes twinkled with amusement. "That you're a dirty little perv with a fetish for big muscles."

I gasped and smacked her again. "I am not."

Perv wasn't entirely accurate, but she had a point. I did love a guy with muscles. Add brains to the brawn and it was a deadly combination, one I was a certified sucker for, and something Murray had, not just in spades, but commercially-sized digger quantities.

She mopped up the maple syrup on her plate with the last of her pancakes. "Don't worry about it, you can pretend all you want, but I know better. I blame myself actually, and the fact we've not been out for a while. You need to blow off some steam. Want to go and see Magic Mike?"

"Ewww, fuck no," I scowled. "I haven't had time to go out in a while. If you remember, I got conned into taking this job just as I was about to enjoy having my life back."

She continued like I hadn't said anything. "Now I come to think about it, you haven't been on a date for a few months since that guy from the gym…"

"The one who only talked about protein shakes?"

"Yep, him. So we definitely need to get back on it. We both know you need more substance than someone who only talks about protein shakes." She pointed her fork at me. "Let's go out next weekend. You think you can get the night off?"

"I can't next weekend because we're going out of the city for Easter, but let's go for drinks on Wednesday. I'm off then."

"Yeah, that works. There's a new cocktail bar in Chelsea I want to try. I'll come over first and get you. I need to maximize my ops for seeing Jackson Foggerty anyway."

I snorted. Jackson Foggerty would not know what had hit him if Payton and her ten-year obsession got her claws in. "Sounds good. So, what's new with you? How's your week been?"

"Not bad, but you know, it's children's books, etcetera,

etcetera. It's why I drink. But as we all know, I'm biding my time until I can move."

I rolled my eyes. All Payton had ever wanted to be was a book editor at Simpson and Mather, one of the world's largest publishing houses. She had *not* wanted to be a children's book editor at Simpson and Mather, but took the job anyway because she thought it would be better to be in the building than waiting to get in. But she'd been waiting six years and was yet to admit that she actually enjoyed her job - and was very good at it.

"I brought you something though." She picked up her gym bag and started rummaging through it before lifting out a few hardback books, the top one covered in a big fluffy bunny with a carrot in his mouth.

I flicked through them, all books which had yet to hit the shelves. "Thanks! These are amazing! I'll read them to Bell later."

"Have you found any jobs yet?"

I shook my head. "No, I haven't had time to look. I need to find a new apartment too."

"I thought the crazy girls were finding one for you." By 'crazy girls' she meant Wolf and Freddie, because since that first phone call, that's how she understandably referred to them, although in reality they were simply excitable and enthusiastic, as well as incredibly loving and loyal.

The waitress came over and cleared our empty plates. "Can I get you anything else?"

Payton looked at me in question, but there was no way I could fit anything else in. "No, we're good, thanks."

She walked off and Payton's attention was back to me, waiting for me to continue.

"Yeah, they said they would. But they've done so much for me already. They organized all the movers the other week and put everything we packed into storage. It's been super busy with Bell, so I haven't really had the time to think, plus I didn't want to take advantage. Columbia called me again too."

"Have you decided what you want to do?"

"Nooooo, but I know I don't want to nanny beyond this job, and I know I don't want to be a kindergarten teacher."

She tutted at me. "You already knew that. You should take the Columbia job. It doesn't matter that they were the first to offer you something, whatever you do you'll be amazing at. And Columbia will look great on your résumé, so you can move on if or when something else comes up."

"I know. But I want some time to have head space and actually think so I can weigh up my options, which I haven't been able to do." The bill was placed on the table and I snatched it up. "I got this one."

Her eyebrow arched at me. "So I should think after being so late we had to do a different class. It's your fault if I can't walk."

My laughter set her own off. "Come on, let's get out of here. Where are you dragging me first?"

Her arm linked through mine as we joined the bustling Sunday crowd on the street. Spring had arrived and the sky was bright and cloudless, enough that I needed to put my sunglasses on. "Let's go and buy some sexy new outfits for our evening out on Wednesday, because we are going to rip the town up and get you laid again."

"Sure, why not?" My phone started ringing and I reached into my pocket to pull it out, Murray's name flashing across the screen. "Pay, hang on."

I hit answer. "Hey, you okay?"

"Hey. It's Murray."

"Yes, I know." I could hear Bell crying down the phone. "Are you okay?"

"Oh yes… well, no. Sorry for calling you, I don't think Bell's well. She's not sleeping or drinking, she feels hot and she was sick again." He was speaking quicker than normal, panic flushing his tone.

My hand shot up to cover my ear as a police car siren went off at the end of the block. "Have you given her anything?"

"No, I didn't know what to give her."

"Have you taken her temperature?"

"No, I didn't know how."

"That's okay, don't worry." I glanced at Payton who was shuffling about on her feet, trying to figure out what was going on. "I can be there in thirty minutes."

"Thank you. I didn't know what to do."

"It's my job, don't worry. I'll be there soon."

I hung up and looked at Payton. "I'm sorry, I have to go. Bell isn't very well and Murray's panicking."

A flicker of anxiety started up in my belly. It was weird, I'd never heard him panic before, and his vulnerability made it feel like my heart was working harder to pump the freshly oxygenated blood through my veins.

"Okay, I'll see you later then. But this means I'm going shopping for both of us, so you will be wearing what I pick out for you."

"Okay, fine. See you Wednesday." I pulled her into a hug, kissing her cheek. "Love you. Send me pics of what you buy."

"No, it's going to be a surprise, guaranteed to get you some action." She let go of me. "Go. Let me know if Muscles has the hots for you."

"I can tell you right now, he doesn't." I waved dismissively as I rushed off. "Bye, Pay."

I walked in the apartment forty minutes later, quietly praying I wouldn't be greeted in the same manner I had been earlier. Definitely hoping I wouldn't be.

Definitely.

I found them in the den, the sight just as good.

Murray had fallen asleep on the giant couch. Bell was also

asleep and looking so tiny on his massive chest. The thick, black rimmed glasses he wore sometimes were hanging loose in his hand, hovering above a pile of newspapers, while the big television screen on the wall had been muted on what looked like a game of England playing rugby.

I stood there watching his chest rise and fall, lifting Bell's with it. I'd never seen him like this before, never had the chance to properly study him, properly absorb his features without being noticed.

If it was possible, he was even more beautiful asleep.

He looked so peaceful, his chiseled face softened but no less impressive. His brow was smooth and relaxed as he breathed in and out, his cherub lips parted slightly, his long lashes resting on the tops of his high cheek bones. His stubble was thicker than usual today, and my fingers itched, as desperately as they had this morning, to stroke along the solid line of his strong jaw.

Instead, I reached out and felt Bell's forehead, holding my fingers against her too-warm skin, leaving them sleeping as I went in search of her medical box. I'd made a couple when I'd arrived, keeping them in the rooms she used the most, and filled all of them with the essentials - digital thermometer, baby Tylenol, gauze, band aids, teething gel, aspirator, scissors... anything that could possibly be needed.

She stirred as I took her temperature, the beeping of the thermometer also waking up Murray. Ninety-nine point four. She had a fever.

"Hey, sorry. She stopped crying and I fell asleep with her. She just wanted to be held." He peered up at me, his eyes intensely green, and I'd never noticed before that the ring around his iris was more navy than black, just like Bell's.

I stood back, needing the space. "That's okay. She's warm though. We can give her some Tylenol and see how that goes."

He sat up straighter as Bell started fussing. "Have you got it here?"

"Yes." I unscrewed the bottle and suctioned out the correct dosage with a pipette. Murray tipped her back so I could administer it to go straight down her throat instead of dribbling out. "See if this helps. I can take her from you if you'd like?"

His hand cupped Bell's back, rubbing it gently, soothing her as she grumbled. "No, that's okay, thank you though. I got her, but stay and we can watch a movie or something. She might go back to sleep."

I hesitated as butterflies started fluttering in my chest, coughing them away. "Okay, let me go sort her bed and get her some water. What can I get you?"

"Just water would be good, thanks," he smiled at me.

I switched on the humidifier in Bell's room for when she went to bed, adding some drops of Vicks Baby to help her breathe, then dropped my bag on my bed and headed back downstairs. Bell had fallen asleep again, and Murray was watching the rugby.

I placed a bottle of water for Bell, along with a glass for Murray, on the side table, and sat down at the far end of the couch, which was practically the other side of the room, but I didn't trust myself to get any nearer to him.

A massive cheer went up from the crowd, even though the volume was on low. "I've never understood this game."

"Rugby?"

"Yep. It's so confusing. And violent."

He laughed softly, Bell never stirring from the movement in his chest. "Come on, you never dated a jock in college? I find that hard to believe. I could easily picture you watching the games wearing team colors, his numbers drawn on both your cheeks." He tapped his finger against his chin as I started laughing. "Although come to think about it, fifty percent of your attention would have been in the latest

Shakespeare you were reading. Yeah, that's definitely how you were in college."

My thighs clenched involuntarily from both his teasing and his comment that he could picture me… That he could think about me in any situation beyond caring for his daughter.

Christ, I had it bad.

I shook my head. "Nope, never dated a sports guy. Payton did though, only for sophomore year, but we did go to games. That was football though, not this." I pointed to the screen where an aggressive pile-on was taking place.

"Who did you date then? Chess club? A guy from the English course? Pre-med?" His lips quivered as he held back his laugh.

"I don't know what impression I've given you, but no, I never dated anyone from chess club. They're bigger geeks than the mathletes, which clearly you were."

He laughed again, a deep rumble rising up as he held it in for Bell.

"No, I dated a philosophy major, but he liked to overanalyze everything. I had a boyfriend for a while who was pre-law, but that's it."

"You didn't miss out. Columbia boys are all pussies anyway. You want a real man, Harvard is where it's at," he winked.

It was like a nuclear reactor was heating up in my core, ready to explode any minute. I was getting so warm, even though I was easily the length of five grown men away from him, I expected to break a sweat any minute. "Thanks for the advice."

He looked down at Bell, fast asleep on his chest and stood up. "I'm going to try putting her down again."

I schooled my expression so he couldn't see how quickly my heart had sunk, because I didn't want him to go. "Okay. The medicine will have helped, so she'll probably go down."

He stood up carefully and walked out. I got up and went back into the kitchen, clearing away all her things and sorting out what I needed for her week ahead. Murray returned five minutes later, heading straight for the fridge door.

"She went down, didn't wake up at all."

I picked up my phone and switched on the baby monitor app. "That's good. You can go and join the guys if you want, I can stay here with her. I'll call you if there's anything to worry about, but I think the Tylenol will have sorted her out."

He closed the fridge, two bottles of beer in his hand, then opened the freezer and took out a tub of ice cream, placing it all on the counter, then went back for another three tubs, all different flavors.

"No, I'm not leaving you or Bell. Thank you though, and I'm sorry I ruined your day off, but I'll make it up to you with ice cream, and I've ordered pizza." He twisted the cap off a beer and handed it to me.

"Thank you." I swigged it. "I'm honestly happy staying though, you don't need to. You can go and enjoy your evening. This is my job."

I wasn't sure why I was trying so hard to make him leave, except for the fact that when I was in his presence it was impossible to concentrate on anything else but him. Especially with the memory of this morning still fresh in my mind.

"No." While his tone said he wasn't budging, his eyes twinkled in amusement. "Come on, or I won't show you what I bought you."

He turned, heading back into the den with the ice cream while I stayed glued to the spot, not entirely sure I'd heard him correctly. He'd bought me a present? It was difficult to decipher my thoughts while my belly was flickering around like a Wi-Fi router on the fritz.

"Kit?" he called, and I hurried after him, finding him back in his spot on the couch, his feet up on the giant ottoman, where a canvas bag with Brown's - a wildly popular, independent New York bookstore – printed on it, lay.

"What's that?" I pointed to it. "You've been in a bookstore? No, that can't be right."

He smirked. "Enough of your cheek young lady, or I won't show you what I bought you."

He clocked the surprise on my face. "Well, for Bells, but also for you. Go on, open it."

I sat down next to him, picking up the bag as I did, pulling out a hard back book – A Midsummer Night's Dream for Babies.

His face had lit up with excitement. "I got it this week. There was a Romeo and Juliet one, but I thought that was a bit tragic. This one is about love, I mean, they're all about love, but this one is the good kind of love."

I raised my eyebrow in question and tried to hold back my smile at how proud of himself he sounded.

"You know, without someone dying a gruesome death at the end." Another big cheer went up from the screen, which was still showing the rugby, and he turned to see what happened.

"Thank you." I ran my palms over the smooth, hard cover before opening it up. The pages were bright and colorful, images of fairies and Puck and Tatiana filling the pages. "She'll love it. It's my favorite too."

"Oh yeah? I did good then?" He handed me a tub of raspberry ripple ice cream with a spoon sticking out.

"Yes, you did." I scraped a spoonful and stuck it in my mouth. "Oh my God, this is good ice cream."

"I know." He dug a spoon into what looked like chocolate chip.

"Do you always eat ice cream before actual dinner?"

"I think you can eat ice cream whenever you want to. It's one of the perks of being an adult. Same as pizza."

He leaned back on the couch, inching closer with the way he twisted his body toward me, his eyes roaming my face before focusing back on mine. "How was your day before I rudely interrupted you?"

I laughed. "You saved me from shopping with Payton, which is my nightmare. But apart from that, it was fun."

"Yeah? How was spinning? Whose class did you do?"

"Mikey's. It was good, really hard though," I grinned. "Do you go there?"

Before I could stop it, my entire body came to life at the visual of seeing him in action, dripping with sweat as he worked his muscles until they strained under his shirt. I took another giant scoop of ice cream, hoping to cool myself down from the inside.

"Sometimes. I helped Emerson set it up. Her husband, Drew, is a good mate of mine. He used to play with Jas and Coop."

His brothers-in-law had been over to the apartment a couple of times since the first day I'd arrived, although I hadn't spoken to them much because I was usually locked in conversation with Diane or Wolf or Freddie. I'd never been a huge hockey fan, but I did remember them from my college days, and I definitely remembered Drew Crawley. He'd been very popular among the girls on campus during hockey season, and between him and Felix Cleverly, they were probably responsible for why the local bars were so full on game nights, because it had nothing to do with the guys watching, and everything to do with the girls.

"That's pretty cool. My dad's actually a big fan of the apparel. I sent him some."

He grinned. "Oh really? I'm glad to hear it. Now if only he'd leave Nike, and come work for us here."

"I think you'd have an easier time convincing Penn to give

up my baking." The teasing smile I offered him dripped in saccharine, because for some reason, it annoyed him that I baked for Penn. Or that Penn enjoyed my baking.

His eyes narrowed in challenge before they flared white hot, "I can be pretty persuasive when I want to be."

The speed at which my core constricted almost winded me, and then I watched him lick another mouthful of ice cream from his spoon, his pink tongue removing all trace of it along with my self-control.

Sweet Jesus.

This was bad.

Really bad.

My thighs began trembling with adrenalin and I shifted uncomfortably to ease the pressure. Yet instead of easing, like a piece of flint against a stone, it created a spark, the tiniest friction. And suddenly I had a fire burning between my legs.

I dug my spoon in again, hoping he hadn't noticed, but my shaking hands as I scooped my ice cream was a dead giveaway.

He reached out, swiping a drop of ice-cream from the corner of my mouth with the pad of his thumb, his pink tongue darting out to lick it off the end. I remained unblinking as his perfect lips suctioned on; removing all traces as though it was blood from a pin prick. And my life began moving in slow motion… Except my heart, which was beating through my ribcage and hammering out of the prison my chest was holding it in, until I bit down hard on my cheek so I could focus on the pain of that instead.

His gaze dropped to my lips, and I held my breath with the absolute certainty he was about to kiss me.

His hand returned to my cheek, his fingers brushing along my jaw, until they reached my pulse point beating harder than it had in my morning spin class, and there was nothing I could do to hide that from him.

"Kit..." he breathed out, leaning into me.

I knew I was about to experience the best kiss of my entire life, the air, intense and thick with tension, practically sealing the deal.

Except for two things...

A piercing shriek from the baby monitor and a loud buzzing from the intercom signaling the pizza had arrived.

Either one would have been enough to break up the moment and bring us back to reality, but we clearly needed both.

I coughed and jumped up. "I'll sort out Bell."

Bell also had other ideas. Three hours and sixteen minutes of crying later, it had killed any possible notion of returning to where we'd been. And if it hadn't been for the intensity still blazing in his eyes as we switched Bell between us, I could have almost convinced myself I'd imagined it.

Imagined chemistry more intense than a chem student's end of term paper.

Which is probably what I needed to do - pretend nothing had been about to happen because no good could ever come from falling for your boss.

And no matter how much I wanted to deny it, I was nearer the edge of that cliff than I ever should be.

9

MURRAY

I rested back in my chair, the front legs tipping as I crossed my feet on the desk and watched the screens in front of me, the bright flickering colors mesmerizing as they rapidly changed from the values and volumes of stock trading live on the global exchanges I was monitoring.

Linking my hands behind my head, I closed my eyes, tired from my sleepless night. And then there she was, arriving as bright and true as she did in real life, bursting into my days, her sunny disposition and unequivocal charm preventing me from any possible chance to sleep peacefully.

Even power nap peacefully.

The hungry, appreciative look she'd given me outside my bedroom as her eyes slowly scanned across my body heated me up as quickly a branding iron thrust into an open flame.

Her pupils flaring under my gaze.

Her pulse beating like a drum through her impossibly soft skin under my fingertips.

Her lips parting as I wiped the ice-cream from the corner of her mouth, her tongue following the movement.

And then the way she sucked in her cheek as I licked it off my thumb.

Her breath hitching.

Nor did I miss her squirming. Only the inflexibility of my jeans stopped my dick from viciously punching out at her.

I'd never seen anyone with such intense desire in their eyes.

And it was all for me.

All of it taking me so close to breaking point I could touch it. Smell it.

Which was why I sprinted out the door this morning before she woke up - because I couldn't see her and not want to finish where we'd left off. I hadn't even been able to reply to the photos of Bell she'd sent through, as usual, because even with fifty blocks between us, she was still clouding my ability to think or craft a perfectly normal and grown up response beyond a very weak 'thanks'. Not to mention the thirty minutes of internal debate I'd had about whether to add an *X* on the end.

My eyes shot open as the door flew wide, Penn and Rafe marching through and flopping down on the black Jean Royère sofa, stretching along the back wall, which Freddie picked out and sent me the bill for later before I'd had a chance to object.

"Come and play with us," demanded Penn, taking a position similar to the one I'd had before they'd barged in.

"No, I can't." My chair legs landed back on the floor and I leaned forward across my desk. "I have actual work to do, which includes making you two a lot of money."

It was irrelevant that I hadn't done any work yet, too distracted by thoughts of Kit and her sweet, perfect mouth. The way her cheeks pinked when I teased her, which had become my favorite thing to do since the first walk we'd been on.

"We already have a lot of money, so we give you permission to play hooky."

I rolled my eyes.

The door opened again, this time it was Joan, my secretary, bringing in coffee and placing it on the table in front of them.

"Thanks, Joanie!" they cried in unison.

Her withering look only amused them more, because they prided themselves on being able to achieve it.

"Feet off the furniture!" she scolded before walking back out.

"God, I love her. I need a PA like that," groaned Penn, as he reached for his coffee, ignoring her order to get his feet off the furniture and remaining prostrate. He did compromise by kicking off his fifteen hundred dollar, Italian leather shoes though.

I got up and sat in the chair opposite them. "To what do I owe this pleasure?"

"I'm hiding from my mother and Pennington is bored, as per." Rafe reached for his coffee at the same time I did.

"Bored from my board meeting, more like. Fuck knows what's going on," he grumbled before shooting to sit upright. "I have a year left before I take control, and my grandfather announced he's changing the terms of the trust. I don't know why they don't give it to Nancy, as she clearly wants the job."

As the only son in the family, with four older sisters, including Nancy, Penn had been primed to take over his grandfather's conglomerate – a sprawling global entity combined of some of the world's largest businesses across real estate, healthcare, casinos, multi-media, and tech - since he was seven years old. You name it, they owned it. To say he didn't want the job would be an understatement. Because by rule, the job belonged to his beloved father, the rightful heir, but it had passed to Penn by default following his father's death when Penn had been little.

"Yeah, you'll clearly run it into the ground," offered Rafe supportively.

Except we all knew that was blatantly untrue because

Penn was genius-level smart. The mid-term he'd failed had been down to him being so hungover he'd forgotten to turn up. This was mostly because it was too easy and he knew that he'd get one hundred percent, so he'd figured why bother getting up early to prove it. The fact that he was right did not appease any of his professors.

But, his moral compass was cemented in place, pointing directly to his strong sense of duty, and he would run the company better than well.

"Right." He raised his coffee cup to Rafe. "Thank you."

"You're welcome."

I tipped my chin up at him. "And why are you hiding from your mother?"

"She wants me to help her with a divorce or something?"

My mouth dropped open. "She's divorcing Chip?"

Rafe's parents collected divorces like Tom Brady collected Superbowl rings. They had gotten divorced when he was a young teenager, for the second time. They'd divorced for the first time after his sister was born, then remarried, had him and his younger brother, Rory, then divorced again. They'd subsequently both been through another three marriages and divorces. Chip was his mother's latest husband and we were all of the opinion he was a sticker, because while he was the most boring and sensible man we'd ever met, he absolutely adored her and treated her like a queen, which we all appreciated.

He shook his head. "No, it's her friend getting divorced and she wants me to represent her."

"Why don't you want to?"

"Because of all the above. It's a divorce case. Anyone could do it, and it's cut and dry. She doesn't need me to do it." He rested back with a shrug. "Anyway, why are you in the office?"

"What do you mean?"

"Why are you here and not at home with Kit?"

I frowned at him. “You came here. I work here. If you didn’t think I’d be here, why did you come here?”

“Hunch,” he smirked and waved his phone, which actually meant he’d tracked me.

I sighed. “I can’t work at home.”

A slow, insolent grin started forming on his lips. “Why can't you work at home?”

“Because Kit’s there. She made croissants from scratch this morning.”

Penn put his cup down dramatically. “Fuck playing, let’s go back to yours. I want croissants.”

“Nooo,” I groaned.

Rafe’s eyes opened wide and concentrated directly on me. It was a gaze that had many of his courtroom opponents breaking into a cold sweat, but I used to see him practice it in the mirror, so its intimidating qualities were lost on me. “Oh fucking hell. You’ve had sex with her.”

I coughed through my inhale. “What? No, I mean…”

“Fuck. I owe Penn a hundred grand now.”

I almost jumped out of my chair. “WHAT?! A hundred fucking grand?! You bet a hundred grand on me having sex with Kit?”

His face dropped in horror at the mere suggestion, his hand placed over his heart. “No, no, of course not. I bet on you holding out because I had faith.” His expression turned devilish. “But clearly, I give you way too much credit.”

I sunk back into the soft cushions, picking my coffee up again. “Well, you haven’t lost any money. We didn’t have sex. We just…”

Actually, what did we do? Nothing.

And now what do I do? Fuck knows.

“There was a...” I tried to find a word that didn’t make me sound as lame as fuck. “And I nearly kissed her.”

“A what?”

“I don’t know. A look? A something? A moment?” God, I

was worse than lame. I rubbed along my brow, trying to ease my swirling thoughts. "She..."

I glanced over at them to find them both staring at me, clearly on tenterhooks, waiting for the rest of the story. "Yesterday morning she went out, but she came back because she'd forgotten something and I bumped into her as I was walking out of the shower, and... I dunno..." I scraped my hands through my hair for the millionth time that morning, "the look she gave me... it was fucking hot, like *I want to fuck you right now* hot. Then when she came back, she was helping me with Bell and we were laughing, and she's so fucking beautiful. So yeah, definitely would have kissed her if Bell hadn't woken up and interrupted us."

And the rest. My dick was getting hard thinking about it. I'd jerked off four times between then and now and it still didn't seem to quench this insatiable want for her currently racing through my veins.

Penn tried hard to mask the grin he very clearly wanted to wear, the one warring with his expression of support. "What are you going to do about it?"

"What d'you mean?"

"You think she's interested in you? And not just your body..." Rafe laughed loudly.

"Course she is, who wouldn't be?" Penn indicated toward me, waving his hand up and down like I was some kind of weather map or visual aid for his presentation. "Finest English specimen you'll ever find. His brain is the sexiest thing about him."

"Thanks. And..." her face swam into my vision again, the look in her eyes as she'd slowly taken in every inch of me. No one had ever looked at me with such unadulterated passion, and if I hadn't had Bell in my arms, who knows what would have happened.

Actually, I know exactly what would have happened...

My dick would have taken exactly what he'd been fantasizing about since she'd moved in six weeks ago.

"Yeah, I'd say so. Yes. But that doesn't mean it's a good idea."

Rafe leaned forward, his elbows on his knees, all serious and businesslike. "As your lawyer, I can tell you it definitely *isn't* a good idea, because then you'll be paying your nanny to have sex with you. If it goes tits-up, then that's a costly shit-storm." He smoothed his fingers over the whiskers above his lips. "But as your best friend, I say you've had a fuck-load to deal with the past few months and you deserve some fun. I suggest you talk to her and we can get her to sign a new NDA and a relationship agreement. But don't fucking do anything until then."

Penn snorted hard. "Wow, Raferty, a relationship agreement? I've never heard of anything so panty dropping. That's going to get her wet right on the spot, my friend. No wonder the ladies throw themselves at you, if this is how you do foreplay."

I didn't disagree. The thought of even bringing it up made my stomach twist into knots.

Rafe responded by flipping him off. "I'm not the one who has legally required apologies issued."

Penn winked, lying back down on the couch, arms crossed behind his head. "You know I like to keep you on your toes. Makes you feel useful."

"I don't know what I'm going to do..."

This was unchartered territory for me, with the potential to be an absolute fucking nightmare.

Penn took in my expression of sheer panic. "Okay, while you think, let's talk about how I was bang on the money about Ace Watson. Did you see him last night? The Yankees are wasting him on the bench as relief. They don't need another pitcher, they should have made him starting catcher.

He fucking smashed it in Spring Training. I don't know why they've brought him up to sit on the fucking bench."

"They're holding onto him. They're doing what they need to do; they've already got Donovan Philips as catcher," Rafe argued.

"Who they should have gotten rid of already." he said pointedly. "They need to let him go. He couldn't catch a fucking cold. Better yet, they should have traded him to the Lions; he's about as good as they are."

The New York Lions was widely recognized as the worst team in baseball, except for 2012 when they were second worst. Consistently bottom of both the National League East and the entire National League, as well as bottom of the entire points table. It was commonly known as the team where players were unofficially retired before retirement. As a lifelong, die-hard Yankees fan, Penn felt that it was more than his right to point out any faults he saw, in order to improve the team - something neither the owner, nor manager, nor coaches, agreed with when he emailed them religiously after every game, pointing out what could have been done better. It was anyone's guess why he hadn't been blocked, or maybe he had and just didn't realize.

"Have you told Steinbrenner? I'm sure he'd welcome your input again this season."

"Yeah, you'd think he would," Penn replied with utmost seriousness, because there wasn't much Penn took more seriously than baseball. "Especially as a season ticket holder, and they lost last night."

"Yeah. And did you see any of the Dodgers game? That homer from Jupiter Reeves was fucking epic. He's already on fire, and this season's only just started."

"Bet he gets MVP again."

"Nah, he'll get Hall of Fame."

"How long's he got left on his contract?"

"Dunno, couple of years maybe? Madness he won't come to the Yankees."

My head went back and forth between them, trying to focus on the baseball chat and push Kit out of my head. But it wasn't working. I couldn't concentrate.

"He's a lifer though. He'll never leave the Dodgers."

I knew I could add to this chat. I'd known Jupiter for a few years through the network of Jasper and Cooper, but my brain wasn't computing.

Nope, definitely not.

I groaned, flinging my head back in the chair. "While I'd love to contribute to this conversation, I'm having an actual crisis here with which I need help."

Rafe returned his attention to me. "Alright, Romeo. What do you want to do?"

"I don't know."

"Well maybe that's where you start."

"Where?"

"Murray, bud," he leaned forward again. "Do you want to date her or fuck her?"

"Ooh, maybe she'll call you 'daddy'." Penn was the only one laughing at his joke.

I clenched my fists.

"I don't want to fuck her." I frowned, hearing the words. "I mean, I do, obviously, but I don't want to *fuck* her, fuck her. It's not about sex. I like hanging out with her. She's different. She's sweet. She doesn't bitch, she doesn't moan or get angry. I don't even think she swears. And she fucking puts up with you two more than she ever should. I like her. So, date I guess."

"But how are you going to date her? Who would babysit?" Rafe smirked.

"Oh fuck off!" I wailed, and it was quite possible I might actually start crying at this rate. "This is serious. If you're not going to help, then leave me alone so I can at least pretend to work."

"Okay, seriously, you want to date her? Is this a settling down situation?"

I shrugged. "I don't know, maybe."

So much had happened in the last two months my head could barely figure out what day of the week it was. Two months ago, settling down was not anywhere on my agenda. The ink wasn't even in the pen, let alone writing it down.

But now?

Could I see myself settling down? Maybe.

Could I see it with Kit? Fuck yes.

I pictured her with Bell; pictured her face lighting up when I gave her the Shakespeare book, the richness of her eyes almost melting to hot chocolate. I'd stood outside Bell's room later listening to her read it, soothing Bell's grumblings with her soft, lilting tone, until my heart squeezed so much it was amazing my ribs were still intact.

"And what if you didn't have Bell? Is this because of her?"

"I dunno. It's a stupid question because I do have Bell. Anyone I date needs to be worthy of being around her, which Kit definitely is. Although I'm not sure I'm worthy of being around Kit. She's fucking smart and funny and..."

"And she bakes," offered up Penn. "I was being serious when I said you should marry her for the baking, and if you don't, I might."

Jealously flared strong and true. I might have very well shot lasers out of my eyes.

"Jeez, it was a joke."

"Am I laughing?"

"No, because you clearly lost your sense of humor when you lost your balls. If this is what happens when you fall in love, then count me out."

I hadn't lost my sense of humor, but nothing was funny

about this hell I was in. I also wasn't about to acknowledge his 'falling in love' comment, because even though it wasn't true, saying it out loud made it too real for comfort. They stopped talking and watched me as I stood up, because I always thought better when I stood up, and I really needed to think.

"Okay, time out. You," I pointed to Penn, "stop being a dickhead. You," I turned on Rafe, "stop being a lawyer. And help me!"

"I've told you what I think as your best friend. But, dude, if you want to start something, you need a new contract which she has to agree to before anything happens. Right now, if things don't go well, it opens you up and I can't in all good conscience advise that - especially as it would cause me a shit-load of paperwork if nothing else."

"I think you should just fuck her."

My eyes rolled to the ceiling while my self-appointed angel and devil continued arguing on the couch. Maybe I should just talk to myself, I'd get better advice.

"This isn't helping. You know what, it's my fault. I've not had sex in months, I'm exhausted and so I'm clearly lacking the proper function I need to make sensible decisions."

"Okay." Penn stood up, placed his hands on my shoulder. "I'm sorry. We're here and we'll help now."

I sighed with relief at the sincerity in his eyes. "Thank you. Rafe, this contract… Can you just tear it up?"

He looked at me like Penn would have done if I'd declared I hated baseball. "No, I can't just tear it up, not without her knowledge, or without mentioning that it's a monumentally stupid idea. She still works for you and she still needs an NDA. You're thinking with your dick again."

I linked my hands behind my head. "Fuck, why's this so hard?"

"Dude, you've never been interested in anyone. Whether you want to admit it or not, Bell is a factor. You know you can be a single dad, right? You don't need to find a wife just because you have a baby."

My mind stopped whirring as I turned to him. "What? This isn't that."

"Okay, just checking."

"This is all Wolf and Franks fault. I should have just let Joanie organize a nanny."

He rolled his eyes at me. "Stop being such a drama queen. Kit seems like a sensible girl, if she likes you as well, then it shouldn't be a problem. But I think you need to figure out first if you actually like *her,* and not just because of Bell."

"What d'you mean?"

"Just figure out what you actually want, then we can decide on how to approach it. So maybe don't say anything to her yet because she's still supposed to be living with you for a few months."

He had a point. It wasn't just me at stake. I was no longer the sole factor of my decisions. Bell was my priority, and the first consideration.

"Seduce her without her knowledge," Penn added.

I blinked, checking I'd heard properly. "What?"

"You know, make it harder for her to say no when the time comes."

I looked between the two of them. "That sounds massively dubious."

"No, idiot. I mean act like a boyfriend would act, but do it subtly. Show her how you'd be as a boyfriend. Win her over. Then when the time comes that you've actually figured out what you want, she'll fall into your arms like you're a Disney prince."

My face screwed up, as did Rafe's, and I assumed it was because we were both trying to figure out what the fuck Disney had to do with it.

Rafe got there before I did.

"What Pennington is trying to say is spend time together

outside of Bell. Get to know her and let her get to know you. Maybe do something nice for her while you're at it."

"That is literally what I just said. Act like a boyfriend."

Yeah, okay. Yes. I could do that. I think.

I hoped.

No, I could. Of course I could. I'd never been a boyfriend before, let alone acted like one, but I'd never been or acted like a dad before either, and I seemed to be doing okay at that.

But this one would also require help.

Seeing as none of us had had serious girlfriends since we'd left college, I needed some actual and sage advice from someone way more seasoned at it that any of us were.

Out of my two brothers-in-law, Jasper was the one who put in the time and effort, more than I ever gave him credit for. Whereas Cooper and Freddie got together in secret over the course of a week, then almost broke up for good due to their own stubbornness. If I needed help with this situation, Jasper was the one I had to ask.

I punched his number into the phone on my desk, the ring coming through loud on the speaker.

"Hey, bud, what's up?"

"Not much, have you got a minute?"

"Yeah, sure. I'm just in the car on the way to pick up Floss from preschool."

"Just wanted to ask you something actually. Um…" Now I was about to say it out loud, it sounded fucking stupid. "When you first met Wolf, it was a while before you actually got together, right?"

The silence on the end of the line told me that yes, it was fucking stupid.

"Murray?"

"Yeah?"

"What's this about?"

"What d'you mean? I was just wondering is all."

"Yeah, okay, sure." He laughed loudly before continuing, "But yes, it was. Three months. Three long fucking months."

"Right. Right. And while you were trying to get to know her, how did you do that exactly?"

"Well, I used to go and meet her after work, which you can't do with Kit because she lives there already."

Penn and Rafe started laughing hard. "Yes, dude."

I rolled my eyes. I mean it wouldn't have taken Columbo to crack the code, but still, the less it got around my family the better.

"But I cooked her dinner a lot which meant we had to spend time together. I used to send her flowers to work, and organized her favorite coffee to be delivered to her every day. I brought her to the games. She really wanted to go around the city, so I was her tour guide. That kind of thing. I listened to what she liked doing and made it happen."

Those all sounded like reasonable and achievable goals. I could listen. I could make stuff happen.

"Excellent. Thanks for the advice. And it was worth it, right? Did you ever think about quitting, seeing as she took so long to give it up?"

"Never. Your sister is the best thing that ever happened to me. I knew it the day I met her, and I know it right now."

"Good to hear. But Jas, don't say anything to Wolf about this, will you? Even if she is the best thing that ever happened to you, can I trust you to keep your trap shut? I don't want this getting back to Wolf and Franks."

"Yeah, don't worry. But I want the full story about this on the weekend, and I've decided we're going to have a boys' night out; you, me, Jamie, and Coop."

"Sounds good to me. See you Thursday."

"Cool, have to go; pulling up at the school."

"Bye, mate. Give Floss a kiss for me."

I hung up and turned back to the guys.

"What's Thursday?"

"We're going out of town for Easter. Jamie, Alex, and the kids will be over too. They're flying in tomorrow."

Seeing as eighty percent of my immediate family was over on the east coast right now, along with two new babies and one on the way, it had been decided that we would spend the long Easter weekend in the Hamptons instead of back in England.

"Fuck, is it Easter this weekend? Shit, I thought it was next weekend." Penn's eyes filled with the kind of annoyance that meant he'd double booked seeing his latest conquest and forgotten he needed to spend a weekend with his family.

"Is Kit going with you?" Rafe ignored Penn's huffing as he got out his phone.

I nodded. "Yep, we're all going."

He shoved his hands into his pants pockets and rocked on his heels. "Good luck with that then."

"Yeah." I scratched through my beard, wondering how I was going to navigate two nosy sisters, one equally nosy sister-in-law, and the nosiest mother, all of whom would be in my business, and worse, in Kit's.

Penn put his phone away, turning to us. "Right, now can we go and play?"

"Yeah, come on." I picked up my jacket and keys from my desk, resigning myself to the fact that I wasn't going to do any more work today. Not that I'd done any at all.

Tomorrow would be more productive.

I hoped.

10

MURRAY

I closed the front door behind me, walked through to my study and dumped my bag, then took the groceries into the kitchen. I'd left the boys playing pool at a local bar we frequented and walked home via Citarella to pick up ingredients for making dinner. Or more accurately, I'd picked up dinner to put in the oven, already ensuring all the preparation had been done.

Selecting a bottle of wine from the cellar off the pantry, I opened it to breathe and set it down on the counter, and went to find what I was looking for.

Who I was looking for.

I could hear them as I padded softly up the stairs, Bell gurgling as Kit talked. Chucking my jacket on my bed, I rolled up the sleeves of my shirt and loosened the top buttons as I followed the noise.

Bell was lying naked on her play mat, cooing up at the fuzzy felt birds flying around on the mobile above her. Barclay's tail started wagging from his bed and he graciously came over to give me a lick. Since Bell had arrived, he'd been staying here during the days instead of coming to the office with me. I'd like to say it was my choice to leave him, but I honestly wasn't sure, seeing as he went to find the baby or Kit every time I looked like I might be heading out.

"Hey, Barc," I stroked his soft fur, "how're you doing? Had a good day with the girls? Protected them from all the baddies?"

"I gotta say, as guard dogs go, he's pretty useless." Kit walked out of Bell's closet and bent down to stroke him. "Aren't you? You're just a big softie."

I tried not to stare at her as she kissed his head, tried not to glimpse the incredible cleavage I wanted to bury my face in, or inhale the fresh and clean sunshine scent that always wafted through the air around her. I hadn't yet figured out how she managed to get through the day without smelling like stale baby formula and vomit like I did, but every day so far she'd managed it, and I was quickly becoming addicted.

"He's very deceptive. Don't let him fool you."

She laughed, clearly not believing me, but I knew better. Her lashes fluttered and my heart gave a heavy thump as she held my gaze. It had only been nine hours since I left, but it was almost like she gave it a fresh surge of energy whenever she was close by. Fuck's sake, I sounded like I was describing the latest Apple tech, but either way, when she was around, my heart definitely beat faster.

I knelt down over Bell, moving the mobile out of the way, watching her face brighten with excitement at seeing me. If I thought Kit had recharging capabilities, it was nothing on Bell's smile. I almost couldn't imagine what life had been like before she'd arrived.

What did I used to come home to?

How did I function without seeing this smile?

Between the two of them, I was rapidly morphing into an entirely new and improved version of myself. Murray 2.0.

"Well, hello there, little one. Have you had a good day with Kit and Barclay?" I kissed her cheek, making her giggle again. "Why are you all naked?"

"She's about to have her bath so I'm letting her have some air before another diaper goes on." Kit called from the bathroom just as a whoosh of water hit the tub.

I smiled down at my daughter, squeezing her chubby little legs. "That sounds sensible, doesn't it?"

Bell blew a spit bubble in agreement. I lifted her up off the mat and carried her through, where the scent of lavender hit like we were walking through a field of it. She kicked excitedly as I placed her in the little bath hammock she had to lay back in. Bell loved bath time, and in the last week, she'd started splashing so much it usually required a change of clothing.

"You're gonna smell so good, Bells." I turned to Kit, "I need to go and sort a few things out, but I'll be back for her bottle."

"Okay," she smiled, kneeling down by the side of the tub, as Bell produced another kick, showering her in water. I didn't turn around as she laughed loudly, not wanting to see what I was positive would be Kit wearing a very thin, white, now wet, t-shirt.

I changed into sweats and went down to the kitchen, pouring a glass of wine and turned on the oven. Kit and I hadn't ever really eaten together before, because as soon as Bell was asleep, she would stay in her room with her in case she woke, and I would stay up reading the markets' news from the day. I had asked her before but she never took me up on it, and I didn't push the point because I always thought it was probably for the best.

That was going to change tonight.

I'd realized when I got to the grocery store I had no clue if there was anything she didn't like, so I picked up a lot. A lot. We'd be eating this for a while.

Luca, the guy who always helped me out whenever I went into Citarella, was aware I hadn't been blessed with the cooking gene and only ever handed me dishes with limited instructions that any idiot could heat up. He'd come through for me once more, because everything was to be heated at the same temperature for the same amount of time.

Easy peasy.

I threw it all in the oven and prayed for success. There would be nothing worse than ruining the first dinner I'd made for Kit, even if she wasn't entirely aware that's what it was.

She was fastening Bell's sleep suit by the time I got back upstairs, the heavy, warm scent of lavender and chamomile filling the air to soporific levels. It didn't go unnoticed by me that Kit had a different, dry shirt on.

"Hello, darling," I cooed softly, collecting her warm bottle from a table in the corner which Kit had turned into the baby equivalent of a mini bar. "Time for bed."

I lifted her off the changing mat and moved to the big rocking chair which Freddie had installed, while Kit started picking up all of Bell's laundry.

She started drinking hungrily and I watched her gulp it down until she closed her eyes in concentration, as she liked to do, her little fists opening and closing while she drank.

"There's a glass of wine for you downstairs, and I've made some dinner for us," I said quietly into the semi-dark room, trying to sound as casual as possible.

She didn't answer immediately but her pause as she bent to grab a sock which had fallen, told me she'd heard.

"Oh, I can grab something later. Don't worry about me; I'll wait until she's properly asleep."

"No, I'll do that. You go and relax, have a drink, and let's have dinner together." I tore my eyes away from Bell and over to Kit. "I'm sorry I left so early this morning; I had a breakfast meeting."

She looked over to me with valid uncertainty, especially after what happened last night.

What *nearly* happened last night.

"Okay. Sure. Sounds good," she answered after a beat, stroking Bell's head softly and placing a cloth on my shoulder. "Night, night, little Bell. Sweet dreams, baby."

"I'll see you downstairs," I called softly as she closed the door behind her, pushing away the nerves that were attempting to make an appearance.

It didn't take long until Bell almost finished the bottle. My daughter liked to eat. Although her nighttime one was never quite empty because she'd always fall asleep before the end. She'd grown so much in the last week, let alone in the six she'd been with me, nearly doubling her weight. Laurie had been around to check on her each week, and she moved to nearly the top of her percentile, like the absolute champion I knew she was. I smiled as her lips suctioned back on when I tried to remove it from her mouth, waiting for the tiny dream cry of protest as I took it away, and laid her across my chest until I coaxed a burp from her.

The things I now felt proud about had changed significantly, because getting my daughter to burp was right up there on the list, along with how well she was growing.

She barely stirred as I kissed her head, then laid her down in the crib and switched the nightlight on. Once I was certain she wasn't going to wake up, I headed back to the kitchen, Barclay hot on my heels, desperate for his own dinner time.

Kit was leaning across the kitchen island, pen in hand and reading over the crossword I hadn't finished, and since the other week, I'd purposely started leaving clues for her to do. Her thick hair fell over her shoulder in caramel waves hiding half of her face, but the second she heard me she glanced up, her brown eyes flashed warm and inviting.

"Hey."

"Hey." I poured out some wine for her, then topped my own glass up before pulling up the nanny cam app so I could hear Bell if she stirred. "How much more did you fill in?"

"Only four." She looked over her glass as she picked up

her wine and sipped, her eyes sparkling in amusement. "Mmmm, this is good. Something smells good too. What is it?"

"A selection of things for dinner. I wasn't sure what you liked so I picked up a few different bits."

"Oh, thank you." She blinked rapidly. "I didn't know you could cook."

I propped myself up near the oven opposite her, so I could look at her and watch what was about to happen. I raised my eyebrow suggestively. "There's a lot you don't know about me."

And there it was, her blush rising over her cheeks, pink like a sunset.

I didn't bother trying to hold in a laugh, because this woman made me happy by doing absolutely nothing but being herself, which right now, was a slightly amused, marginally uncomfortable, sexiest fucking woman I'd ever met. "I don't. I'm a terrible cook but I can reheat like a champion. I thought it was about time we at least had dinner together."

She chewed down on her cheek like she did whenever she was slightly nervous. I hoped that was a good sign.

"Well, what have you heated up then?" she smirked, before her face softened. "Thank you, it's really sweet of you."

I gave myself an internal high five, feeling like I'd won a small point. Maybe I should have pushed harder earlier, but we were here now and about to have our first dinner together.

"You're welcome." I walked into the pantry, Barclay following because he knew he was about to be fed. "How was your day? What did you do together?"

"We had a long walk up to Riverside Park this morning; she had her first nap there. We went to the market I used to like going to at college, bought some apples for a pie."

I placed Barclay's bowl down and left him scarfing his food up. "Have you been baking again?"

"No." Her cheeks rounded, her mouth open as she chuckled loudly at me. "Just for when I have some time."

"Have you always baked?"

She shook her head. "No, but when Payton and I lived together we used to be obsessed with that show you have in England - The Great British Bake Off – and we used to try and make whatever they made. We weren't always successful though."

I chuckled imagining her covered in flour as she tried to grapple with whatever she had been trying to bake. The timer on the oven buzzed, and I grabbed the kitchen towel to pull out the trays. "Well, speaking as someone who's terrible in the kitchen, I think it's pretty cool. Maybe you can teach me some of your skills."

"I can try, but I'm no miracle worker. Although," she sipped with a grin, her eyes lighting up as I placed the food on the counter, "your heating up skills seem to be on point. This looks amazing."

She jumped off the stool and grabbed some plates from the cupboard.

"What have we got then?"

The individual fragrances of the steaming dishes mingled in the air until my mouth filled with saliva; a low rumble let out from across the counter and Kit grabbed her stomach with a giggle.

"That sounds like approval, but let's taste it first," I grinned, pointing to them all, placing another tray of food down. "Eggplant parmesan, fennel meatballs, chicken escalope, and mushroom stroganoff. Plus mashed potatoes and roasted vegetables."

She looked toward the door, then over her shoulders before back at me with confusion. "Who else is coming for dinner?"

I held my hands up in defense. "Hey, I didn't know what you would like."

"It's perfect, thank you." She took the serving spoons I was holding out for her, before squinting at me. "Are you going to judge me if I have something of everything?"

I gasped loudly in faux shock, making her laugh again. "Nope, because that's exactly what I'm going to do. Dig in."

She filled her plate to impressive levels, and it dawned on me that I wasn't entirely sure I'd ever had anyone to dinner here that wasn't my family or the boys. I certainly hadn't ever cooked for anyone before, given that my abilities were limited to toast and bacon sandwiches.

I'd also not been out for dinner with a woman often, unless it was somewhere private, because it would inevitably end up in a gossip column somewhere proclaiming us as getting married. This would then result in a conversation along the lines of *this is strictly casual,* because I felt it important to clarify, but which never went down that well and usually put an end to whatever it was that had been going on.

But here I was, in front of a woman who had never tried to impress me, didn't agree with everything I said, nor adapt her personality to fit what I liked, or coax me into being seen together in public, and it felt more serious than anything I'd ever had.

And as someone who would be out every night of the week, if this is what staying in looked like, then I was into it.

"Oh my God, these are the best mashed potatoes I've ever had. Good job with the reheating." Her eyes twinkled as she grinned in a way that made my dick twitch and I ignored it as best as I could, seeing as how my sweatpants weren't about to hide anything. I loved that she could also give as good as she got, even if she did blush up a storm every time I teased her.

"The best in New York." I scooped my own mouthful. "Everything from Citarella is amazing."

We ate in silence for a minute, both too busy feeding our hunger to take a breath, although I was watching her eat more than I seemed to be concentrating on my own food. I topped up her empty glass.

"Thank you. What did you do today? How was work?"

I wasn't about to tell her that I did nothing because I couldn't think of anything except her and my dilemma.

"It was good. The boys came by though, so I didn't get much done."

"Don't they have their own work to do?"

"You'd think, but not today it seemed."

"They're funny. The three of you are like an old married couple. Actually, throuple?" Her low growly laugh added an unnecessary level of dirtiness that only served to fill my mind with visuals of her that were wholly inappropriate during dinner time. "They're very sweet with Bell too."

"Yes, they are. We all look out for each other." I forked up a meatball. "What about Payton? When's she coming over? I want to meet her."

"Really?"

I sipped my wine. "Yep."

"She's going to come on Wednesday. We're going out for drinks in the evening, if it's still good for me to have the night off?"

I cringed internally at the reminder of the true nature of our relationship.

"Yes, of course it is. The boys are coming over anyway to watch a game."

"What's the game?"

"Yankees at the Red Sox." I spooned more potatoes onto my plate. She was right, they were the best.

She raised her eyebrow. "Ooh, is that a hard one to pick seeing as you spent your formative years in Boston?"

"No, Penn is an avid Yankees fan. We were never going to be supporting another team."

"Really? He must have been pissed the other night when they lost."

I tilted my head as another nugget of information about her came to light. "Are you a baseball fan?"

She shrugged. "I'd go and watch a game because it's fun, but I don't really care who wins."

My eyes opened wide with mock warning. "Whatever you do, do not let Penn hear you say that. You will never hear the end of why baseball is the greatest game in existence, the history of baseball, and its importance in American culture."

"Seriously?"

I pointed my finger at her. "Yep. You've been warned, Columbia. And no amount of baked goods will shut him up."

"Noted." She ran her fingers across her lips, twisting at the end, handing me the invisible key.

"Actually, that reminds me, you said you liked going to the new exhibits at the Met?"

"Oh yes, I always try and get tickets for them."

"There's a Picasso one coming up soon I think." I did a quick memory check. "Yes, in a few weeks."

Her eyes took on a distinctly dreamy but sad look. "Yes!" she exclaimed. "It totally sold out though. I was too late."

My lips twitched at the corners. "Lucky you know someone who can get you in then, don't you?"

Her jaw dropped open. "You?"

Picking up a green bean, I crunched down on it. "Yep. Penn's family is sponsoring it, they've loaned a few pieces to it, so I'm relatively confident that means we'll get some viewing time if you'd like to go."

She put down her fork as her brow shot up. "They've loaned some pieces?"

I nodded with a grin.

"Then yes, please. That would be amazing."

"No problem…" I held her gaze, "Maybe we can go together."

She shifted slightly on the stool, her eyes darting away before returning to mine. "Yes, I'd like that."

"It's a date," I added casually, trying not to convey any of the weight that I wanted it to. Because it would be a date. A proper one. I'd already started planning it in my head.

"Where are you going for drinks on Wednesday?"

She shrugged, her button nose wrinkling up in a way I'd not seen before. "Some new bar Payton wants to go to, called Vitamin D I think. You know it?"

Not only did I know it, I part-owned it. I added another to-do item to my Kit List, making sure I called Leon, the manager, first thing in the morning, to set her and Payton up in the best space on Wednesday.

"I do. It has a great roof terrace."

Her eyes opened another degree, as she correctly read the grin I'd offered her.

"Is there anything in this city not touched by you?" she teased.

My heart, my mind, and my dick were all fully aligned on the answer to that question, but it probably wasn't the right time to tell her that. Instead I went for a slightly vague... "I can think of one thing."

She coughed into her glass of wine, making me laugh. Fuck, she was sexy when she blushed.

My heart, my mind, and my dick all responded accordingly. I swiftly decided to change the subject before we all became uncomfortable.

"Then we're off on Thursday. Hope you're prepared, it's the entire family."

Her wry smile told me she didn't think it would be as bad as I was certain it would be, but then again, she didn't have the knowledge I did, nor would she be subjected to the same levels of interrogation about our relationship. "I'm sure I'll be able to manage it."

"You say that now, but you'll be begging me for an early breakaway back to the city."

"I'm pretty tough when I want to be," she chuckled, before forking in a final mouthful of meatballs.

"Oh yeah?" I challenged.

"Yep." She held my gaze with her eyebrows raised, and it did nothing for the problem in my pants except make it worse.

"Well, I look forward to the day I get to witness that." I lifted my glass in salute and leaned back on the stool, trying to ease my belly which was now very full. And I could eat a lot.

She pushed her own plate away, looking down at the dishes which weren't empty, but looked like we'd made every attempt to. "God, I can't believe how much we've just eaten. Good job I only need to walk up the stairs."

"I know. I might end up in a food coma."

"It was all so good, but I think the meatballs were my favorite."

I filed that away for future use. "Me too."

Her arms lengthened out over her head in a stretch and she stifled a yawn before standing up and started clearing away our empty plates. I put my hand over hers to stop her.

"Don't. I'll do this. You clear up all day after my baby, you don't have to clear up after me too."

"You heated it up, doesn't that mean I clear?" She winked, "Let's do it together." She opened the dishwasher and started loading it. I followed her lead, clearing the counter and covering all the leftover food, moving around her as she took them from me and put them in the fridge. It was the most domesticated I'd ever been in my own kitchen.

I turned to find her leaning back against the counter finishing the last drop of her wine. "Thank you, Murray. It was all delicious. I should probably head to bed for a bit of sleep before Bell wakes for her midnight feed. Next time, I'll cook."

I draped the damp tea towel over the oven rail, torn between wanting her to stay and not coming on too strong. I settled for the latter. "I'll hold you to that. Sleep well, Kit."

Next time. I wasn't about to fixate on those words because there *was* going to be a next time. And one after that. And one after that.

I'd never met anyone I'd wanted a *one after that* with. And this wasn't about Bell. I knew it as well as I not only knew my heart, mind, and dick, but also my own soul.

If Bell wasn't here, I'd still want her.

I hadn't been looking for her, but somehow I'd found her.

And now I was going to show her I'd be worth wanting, too.

11

KIT

Bell squeezed hard on the rubber giraffe I'd handed her while I waited for her bottle to cool, the high pitched squeaking causing Barclay to get up from lying underneath the bouncer on the table and move to his bed in the corner. The air was still chilly as I opened the patio doors, but the sky was blue and cloudless, and the flower boxes which lined the length of the enormous outdoor terrace were already well in bloom. The trees lining Central Park were getting thicker with new leaves, and I could just make out the buds of blossoms coming through. It was going to be a beautiful spring day.

Murray strode into the kitchen, momentarily stealing my breath because whenever he was in a suit, his hotness topped the Scoville scale, most certainly qualifying him for five flame emojis. The hotness scale was in direct contrast to my disappointment scale, because his suit meant he had a meeting today and I hadn't realized, hoping instead he'd be around so we could go for a walk together.

It had been three days since our *almost kiss*.

I'd spent the first day doing my best impression of a ball-bearing in a pinball machine, ricocheting between wishing I could have experienced the feel of his lips on mine, knowing I'd missed out on the type of kiss that wouldn't just curl your toes, it would melt you like a candle until you were nothing but a pile of hot dripping wax, and knowing how bad an idea it was. Coupled with the fact that he'd left before I'd seen him that morning, reducing me to a ball of anxiety and one of those girls that second guesses every single minute we'd been together, analyzing it so thoroughly I could now most certainly moonlight as a Freud expert in any court of law.

I was then abruptly yanked out of the spiral I'd spent the day in, when the fun, teasing Murray I'd come to look forward to every morning returned later that day, with the most delicious array of foods for dinner, all because he hadn't been sure what I'd like.

Now it was day three, and I was still no closer to figuring out if something was happening between us. It wasn't, and the almost kiss had not been mentioned, but it also wasn't *not*, because his attentiveness and insistence we spend time together while he peppered me with questions had notched up several degrees.

"Earth to Kit..." he waved at me.

I jolted out of the trance I'd locked myself in, which happened far more than it ought to whenever he was around. If I could moonlight as Freud, Murray could moonlight as Derren Brown.

"Sorry, what did you say?"

"Your coffee." He pointed at a mug on the counter with his own as he sipped. I'd been staring so long he'd had time to finish making them. "I haven't filled it quite to the level you usually do, so you should be able to lift it without spilling it everywhere."

My cheeks warmed as they always did at his teasing, and the fact that he'd noticed how I never managed to gauge the coffee and milk ratio. Good job he took his black and the coffee machine did all the work, because otherwise I'd be in trouble.

"Thank you."

His eyes crinkled in amusement as he drank.

"You have a meeting today?" I tried to keep the tone in my voice as casual as possible.

"I do." His coffee cup went down on the counter, all without breaking eye contact. "But I'll be back early afternoon, and the guys are coming over."

"Okay, sounds good."

He leaned over Bell, grabbing her feet and kissing them. My ovaries still hadn't grown back since that first week, and I still hadn't gotten any closer to being used to seeing them together. He was so fucking adorable; adorable with a capital A. For someone who became a dad overnight with no forewarning, he was a natural. "What are you girls going to do?"

"Just the usual, go and hang out in the park, take Barclay for a walk. Payton is coming over to join us."

"Sounds like fun, I'm jealous." He slid back the crisp white double cuff of his shirt, his gold cufflinks catching the glare of the sun, looking at his watch. "I have to shoot off." He picked Bell out of her bouncer, kissing her cheek. "Bye, little girl. Be good."

Since Sunday, I'd been counting how long he held my gaze before speaking. Right now as he handed Bell to me, it was four seconds. And each one heated my body until my internal thermostat hit max.

"You too, Columbia. Be good." His wink took me to feverish levels. "Call me if you need anything though. Or just want to give me a play by play, I enjoy those."

I grinned. "I can do that."

"Good. See you later, Kit."

He gathered up his briefcase and headed out, leaving behind a trail of his woodsy, heady, delicious man scent. It was still lingering in the air two hours later as Payton arrived, just as I put Bell down for her first nap of the day.

"This place is incredible." She'd already opened up all the doors in the kitchen, rummaged through the pantry for snacks and was now ensconced on one of the very squashy and comfy loungers on the patio. She'd also taken herself on a tour of the artwork, including originals of several prominent British artists – Tracey Emin, Damien Hirst, Banksy, and Harland Miller. His apartment doubled as a very private and exclusive gallery of modern art, worth millions.

I placed some coffee down in front of her. "I know. It's really beautiful."

"But the décor - it doesn't scream bachelor pad, or man with money and no taste or clue. I could move in here and not do anything."

"Freddie's an interior designer, she did the place."

"I like it." A crumb from the chocolate chip cookies I'd made yesterday fell to the floor as she bit into it. Barclay quickly hoovered it up then waited patiently for the next bit. "This is good."

"They are." I picked up my own from the pile she'd put on a plate.

"Which one is Jackson Foggerty's place?" She looked up, but there was only one more floor above the one we were on, and that was Murray's too.

"He's round the other side. I don't know if it's the same layout as this one, though I assume it is."

"Have you seen him again?"

"Not since you asked me this morning." In what may have been a record, it had been three hours since she'd asked me, because she seemed to think I spent my life going up and down in the elevator - something she'd very seriously asked me to consider. "The second I see him again, I'll let you know."

"If he's going out, can you follow him?"

"No, I fucking can't. I have better things to do."

"Alright, calm down. You never know unless you ask."

I rolled my eyes, standing up as I heard the intercom, Barclay following me in.

"Hello?"

"Hi, Kit, it's Graham from the front desk. There's a guest here to see Murray, but I think he's gone out. She says she's come to collect something, but he didn't leave anything with us and he normally would, so I wanted to check."

I frowned, pretty sure I hadn't heard him tell me this, although if he had, it was entirely possible it would have been during one of my zoning out episodes, so hadn't heard a single thing he'd said. "Yes, he has gone out. He didn't mention anyone coming by, and I don't think he's left anything. Do you know what it is he's supposed to have left?"

"No, ma'am."

I chewed on my lip. "Okay, it's fine if you want to send her up."

"Are you sure? I can ask her to come back."

This wasn't the first time someone had come over to see Murray, and after what happened with Bell, the concierge was always overly cautious. Especially Graham, who I'd sort of become friends with.

"No, don't worry. Maybe it's here but I didn't realize."

"If you're sure. Please don't hesitate to call if you need anything."

"Will do."

Payton wandered in. "What was that about?"

"Dunno. Someone downstairs says they've come to collect something Murray's left for them, but it wasn't at the front desk and I don't remember him saying anything to me about it." I shrugged. "Probably a courier."

Her mouth dropped dramatically. "You shouldn't have let them up. What if it's a hit man?"

Sometimes I had no idea how her brain worked. "What?"

"You know, they've conned their way in."

Then I remembered her current fixation was mafia romance.

"Pay, Professor Grady would turn in her grave if she knew about your mafia obsession."

"She isn't dead."

"She would be if she knew you had a mafia romance fetish!" I called behind me on my way to the door as the bell rang, leaving Payton to hypothesize over who was there.

It wasn't a courier. What it was however, was a strikingly beautiful, slightly familiar, very tall woman, dressed head to toe in black, with hair so dark and shiny I wanted to ask what her hair care regimen was. Instead, I waited as she gave me a very slow and thorough once over that immediately made me feel like my spine had just infused itself with a titanium rod, pulling my shoulders back hard in defense.

The temperature of the air around us dropped significantly.

"Can I help you?"

She peered down at me then plastered on a not-very-well-practiced fake smile that didn't reach her eyes. At least I didn't think it did, but I couldn't be sure because I also detected a subtle amount of Botox. No one's skin was that smooth.

"You must be the housekeeper."

I was about to respond that no, I wasn't the housekeeper, when Barclay barged in next to me with his hackles raised and began growling.

Huh.

Maybe he wasn't a terrible guard dog, because this woman was anything but friendly, the attempted fake smile only making things worse. She glared down at him, and I swear I caught her snarling back.

Who the fuck was this woman?

I was tempted to look around for a broomstick, because

those were definitely the vibes she was giving off. Payton then added to the mix, pulling the door open wider, assessing the scene, which to the average onlooker must have appeared like some kind of Mexican standoff.

"Who are you?" asked Payton.

She gave Payton as much of a once over as she had me, before her overly shaped eyebrow arched unnecessarily. "I'm Murray's girlfriend."

"What?!" Payton scoffed, while I tried to remember how to breathe from the sucker-punch I'd just taken in the gut. "I don't think so."

No. This can't be right. He can't have a girlfriend. Someone would have mentioned it. *He* would have mentioned it.

Wouldn't he?

He'd had plenty of time to mention it in the six weeks we'd been living together, during our conversations on all the walks we'd been on, or conversations period, not including the evening of the almost kiss; the night he brought home dinner, or at any point during all the time we'd spent together recently.

"Murray's not here, but I'll let him know you stopped by." I held onto Barclay who was now openly snarling at her, giving me a legitimate concern he might eat her. The only objection I had to that was the fact I'd have to clean up the mess afterward.

For the second time her smile failed to reach her eyes. "No, don't worry. I said I'd meet him here, but maybe he's at the office. Silly boy must have got it mixed up. I'll go there."

Was *she* the meetings he'd been having? Bile started swirling around my stomach and jealousy leached through my veins.

"Cool, bye." Payton slammed the door in her face, heading back toward the kitchen like the Daughter of Evil had just knocked on the door, only to turn around when she realized

I wasn't following, because I was glued to the spot. "Kit, what are you doing?"

What was I doing? For the first time, I had no clue.

"She said she was his girlfriend."

Payton's head tilted as she studied me with a frown. "Don't tell me you believed her."

"Why would someone say that if they weren't?"

"Because she a crazy bitch! Everyone knows it."

I shook my head, not really understanding what she meant or why she was so casual about everything. "What?"

"You know who that was, right?"

Did I? I didn't think I did. "Should I?"

I'd dismissed my earlier notion that she'd been familiar, writing her off as an identikit Eastern European, but Payton was about to correct me.

"That was Dasha Novikoff. She used to model quite a lot, one of those girls you always see in pointless articles about how they decorate, shit like that. She always dates dodgy Russian gazillionaires, and she hasn't appeared in much recently, except articles by her old assistants saying she used to throw shoes and stuff at them. I think maybe one was an iPad. Anyway, she's nothing but a Malevolent knock off, and she's full of shit."

"How do you know this?"

"People and Us Weekly," she replied, like it was obvious.

I rolled my eyes at my stupid question, because of course she did. Payton read People and Us Weekly like Murray read the financial pages.

"Hey, I need to break up the monotony of children's books with something more entertaining." She pulled me into a hug. "Kit, she's not his girlfriend. I'd bet my entire shoe collection on it. Also, look at how Barclay reacted. If that had been me, I'd have been running for my life."

She did have a point there, I'd never seen him like that, and he was still sitting by my feet just in case I still needed protection from the Wicked Witch of the West Village. But it didn't make me feel any better about what had unfolded in the last five minutes.

"You know what. Even if she isn't, she's clearly the type of woman he goes for. And I'm not."

Payton looped her arm through mine and guided me into the kitchen, sitting me on a stool like I was a toddler. "What are you talking about? You're amazing! She's nothing except someone with hard edges and pointy elbows and a clear attitude problem. Oh, and the obvious need for a decent meal. Maybe if she ate she'd be more pleasant, though I doubt it."

When we'd lived together through college and beyond, anything shitty that happened was always made better with milk and cookies, because that was what both our moms had done for us. I watched her make her way around the kitchen as she put it together again, pouring out two glasses of milk and fetching the rest of the tub of cookies I'd made, although she hadn't noticed the irritation currently forcing my brow to furrow.

"That's not what I meant, but thanks for the veiled insult. I meant aesthetically we're totally different. Based on the three minutes I experienced of her stellar personality, I'd say were also *totally* different. Even if she's not his girlfriend, she was confident enough to proclaim that she was which means they've obviously slept together." My lips curled in revulsion at the image of her touching his perfect body, but also at how visually perfect they'd look together, like they'd fallen straight out of a Calvin Klein campaign.

"And that's not what *I* meant. Even if they have had sex, it means nothing. She just lied about being his girlfriend, so that should tell you how desperate she is. Murray is into you, I can tell. Look at what happened the other night, and then dinner."

I didn't want to think about the other night, about the almost kiss, or the dinner, or the flirting or this morning. I was already feeling foolish, and thinking about it all would only make it worse, because even if there had been a connection, even if I hadn't imagined it, I'd clearly built it into more than I thought it was.

So no, I wasn't going to think about it.

"It's not a good idea. This is a sign, a sign that I'm playing with fire and I shouldn't be contemplating an affair with my boss; a fantasy which has been living only in my head. What we are going to do is go out and we're going to have fun, and I'm not going home until I have several numbers to call."

"I'm not arguing with that, you deserve it. We had one night out between you finishing your exams and this place."

"Good. This dress you bought me better look slutty."

She scoffed. "Would I have bought you anything else? You want to see it?"

"Damn right I do." I caught the time on the kitchen clock. "Quickly though, Bell will wake up soon."

She ran to the front door and came back with a Bergdorf's bag and I was almost thankful I'd been called away to a sick baby because a trip to Bergdorf's with Payton was akin to Hell on Earth. I'd learned a long time ago that it was much easier for her to shop for me than for me to go with her. My favorite thing was when she sent me the links to things she'd think I'd like, so I could shop from the comfort of my couch. Or the coffee shop. Or the back row of a lecture on eighteenth century poets.

She pulled it out of the bag and I waited for her to pull out the rest, only there wasn't any rest.

"Jesus. I said slutty, but I don't think I'd get this over my head." I reached for it, holding it out in front of me by the sheerest of spaghetti straps. The dress was the darkest green silk, reminding me of the color Murray's eyes flared when he looked at me. It was so delicate I could very easily rip it with a deep breath, and calling it a dress was perhaps a generous description. A scrap of material was more accurate.

"It will. I tried it on and it was a bit too small for me so it'll fit you perfectly."

I didn't hold the same level of confidence she did, and I doubted it would even cover my ass. But fuck it. I'd simply require a lot of alcohol.

A shrill cry let out from my phone, turning into a loud and steady grumbling. "Shit, Bell is awake. I need to go and feed her."

Payton jumped off her stool. "Okay. I have to head off anyway, but I'll come by about five."

Five was early, but seeing as Murray would be home with Bell and I wasn't currently in the mood to spend time around him, I didn't object.

We walked out together. "Love you. Thanks for the Band-Aid I'll be wearing tonight."

"Oh, it's gonna fix you right up," she cackled.

"That's not what I meant, and you know it."

I closed the door behind her and ran up the stairs to Bell, the heaviness lifting with each swing of the Bergdorf bag. I might not have meant Band-Aid in the traditional sense, but Payton had been right. If anything could fix my bruised ego and dented heart, it was this dress.

A night out was exactly what I needed.

12

KIT

The biggest bunch of pink roses I'd ever seen in my entire life floated into the kitchen.

No, Murray was carrying them.

But that's how big they were because they'd completely blocked him from my view until he placed them on the island counter, smiling at me like he'd won the lottery.

"I picked these up for you on the way home." He pulled a single stem out of the thick brown paper they were wrapped in. "Except this one. This one is for Bell."

He looked so handsome standing there waiting for me to respond, but my mind was travelling the speed of light, and I couldn't get a grasp on any thought I'd had between what happened this morning and why he would bring me roses so enormous I could smell the fragrance of them from where I was standing across the kitchen in stunned silence.

The only thing I could manage was to gather them up, inhaling the floral rose scent before putting them in the sink. "Thank you."

Murray followed me into the pantry to where the vases were kept, coming up behind me to grab the biggest one from the top shelf when I couldn't reach it. "You're welcome.

Bell looked so cute in the picture you sent me. How was your day?"

How was my day? *It was fine until some psycho who may or may not be your girlfriend turned up,* but his nearness was too much for me to think clearly.

"It was good, thanks. Non-eventful." I moved past him so no part of him could touch me, because the smell of him was already overpowering that of the roses and serving no purpose except fogging my senses, reminding me of that first week I lived here when I did everything I could to avoid it.

He followed me out, as close to my heels as Barclay whenever food was involved.

"Are you okay?"

I turned the faucet on loud, filling the vase, hoping to drown out both my thoughts and his staring at me.

"Kit?"

Damn.

I looked up at him, plastering on the cheeriest smile I could muster. "Yep?"

"Are you okay?"

"Yes, all good." I unwrapped the flowers, placing them carefully in the vase. Fuck's sake, may as well get this over with. "Oh, I forgot. Your girlfriend came by, but she said she must have got the plans wrong and she'd find you at the office because that's where she usually meets you. Hope she did."

Actually, I hoped she'd been swallowed by a sink hole, but as I hadn't seen anything on the news about one appearing, I suspected she'd gone to find him at his office. I dared to glance up at him, a tsunami sized wave of relief washing over me at the expression of genuine confusion on his face.

But it changed nothing.

Anything between us was a stupid idea. All I needed was a night out with Payton, and in the morning, whatever I'd imagined between us would be a distant memory.

I hoped.

"My girlfriend? I don't have a girlfriend."

"Oh, well, it's none of my business, although she seemed quite insistent." I placed the very heavy vase at the end of the kitchen island. They really were stunning. I loved pink roses, a fact I'd suspected he'd remembered from the time we'd walked through a flower market in Riverside Park weeks ago, and my smile was utterly genuine this time. "Thank you for the roses, it was very sweet of you. I'll take Bell's to her room."

"Kit?"

"Yes?" I turned around to find him standing in the same spot he'd been in since I dropped the news about his visitor, two lines creasing his brow.

"I don't have a girlfriend."

"I know, you just said."

His eyes narrowed and his creases deepened. "Then why does it feel like you don't believe me?"

"I believe you Murray, you told me. But it's none of my business what you get up to in your private time." I thumbed behind me, wanting to leave this conversation as quickly as possible so I didn't have to admit why it had upset me. "I need to go and get Bell for her bottle."

It didn't take him long to follow me upstairs too.

"What time are you going out?" He picked up Bell's bottle from the side table and sat in the rocking chair. I placed her in his arms, having difficulty with the intensity of his gaze being trained on my face, even though I was looking at the baby.

I stood back, making sure there was the minimum amount of distance between us needed for me to meet his heavy scrutiny. "At five, if that's still okay?"

"Of course it is." The soft voice he reserved for whenever he was holding Bell echoed around my muddled head. "I've got Bell now, you take off or whatever it is you want to do."

I wasn't about to argue. I needed to gather my thoughts and I couldn't do it with him watching my every move. "Thank you."

I handed him a burp cloth and walked out through the bathroom into my room, feeling his eyes boring into me with every step.

The dress was hanging where I'd left it on the closet door and renewed my sense of determination to shed this entire day like old skin washed over me. I checked my watch; I had time for a very quick run. Grabbing my gear, I laced up my sneakers and took off.

Kit: *I can see my ass!*

Payton: *Good thing it's a mighty fine ass then. I'm five minutes away.*

I turned again to see myself in the full length mirror. Yep, I could definitely see my ass. I had to hand it to her; this dress was beautiful and fitted perfectly, even if I did have t-shirts longer. With my hair flowing in thick waves over my shoulders hiding the spaghetti straps, it looked like I was wearing even less than I was. I rummaged in my closet, shrugging on my leather jacket when I found it, working to add a bit of edginess to the entire ensemble which included a pair of grey Manolos Payton had loaned me, a key part of the collection she'd bet me earlier. I added one final coat of mascara and a slick of lip gloss, grabbed my clutch, and took off.

Loud laughter was coming from the direction of the kitchen. The boys had arrived at some point while I was getting ready, and given the state of what I wasn't wearing, I didn't really want to follow the volume of chatter and subject myself to the watchful stare Murray trained on me earlier. But I also couldn't leave without telling him.

Kit: *Heading out, back later. Enjoy your evening.*

I gingerly made my way down the stairs, gripping the handrail because breaking my ankle before I'd even left would not be an ideal start to the evening. I should have carried these goddamn shoes and put them on in the elevator like a sensible person would do. Instead, to pay my idiot tax for the day, I'd taken so long to get to the front door that Murray was already standing there, his thick biceps bulging under his shirt as his arms crossed over his chest.

"You were going to leave without saying goodbye?"

I couldn't tell whether the inflection in his voice was from annoyance or hurt.

"I didn't want to disturb you with the guys. Payton's downstairs waiting for me."

If the once over from Dasha froze me to my core, the once over from Murray laved every inch of my skin from the inside out until I was a bubbling, conflicted mess.

"You look… beautiful."

"Thank you."

I startled as he took my hand in his, staring at me like he was on the verge of saying something until a buzzing started up in my clutch, breaking whatever moment we were in the middle of.

"I need to go. Payton is downstairs." I closed the door behind me, preventing any plans he may have had to watch me until I got in the elevator, because I had the distinct feeling that's exactly what he was about to do.

I pressed the button for the atrium, leaning against the mirrored walls, closing my eyes in an attempt to make sense of the confusion jumbling my brain; losing myself in trying to figure out what had been flashing across Murray's face as he held my hand.

I was so lost I didn't notice the elevator doors hadn't closed, or that I was no longer alone, with only with my thoughts for company.

"Well if it isn't the nanny. And you are looking exceptionally beautiful tonight if I do say so myself."

My eyes flew open to find Jackson Foggerty standing opposite me, staring like the Big Bad Wolf he played in a remake of Red Riding Hood. And I now knew why he'd won his Academy Award, because he genuinely made me believe he was about to eat me.

"Thanks."

"Where are you off to looking like a smoking hot pixie?"

Having met him twice now, I felt I was authorized to say he was actually kind of a creeper, negating any attractiveness he had. He might be an award winner, but the way he was currently looking at me was making my skin crawl.

"Sorry? What did you say?"

His snort carried undertones of derision. "Wow. He must be more amazing in the sack than the rumors make out."

His cryptic comment did nothing to change my mind, not that I understood it either. "What?"

The door pinged and opened before he replied. "Ah, saved by the bell."

I hurried out to find Payton waiting for me in the atrium, looking like a goddess in a golden jumpsuit which deepened her olive skin perfectly, giving her legs for days. Her hair was curled into big, dark waves, flowing around her like she had her own personal wind machine.

"Finally! Let's go!"

I could almost hear Jackson Foggerty's jaw hitting the polished marble floor, which was a split second before she noticed him behind me, and my plan for a rapid exit from both him and the building were foiled.

"Holy shit. Do you two come as a pair?" he drawled.

She put her arm around me. "Yes, we do." She gave him her most flirtatious smile, one I'd seen before, although I was actually impressed she hadn't completely lost her mind considering a guy she'd been lusting over for a decade was now standing in front of her.

But you know what they say about fantasies: they never meet expectations, not by a long shot.

His eyebrow rose with more than a little interest. "Does that mean you come with a warning too?"

She frowned. "A what?"

"A warning, like this one." He tipped his chin in my direction.

Now it was my turn to frown. "What's a warning? What does that mean?"

"Your boy, Murray, said he'd cut me off if I go anywhere near you. Fucking ruthless," he shook his head, "but he makes me a fuck ton of money and I ain't gonna be acting forever so I need to steer clear of you, no matter how desperately tempting you are because the three of us together..." he groaned leeringly at our stunned, silent faces. "Fuck me. Anyway, I bid you *adieu*, ladies."

He walked out and stepped into the back of massive black Lincoln Navigator which swept him away into the Manhattan traffic as soon as door slammed shut, before Payton and I had even had a chance to take a breath, let alone make any sense of his parting words.

"Wow. That was…"

"What the fuck just happened?"

"I'm not sure."

In my periphery I could see that she was still glued to the spot, staring straight ahead to the point where Jackson Foggerty just left. "What did he mean about me coming with a warning?"

"I'm not sure."

"And he offered us a threesome?"

"Yep."

"I need a drink."

"Yep."

The doorman hailed us a cab, and two minutes later, we were lost in a sea of yellow and a cacophony of loud honking. Payton smoothed down her jumpsuit, crossing her legs with a *tut* almost as loud as the honking.

"No offense, but I wouldn't have a threesome with you. It would be too weird."

"I'm not offended. I wouldn't have a threesome with you either."

"Why not?" Her tone was incredibly indignant considering she'd just told me the exact same thing.

"You want me to list the reasons?"

Her eyes bugged far too dramatically for a hypothetically based chat. "There's a whole list?!"

"Okay, this is a stupid conversation. What's wrong?"

Her huff summed up our days exactly. "Jackson Foggerty is a huge dick. God! Why did he have to be such a dick? Now I need to find someone else to fantasize over."

"I'm sorry, babe. Some people are dicks." I put my arm around her in comfort. "We just need to drink the day away and have some fun."

"Yeah, you're right. Oh look, we're here."

Payton knocked into me on my side of the cab as it swerved to a sharp halt outside the orange door signaling the entrance to Vitamin D. She righted herself while I passed a twenty to the driver and hopped out behind her.

We found a sharply dressed hostess standing by an elevator inside a very small entrance, so small it only contained the elevator doors. She was so sharply dressed it made me feel less overdressed, or at least less aware of how little I was wearing, and how high my heels were.

"Ms. Hawkes?"

"Yes?"

"We've been expecting you. Welcome to Vitamin D, this way please." She pressed the button and the doors opened immediately. "Your table is waiting."

I felt my attempt to not show any shred of surprise that this woman didn't only know my name but also had a table waiting was award worthy, maybe not a Jackson Foggerty Oscar, but certainly a Golden Globe.

"Thank you."

Payton pounced the second the doors closed.

"Did you book it? How did they know your name?"

I figured it out as we were shown to our table, easily the best in the bar with views heading out toward the East River on one side, and the Empire State Building on the other. It was confirmed when a bottle of champagne we hadn't ordered arrived with compliments from Murray Williams.

"Wow," Payton sipped, "this is seriously cool. You didn't tell me he owned the place."

I crossed my legs awkwardly, trying to stop my panties from showing, but however I moved, I was certain they did. "I don't think he does. I think he said he invested in it, whatever that means."

"He didn't have to do this. This is seriously nice of him." She took a long sip. "What happened when he got home?"

I stopped fiddling and focused on Payton with a heavy sigh. "I know. He is kind. He's kind and sweet and smart and funny. And when he got home, he'd brought with him fifty one enormous long stemmed pink roses, fifty for me and one for Bell. And then when I told him his girlfriend had stopped by, he looked so confused and said he didn't have one. I believe him, Pay."

"Fucking hell. Fifty roses? And the one for Bell is adorable. "

My shoulders dropped, weighed down with the tension I'd been carrying since Fatal Attraction had rung the doorbell this morning. I should have let Graham deal with her.

"Yes, it was."

"What happened?" She leaned forward, waiting for me to answer.

I picked up my glass and took three large gulps, needing something to take the edge off. Almost immediately, a waiter appeared to top us up.

"He said he didn't have a girlfriend. Several times. He followed me around the house and kept repeating it until I believed him. I do believe him, I do. But that woman... How could he have been with her? She was awful."

Her hands shot out in a *who fucking knows* gesture. "People do stupid things and make mistakes, especially when it comes to sex. I've done it plenty."

"You've never slept with your boss."

"If I had one who looked like Murray, I might," she shot back with a grin.

"It's still a stupid idea. And I have two months left there."

She sat back, twisting the stem of her champagne flute between her fingers. "You didn't even want the job anyway, so if something starts to properly develop between you, then find him a new nanny and quit. If he's that into you, then he'll go along with it."

She may as well have been voicing aloud thoughts I only had when I allowed myself the fantasy. "I dunno. I don't even know want he wants with all this. I don't know what any of it means."

"Speaking as someone who's dated plenty and never received fifty roses of any color, I'd say he likes you." She may as well have told me one plus one equals two, with the tone she was using.

My mind went back to the past few days, even the past few weeks, because if I really thought about it, that almost kiss didn't come out of nowhere. He hadn't given a single shit that I'd caught him wearing nothing but a towel, and the smirk on his face from my reaction wasn't arrogance or the look of someone who was used to women salivating over his naked body. No, it was... pride? Happiness? Relief?

So maybe he did like me.

Maybe.

"Do you think that comment from Jackson Foggerty was about me?"

"Absolutely."

"As in more than just because I'm always with Bell?"

"Yes. It's because Jackson Foggerty is undoubtedly a sleaze, as much as it pains me to say it."

Her exaggerated sad face made me laugh, loosening the tight churning in my gut. "Yeah. I'm sorry your day has sucked as much as mine."

"That's okay, I'll get over it." She rubbed her hands together, "But let's try to forget about them and get on with our evening, because we both look smoking hot and we're not wasting it by mooning over stupid boys. We're here to have fun."

Which is how we found ourselves sharing our table with a group of guys who'd waltzed straight in and sat down next to us like they owned the place, and apparently this was their usual table. Payton and I didn't correct them, nor did we move, but every few minutes she threw me a look which told me exactly what she thought about them. The guy next to Payton was waving around his platinum Amex and talking to her about stock, and she was listening like it was the most fascinating thing she'd ever heard.

It wasn't.

I'd initially had the pleasure of sitting next to Mike in the pink striped shirt, who was much less vocal about his bank balance and couldn't stop looking at my legs. But then he left after seeing someone he knew, and his place was taken by Blake, the one I'd decided was the most genuine, and probably would have been interested in if his eyes hadn't been a shade of green joltingly similar to Murray's, but without the shine and sparkle. Although when he moved nearer, I realized they were more of a sludgy khaki which was nothing like Murray's, but then I had Murray on the brain, and no matter how hard I tried to follow what Blake was saying and listen with rapt enthusiasm, I couldn't stop myself from comparing the size of his biceps – smaller – the broadness of his chest – smaller – the width of his shoulders – smaller – with Murray.

Have you ever noticed how easy it is to get drunk when someone else is doing all the talking? The bottle of champagne was long gone, so were the two rounds of tequila sodas.

"I'd love to take you out," Blake's body shifted nearer to mine, his arm going round the back of my chair. "Are you free this weekend?"

"Yes, she is," slurred Payton, ungluing herself from Platinum Amex guy for a second before resuming her position.

"I'm not actually. I'm going out of town for Easter weekend."

Even though it was true, it sounded like a blatant lie after Payton's outburst.

"Nice, where are you going?"

"The Hamptons."

"Me too! Let me take you out." The excitement in his voice would have been endearing if I'd been able to focus properly, less to do with the alcohol and more to do with the man I knew would be waiting for me at home

"I don't know what the plans are yet, I'm not sure if I'll have time."

He ran his hands through his thick, dark curls. "Can I have your number? I'll message you and you can decide if you're free."

I was expecting my inability to say no to kick in, but miraculously, I pushed through. Kind of. "Why don't you give me yours, and if I'm around, I'll let you know."

He hesitated for a second before reaching into his pocket, pulling out a thick cream business card with his number embossed on it.

"Okay, but you'd better call." He waved it at me, then laughed, "Unless you're trying to let me down gently and I haven't been able to take the hint?"

"No, honestly, I really don't know what I'm doing this weekend."

His preppy cuteness intensified from his toothy grin.

In the distance, the lights on the Brooklyn Bridge were twinkling in full force. I hadn't noticed how late it had gotten, especially as the powerful patio heaters had fought off the evening chill. I checked my watch then turned to Payton.

"Pay, it's time to go."

A chorus of *boos* and *it's still earlies* went up from the rest of the table.

"She's right boys. We've been here a lot longer than you." Payton stood up and smoothed down her jumpsuit. "But if you're lucky, we'll see you again."

We said our goodbyes, and I wrangled my arms into my jacket which had been resting on my shoulders, as we walked off.

"We're not seeing them again," Payton whispered.

"I know."

We stopped by the reception desk on the way out. "Excuse me; we need to settle our bill."

"Oh no, Ms. Hawkes, your bill was already settled by Mr. Williams," she smiled.

I shouldn't have been surprised but I was. "Not just the champagne?"

"No, ma'am. Everything."

"Oh, thank you." A little dance of happiness started up in my belly that wasn't anything to do with champagne or tequila, even though both those drinks were the epitome of happiness.

"We hope you enjoyed your evening."

"We did, thank you." I met her smile with a wider one. "It's been wonderful."

A line of cabs was stationed outside the bar as we exited.

Payton hugged me then jumped into the first cab. "Speak to you tomorrow. Love you!"

"Love you."

I was back in the apartment fifteen minutes later, marveling that it would have taken me another thirty minutes to get home if I still lived out in Williamsburg. It was only after two attempts to get the key in the lock I realized I may have been more tipsy than I thought.

"Whoops!" I rebounded off the wall, avoiding Barclay who'd run out to greet me as I walked into the kitchen to grab a bottle of water, grinding to a halt when I spied Murray, Rafe, and Penn sitting at the kitchen table, each with a large pile of poker chips in front of them.

"Oh, hey there."

Rafe and Penn looked up, identical smirks appearing almost immediately. Murray, however, still had his back to me.

"No wonder you were worked up," Penn muttered quietly across the table before clearing his throat. "Kit, you look beautiful."

"Thank you."

I glanced over to Murray's now turning back, expecting a look which agreed with Penn's assessment. What I got instead was a glare of pure loathing, darkening with every second his eyes stayed on me, and the dancy, happy feeling I'd been floating on since we left the bar sunk like a lead weight.

"Are you drunk?"

"No." I frowned, peering past him to the table where an almost empty bottle of whiskey stood, along with almost empty glasses. I'd seen that bottle in the cellar earlier – it had been full. "Are you?"

He stood up, leaning against the table. But I didn't miss the way his eye twitched as he answered. "No."

"Well, that's good then isn't it?" I went to move past him, but it was no coincidence he was now blocking the way. "Excuse me. I'd like to get some water."

He moved his arms and shifted the smallest amount required to let me pass, holding my breath as I did so I wouldn't be assaulted with his heady, Murray scent. It put me, once again, under his watchful glare as I took a bottle of water from the fridge, needing to gulp it down to quench my sudden thirst. But it wasn't working, because the longer he stared, the hotter I was becoming.

"Were you out with Jackson Foggerty?"

Penn and Rafe pushed back from their chairs, noisily screeching them along the hardwood floor. "Okay, this is our cue to leave."

Murray didn't even blink as they walked out, his eyes laser focused on mine like we were in a staring contest I hadn't meant to enter. I was finding his contemptuous glower hard to hold, but the second I actually thought about his question anger started to bubble inside me because how fucking *dare* he?

"No."

His jaw gritted hard under his thick stubble. "Well, that's not what he said. I told you to stay away from him."

It took me a second to breathe through my rapidly ascending rage and stay calm. "First off, what I do in my spare time is none of your business, and second, unless it's related to Bell, you don't get to tell me what to do." I glared back before remembering Jackson Foggerty's bizarre comment, which seemed to make more sense under the circumstances. "Nor do you have any right to warn people away from me. What is your problem?"

The green eyes I'd been fantasizing about all evening

narrowed. "You! You're my problem. Ever since you moved in, you've been my problem!"

I stopped a gasp from escaping, but could not stop my chest splintering into tiny shards. His words were a hard slap to the face and ones I wasn't expecting, couldn't even have dreamed him saying. Even in my slightly liquored up state, the pain was real, and I swallowed down the tears which threatened to fall. I wasn't sure what I'd suddenly done to deserve this version of Murray, this vicious, angry man in front of me doing his best impression of a fire breathing dragon.

The alcohol I'd drunk added a level of bravado I wouldn't have normally had. "Okay, well, that's a simple problem to fix. I'll move out while you go away for Easter and you can start looking for a new nanny. Bell almost sleeps through night anyway, so I'm sure you'll be able to cope." I turned away at the same time he did. "Or perhaps your girlfriend can help." I murmured angrily under my breath, but not quietly enough.

A cupboard door slammed shut. "I TOLD YOU, I DON'T HAVE A GIRLFRIEND!"

His voice was loud enough to wake up Bell, even though she was one floor up and across the other side of the apartment.

My entire body whipped round so quickly I heard my spine crack. Under normal circumstances I'd have likely flinched by someone shouting so loudly at me, but the tequila had taken the edge off, not to mention I was equally as annoyed with him. The bottle of water I was still holding got slammed down so hard it erupted like a geyser.

"Well that's not what she said when she was standing at the front door looking at me like something she'd trodden in!"

Even with his nostrils flaring he looked sexy. Why did he

have to look so fucking sexy when he was being an unbelievable asshole? And why was I finding his fury such a turn on?

"Are you saying you don't believe me?"

"You didn't believe me when I told you I didn't go out with Jackson Fucking Foggerty. HOW IS THIS ANY FUCKING DIFFERENT?!"

His neck jerked back in surprise, his eyes gaping before a grin came out of nowhere, splitting his face in half, which only served to make me even angrier.

"What's so fucking funny?!"

His booming laugh was the cure-all for diffusing tension, but only in the air, because inside me, there was now a different tension building… One I was trying to ignore.

"I've never heard you swear before. I've never even seen you angry."

"I swear." I mustered up as much annoyance as I could, but my tone had lost all wrath.

"No," he shook his head slowly, his demeanor relaxing back into the Murray I was familiar with. "I've never heard you swear. Or shout."

"Yeah, well, you've never pissed me off this much before." My arms crossed over my chest of their own accord, and I glared again until his smirk turned devious in a way that set off a deep, traitorous throbbing between my legs, soaking my panties.

"Pissed you off, hey? Who are you and what have you done with my cookie baking nanny?"

He took a slow step toward me while the rest of his body remained deathly still, reminding me of an Apex predator waiting to pounce, and I was his prey. The throbbing intensified, along with my need to take a full breath. I was suddenly desperate to suck in all the oxygen I could, knowing I wouldn't get another chance any time soon.

"Kit, I don't have a girlfriend." He emphasized every word

to make sure I understood, and in a tone I'd never heard him use; gravelly, voracious and dangerously sexy.

"Okay." I rolled my eyes, trying to look away and diffuse the unbearable tension that was causing my heart to beat faster than a rocket during take-off. I tried to focus on anything but him getting infinitely closer to me.

"I. Don't have. A fucking. Girlfriend." His words were slow and punctuated with each step he took, bringing him closer to me. I found myself backing up, hitting the cool, flat surface of the refrigerator.

"Okay, I heard you the first time."

"I have Bell. I have you. And that's it." His bare feet stopped on the outsides of mine, boxing me in as he dipped down to nearer my height, which was closer than usual seeing as I still hadn't taken my shoes off.

"Me?"

"Yes, Kit. You." His finger pushed a stray hair away and tucked it behind my ear before grasping my chin gently between his fingers, forcing the direction of my attention back to him. "You."

"Murray..."

His other hand moved to the pulse pounding below my ear, tracing along the column of my neck with a featherlight touch, his long fingers wrapping around my nape and pushing into my hair. His thumb started stroking along my jaw line, and I forgot how to breathe. It was entirely possible I hadn't taken a breath for a while and was on the verge of passing out.

His eyes dropped to where my bottom lip was caught between my teeth, using his thumb to pull it free.

"For weeks I've been desperate to know how you'd feel, how you'd taste on my tongue. After Saturday..."

I finally managed to breathe but it caught in my throat.

His eyes shot up to mine, the emerald had turned dark

and stormy like a forbidden winter forest. "Tell me no. Tell me to stop if you don't want this."

I could barely hear him over the thrashing of my heart, of the blood whooshing in my head.

"Tell me, Kit."

But my ability to speak had vanished along with my ability to think, breathe, or do anything that didn't involve being utterly consumed by him.

"Tell me."

"I want this." If I'd thought Murray's voice had been unrecognizable moments ago, it had nothing on the croak I'd just let out.

My words were a starting pistol. His mouth crashed to mine, and I had no power to do anything but let it. With a single groan, he gained access to my mouth, the warmth of his tongue tingling as he stroked against me, tasting like expensive whiskey and the best decision of my life. Because with one swipe of his tongue, my worries, my self-warnings that making out with your boss was a bad idea, were silenced.

But I *had* been wrong about it being the best kiss I'd ever had. This was the best kiss *anyone* had ever had. The best kiss in existence. His lips were better than I'd imagined them to be, soft and firm all at the same time, consuming me, owning me with his mouth. Taking exactly what he wanted.

And I wanted to give it. I wanted to give him everything.

My moans echoed off the hard surfaces of the kitchen as his hands moved under the shortest dress in existence, grabbing my ass and lifting me until I was wrapped around a minimum of twenty-five square inches of solid, hard-earned muscle. Sandwiching me against the fridge, his hands threaded through my hair, tilting me for more access because the past three minutes hadn't given him enough. A profound rumble let up from his throat, adding kerosene to the fire already burning inside me, desperate for some friction against the flimsy scrap of material that were my soaked panties and what I knew was his rock hard cock.

His strokes slowed, becoming more gentle but no less intense until he pulled back, taking my lower lip with him as we broke apart.

"Kit…" he growled, his lips moving to my neck before inhaling deeply, "we need to stop. I need to stop now or I won't be able to stop."

He looked up, his eyes lust-drunk and hooded, his lips as swollen as I knew mine were.

"Murray?"

His forehead fell against mine on a heavy exhale, his breath warm against my already burning skin. "I need to stop. We need to stop. We've both been drinking and I don't want that on my conscience. When this happens, I want it to be with a clear head."

I loosened my grip around his waist and he put me down. I didn't dare look at what I was certain would be a very large wet patch against his shirt. I wasn't entirely sure where to look, because I didn't want him to see the disappointment stinging in my eyes, but he took care of that with a tilt of my chin.

"Kit, it is going to happen again." His lips brushed mine in a gesture that melted the vestiges of my insides that hadn't been eviscerated the first time round.

"Okay."

He moved me out of the way of the fridge, opening it and retrieved two bottles of water, handing me one. "I'm going to walk you to your room and say good night, before going to my room and getting into bed," he grinned, "and I'll pick you up in the morning for our road trip."

I did a poor job of holding back a massive smile. "Okay."

He threaded our fingers together, leading me out of the kitchen and up the stairs, slowly, because I still hadn't taken off my shoes, and stopped outside my bedroom door.

"Sweet dreams, Columbia." His lips lingered on my cheek as he reached behind me to turn the doorknob. "Don't forget, I'll sort Bell in the morning. Enjoy your lie-in."

"Are you kidding? I'm never going to forget a lie-in. Thank you," I stepped back into my room and watched him walk away with a smile. "Good night, Murray."

I jumped into the shower, not able to hold back the grin. It was still there when I dried off and brushed my teeth. It was still there when I threw on panties and a shirt, as I got into bed.

And it was there an hour later when Bell woke for her one a.m. bottle.

As I held her, Barclay pushed open the door, which he was given to do. Except… when I got up to close it behind him, I could make out a darkened figure running down the stairs, followed by the distinct sound of the front door opening and closing.

The sound of Murray leaving in the middle of the night.

When I got back into bed, my grin didn't follow, but the sinking feeling I'd carried all day did.

13

MURRAY

According to the clock on the bedside table, I'd slept a total of three hours, give or take. Yet as someone who cherished sleep over almost every single thing in his life, and should not only be exhausted, but grumpy too, I'd never felt more awake.

Or so overcome with excitement, or happiness, or anticipation.

My body had been buzzing like a livewire all night, my source of energy coming straight from the resident of the room at the other end of the hallway, and the white hot kiss we'd shared.

Even if it was the stupidest, most impulsive reaction to weeks and weeks of not being able to have what I wanted.

After she'd left and Jackson fucking Foggerty had called to tell me how smoking hot she looked, my entire evening had been consumed with thoughts of them together, my brain immediately frying with jealous rage that she was with him, that he'd been able to lay eyes on her looking like *that.*

My mouth had dried up the second I'd clocked her walking into the hallway ready to leave, looking like a goddess, a siren beguiling me in a way no one ever had. Ever.

Walking like Bambi on impossibly high heels; her lithe, creamy legs made even longer by the tiniest dress known to man, one that would tempt the Devil himself. She'd looked nothing like the Kit I saw every day, the Kit I'd been coming home to every evening, the Kit I'd walked in the park with, made dinner for, the Kit who dressed exclusively in yoga pants.

Then Jackson fucking Foggerty had taken a match to the fuse that was my patience, with one sly little dig about keeping her on a leash.

But I shouldn't have done it.

I shouldn't have kissed her.

Because once I had, I couldn't think of anything else. Anything more perfect than the taste of her on my tongue, her moans echoing round my mouth as I breathed them in until they rooted themselves deep in my core. All that… from a kiss. A kiss I'd never in my life experienced.

But I shouldn't have done it.

After I'd walked her to her bedroom door, the reality had hit, and so had the text messages coming in thick and fast from Rafe, repeating everything he'd been attempting to drum into me all evening. If all I could think about was our kiss, all I could hear was his voice until it became louder and louder, drowning out all memory of her lips until my only thoughts were about what would happen when she woke up.

That I hadn't been sober, but was still in full grasp of my actions.

That she had bounced off the kitchen wall and would be sporting a pretty big hangover.

His voice advising me to slow down, asking me to decide first about how we'd navigate the next part; the employer/employee relationship part. He'd been right. I shouldn't have kissed her, but my self-control eviscerated the second I saw the fury burning in her eyes, aimed directly for me. I'd been a goner.

And now I needed to figure out my next move. I needed to think.

All through school, and college, and my entire career up to the point Bell had arrived, I'd swam. I'd push myself to the point of exhaustion, where my lungs were on the verge of collapse and my head was clear of whatever needed untangling and thoughts made sense.

So that's what I did. I'd forgotten the power a midnight swim could have. By the time I was done, my decision had been made.

I shouldn't have kissed her, but now that I had, I was planning on doing it again, then again and again. Until I died, kissing her.

It was six thirty-four a.m., I was wide awake and couldn't fucking wait to see her, except she was having a well-deserved lie-in, so I was going to have to dig deep and find my patience once more. Not to mention my daughter would be up very soon and want her breakfast.

It took me less than seven minutes to brush my teeth, grab some sweats, put the coffee on and have a steaming mug in my hand while I warmed a bottle for Bell. It took me another hour to feed her, dress her, strap her into her Baby Bjorn, then walk down to the corner bakery and buy a selection of plain and chocolate croissants, along with muffins for breakfast, as well a couple of loaves of the best sourdough in New York to take away for the weekend.

I'd put Bell down for her morning nap and completed half of the crossword, filling the boxes to answer *'Diamond'* for *'Hardest Substance on Earth'*, when she walked into the kitchen, dressed in her uniform of yoga pants and tank, her face devoid of make-up, returning to the fresh, clean glow I was accustomed to. Her apple cheeks pinked as she spotted me, followed with an awkwardness I wanted to put an immediate halt to.

"Hey." She bit down on her cheek and my dick thumped

with plans to kiss away her shyness and bring back the loud, self-assured woman I usually met first thing in the morning. I gave her the biggest smile I could muster without coming across as a weirdo and jumped up from my chair.

"Hey, let me make you coffee. Come sit down. I got us fresh croissants from the bakery across the street." The smile turned into a face splitting grin, "I can warm them up…"

The awkwardness dropped slightly as her face brightened with a smile which raised an even bigger thump in my heart. "You've been out already? I'm impressed."

"I can't compete with your baking skills, but the bakery gives it a fair go," I teased, earning myself a twinkle of amusement in her eye. "How did you sleep?"

She looked away and busied herself rummaging through the bakery bags on the table, selecting a banana muffin. "Okay… how about you?"

"Not too bad."

I placed her coffee in front of her and she picked it up in silence. That she wasn't meeting my eye when she spoke wasn't sitting well in my stomach. It only took the longest thirty seconds of my life, watching her mindlessly fiddle with the corners of the newspaper, to kick-start my resolve to face this head on.

"Kit. Look at me."

She gave a heavy blink as she glanced my way.

"About last night..."

"Don't worry, I got it," she interrupted, bitterness biting at her tone.

My head tilted. "Got what?"

"That we were drunk and you want to take it back."

I balked at the hardness of her expression, while my stomach dropped another degree as Rafe's warnings started up in my ear again.

"I want to take back nothing," I pushed on, willing her to make eye contact. "Is that what you want?"

The cheek chewing started up again.

"Kit? Is that what you want?"

She took a deep breath and began tracing her fingers around the edges of her mug. "Where did you go last night?"

"What do you mean?"

Now she looked up at me, but her usual warmth was missing. "Murray, I saw you leave in the middle of the night. I heard the door."

"Did I wake you?"

She shook her head. "No, I was feeding Bell. Murray, where did you go?"

"I went swimming."

Her narrowed eyes, jutted chin, and pursed lips did a good job of telling me she thought I was full of shit. To be fair, she had a point, but I still didn't like the fact she didn't believe me.

"I couldn't sleep and needed to clear my head. I used to do it all the time, but haven't done it in a while."

"Where did you go swimming?"

"My club is open twenty-four hours." I frowned. "Kit, where did you think I'd gone?"

"Not swimming."

"I understand that, but where did you think I'd gone after I kissed you goodnight?"

"Who was that woman who turned up at the door yesterday and said she was your girlfriend?"

I sighed deeply. I'd talked about it with the guys and we only came to one conclusion. Dasha.

I'd been expecting Kit to ask more about her, and I'd planned to tell her everything, it just hadn't been part of my plan this morning. However, we weren't going to get anywhere if she continued answering a question with a question, and I wanted to rid of her any insecurity she was holding on to.

"Was she tall, dark hair?"

Her mouth fixed into a hard line. "Yep. So, you know her?"

"I do. Her name is Dasha. We briefly… we slept together for a few weeks last year… it wasn't anything more than that. I'm sorry she came over, it won't happen again. And she's not someone you ever need to worry about."

Along with speaking to Graham about never letting her into the building, Rafe was sending her a warning letter to stay the fuck away, but in better worded, legal terminology.

"I'm not worried." The slight shift in her seat, along with a flick of her hair told me otherwise, and it only served to make my insides flicker with hope that I hadn't fucked things up.

"Kit?"

"What?" she huffed, making me chuckle. This truculent Kit was one I was enjoying more than I ought to.

"I'm sorry about Dasha, I really am, but you haven't answered my question."

"What question?"

"Is that what you want? You want to take it back? Take back our kiss? Our perfect kiss?"

The sucking in of her cheek recommenced and I let out a groan.

"Please stop doing that, it drives me crazy."

She stopped immediately, her cheek still indented, her mouth dropping slowly back with a smirk and a shake of her head.

Fucking. Yes.

"Good, because I want to kiss you again."

Her eyes flared slightly. "You do?"

"Yes, I do. So fucking badly."

"Okay."

With the way she gasped, I don't think she realized I'd meant right that second. Her eyes widened as I reached between us, grabbing the seat of her chair to pull her toward me until there was less than a couple of inches between us. Every time I looked at her, her eyes seemed to change color, and right now, they were as dark and warm as the melted chocolate in the croissants, and her gaze dropped to my lips. I could see her fighting against the instinct to bite her lip, so I decided to help her out.

My fingers pushed through her hair until my palms framed her face, my thumb running along her plump lower lip as our eyes trained on each other. If I'd thought it once, I'd thought it a thousand times; I'd never seen anyone more beautiful. I was so fucking lucky to have the chance to kiss this woman again, and I was absolutely about to make the most of it.

I stole her last breath, inhaling her as my mouth covered hers, owning it, tasting her on the tip of my tongue as it ran slowly along the seam of her lips until she opened up for me. Teasing her softly, I kept the pace languid so I could explore her properly, lazy, like a Sunday morning, even though it was Thursday.

I discovered that when I pulled her hair back so I could roam deeper, her moans shot straight to my dick. And when I moved my kisses along her jaw line, her pulse ratcheted to the point where she grabbed my face demanding my lips back on hers.

Soon, it wasn't enough.

Leaning forward I scooped her up, moving her so she straddled my thighs, our connection never wavering. My hands moved under her tank, stroking up against her impossibly soft skin, my thumb moving of its own accord, caressing the stretch of silken warmth under her boobs, itching to move higher to the pebbled nipples I could feel rubbing against my chest.

Her weight shifted as she rocked against me, and I could have legitimately changed the answer in the crossword to *My Dick*.

I needed to slow this down before one of two things happened; I blew in my pants or I ended up fucking her on the table. Neither of which she deserved. I took hold of her face again; easing back so I could look at her lust-drunk expression, which was a million times more pronounced than the one I'd witnessed last night. She released my bottom lip with a wet pop that almost had me changing my mind.

I smoothed down the back of her tank top, not ready to let go of her entirely. "That... was even better than last night."

I meant it; last night had been beyond my imagination. In the time we'd lived together, I'd seen nothing but a kind, sweet, caring, baking, sexy as fuck woman. I'd never expected her to be so fiery and passionate and obstinate too. But our second kiss, feeling the warmth of her skin under my palms as she rocked in my lap while her tongue stroked hungrily against mine, was on the verge of mind-blowing.

"It was." She looked down at me, wanting to say something but it seemed stuck in her throat.

"Tell me."

"You really meant it? You don't want to take this back?"

Not a chance. After that kiss, wild horses couldn't drag me away.

"I really fucking meant it." I tugged gently on the bottom of her hair I'd curled around my fingers.

Her smile was as bright as the sunshine streaming through the windows. "Then what are we going to do this weekend?"

I frowned. "About what?"

"This." She gestured between us. "With your family..." She paused again. "Would you mind if... can we not say anything?"

I gasped with faux shock. "You mean keep us a secret from my interfering and meddling family?"

She gave me a sheepish grin. "Yeah. Is that okay?"

"That's more than fine." I cupped her cheek, "I know we

have some stuff to figure out, which I want to do before anyone starts weighing in with their own opinions. And you've met my sisters and my mother."

She burst out laughing before turning serious again. "Murray, why did you go for a swim? What did you mean when you said you needed to clear your head? And last night, what did you mean when you said I was your problem?"

My shoulders dropped in a sigh. I'd regretted it the second I'd blurted it out, wishing I could take it back, but I'd been so fucking angry. At her, at Jackson, at the entire situation, when all I wanted to do was take her in my arms and kiss her until she couldn't stand.

Which I then fucking did.

"I'm sorry I said that." I began twirling the ends of her thick, silky hair around my fingers, just like I'd always wanted to do. "I didn't mean it."

"But why did you say it?" she pressed.

"Kit…" She stared at me while I took a second or five to think how to word this without sounding like a dick, but there was no way around it. I'd promised myself I was never going to lie to her, although I briefly wondered what shade of grey stretching the truth would fall into. I looked at her, waiting patiently for my answer.

"Okay." My hands started stroking her back again, soothing me. "I work hard, and up until a few months ago, I played hard. You know that Bell is the result of one of those plays. I have an amazing life and I enjoy it. I have more money than I know what to do with, and if I've ever wanted something, I take it or find a way to take it. Life is too short otherwise."

She didn't say anything, although her expression was one of understandable confusion because she had no idea where I was going with this.

"But things changed when Bell came along, and she became the single most important factor in my amazing life, along with any decision I made. Then you came along, too. And since the second time I laid eyes on you I've wanted you, but for the first time ever, I couldn't do anything about it. You don't belong to me, you belong to Bell. It was all new to me. I've never done this before. I've never been patient or had to be patient. Since you moved in, you've consumed me, and I've found it incredibly hard to handle."

Her brows drew together. "The second time?"

I curbed my smile. "The day you moved in, I was too tired to see straight."

She looked at me for a beat before bursting out laughing.

"But," I continued, "if it makes you feel better, every single person in my family predicted this."

Her jaw dropped in horror. "Oh my God, they all think something's happening? Please say no."

"No." Which was technically true.

Her hands shot up to cover her face, not believing me. "Jesus. I'm such a cliché."

I peeled them away so she could see the sincerity in my eyes. "No, you aren't. But if you are, then I am too, and there's no-one I'd rather be a cliché with."

The magic broke when she quickly jumped off my lap as though it would make us less of a cliché if we weren't touching. I immediately missed the curve of her taut ass resting on my thighs, even if it did give my dick minimal reprieve.

"Kit," I took hold of her hand, "it'll be fine. No one knows, but I cannot emphasize enough how happy they'd be if they did."

"Why?"

"Because my sisters like a project and they've decided trying to marry me off is their next mission."

"Marriage..?!" Her eyes bugged wide.

Fuck. She looked more freaked out than I'd been when I'd found Bell. Although considering every other woman I'd been with had tried in some capacity to trap me into committing, that I was now in front of someone who seemed actively horrified by the idea, was novel. What was more novel was that the idea of marriage to her wasn't freaking *me* out.

"No, no, it's just an expression. It's my sisters, and you and I would both do our best to ignore them." I ran my fingers over her creased brow, smoothing it out and hopefully removing her panic. "It's not ideal we have to leave for a weekend away when all I want is to keep you to myself, but we'll figure it out. I know it might seem complicated, but it won't be. I promise."

She took a breath, reading the earnestness in my voice, and gave me a soft smile which pulled tight in my chest.

"Okay." She glanced over at the kitchen clock. "I should probably go and wake Bell. What time do we need to get there?"

"We'll be there in time for lunch. Are you all packed?"

She nodded. "Yes, and Bell's is done as well. We just need the bouncer and a couple more bottles."

"Perfect. If you can sort Bell and get her dressed, I'll sort out Barclay, get the bags to the door, and call Graham to collect everything and stick it all in the car. Then we're off." I brushed my knuckles across her cheek. "Reckon we can do it in under thirty minutes?"

She grinned. "I'd say so."

She went to move away from my grasp, but instead, I used the opportunity to pull her in, taking her mouth once more for a quick sweep of her tongue against mine, the novelty that I could zipping through my veins.

"Might not be under thirty now." She moved away with a wink, leaving me sitting there, and five minutes later, I was still wondering how the fuck I'd managed to get her, and what legitimate excuse I could come up with to skip lunch if it meant I'd get a few more uninterrupted hours of her lips.

14

MURRAY

We pulled off Route-27 at the 'Welcome to Bridgehampton' sign, taking a left at the long line of maple trees which signaled the entrance to the town. The house we were staying in belonged to a friend of Freddie and Cooper's, Freddie having spent almost a year renovating it for them.

An uncomfortable churning started up out of nowhere, deep in the pit of my stomach, and it suddenly dawned on me that the house was right up the beach from Rafe's family home, where I'd been the night Bell was conceived. Over the last two months, I'd tried so hard to remember what had happened, remember that woman who'd left *my* daughter on *my* doorstep, but I couldn't. Even Rory hadn't been able to shed any light on her, and he'd brought her along. I'd also tried so hard to let go of the anger I felt toward her too, and I vowed to ensure Bell never went a second without knowing how much she was loved by me and my family, even if the woman who gave birth to her couldn't have given a shit.

As if she could sense my imminent spiral, Bell let out a loud gurgle. I glanced in the rear view mirror to see her blowing bubbles, the sight immediately pushing out any worries, reminding me I now had something infinitely more precious than anything else in my world. And that's all that mattered.

"So, how's this weekend going to go?"

I took my eyes off the road momentarily, turning to Kit with a raised eyebrow. "Come on, you've met my family. You must know."

"Yes, but there'll be more of them now! Tell me about the ones I haven't met yet."

I lifted her hand and kissed it. I'd spent the entirety of the journey with my hand firmly on her thigh like it was something I'd always done, and this wasn't our first time in a car together, and we weren't twelve hours into a new stage of our relationship.

"Jamie and Alex?"

"Yes, what's your brother like?"

"Not as good looking as me for one, so don't get any ideas."

She laughed. "Nothing wrong with a girl keeping her options open, and I'm not about to make your ego any bigger than it needs to be. I see you turning every single head, women and men looking at you."

"No one's ever looked at me the way you did last night, or again this morning, so I'd say we're safe." I bit the tips of her fingers making her squeal, stopping the air from getting too heavy with anything else I shouldn't be admitting quite yet. "And if you think I'm going to give you up after that, you've got another thing coming."

"Really?"

"Yes, really. I told you I want you and I always get what I want, even if this did take me a little longer than usual." I glanced at her again. "And don't try to deny you don't want me."

She chuckled softly. "I'm not; I'm just getting in the practice now before we arrive."

I stroked her flushed cheek. “We’ll figure it out.”

I turned left down the road which led to the house, passing by a couple of huge gates before pulling up to the biggest gates on the road and tapped in the code on the keypad, waiting until they swung open.

“Wow, this place is incredible,” Kit exclaimed as we drove along the immense driveway lined with more maple trees, expansive lawns on either side beyond them. Then the drive opened up right before we reached the house, the Atlantic Ocean looking remarkably calm in the distance, a stretch beyond the beach. “Holy fuck! Look.”

“You know, for an English major, I’d have expected something a little more poetic than ‘holy fuck’.” I winked.

Her face was filled with challenge as she turned to me. “As an English major I can tell you that ‘fuck’ is the most versatile word in the English language: adjective, noun, verb, pronoun, modifier, adverb… I could go on.”

The front door opened as I pulled to a stop, my mum and Wolf running out. I leaned into Kit, whispering to her before they reached us. “I look forward to using it as a noun and a verb.”

My prize was a blush of the deepest red, which made me throw my head back in laughter. “Come on. Let’s find the rabble.”

No one came around to my side of the car to greet me; instead, my mom couldn’t get to Bell quick enough, while Wolfie grabbed Kit in a massive bear-like hug, which made me smile more than it should have. I opened the trunk for Barclay to jump out.

“Come on, Barc. We’ll stick with the guys this weekend.”

He *woofed* in agreement.

“Wey hey, there he is! Dad of the year.”

I put down the bags I’d picked up, just as my brother, Jamie, scooped me into a hug almost as big as the one Kit had received, slapping me hard on the back.

"I am goddamn Dad of the year. I honestly don't know what you lot have been whining about all these years, sleepless nights, schleepness nights."

"Ah, my baby brother, the comedian." He bent over double with loud, forced laughter before righting himself and giving me a thorough assessment. "You look good though."

I rolled my eyes. "It's only been three months since I was last home."

"Yeah, but look at how much has changed." He turned around, spotting no one because they'd all gone inside. "Speaking of, where's my niece? Lemme hold her."

"You snooze, you lose buddy. I think mum already took her."

"Jesus, I'm not going to get to hold her all weekend, am I?"

"Yeah, good luck with that." I heaved another bag out of the trunk. "Jay, make yourself useful and help me carry all this in, will you?"

"You might be Dad of the year, but I'm Brother of the year," he said, picking up one of the many bags full of Bell's things. Babies didn't travel light, that was for sure.

"Yeah, yeah, make sure you pick up the heavy ones then I might consider voting for you."

He gave me a massive grin then loaded up with as much as he could carry, and seeing as it only took another two trips instead of what would likely have been five, I was seriously contemplating on creating the award just so I could vote.

I couldn't even see Kit, or Bell for that matter, for the sea of women in my family fussing around both of them. Or at least that's what I assumed was happening when I walked into the backyard after dumping all the bags in the hallway, and where I found eight adults, seven kids, and a dog, which made up the rest of my family. Sam was being followed by a soaking wet Barclay, who'd clearly made the very large swimming pool his first port of call. It was also where Florence was currently ordering my dad to throw her higher, taking it in turns with Noah, Maggie, and Mia – Jamie and Alex's three kids. I couldn't see Macauley, but I assumed he was part of the loud gaggle over by the veranda.

I picked up a beer from the ice trough and headed in the direction of the barbecue, where Jasper and Cooper were manning a dozen T-bone steaks.

"Hey, man. How're you doing?" Cooper slapped me on the back, following my line of sight to the veranda, misinterpreting it. "Yeah, you need to come to terms with the fact you won't get to hold your baby at all this weekend."

"You think?"

"I know, especially in this family."

Jamie joined us at the grills and then almost in sync, the three of them turned to face me until it became clear they were waiting for me to answer a question they hadn't yet asked.

I took a long swig of my beer. "What?"

Jasper crossed his arms, followed by Jamie, then Cooper, as though I was about to get embroiled in some kind of shake down. And I wanted to spill the beans; I just didn't know what beans they were after.

"Explain your call."

Then it became clear exactly why they were behaving like fucking mafia thug wannabes, except dressed in their Loro Piana cashmere hoodies and Orlebar Brown shorts, they weren't credibly threatening.

"Jas, you fucker, you promised you wouldn't say anything."

He shook his head slowly, a sly grin framing the corner of his mouth. "No, I didn't. I said I wouldn't say anything to the girls. I also said that we'd be having a boys' night out at which you will tell us what's going on, and that we were all correct."

I took another swig of my beer, looking past them and over to the girls where a small gap in the group allowed me to watch Kit, laughing with my family, fitting in like she'd always been with us, and holding her own against the rising volume. As she turned to my mum she looked over, her eyes locking with mine, our secret passing between us until she sucked in her cheek, followed by a grin so wide it could have been seen from any of the boats far out on the water.

"Oh, man, we are so fucking correct. You are in deep shit," Cooper chuckled as he twisted the cap off a fresh beer.

"Fuck off." Even if I'd wanted to, I couldn't hold back my grin. "Where're we going tonight then?"

"Tiger," Jasper replied, naming a notorious and extremely popular club along the beach. Even though a lot of places didn't open until Memorial Day Weekend, Tiger was renowned for its all year round parties.

"Are the girls going out?" I didn't need to ask whether Kit was going with them too, because I knew she would be whether she wanted to or not. I had no doubt the evening would be some form of interrogation for her, especially as she hadn't met Jamie's wife, Alex, yet. And even though none of them knew what had happened, that didn't mean they wouldn't be quizzing her on every element of us living together.

"Yes, but not sure where and not with us. They're going for dinner somewhere I think."

"Who's looking after the kids?" I frowned.

The thing about Tiger was you never came away without a monumental hangover the next day, which was all very well, but hangovers and babies do not mix.

"Your parents, plus Greta and Sylvia are staying." Coop took in my skepticism. "Don't worry, it'll be fine tomorrow."

"Just making sure."

"How long until lunch?" yelled a voice from across the garden, which sounded like Freddie.

Jasper examined the steaks. "Ten minutes."

Everyone on the veranda jumped into action. The kids were hauled out of the pool and dried before being settled in their various seats at the long table which stretched along the back of the house, already heaving with copious amounts of food. Freddie waddled over, bump protruding, and handed over a large platter to Cooper, then turned to hug me.

"Was wondering when you'd bother to come and say hi." I hugged her back without squashing her.

"Hey, I had priorities. Your daughter and Kit are much more interesting."

She had a point.

She studied me in the way big sisters do - or the way she always did, thoroughly inspecting with eyes narrowed, looking for some kind of change she could pick up on. "Fallen in love with her yet?"

That was not the change I'd wanted her to pick up on. Not that there was any change at all, and certainly not that, but tact was not Freddie's middle name and I tried to hide my sharp inhale with a cough, while Jamie, Cooper, and Jas smirked into the grill.

"Just as I thought." She answered her own question with a raised eyebrow.

"There's nothing to think. And for the love of God, don't fucking ask her either."

At least I'd done some sort of job in pre-warning Kit about the head space my sisters were in, but given she'd freaked out at the mere mention of them knowing, it was something I wanted to protect her from. I glared as hard as I could, trying to convey my annoyance, but Fred had always done what she wanted so it would be relatively ineffectual, and I'd put nothing past Freddie on a mission. Or Wolf for that matter, and after my thirty-two years, I was still undecided who was worse.

"Can't promise anything," she replied, making me groan with more than a little semblance of despair.

In all honesty, however, I didn't really give a fuck who knew. Not the falling in love part, obviously, because that was... well, not the case... yet... and I would prefer to have the time for us to acknowledge it before they did. But they'd find out about us sooner or later, and after this morning, I was more determined than I'd ever been. I wanted her, all of her. Falling in love was an inevitable part of that, and for the first time in my life, I was ready.

I wanted her to be mine.

And I was going to Bring. It. The fuck. On.

We all took a seat at the table and I looked around to find Bell in Alex's arms, guzzling down her lunchtime bottle. Kit was deep in conversation with Freddie, and even though I tried to catch her eye, she was too engrossed in whatever they were talking about. It was probably pointless praying it wasn't me.

Someone dropped a steak on my plate, and from then on, my attention was taken by food, something I had in common with Bell.

"Fuck, these are good steaks. Nice job, bud." I raised my beer to Jasper sitting across from me.

"Agreed." Jamie scooped a massive portion of sweet potato onto his plate. "And it's good to be over here. I plan on eating myself into a food coma this afternoon, then starting all over again tonight."

"Think we could all do with a nap."

Napping wasn't what I had in mind, not by a long shot. However, as much our relationship had changed in the last twenty four hours, Kit was still working for me, and until I managed to have the incredibly awkward and uncomfortable conversation about her contract which Rafe had been pushing, I wanted Kit to take the lead, to decide what was right for her. I didn't want her to feel pressured by me in any way, because if it was my choice, we'd spend the rest of the weekend in bed where I'd explore every single millimeter of her heavenly body, discovering exactly what pushed her to the brink of explosion, and do it over and over again until we needed resuscitating.

I pushed away the visual of her riding me, sweaty and naked, before lunch became very uncomfortable. I glanced over to Cooper to find a shit eating grin on his face.

"What's so funny?"

"Nothing, just that I've been looking forward to this moment for a long, long time."

"What moment? What's happened?"

His fork twirled in the general direction of my face. "That look you have. That's what I've been waiting for, what we've all been waiting for. Never thought I'd see the day when Murray Williams willingly hung up his rubbers."

"Whatever." It was the only response I could come up with. It was irrelevant I hadn't had sex in months, or that I was a willing participant in my abstinence because that's not what he was talking about. "Not like you didn't cry like a baby when you met Freddie."

"Not denying I did. I just never thought I'd see it from you."

I shrugged, not caring. And I didn't, I really didn't. It wasn't just sex I hadn't had in months; I hadn't even looked at another woman in months, which had nothing to do with Bell.

Jamie peered down the table to where the girls were either side of the kids and my parents, except Samson who was now sitting on Cooper's knee.

"Come on then, tell us what's happened."

"Nothing's happened."

"Bullshit."

I was stuck between the rock that was the three of them not giving up until I spilled the beans, made rockier by the fact that I'd called Jas for advice, and the hard place that was my word to Kit we wouldn't make it widely known. Although we hadn't actually discussed our own behavior this weekend, I very much hoped that I'd still be allowed to sneak in a few kissing sessions. A boob squeeze too, if I was lucky.

I made eye contact with each one of them individually. "How much of what I tell you goes straight back to the girls?"

To give them credit, they were all solemn and genuine in the crosses over their hearts. "None of it."

"Fine. We kissed last night. And then this morning."

"Yeah you did," Jasper smirked through the sip of his beer. "Then what happened?"

"Nothing, we drove up here."

"What's going to happen this weekend?"

I shrugged. "What d'you mean?"

"Is it a separate bedrooms situation and we'll find you sneaking in the hallway in the middle of the night? Or actual separate bedrooms? Because if it's the former, give me advanced warning - I don't want to run into you in the night with your dick hanging out."

Cooper snorted so hard he inhaled whatever he was eating, and Jamie had to give him a firm thwack on the back to help him stop coughing.

"Are you okay, Papa?" Samson looked at him with wide eyes.

"I'm good," he croaked, his eyes watering. "Uncle Jasper just told a funny joke."

"Oh," he replied, then looked at us all and started laughing himself. "Funny."

"Jesus," I hissed, glancing down to the other end of the table, hoping they hadn't noticed the commotion. "It's actual separate bedrooms. We're taking things slow, not to mention she works for me, and Rafe keeps banging on about her contract. He wants me to have her sign a new one before anything happens."

"Just fire her," Jamie suggested with a grin, which I ignored.

"What made you decide to go for it?"

I groaned. "She bumped into Jackson Foggerty in the elevator and he called me to say she looked smoking hot, and he'd suggested a threesome to her and the friend she was with, and they were up for it. I saw red, or rather green."

Jamie's beer slammed so hard on the table it frothed. "That guy is such a dick. You should definitely fire *him*. We don't need him or his money."

"I know. I'm getting the paperwork started this week. But last night he pushed my fucking buttons because I'd already warned him off, then she came home and I lost my shit."

"What did you do?"

That first taste of her was still on the tip of my tongue. I groaned before cracking a wide grin. "Shouted at her, then pinned her against the fridge and kissed her until I forgot my own name."

Jamie didn't even bother to contain his laughter. "Sounds like you need to send Foggerty a case of whiskey for lighting a fire up your ass."

"I'm sending him nothing except termination papers. I've made him enough money."

The volume levels had dwindled considerably. I leaned back in my chair surveying the mess, and the survivors. Kit and Bell were missing, along with Wolf and Mac. Samson was on the brink of falling asleep on Cooper, his eyelids heavy. I could hear someone else crying in the distance, and the older kids were back in the pool.

Lunch was over.

I stood up, picking up some of the empty dishes. "I'm going to clear up and find my daughter."

I took as much as I could carry and deposited it in the kitchen, thanking the permanent housekeeping staff as they took over, and then went in search of my room. Up two flights of stairs, I found it with a little label on the door handle with my name on it, our cases lined up neatly by the wall. I picked up Kit's and Bell's, heading along the rest of the corridor until I found a tag with her name. I knocked but she wasn't there, only to discover her a little further down with Alex, Wolfie, and Fred, in what I assumed was a nursery, given the walls were painted in farmyard animals.

They looked up as I entered and all immediately stopped talking, in the way that people did when the subject of said conversation is standing in front of you. Given that Freddie made it clear she'd be saying something, I didn't think I was being paranoid.

"Hi ladies, all okay in here?" I tried to meet Kit's eye just to double check she was really alright and not being forced into a confession at the hands of my sisters.

"Yes, thank you, Murray. We're good," replied Wolf, who was feeding Macauley.

"Okay, do you need anything?" I tried again, holding up Bell's bags, "I'll leave her stuff here."

I received a small, unreadable smile, and a mouthed thank you from Kit.

"Murray, could you check Coop is good with Sammy?" asked Freddie innocently, but I knew better. If that wasn't a clear cut sign I wasn't welcome in this room, I don't know what was. Maybe sneaking around this weekend wouldn't be hard as I thought, given it seemed highly unlikely I was going to get any time with Kit at all.

"Sure."

I huffed off down the corridor in search of boys and beers, the peals of laughter coming from the room immediately as I exited only upped my paranoia. Kit would just have to hold her own, something I didn't have any doubt she was capable of.

15

MURRAY

An ice bucket, four heavy glasses, and a bottle of Gran Patron was placed in the middle of our table, overlooking the crowded dance floor of Tiger in a private area of the club.

"Let me know if you need anything else, gentlemen."

"Thank you." I smiled at the waitress before she walked off.

Cooper pulled the stopper from the bottle with a loud squeak and poured it out, each of us taking one. We'd arrived here not long ago, following dinner at a local fish bar which sold the best lobster rolls on the north-east coast. The girls had also gone for dinner, and the rest of the day followed much the same route as after lunch had done, where they'd all but deserted us for their gossiping and girl chat.

Not that I minded them having their time together.

What I did mind however, was the fact I'd barely laid eyes on Kit since we'd arrived at the house, let alone had the chance to kiss her again, or even talk to her. I'd been tempted to bang down her door for a quick brush of her lips, but she hadn't been in there when I'd tried. Instead, I went for a nap, the midnight swim and three hours sleep finally catching up with me.

"Does anyone know where the girls went this evening?" Jamie peered around at us all.

Jasper put his glass down. "Somewhere in town, but I'm not sure what Wolf said it was called. I don't think they're having a late night though."

"What makes you think that?" I laughed.

He rolled his lips. "Wolf said she didn't think it would be late."

Jamie scoffed. "I saw Alex just before we left, and she wasn't dressed like they were planning an early or demure evening."

"You, my friend, have been played." I raised my glass to Jasper.

"Nah, your sister can do whatever she wants. But I might lay off too much of this stuff," he tipped his glass. "A hungover Wolf is not something anyone needs. I learned that lesson a long time ago."

All of us started laughing, hard. It was widely known that neither of my sisters was great with a hangover. I mean, who was? But those two really set the bar low for levels of tolerance.

"At least Fred won't be hungover."

Cooper grinned into his glass. "Nope, she'll just be tired."

"Who'll be tired?"

We all spun at the same time to see Wolf, Freddie, Alex, and fuck me… if I'd seen Kit before I'd left, I wouldn't be sitting here right now. I wouldn't have come out at all. I'd have locked her in her room, or my room, or any room, because she wasn't just breathtaking, she was absolutely blinding. And I thanked all the stars, lucky or not, that she'd had the foresight to pack it.

I'd assumed the dress she'd had on yesterday was the epitome of sexiness, but this outfit blew it out of the water.

The tightest leather pants hugged her lean legs, sitting snug over her hips in a way that only accentuated her perfect hourglass figure. A cropped black strapless top stretched across her torso, making her boobs look so fucking cuppable that I gripped my glass harder just to stop myself from reaching out. As it was, my dick was wildly uncomfortable, doing a good job of reminding us both that it was a fucking inconvenience we were trying to keep things a secret. Pouring my gaze over every inch of her, my memory jogged to something Rafe had said a while ago about teachers not being innocent, and I had to agree with him, because right this second, she looked like she wanted to be dirtied all night long, making me think this whole ensemble was for my benefit entirely.

I knew I was right when I saw a dark, sly curl on her lips, just as I met her own stare. Her long, thick black lashes and kohl rimmed eyes only framed the heat flaring in them as she held mine. I would be looking at nothing else all night long, my attention focused solely on her, but given we were now a party of eight, I was in for a painful time until I could get her alone.

We all shifted around, making room for the girls to plonk themselves down next to us, Kit next to me. My arm found its way along the back of the couch, and just as subconsciously as my fingers slipped through the ends of her silky waves and twisted them round, she leaned into it.

"You, Francesca," Cooper patted his lap and Freddie slipped onto it.

"I'm not tired."

"You will be in the morning, baby." His arms snaked around her as she leaned back onto him.

I snagged the server as she strode past. "Could we get four more glasses, a couple of bottles of sparkling water and a non-alcoholic cocktail please?"

She nodded. "Yes, sir. I'll bring them shortly."

Wolfie picked up Jasper's glass, knocked back the contents without a single wince at the strength, and then refilled it along with everyone else's. Jasper chuckled quietly from beside her, catching my eye.

"Come on girls, drink up before she comes back and let's get a dance in," she ordered the group, and they all followed both her instruction then her, and we lost them to the crowd on the dance floor.

"Dude, they're fine."

"Huh?" I shifted around to where the voice had come from, until I recognized it as Jasper's.

"You've been staring at the dance floor." He pointed to the girls, where I'd not been able to find them. "They're right there. I can see them, and they're fine."

I frowned, and he dropped his head with a shake, but I didn't care because yes, I was trying to find Kit.

"You need to chill out." Cooper casually leaned back into his seat opposite me. He was looking straight at me but not for a second did I think he also wasn't aware of exactly where Freddie was, his killer instinct from years of playing in the NHL kicking in. "You're supposed to be sneaking around, but the drool hanging down like shoelaces says otherwise, and everyone can see it."

I wiped my mouth even though I knew there was nothing there.

"Muz, seriously, what's the big deal with us knowing?"

I momentarily gave up and focused back on the boys. "It's not a big deal, but our new relationship is only hours old and I don't want to fuck it up. I've never felt like this before. It's like something's sitting on my chest when I'm not with her."

All three of them looked at each other with a knowing grin, except *I* didn't know.

"All I'm saying is, being with her, it's better than anything I've known, but all I'm getting are other people's opinions right now, and we need to figure out the next step before we listen to anyone else."

Jasper topped up my glass. "Okay, but you know we'll all be happy for you."

"Yeah, I know, and I'm grateful, but everyone's been trying to marry me off for years, so I just want a bit of time without that pressure and everyone – by that I mean the girls – freaking her out by talking about marriage."

He nodded solemnly, "Say no more, we got your back. But if you don't want the girls to know, you might want to cool it."

"I'm not cooling anything; just tell them I'm not looking for their opinions."

Jamie snorted through his laughter, raising his glass to us all. "Hey, it's my baby brother, the comedian, again."

Freddie reappeared as quickly as they left, flopping down on Cooper again, "What's Murray being funny about this time?"

I looked around but no-one was following her. "Where're the others?"

"Still on the dance floor. I wanted some water." She picked up a bottle the server had brought back while they'd been gone. "What are you being funny about?"

"What am I not funny about?" I deflected with a smirk.

"True." She sipped her water, and subsequently burped from the bubbles. "I just assumed it had something to do with the way your tongue was hanging out when you saw Kit, but then tried to hide it."

I schooled my expression to stay as blank as possible, something Rafe would have been proud of.

"You know," she continued sweetly, fooling no one, "she's been very popular this evening."

That made me pay attention. "What's that supposed to mean?"

She shrugged, sinking back into Cooper's arms. "Just that

a lot of men have noticed her. Not wanted, I should add, but more than a few tried to slip her their number."

My blood went from ninety-eight point six degrees Fahrenheit to boiling in under a second. "Why are you telling me this? Jesus, Franks, you're such a shit stirrer."

She laughed in my face, "You're so predictable."

There was no one who could wind me up as much as Freddie, mostly because she knew me better than anyone else. If I'd been standing I'd have stomped my foot, just like when we were kids.

"No, I'm fucking not."

"Yeah, you are. But it's good, we're happy for you."

Knowing Freddie as *I* did, there was a good chance she didn't know anything and I was about to fall into her trap. Sometimes I wondered if she'd be a better lawyer than Rafe, if she'd gone to law school.

"What do you know?"

Her eyes twinkled deviously. "She told us what happened."

"Yeah, told you what exactly?" I had more faith in Kit than Freddie was giving her credit for. She was strong enough not to crumble under Freddie's cross examination.

I held her stare, waiting for her to break. Then she did, giggling into Cooper arms, amusing everyone else in our group just as much as she was amusing herself.

I rolled my eyes. "You're a dick."

"I know something happened," she shot back.

"You know nothing."

"I wasn't kidding about the numbers. She's looking fucking hot tonight, so many guys have hit on her and she's batted every single one of them away. That's how I know." Her black brow arched pointedly. "Think there's only been one man she wanted to notice her tonight,"

I turned toward the dancefloor again, still not finding

them among the heaving throngs of people. It was so fucking busy.

"If nothing is happening, you're an idiot. She's perfect for you. She likes you and I've seen the way you look at her. You need to marry this girl."

Cooper slapped his hand over Freddie's mouth. "Francesca, give it a rest and leave him alone."

I shot a look of gratitude toward him as Freddie finally shut up. Contrary to what my sister thought, I hadn't needed to hear anything she'd said. It served as no reminder of how beautiful Kit looked tonight, how beautiful she always looked. I had no doubt that she'd been hit on, and I was under no illusion how fucking lucky I was that she'd turned them down, nor why I was overwhelmed with immense relief that she had.

I stood up and leaned across the railings overlooking the rest of the club, searching until I finally spotted her, shining bright under the glare of a spotlight. She was waving her hands in the air, jumping around with Wolfie and Alex, totally carefree, her caramel locks flying around her. She was like no one else on the dancefloor, and now I'd found her, I don't know how I'd missed her, much in the same way I don't know how I'd missed this side of her in the time I'd known her.

She'd opened my eyes, to more than just her... To the possibility of a whole new life.

Soon, watching her wasn't enough, especially as I'd also borne witness to more than one guy attempt to get in her space, lowering my tolerance to non-existent. The next guy would get a fist in his face. I thought I'd experienced jealousy before, but then it had been more of an irritation, a mild inconvenience, that I got over as quickly as I moved on. What I'd never experienced was this possessive, overpowering, ugly sensation that surged through me like a tsunami, destroying anything in its path and sucking the air from my lungs, taking me back to the day in the elevator when it had first engulfed me.

Luck was on my side again when I spotted the girls leaving the dancefloor and I made it my mission to cut Kit off before she managed to get back here, because I was done with not being able to touch her.

"I'm going to the bathroom." I took off down the stairs before any of them could pass comment, which I knew they'd be doing.

I waited until I saw them head my way, stepping to one side as Wolf walked right past me without a second glance, followed by Alex. Before Kit could follow, I caught her wrist in mine pulling her away while simultaneously ducking from the swift right slap her hand was about to deliver, until she realized it was me. Her dropped jaw only made me laugh harder.

"Oh my God, I'm so sorry! I nearly smacked you."

"I'm not complaining if that's what you do every time a guy tries to hit on you. I was about to do the same." I wrapped my arms around her waist, pulling her into me, but it wasn't close enough. I forced her to take a step back until I was pinning her against the wall we were standing by.

Her brows furrowed, as she peered at me through an amused glint in her eye. "What guys?"

"Freddie might've mentioned you'd been offered a few numbers."

"Did she indeed?" she asked with faux innocence.

"Yes. Not that I blame them, but it's a strictly 'look but don't get fucking near enough to touch' situation. Only I get to touch you," I growled, leaning away to fully assesses her now she was back where I'd wanted her since we'd arrived at the house; in my arms, "I've not had the chance to tell you how fucking incredible, not to mention beautiful, you look tonight. I wish I'd seen you earlier, before anyone else got to see you."

"Thank you." She tilted her head taking a closer look at my pained expression. "Wait, were you jealous?"

"Yes, I fucking was. I have no problem admitting that."

"Really? That's why you came to find me?"

"Yes and no." I offered a one shouldered shrug. "Yes, because I was watching you on the dance floor and couldn't stand it any longer. No, because I wanted to come and find you anyway. I've barely seen you all day and you turned up tonight like a fucking knock-out and I'm a weak, *weak* man. I don't have the strength to stand on the side lines and watch. Not to mention I've only been able to do this..." I bent down, running my nose along her jawline, inhaling her sunshine and spring scent, "and this..." my lips moved along to her pulse hammering hard with the bass of the music, tasting the saltiness of her exertions. Her head tilted, giving me better access, along with a low moan which rumbled up her throat, "and this..." I sucked on her ear lobe, my voice deep and growly, "for a mere twenty-four hours, and if you think that I'm going to let someone else swoop in and take what's mine..."

It garnered the same reaction it had this morning, reaffirming that this was something I'd be doing over and over as I explored every nook and crevice of her body. She grabbed my face, pulling my lips into a collision with hers amid a passion and intensity that I matched. Her hot tongue swiped against mine before she properly opened up to me, as her fingers moved to the base of my neck and thrust into my hair.

After weeks and weeks of fantasizing about how fine her ass was, I'd finally discovered last night how it felt to have it fit perfectly in my hands as I cupped her cheeks, and that's what I did again. Lifting her against me, I pushed her further into the wall using my body to shield her from passers-by.

She shifted to lock her legs around my hips and a thunderous groan rolled through me as she rubbed up against my dick, making it even harder than it already was. I groaned again when she removed her lips from mine, and looked at me with both mild amusement and deep seated arousal, her eyes so dark brown they were almost black.

"Can we go somewhere quieter? Someone might see us."

"Let them see us. I don't care." I was beyond caring. My lips found the long slender column of her neck.

"Murray…" she pleaded and I could deny her nothing, even though I wasn't convinced I could walk.

"Come on." I put her down, holding her hand tightly in mine with no intention of ever letting go, leading her away from the dancefloor and noisy hordes walking past us. I'd been in this club enough times that I knew where we could be undisturbed.

"Where are we going?"

Taking a left at the stairs to the VIP section, we continued a short way down the corridor until I pushed open a door I knew wasn't alarmed, to a place I'd been more than once before. It was a dressing room of sorts, a room which was used for any visiting bands or artists on the nights they had live music. Vanity mirrors surrounded by big Hollywood bulbs ran along one wall above a bank of tables, half of which were lit. Full length mirrors covered the walls at the end and combined with the muffled music and heavy vibrations created an eerie carnival feel.

"How do you know about this?"

That I'd taken other women here too wasn't something I had any inclination to share with her right this second. Or any second.

"I know the owner of this place." I kicked the door shut as she walked further in and turned around, the mirrors giving me a perfect view of her perfect ass.

"Of course, you do."

Her chest was still heaving from our kiss and the speed at which I'd led us here, her tight nipples straining against the strapless top. It was beyond me how I'd managed to get her, but I'd stopped questioning anything happening in my life since I got home to a baby on my doorstep.

Two strides and I was back to where I'd been, as far in her personal space as I could get. I reached out and ran my thumb against her exposed belly button, circling it until she melted against my touch. Being somewhere private was both the best and worst idea she'd ever had, because I was unsure how strong my willpower was. I knew I was less likely to fuck her up against the wall by the dancefloor, but it wasn't totally out of the realm of possibility. Here, however…

"Fuck, do you have any idea how crazy you've been driving me? How badly I want you? You blow my fucking mind, Kit Isobel Hawkes." My hands were unable to stay still, running all over her body, including her leather clad ass.

Her head tilted back so she could look up at me through thick, sooty lashes. "It's the same for me."

"Really?"

"Yeah, since our first walk. When we got back, I realized what a massive crush I had on you."

A crush? Jesus Christ. I wasn't sure what was zipping through my nervous system at g-force could be described as a crush, although it *was* crushing me. No, this was more than a fucking crush. This was a… consuming.

No woman had ever consumed me like this.

My mouth found hers again, the tip of my tongue running along the seam of her lips as she opened up and I took my time to roam around, while my hands never ceased on their journey to map out her body until I memorized it. Her breasts felt as good in my hands as I thought they would; firm, pert, round and absolutely incredible, then my thumbs brushed against the tightest nipples I'd ever known, producing a deep, appreciative moan.

"You like that?"

She nodded through a haze of heightening arousal; her

responsiveness to my touch was all the assurance I needed. She wanted me as much as I wanted her.

I locked on her face as I slowly repeated the movement, watching her jaw slacken; it was the sexiest goddamn thing I'd ever seen. Then I realized she wasn't wearing a bra and my dick hardened by an impossible degree.

I picked her up and carried her to one of the dressing tables, setting her down. My eyes tracked the movement of her soft pink tongue darting out as she chewed her lip. I wanted that tongue on my cock while I slid down her throat; I wanted those lips wrapped around me as I fucked her mouth. But good things come to those who wait, and I wasn't going to rush this. What I was going to do was make her see stars.

I spread her legs wide and stood between them, knowing she could feel how hard I was for her. How much I wanted her, how desperate I was for her.

"Murray..." It wasn't a moan, it wasn't a whisper, but I swore to myself I'd hear her say it again. Just. Like. That.

I stepped back, drinking her in. She was looking at me like I was the first and only man she'd ever seen, and I had plans to keep it that way; except that I would also be the last man she'd ever see, the last man she'd ever look at with her rich, chocolate browns.

"I know, darling," I groaned. "Fuck, I'm going to make you feel so fucking good."

I was going to blow her mind, and maybe mine in the process.

But I wasn't about to fuck her in this room, I didn't even want to get her naked in this room. I had no desire to add her to the list of those who had both been fucked and/or naked in this room. Not all by me, not by a long shot, but still... I wasn't adding her to the list. She belonged on a list of her own, right at the top, with no one following.

I brushed a lock of hair from her face with the end of my

finger, tracing it on a path along her jaw and down the curve of her neck. Her breath hitched as I ran along the swell of her breasts, dipping under the flimsy material, feeling her soft skin with the back of my hand. Returning them to the fronts of her thighs, I ran my palms up and down the smooth leather. She was yet to let out a breath as my fingers dipped under the waistband, which was when it occurred to me that as sexy as these pants were, they were too fucking tight for me to get my fingers anywhere near where I wanted them.

How the fuck did she get them on?

More to the point, how the fuck do I get them off? Or at the very least, get her off?

They were nothing more than a sexy as fuck chastity belt, except even the sexiness factor was on a swift decline with how long it was taking me to get in them.

I shifted her to the edge of the desk, spreading her legs wider. I had no doubt that if I could slip my fingers in there she'd be soaking wet. Drenched. I could smell her and my dick punched hard in my jeans, making them almost as tight as her pants. I rubbed against her.

This was not going to work. She needed friction and dry humping my dick wasn't going to do it.

I lifted her off the table and led her over until she stood in front of the long mirror, my hands running along her bare arms as she leaned back into me, the scent of her shampoo heavy in the air. Even with her heels, she only came up to just above my shoulder, but it also meant my lips could brush over the shell of her ear, sending a cascade of shivers over her body.

She watched intently as my arms wrapped around her, my palms running across her stomach, skimming the top of her pants until they stopped to unfasten the button. The bass of the music was vibrating through us, but it had nothing on her heart hammering against her ribs while her eyes stayed trained on my fingers as they slowly pulled down the zip, opening up a clear path to her panties.

"Watch me," I whispered unnecessarily, because her eyes were glued to my movements, but I wanted to feel her chest hitch against me at the sensation of my breath against her, which it did. "I'm not taking these off because I'm scared I'm not going to get them back on, so you're going to watch what I'm doing. And you're going to feel everything."

I wasn't sure whose groan was whose as I eased into the silky fabric. I'd been right, she was fucking dripping, and slipping further down I found what I was searching for as she buckled under me.

"Murray… fuck."

"Shhhh." My lips grazed her ear lobe.

I held a steady grip across her chest with my other arm as my fingers started a slow circle of her clit, unable to move any further, restricted by goddamn leather. Her eyelids fluttered as I kept up a steady rhythm, the tiny nub under my fingers as hard as my cock.

My other hand busied itself separating her top from her incredible tits, peeling it down until I finally managed some skin-to-skin action. Her nipples were the color of warm toffee I wanted to bite down on, but instead, I rolled one between my finger and thumb which elicited another deep groan. Her eyes closed as her head fell back.

"Nah-uh, you watch me." I stopped still until her lids fluttered open, then she fixed her gaze on me as best she could with heavily glazed eyes. "Good girl."

She began trembling, her breathing growing shallower with the increased pressure from my finger, easily sliding over her slick, hot skin, drenched with her juices. She was so aroused that I almost wished I could make it last longer; the feel of her under my touch hot and slippery and so damn sensual that I didn't want to stop. Her arm flung back around my neck as she held on, her legs shaking as she tried to stop the power of her impending orgasm.

"Let go, Kit. Come for me."

The sensation of my breath against her ear as I tweaked her nipple and increased the pressure on her clit was too much. I gripped her tightly as her legs gave way and she fell limp against me. Even without being inside her, I could feel the force of her convulsions and ignored the savage weeping of my dick at having to wait to experience it for himself.

I wasn't sure when I'd last blinked, not wanting to miss any part of the ecstasy spreading over her gorgeous face, now flushed a shade of pink I'd never seen before. "You are so beautiful."

I watched her come back down to earth, felt her legs strengthening up again, though I was less keen to loosen my grip.

"So, that's how the Harvard boys do it," she chuckled softly, her eyes refocusing. "Maybe I did go to the wrong school."

My irrational jealousy reared its ugly head again at the thought of any fumbling freshman getting their hands near her. I'd almost got used to it, but now I'd actually had my hands on her it seemed to have increased a hundred-fold.

"Oh, Columbia, no," I reluctantly pulled my fingers free from her warmth, zipping her pants back up and fastening the button. "That's how *I* do it."

"I like it."

"I know. I felt it," I smirked, spinning her round and kissing her full on the mouth. "But I'm telling you, I don't care how hot they look, these fucking pants are going in the trash as soon as we're home."

Her eyes twinkled but she stayed silent.

"Come on," I took her hand in mine, kissing her palm. "Let's go find the others before they send a search party."

The hand I wasn't holding flew to her face. "They're going to know what we've done."

"I don't care who knows." I opened the door. "And if you're going to be part of this family, you need to know how to take on my sisters."

Her combined expression of confusion and horror had me laughing all the way back to our group.

16

KIT

I picked myself up and rubbed my bruised ass, collecting both my phone from where it had fallen and my thoughts, which were all over the place, and ran to the en-suite.

Payton: *WHY ARE YOU NOT CALLING ME BACK? I CAN'T BELIEVE YOU'RE GIVING ME RADIO SILENCE. I NEED AN UPDATE.*

The buzz of Payton's message had woken me up, and as I glanced at the screen, I could see it was the latest in a series of messages, each becoming more insistent than the last. Then, noticing the time, I simultaneously jumped and proceeded to fall out of bed in shock at how long I'd been asleep which is how I'd found myself with a sore tailbone and an impending headache, although the headache had nothing to do with me falling out of bed and everything to do with how much I'd drunk last night.

I propped the phone up on the counter and dialed her, knowing if I didn't she'd only keep calling.

"Oh my God, finally!"

I rolled my eyes and squeezed some toothpaste onto my

brush. "You really should have been a drama major, you know."

"Yeah, yeah. So...?" She stared down the phone.

"So?" I replied my mouth foaming as I brushed.

"Kit, don't make me wait any longer. What happened after the kiss the other night?"

I chuckled and spat everything into the sink, taking my time to rinse my mouth knowing how much it would annoy her. In her defense, we hadn't spoken at all yesterday which was unusual in itself as we spoke every day, so it was only my own doing that she was on the verge of a breakdown at not knowing the gossip. Not that this was gossip, or that Murray was gossip, and weirdly, even though we spoke about everything, I wasn't sure how much I wanted to share right now, or at all.

Yesterday had been a lot. A LOT. Starting with another perfect kiss, and ending in one of the hottest, most intense sexual experiences of my life. No, not one of. *The* hottest. But throw into the mix the fact that we were away with his family for a few days, all of whom seemed to have a vested interest in Murray and I being together, it added up to A LOT. It would require a little time to wrap my head around.

I couldn't stop the grin, however. "When I woke up yesterday, he'd been to the bakery for breakfast and made me coffee…"

"Cute. And?" she snapped impatiently, wanting me to get to the good stuff.

"And we kissed again."

I snatched my phone up to turn the volume down before everyone heard her shrieking. "Oh my God, this is amazing. I knew it! Then what happened? What's it like being away?"

"I didn't really spend any time with him yesterday. I was with his sisters and the kids. Then we all went out separately, but met up later in a club." I sighed, heavily, which hopefully conveyed everything I was feeling. "Jesus, Pay, he's so hot."

"Did something else happen?"

I tried to school my mouth into a straight line, but it was virtually impossible. I could still feel his hands on my skin, his fingers travelling everywhere, caressing me until I was nothing but liquid. And she could see it.

I nodded, which caused another shriek. "Shhhhh."

"Does his family know?"

I worried my lip as I thought about it. "I'm not sure. It's weird because I get the impression his sisters really want us to be together, like *really,* really. They haven't come outright and asked, and they haven't said anything, but there was so much insinuation in their questions. But UGH, he's so hot, I can't help myself. And the way he looks at me…" I started to trail off into a daydream about exactly how hot he was, until Payton snapped her fingers for my attention. "Yeah, we need to figure it out, I guess."

"What's to figure out?"

My brows knotted. "I work for him, for one. You know, what happens now? He pays me and we're in a relationship? Or he stops paying me and I stay and look after Bell, or he gets a new nanny and I carry on with what I was planning to do in the first place? Or is this just while I work for him, then we go our separate ways? I dunno, just feels a bit…" I couldn't find the word I was searching for, but there was a niggle in the back of my head which caused some nervous knots to make themselves known. "I wasn't expecting it to all happen so quickly, and he talks like this is our future and we haven't even had sex yet. Or maybe he doesn't want to have sex."

She stared at me so long I thought the phone had frozen. "Wow, that's some hole you've gone down. Way to take all the fun out of it... You're thinking too much, just go and enjoy it. He's hot, you're hot, there's no way he doesn't want to have sex with you. So please go have some hot sex," her eyes glinted devilishly, "and don't worry about being a cliché."

I rolled my eyes. "Thanks for that."

"Anytime, what are best friends for?"

I could hear some distant shouting coming from the pool. "I have to go, I've slept so late. I need a shower and make myself more human and presentable."

"You do. You've got a hot, single dad to keep now."

I inwardly cringed. "Ugh, shut-up."

"Bye, love you."

"You too." I hung up, stripped, and jumped in the shower.

Twenty minutes later I entered the kitchen, somewhat sheepishly, with no idea what to expect. My only saving grace was that Wolfie and Alex had maybe been as drunk as me, something which was confirmed when I found Wolfie head down on the table, resting on her arms. I definitely didn't feel that bad.

"Morning."

She raised her head with a groan. "Hey. Tell me you feel as bad as I do."

"I don't think I do," I chuckled. "You want a coffee?"

"Yes, please. I didn't have the stomach for it earlier, but I could probably manage it now."

Luckily the coffee machine in this kitchen was the same as Murray's, which I could work, even though it had taken me the whole of the first week to figure out. I flicked it on.

"Why do you feel so bad?"

"Why do you not?" she shot back, "Don't you remember free-pouring tequila while we were dancing on the table?"

My eyes bugged. "What?"

Then it all came flooding back. Cooper had left with Freddie, but the rest of us had stayed, another bottle of tequila was brought over and the wheels had come off. Alex, Wolfie, and I had ended up on the tables, and Wolfie had refused to get off when it was time to go home, so Jasper had fireman lifted her to the waiting car.

I joined her at the table, head in my hand. "Oh my God."

"I see you two feel as bad as I do." I looked up to find Alex leaning against the patio doors, sunglasses on, and looking like what I wanted to name 'English Country Chic', in a long, floaty peach dress. And for the first time, I noticed what a beautiful day it was outside. The warm breeze coming in from the beach was more suited to June than early April.

"Wolfie feels worse; I just had a memory jog to what happened."

"It was fun. Haven't had a night out like that in ages," she laughed, "and I'm thankful my kids are old enough that I don't need to get up in the night with them."

Wolfie groaned again. "Macauley will be on formula until my milk doesn't resemble grain alcohol."

Oh God, the kids. Maybe I was more hungover than I felt; I'd completely forgotten about them. "Where are the kids?"

"The boys have them, they're in the pool. The babies are with the grandparents."

"Shit, I'm the worst nanny. I should be with Bell."

Wolfie tried to lean over and pat my hand but gave up half way. "No, you should be hungover with us. There are plenty of adults here, not to mention grandparents, who don't really want us near the kids. This is their time to shine, and I'm here for it."

"Where are Sylvia and Greta?"

"They have the morning off. I think they went into town."

That made me feel slightly better, seeing as I was also a paid employee even if I wasn't behaving like one.

"Come outside for breakfast, it's all laid out." Alex gestured behind her. "There's coffee and everything."

That was enough to persuade me, seeing as I hadn't actually started making ours, plus I was hungry. Coffee was all Wolfie needed to hear too, and we all wandered out to the veranda, where my attention was immediately taken, not with food, but with the view. And by view I wasn't talking about the smooth stretch of beach and ocean. No, by view, I was talking about the four male specimens jumping around in the pool playing volleyball with the kids. All the thoughts I'd had whirring around my brain since I'd woken up stopped dead. It had been silenced.

I couldn't remember a time I'd seen so many finely honed muscles all in one place, maybe I'd never seen them. Not like this, anyway. Not so gratuitously wet and glistening. There were four guys in the pool, but my attention was only on one. I could only see one. Murray. Standing tall, he currently had his back to me, his strong, thickly defined back and shoulders, which Maggie was sitting on as she tried to catch the volleyball Jasper and Mia had thrown over the net.

I'd seen how spectacular his body was the morning I'd bumped into him, and even though I'd been wrapped around him while he kissed me, held onto his tight muscles, felt them flex under my fingers as I clung onto him while he brought me to orgasm, I hadn't actually been skin-to-skin. The heavy throb at the apex of my thighs told me I needed to rectify that, soon.

"Kit, coffee?"

I turned around to find Wolfie holding the pot up, unsure of how long she'd been standing like that. "Yes. Please."

She started pouring as my attention then focused on the breakfast set out for us along the wall, where it should have been. Bowls of enormous strawberries and juicy blueberries; Kilner jars filled with granola; yogurts, preserves. Lifting the lids on the burners, I found stacks of waffles, eggs, bacon, sausages, and hash browns.

My stomach rumbled loudly. "Who did all this?"

"The chef."

I had seen a couple of housekeepers yesterday, but no one apart from that. Naively perhaps, it never occurred to me there would be staff this weekend, but a house of this size, built for entertaining, would need a staff. It was too big for one person to run it. This was a life I'd never lived before; this was Murray's life though. This was what he was used to, what he was comfortable with, although he seemed to manage to get by with a housekeeper who came a couple of times a week. And considering his cooking skills were zero to none, I was surprised he didn't have a chef.

I sat down with my heaped bowl of granola and fruit, reaching for the coffee Wolfie had poured. "How many staff are there?"

"Six here right now. But I think when the family is here, there's ten or twelve plus security. Freddie would know, she renovated it. There's a whole staff quarters and kitchen."

That would explain why I'd not seen anyone. Freddie waddled over and pulled out a seat before I had time to quiz her on any more.

"You three are a sorry state. I'm so jealous." She rubbed her belly, "God I can't wait for this baby to come out."

"How long have you got left?"

Freddie was so small that her bump was deceiving. In fact, her whole size was testament that you should never judge a book by its cover, and she certainly made up for it in personality.

"Still another month," she groaned.

Samson joined us with Barclay in hot pursuit. Freddie picked him up to sit on her knee and he immediately dived into the bowl of blueberries on the table like he'd been starved for days, stuffing them in his mouth. Except, every other blueberry fell on the floor which Barclay then inhaled. We all watched them, back and forth, no one really having the energy to speak.

"Why don't we leave the kids here and go for coffee in the village?" suggested Alex, breaking the silence.

"Yeah, good idea," Wolfie agreed. "A walk would do me good."

"Me, too." Freddie stretched, and then cackled. "Stare any harder and you'll give yourself eye strain."

I realized she was talking to me and was about to turn to her, but then Murray spun round in the pool, water flying everywhere, and caught me staring. The combination of the sly grin and the immediate fire in his eyes made it feel much more like the height of summer in the Middle East instead of a balmy April Friday in the Hamptons.

He jumped out of the pool without looking back, grabbing a towel as he sauntered over to our table.

"Come on," I heard Alex say through my Murray induced fog, "Let's go and get our stuff together… Kit, we'll see you in ten to leave…" I heard chairs move… "Freddie, come on."

"Fucking hell, I just sat down. You know how long it takes me to get back up," she grumbled.

They were all gone by the time Murray reached me, towering over me, droplets of water running down his chest.

"Something I said?" He took the chair Wolfie had left vacant; moving so close his knees surrounded mine then leaned forward and kissed my cheek. He smelled like swimming and sunshine, his skin warm from the water and his exertions, and I leaned into his lips. "Hey."

"Hey," I smiled back.

He took my hands in his and placed them on the soft, red striped towel covering his lap. "How did you sleep?"

"Good. You should have woken me."

"You deserved to sleep in." His fingers brushed my jaw.

Wasn't going to argue with a lie-in, but that was two days in a row and I'd yet to see the baby.

I couldn't tell if it was guilt or the hangover creating unease in my belly. "How's Bell? Where's Bell?"

"She's fine, she's with my parents. This weekend is as much for you to relax as everyone else."

I'd never worked for a family that gave time off, beyond a couple of hours at a weekend, because my stints were short and intensive with the only goal of getting the baby on a schedule. But nothing about my time with Murray had been usual.

I squeezed his hand. "This is my job, I'm her nanny."

The only way I could describe Murray's reaction to that, was pained. Nor did I understand it.

"What?"

He shook it off. "Nothing."

If anyone looked over they would not have seen an employee/employer having a conversation. They would have seen a couple, having a private moment with more than a little lust burning in their eyes. Thankfully, no one was paying us the slightest bit of attention; the rest of the boys still going strong in the pool, and the girls were off getting ready to leave. I rubbed his thigh, "How are you doing?"

"I'm good." He cupped my face and kissed me, his tongue stroking against mine for less time than I wanted it to. "Now, I'm fucking excellent."

His grin spread wide across his perfect face, showing off his perfect teeth, and I once again forgot about anything I'd had concerns about; the anxiety in my belly replaced by fluttering butterflies.

"Did I hear Alex say you're all going out?"

I nodded, "Yeah, we're going to go for a walk to the town. Is that okay?"

His brows shot up. "Kit, you don't need to ask my permission. Of course, it is."

"Murray," I frowned slightly, "I work for you. I can't just take off without asking."

He made that face again. "Okay, go. Of course, it's fine. But let's talk about this later." He leaned forward and kissed me. "I'd say don't let Wolf and Franks push you around, but I think you're good there. Enjoy yourself, relax."

"Thank you." I stole a kiss but kept it chaste on the cheek. "I'll see you later."

He stood up with me and followed me into the house, where we found the girls waiting.

"Ready?" asked Wolf.

"Yes, let me grab my bag and sunglasses."

I ran up the stairs, and when I returned, Murray was in a whispered and heated conversation with the three of them. They jumped apart as I rejoined them.

Alex clapped her hands. "Let's go."

Murray threw me a wink as I followed them back out to the poolside and through the gate leading to the beach, each of us carrying our shoes as we walked along the waterline. Unsurprisingly, given the weather, it was busy with kids and dogs and joggers.

"Do you guys do this every year?"

"Come out here?"

"Yeah."

"No. We usually spend Easter together but it's been back home in England the last few years, since the boys finished playing hockey. But as our parents were here already and we were offered the house, we thought why not?" Wolf picked up a stone and threw it in the water. "It's beautiful here, and much warmer than it would be in London."

I could see Freddie looking at me from the corner of my eye. "So, what's going on with our brother?"

I threw my head back, laughing loudly. "Wow, that's taken you twenty-four hours."

"I know. This baby's made me lose my touch." She rubbed her belly. "I give you credit though, you've been here twenty-four hours and still not spilled the beans on what's happening."

"Why are you assuming something is happening?

It was her turn to laugh, Wolfie and Alex joining in. "Because we know our brother."

I wasn't sure what that meant. "What was he saying to you when I came back down the stairs just now?"

She grinned, conspiratorially, glancing to Wolfie for a second before she answered. "He told us to behave."

"What does that mean?"

"It means that Murray likes you," she nudged me, "and we know you like him, if only based on the outright perving on him in the pool just now, so spill..."

I couldn't deny my perving. Instead, I kicked the sand under my feet, inhaling a deep breath of fresh air. "Yes, I like him."

It had started with a crush, but after this week, I knew it was more than that. My feelings were rapidly steamrolling through me into something I wasn't sure I could identify.

"And?"

"And, what?"

"Okay, look, I don't want details about my brother, but tell us if something's happening."

Not once had Murray appeared to give a shit if anyone saw us together, including his family. I was also certain the boys knew. Our agreement to keep it between ourselves had become redundant. "Yes, something's happened."

The collective gasp of excitement would have rivaled One Direction's fans.

Wolfie clapped her hands together, momentarily rising out of her hungover stupor. Her eyes, so like Murray's, lit up with glee. "This is so amazing! What happened? How did it happen? How long has it been happening?"

"Wow, give her a minute. You guys are so full-on." Alex put her arm around me, giving me a gentle squeeze. "As someone who's also come into this family, I can tell you I know what you're going through. Feel free to ignore these two nosy parkers, although I do hope you don't because I want to know too. You guys make the best couple. We're so happy Murray finally found someone worthy."

I laughed, grateful for her but also very amused at how eager everyone was about it, or why it was such a big deal. I'd been prepared for the cross examination, but was probably going to need something stronger than coffee at this rate, and I wasn't giving the information up for free. Even though Murray had consumed ninety-nine percent of my thoughts, the final one percent had been taken up by someone else since Wednesday morning.

"I propose a trade of information. So before I say anything, what do you know about Dasha?"

"Who?" Alex and Wolf looked confused, while Freddie's features deepened as she thought about it, chewing on her cheek as she did.

"Dark hair, abnormally tall?" Her hand shot up above her head.

"Yes. Her."

She shrugged. "Not much, we've never met her. But what I do know about her, I don't like. Why?"

I was thankful she shared the same opinion I did, because I hadn't been totally sure how she'd react. For all I knew they could be massive Dasha fans, welcoming to anyone new, although I somehow doubted it given how Barclay had almost made her his next meal.

Wolfie looked between the two of us. "Who is she?"

Freddie glanced at her. "You know, that girl Murray was in a photo with last year, the one you kept taking the piss out of at the Halloween party because she wouldn't stop following him around."

It took her a second to remember. "Oh, her?" She turned to me. "Why d'you want to know about her?"

"She came to the apartment the other day saying she was his girlfriend, and that he'd told her to meet him there."

The three of them stopped in their tracks, Wolfie throwing her arm across me in a halt, like we'd braked suddenly.

Freddie pulled her glasses down her nose. "Shut. Up. She did not."

I smirked at the incredulity on her face. "She did."

Her mouth fell open, and I already knew that shocking Freddie wasn't a common occurrence, but I'd managed it with this news. "And what did you do?"

"I was kind of in disbelief because he's never mentioned her, and I was holding onto Barclay, but my best friend, Payton, was with me, and she slammed the door in her face."

Her eyes widened further. "Wow, I wish I'd seen that."

"Yeah, just in time before Barclay launched himself at her."

"Barclay?" Wolfie asked. "He likes everyone."

"He didn't like her."

"Wow."

"I know. She made Regina George seem like Mother Theresa."

The three of them laughed loudly and we started walking along the beach again.

Wolfie hugged me with one arm. "You really are going to fit well into this family."

I frowned. "Why does everyone keep saying that?"

"What do you mean?"

"That I'm going to fit in well. Murray said it, too."

"What? He did?" She dropped her arm to look at me properly as we walked.

I nodded.

"Wow. That is..." She rolled her lips, but didn't seem to find the words she needed for the rest of her sentence, and I didn't push it because we'd veered off topic

"Anyway, what do you know about Dasha? And them?"

Freddie shook her head. "Nothing. Murray never tells us about anyone he dates. We don't even know if he dates or just sleeps around. The only time we know he's been with girls is when he's photographed and it turns up in the paper.

She's definitely not someone you need to worry about; there's been a couple more since her."

"Oh." I wasn't sure if that made me feel better, because it still didn't shed any light on how our relationship was different, seeing as we hadn't been out either. And it wasn't like he could hide me, even if he wanted to, because they'd hired me. They'd known about me before he did.

"Kit, this isn't that," Wolfie said reassuringly, taking in my slight dismay. "That's how we know something's happening."

"What do you mean?"

She smiled as she watched a dad running to catch up with his toddler who'd made a bolt for the water. "It's been a lot for him the last few months, but you seem to have made it… I don't know, bearable? Easy? We've never seen him behave like this, or be like this…"

"Like what?"

"Protective, possessive," she smirked, "all moony-eyed. He never stops staring at you."

"No, that's because of Bell."

She shook her head. "It's not Bell, it's you. Freddie said he was watching you like a hawk on the dance floor last night."

"She's right. Jamie told me that Jasper told him that Murray called him at the beginning of the week, asking for advice on dating. But I'm not supposed to know that," Alex added.

Wolfie gasped, slapping her arm. "I didn't know that! He didn't tell me."

"Probably because he knew you'd make a big deal of it. I only found out last night when we got home."

The Williams' family rivalled Payton for how much she loved the gossip, although theirs seemed to be exclusively involving the family. They didn't seem to care about anything else. While I didn't want to add to the fire, I was intrigued to hear more, and knowing Murray had been thinking of me so much he'd asked for advice started up the butterflies again.

"Yeah, we've wanted him to settle down for a long time."

I put my hands behind my head, as I always did when I needed to think, because there was something I couldn't put my finger on... And again, they were almost determining that this was what would happen, that it was a given we'd be together when I didn't even know myself. Then it struck me that maybe there was more to this.

I stopped walking.

"Why did you hire me?" I looked between Freddie and Wolf, wanting the truth, because I knew it was more than to care for Bell. My suspicions were confirmed when their expressions turned shifty. "Come on, why did you really hire me?"

Wolf wouldn't meet my eye, and Alex was openly grinning at her squirming. "Murray needed help."

I shook my head. "There were plenty of better qualified nannies who could have done the job, but you requested me from Marcia, and she wouldn't let me say no. I wasn't planning on nannying again, and you're paying me double what you needed to. Give me the real reason."

I crossed my arms over my chest, waiting for the honest answer.

"Fine, we liked you. We thought you'd be perfect for each other, and we wanted to give Murray a nudge in the right direction."

My nose creased up. "What does that mean? What direction?"

"You've seen the kind of girls he goes for..." She left it hanging in the air until the silence bordered on awkward. "We wanted him to spend time with someone who didn't have a giant stick up her ass or daily Botox injections."

I laughed, but I was also unsure how I felt about this admission. I tried not to delve too deep into it, because it sounded like I'd been set up for a blind date I hadn't know about, which could have gone drastically wrong. Living together, just the two of us, was intense to begin with, and even though I knew something was unfolding between us, was it only because we were stuck together? I didn't appreciate being puppet to their puppet masters, or the playing fast and loose with my feelings part of it. Or Murray's for that matter, unless…

"Does Murray know?"

Freddie nodded. "Yep, but not right away, and when he found out he was pissed."

"Really?"

"Yes. Really pissed. But we were right. You are perfect, and he knows it too."

It mollified me slightly that he'd also not been happy, but I stood fast, holding my ground. "That's a risky move, you know. I'm not sure if I should be pissed, too."

Alex laughed loudly, pulling me into a hug. "You're definitely going to fit in well with this family if you can take these two on."

I rolled my eyes. "Murray and I haven't talked about this at all. Nothing's happened beyond a kiss," I ignored Wolfie clasping her hands together with unadulterated glee, like she'd won a grand prize. "Could you please stop planning our lives out before they've started? I work for him, and it could go really wrong."

"It won't."

I glared at Freddie, and she held her hands up in defense. "But okay, yes, we promise to stop planning your lives out."

"Thank you."

"Let us just say one final thing." I didn't bother to argue because she was going to anyway. "Murray might be our brother, but we do know how amazing he is, and he's also a lot of fun. So just have some fun this weekend, you both deserve it."

I didn't disagree with that.

Alex looked at her watch. "Hey girls, I think we've missed the boat for coffee, but Bloody Mary's could be calling us."

I didn't disagree with that either as we veered off the beach and onto the path toward the town.

17

KIT

"Mama!" Florence ran forward, her arms raised high, as we walked back into the compound.

"Hi, baby! Are you having a fun morning with Daddy?"

"Yes, except he said I can't be thrown in the pool again 'til later!" she cried, shrilly. She had mastered Wolfie's clipped English accent, bar a few words, which couldn't be mistaken for anything other than American.

Wolfie picked her up. "Why not?"

"Because I was sick."

"What? You're not well?" Wolfie felt her forehead.

"Daddy said I drank too much pool water, and now I have to wait," she sulked, her lip protruding dramatically.

"That child is too precocious for her own good," Freddie whispered in my ear as we rounded the corner to where everyone else was sitting round the pool, and received a rousing cheer as we did.

"Hey, there they are!" Jasper's eyebrow shot up, "How was coffee?"

"It was good, thanks, good walk along the beach. Feel much better. Thanks for holding the fort." Wolfie bent down to kiss him before he could say any more.

I perched on the edge of the sun lounger Murray was playing with Bell on. "Hey, how are you?"

"Good. Did you survive?"

"Just about," I laughed, tickling Bell's tummy. "Hey, little lady, how are you? I've missed you."

"We've missed you, too." He held my gaze until I had to bite down on my lip to stop myself from glowing pink.

"It's nearly nap time for her."

"Yes I know, I was about to take her in."

"I can do it."

"We'll both do it." He stood up, lifting her from the lounger as he did. "Come on you two, nap time."

"Lunch time in thirty," called Jamie as we passed.

"We'll be back, just putting Bell down for a nap."

Or we would have put her down for a nap if Diane hadn't been in the kitchen as we walked through, but the pull of the grandmother was too strong and she relieved Murray of his daughter to do it herself.

His strong hand gripped my wrist as I turned to head back to the pool. "Come with me. We now have a free thirty minutes before lunch."

Just as I had last night, I let him guide me down a corridor I'd not ventured along yet and lead me into a room at the end, my mouth dropping open as I took it in. "Holy fuck!"

"Bollocks, this was the wrong room to bring you into for some attention." He laughed loudly.

I stepped to the middle, barely registering the click of the lock, and turned round, staring at the stacks and stacks of books lining the double height walls, a ladder propped on the rails to reach the upper shelves. Walking closer, I spied an entire collection of Charles Dickens first editions, lightly brushing my fingers along their spines, too scared to properly touch them.

I turned to find Murray staring at me with both amusement and delight. "This room, it's incredible."

"It certainly is. I'd have brought you in here sooner if I'd known it was here."

"Would you?"

"Columbia, of course I would." He stepped closer to take a better look, "This is your Disneyland."

I grinned. "You're right about that."

He reached over, dragging the ladder along its tracks to us.

"See what's on the top shelf." His innocent tone contradicted the fire burning in his eyes and the sly amusement shaping his lip. "Read them out to me."

"Okay." I narrowed my eyes at him, slipping my sandals off and climbed up the first five rungs of the ladder to take a look. "There are some copies of Dante's Inferno."

"And what else?" Shivers ran across my body at the feel of his breath on my legs. I tried to read the next section, desperately wanting to concentrate on what I was looking at, but it was impossible, especially when his hand began sliding up my leg. If he went any higher, he'd be greeted with my soaking wet panties, something I was certain was his goal.

I tried to say his name, but that was also impossible, coming out as a moaning whisper and the very immediate need to stay standing while I was six feet up a ladder became my priority.

I stepped down a rung, then another, until he stopped me.

"Turn around."

We were eye to eye, my breath catching at the intensity in his, the heat shooting out of them scorching my skin. He straddled my legs on either side of the ladder, getting so close to me I needed to grip onto his shoulders before my balance went.

Cupping my calves, he ran his palms up the backs of my

legs. "This dress is much more to my liking, and now I get to do what I couldn't last night because of those fucking pants."

The throbbing in my clit travelled the length of my body until I was shaking so ferociously he winced from my nails digging into his shoulders as I tried to hold on.

"Did anyone ever make you come in the Columbia library?" His head tilted inquisitively, but I didn't miss his eye twitch. "Actually don't answer that. I don't want to know about you and any other guys. Ever."

He leaned forward, inhaling the last remainder of the breath he'd already stolen from me. His lips touched mine so softly I wasn't sure they were even there, until I felt the soft edge of his tongue probing me, asking me to open up for him. I willingly complied, wanting to give this Harvard boy everything I had and more.

My tongue swept against his as he took my mouth as his own with a delicious rumble at the base of his throat. His hard body pressed into me until I knew my back would be indented with the rungs of the ladder, and I let him, needing to be marked by him.

He moved back, his hands sliding from above my head down my body, returning to where they'd been.

"Kit, tell me again, how good was last night?"

His thumbs were slowly brushing the insides of my thighs, back and forth in a delicate swiping movement. I wanted to push myself down onto him to feel that swiping higher up.

"It was amazing." I managed to find the words somewhere to string a sentence together.

"Fuck, look at you. You're so perfect." His thumbs kept up their rhythm and a trickle of wetness seeped out of my panties, coating the skin where he could feel it.

"How badly do you want it? Tell me, I need to hear it."

"So badly."

He was mesmerizing, leaning over me, almost incandescent with arousal, his green eyes mossy dark and hooded. I could feel how hard he was, his swim trunks doing a poor job of holding in what was clearly a very impressive dick. A dick I desperately wanted to feel inside me.

His hands finally moved up, his fingers slipping under the elastic of my panties. My breath stopped as he slid them slowly down my legs, dropping them on the floor to the side.

"Do you trust me?"

I nodded, beside myself with anticipation. "Yes, of course."

"Lift your hands above your head and hold onto the ladder. Don't let go."

I did as he ordered, which pushed my boobs closer to his face. Another sly smile passed over his lips, and he pulled the top edge of my dress down, taking my bra with it.

My head hit the back of the ladder as his mouth closed over a nipple, my grip on the rung the only thing holding me up as my legs practically gave way.

"You are the sexist thing I've ever seen." The timbre of his low, gravelly voice vibrated across my skin, sending goosebumps from the tips of my fingers to the ends of my curled toes.

I couldn't answer. Just like last night, he'd stripped me of all my abilities, stolen my voice along with my inhibitions. I stopped breathing altogether as he pushed my dress up, exposing me to him, completely naked in the glow of the midday sun bursting through the windows.

He pushed my legs as far apart as the ladder would let them. "Jesus Christ, if I'd known last night that this is what awaited me, I would have ripped those fucking pants off there and then."

He stood back, studying me, I could feel the heat of a blush coursing through my body, but I was too far gone to care. I wanted his hands on me and I wanted them now.

"Murray, please…"

"It's okay, darling. I've got you."

His thumb brushed against my clit and I couldn't shoot back any further than I already was, but my head hit the ladder again as it fell hard, and all I could see was my knuckles, white as snow, and gripping the rung like I was on a ride. Which, I was. The ride of my life.

Using both his hands he parted my folds, taking another long look. "You're dripping wet, dripping… Later, I'm tasting this. Later."

My toes were curling, my thighs were shaking, and he'd barely touched me. Was this an out of body experience? But then one of his thick fingers slid inside me, followed by another, curling up inside me, bearing down with just the right amount of pressure and my entire core clenched on itself.

No, this was my out of body experience.

"Fuck, Kit, you're squeezing me so hard. Jesus, my dick is going to need CPR."

I groaned so loudly the island of Manhattan would have heard me.

"Oh, you like that? You like the thought of my dick being so tightly fitted inside you it's going to need your mouth around it, bringing it back to life?" His fingers kept a steady pace, sliding in and out, his gaze fixated on the movement as intensely as I was fixated on the sensation.

I hummed in response, barely managing to stay conscious, my body shaking so viciously I could be having a seizure.

He leaned forward, his lips almost touching mine but not quite, the heat of his body sending mine into red zone levels. "I've thought about it so much, what you'd feel like wrapped around my dick. Your mouth, your pussy, it doesn't matter. I want to feel you wring the life out of me."

He added another finger, filling me up, all three

pressing inside me as his lips found a nipple again. I couldn't hold on any longer. My orgasm hit me at Mach speed, Murray's one free arm tightened round me as my legs gave way and I slipped down the ladder, while my body spasmed like it was being exorcised. His lips crashed down on mine swallowing my cries, taking control of my mouth like he'd taken control of every other part of me, heart, mind, soul… and now my vagina. He owned every facet of my life.

"Murray…" My hands had frozen in placed, my muscles liquefied. A curl, lazy and smug lifted the corner of his mouth as he straightened my dress and lifted me down. Bending, he picked up my panties and helped me step into them, first one foot, then the other, my hands still gripping onto his shoulders for much needed balance.

His fingers brushed my knees as he stood up, rearranging himself in his shorts.

"That worked up an appetite," he growled into my neck.

I moved back so I could look at him properly. His rugged face was softened with lust. It amazed me that he got more beautiful every time I looked at him. And he was beautiful; he'd surpassed handsome weeks ago.

"Murray?"

"Yes?" he smirked, kissing my neck and I almost forgot what I was about to say, then he stopped me again with another kiss. "Come on, let's go have lunch."

I took the hand he was holding out to me and allowed him to guide me from the room, meekly following like he hadn't just eviscerated my world for the second time in a little over fifteen hours. And I'd done nothing. He'd not asked me for anything, not expected anything from me in return, for making me come like no one ever had before him. For blowing my mind. He'd also not given me the opportunity. And I wanted it, I wanted that opportunity. More than I'd ever wanted anything.

"There you both are," Diane exclaimed as we made our way back outside. "Wondering where you'd got to."

The whole family looked up from the table as we stepped onto the veranda, Wolf and Alex beside themselves with satisfaction they were right. I could still feel my body glowing in the embers of my orgasm and I had no doubt it was visible to the two of them, too.

"I was showing Kit the library, because she loves libraries."

I almost choked on my inhale as he gave me the dirtiest most suggestive wink I'd ever seen, before he pulled me into him and kissed my head, making me blush even more. "It's actually really cool, all first editions."

No one seemed to care that he'd kissed me, which clarified that everyone either already knew Murray and I were something, or assumed it was about to happen and didn't care.

He pulled out a chair at the table for me to sit down and then took a place next to me. Wolf poured me a glass of wine.

"You love libraries?" she asked with pointed amusement and a tilt to her head.

I nodded. "I mean, not like a weirdo, but I studied English and I've spent a lot of time in them. The one here is really impressive."

Not that I'd properly had a chance to look. I'd have to go back in when I wasn't accompanied by my own personal sex pest.

"You loved this one," Murray whispered, for my ears only. I shifted uncomfortably in my seat. I don't know how he'd done it, but only ten minutes after I'd seen stars, I was already desperate for another round, desperate to feel him inside me.

I hadn't realized Jasper and Freddie weren't at the table either until they walked out and sat down. "All kids that are supposed to be asleep, are."

There was a unified sigh of relief and everyone tucked into the enormous spread of giant salads, Snapper, freshly baked bread, vegetables, cheese – the chefs had outdone themselves. I could certainly get used to this.

"What's everyone doing this afternoon?"

There were cries of pool, beach, and naps.

"I'm taking Kit and heading down the beach, into the town. We'll go when Bell's awake and take her and Barclay." Murray's voice carried an undertone making it clear it wasn't an open invitation.

I shifted again as one of his big hands squeezed the top of my thigh.

It was like he'd read my mind. A walk along the beach was exactly what I wanted to do. As much as I loved this family, I needed alone time with Murray.

Barclay raced down to the water, jumping about in the surf as Murray and I walked out of the compound gates and down to the beach. Bell was strapped to his chest, facing forward, and wearing the cutest striped sunhat while his big bicep rested against my neck, his fingers dangling down the straps of my dress.

It was busier than it had been this morning; more families, more dogs. A lot of people had taken the day off to enjoy a long Easter weekend.

"It's beautiful here."

"Yeah, it is."

"Do you come here much?"

He was silent for a second before answering. "Yes. Rafe's family has a house a little bit further down than where we are. The three of us have been coming here every year for Memorial Day since we were in college."

"Oh, that sounds like fun. Is it just the three of you?"

"Usually, yes. It's our weekend rule. We party in the town, but the house is just a boys' weekend."

"Usually?" I watched Barclay digging in the sand.

"Last year, Rafe's youngest brother, Rory, came along with some of his Varsity mates, and they brought some girls…" His voice trailed off and my stomach dropped, not knowing what was about to come next. "Last Memorial Day is when Bell was conceived."

"Oh." I hadn't expected that. I was also surprised I hadn't known, or that we hadn't talked about it. I stopped and turned to him. "Oh, and you haven't been back since? Is this hard for you? Has it been hard to be here?"

His soft smile made my heart thump double time.

"No. I hadn't thought about it at all until we were driving down the road yesterday. So much has changed in my life since Bell came along," His fingers brushed my cheek, "Since you came along. I live a very privileged life, as you can see. I worked my ass off building my business from scratch, but I still do appreciate that I have a lot more than most. However, until Bell, I don't think I ever realized that something was missing. Bell and you, you've changed my whole world."

He spread his legs slightly, a new move he made whenever he was trying to get closer to my height. His arms snaked around my waist and he pulled me into the side of him without squashing Bell. "This past week, and now having you here with my family and Bell, it's been the best week of my life. It feels like everything is slotting into place, where I didn't understand it before."

His mouth fell onto mine, soft and full, capturing my lips and parting them with his own. His tongue tangled against mine, hot and sweet, then softly moaned before letting me go. His eyes met mine when he moved back.

"What?"

I hadn't planned to say anything, or hadn't planned to say anything right this second and spoil this perfect moment between the two of us, because if I was honest, he'd changed my life too. I hadn't been looking for a relationship; I definitely hadn't ever expected one to come from this job. Hell, I hadn't even *wanted* this job, but even with all that, the breakneck speed with which it had moved over the past few days was festering in the back of my mind, like spoiled milk. Because the faster you rise, the faster you plummet.

And no one survives a plummet.

"This morning, Freddie and Wolf told me about the set-up, about hiring me for you, more than you needing a nanny."

He groaned loudly, his hands letting go of me and pushing through his hair in frustration. "I had nothing to do with that. I was so mad when I found out because all they try to do is marry me off." He kissed my nose with a smile. "But it's all worked out."

I didn't know what he meant by *it's all worked out* but I didn't want to ruin the moment by pushing the points of my spiraling maze of thoughts.

I straightened Bell's sun hat, and Murray's arm slipped round my shoulder as we started heading down the beach again. Barclay ran back to us, shaking off a torrent of sea water, the droplets creating a rainbow effect around us.

"Ugh!" I jumped out of the way, nearly colliding with an older lady walking past in the opposite direction. I wiped myself off, making Murray laugh. "Thanks, Barc."

"Dogs! Can't remember the last time I wore something that was clean for longer than a few minutes," she chuckled, nodding at her own dogs, although I wasn't sure a Labrador and a Chihuahua was a fair comparison.

"I know, right?"

She smiled at the three of us. "You have a beautiful daughter."

"Thank you," Murray replied, with a smile so wide it could eclipse the sun.

"You're a lucky boy to have such a beautiful wife and baby." She shook her finger at him, teasingly.

"Yes, ma'am, and don't I know it." He pulled me in and kissed my head.

"Enjoy your day," she said, leaving us to catch up with her dogs who'd moved pretty far down the beach considering how small their legs were.

"There's a great ice-cream parlor round here. Let's see if it's open." He carried on walking as though nothing had happened.

I stopped, trying to figure out why it bothered me so much that he dismissed comments about us so easily. I understood that it was probably simpler for him to go with whatever people assumed, but that didn't mean I was assuming, or even knew what we were. Were we dating now? Were we in a relationship? We hadn't even had sex. Or maybe I'd been right and he didn't want to. Twice he'd left me at my door when any other guy would have jumped at the chance to come in.

"Murray?" I stopped again, my brows knotted together.

"Yes, darling?"

"That woman, she said we were a beautiful family..."

"I know." He held his hand out to me. "Come on, let's find the ice cream."

He strides became purposeful, because once Murray was on a mission, there wasn't much that would get in his way.

"Wait, hang on." I ran slightly, trying to move round to the front of him so I could block his path.

"Are you okay?" He frowned.

"Yes, I am. I'm good. But you didn't correct her, and this morning you said we'd talk."

His shoulders dropped with a sigh, considering me for a second before answering.

"I know." He brushed my cheek. "I did, I'm sorry. We haven't exactly had much alone time though."

"I know we haven't. I know the time we've had, we've..." I trailed off, not really sure what I was asking. "Last night, and then just now, was incredible. Your family obviously knows something is going on. But *I* don't know what's going on. I work for you, I look after Bell."

His frown deepened, creating lines on his forehead that weren't usually there, because he rarely frowned. He was always so happy and jovial.

"I don't want you to feel like you work for me. You're more to me than that; you've been more to me than that for a long time, and I'm sick of fighting it. Kit, I want you, more than I've ever wanted anyone. Believe me when I say you're all I think about and I've tried being a gentleman, but fuck if it's the hardest thing I've ever done. We'll figure it out soon, I promise. I'm already working on it with Rafe."

I had no idea what Rafe had to do with it, or why he was working on our relationship with him, but his eyes shifted to somewhere in the distance and a twitch flexed in his jaw. It was clearly troubling him as much as me, so I left it alone because my focus had zoned in on something else he'd said.

"Okay..." I bit my cheek, my eyes glancing down to the smooth, soft sand. It was too much to look at him directly. "You can stop being a gentleman now..."

"Kit..." I could feel the heat of his gaze on me, "I don't want to rush you into anything. I don't want you to think it's all I'm after. This isn't about sex for me."

I crooked an eyebrow, "Seriously?"

He held his hand across his heart. "I promise."

I wasn't sure if this was some type of reverse psychology; but if it was, it was working. And it wasn't a case of wanting something more because you'd been told you couldn't have it. I wasn't sure I could want him more, the intensity and chemistry between us was off the charts.

"I don't need you to do that."

In a split second his eyes lost all their sparkle, turning

dark and fiery, burning through me like a laser. A thick lump stuck in my throat from his predatory glare, the one which caused my pulse to shoot up, the flames already licking me where I yearned to feel his tongue.

His fingers traced along my cheek and under my jaw, tipping it up to his face so his lips could snare mine. "Are you sure?"

I swallowed thickly, "Yes."

His head tilted and his eyes narrowed again, while he contemplated. "Ice cream, then we're heading back. You should have a nap; you're going to be in for a long night."

It wasn't the first time he'd shocked me into silence.

He kissed my mouth, which had fallen open. "Come on, let's go."

I hadn't had a nap. I'd tried, but I couldn't sleep. I'd also tried calling Payton so she could talk me out of the anxiety knots I'd built up, but that had only caused her to shriek down the phone with excitement, and I'd hung up because I obviously hadn't learned my lesson from earlier this morning.

I'd had sex before, not *a lot* a lot, but enough to have the knowledge of how good it could be. Yet in all my years of having 'the sex' , I'd never been as turned on or as desperate for an evening to be over in order to get to the next stage as I had been for this one.

I'd spent the day subjected to absolute torture, suffering endlessly at the expert hands of my tormentor. He'd purposely kept me from falling over the cliff edge, never quite letting me go; furtive touches against my skin, lips pressing my ear as he leaned in close, knuckles brushing my nipples as he moved past me. Once, during the afternoon, we'd all been in the pool and his fingers slipped into my bikini, teasingly searching until he found what he was looking for, and I was ready to declare him the winner of whatever game we were playing.

"You're going to be so much wetter than this later," he'd promised, and I lost the ability to breathe.

In the end, I'd had to feign an early night, not caring that anyone suspected what was happening, because I was no longer able to concentrate on anything that required me to be mentally present. I had no idea what was about to happen, but having already sampled at the Murray buffet twice, I knew this wouldn't be like anything I'd experienced before. The expectancy and anticipation was enough to make my heart hammer so hard in my chest I could see it as I stood in front of the mirror, my naked body on full display.

Throughout the course of the evening, I'd soaked two pairs of panties. I'd showered twice, lathered my body up using almost the entire bottle of outrageously expensive wash which had been left for me, then dried and lathered again in an outrageously expensive lotion.

I'd almost didn't bother with a third pair before Murray arrived, seeing as he would simply remove them anyway, but decided that was a fraction too brazen for our first time.

I walked over to the armoire where I'd laid out my favorite dark gold lace, the color of his hair, and slipped them on, sat down and watched the clock until it struck eleven p.m.; the hour of our agreed rendezvous.

This was not like watching a clock where time stands still. No, this had the opposite, almost warp like speed effect; the door opened softly and he was standing there, stealing what little composure I had left. It clicked behind him and he leaned against it.

He was wearing nothing but a pair of soft, black cotton shorts. His hair was wet from a shower, his golden skin darker from a day in the sun. The shadows from the dimmed sconces flicked across his tight abs and thick pecs, his enormous biceps flexed with power as he casually pushed his hands into his pockets. But that was the only thing casual; because the way he was looking at me… there was only possession and danger. I knew I could do nothing but surrender to him. I didn't want to do anything else.

He was magnificent.

His dick was already straining against his shorts, but he paid it no attention, his hooded gaze focused solely on me. My mouth filled with saliva and my fists clenched into themselves, hoping the pain of my nails digging in would stop me from passing out from the speed at which my pulse was racing.

"Kit…" His voice was warm and soft, coating my body, sweet like honey, "Come here…"

I followed his crooked finger, noticing his breath catch as I stood up which calmed my fraying nerves, thankful I wasn't the only one feeling like this. He smelled like oak and sandalwood, and him. And I wanted that smell on me, I wanted him on me.

I stopped inches away.

"Shhhhh, darling." He placed his palm on my chest, then took my hand and mirrored the motion. Under my fingers I could feel his heart beating as fast as mine. "See? I'm the same."

I finally managed to suck in some air, calming myself in the process.

"You are so beautiful like this, so goddamn beautiful." His fingers laced through the ends of my hair, carefully curling it around his fist. His lips brushed mine so gently I almost wasn't sure they'd touched. "This is what's going to happen. First, I'm going to remove this flimsy excuse for a bra…" His fingers slid under the straps, allowing them to fall off my shoulders. Warm hands skimmed my back as he unhooked my bra with the expertise of a seasoned professional. He caught it in his hands as it fell from my body, lifting it to his nose and breathing deeply. He was close enough to me that I felt his dick twitch against my leg.

Once more I was glued to the spot, unable to do anything except take shallow breaths as his thumbs ran over my nipples before a hot tongue took the place of one. My loud groan broke his trance and he lifted me up, taking four large strides and threw me on my bed, which was big enough to sleep a family of six.

He rose, crawling over my body until he hovered above me. "We aren't alone in this house, Columbia. You can scream all you want when we're back home, but here you need to keep quiet. I don't want anyone to hear your moans except me, every single one belongs to me. I've earned them and I'm not sharing."

His hungry mouth crushed mine, and if I hadn't already been lying down, I would have been after this kiss, my body melting as quickly as our ice creams had in the sun. His tongue swept round, engulfing me, taking no prisoners as he tasted every corner of my mouth like it was his appetizer, and I was the main meal.

He swallowed my next groan. I didn't know how I was going to remember to keep them in when I could barely remember who I was or where I was.

"Don't make me gag you." He nipped my neck, chuckling darkly, although I wasn't sure he was joking.

My back arched off the bed as his lips found my nipple again, his fingers rolling the other with equal pain and pleasure as each bite was followed by a soft laving. "Jesus, fuck."

His hot breath left a trail of condensation on my skin as his mouth moved downward. "There's that word again. I did say I'd use it as a noun and a verb, so maybe I should make good on my promise... What do you think, Columbia?"

The only thing I could think was that my body was about to be ripped in half; igniting from his touch.

"Please..."

He sat back on his haunches, his fingers hooking under the elastic of my panties. I wanted to watch but I couldn't muster up the amount of consciousness needed to do it.

"Look at me."

My eyes flicked up at his order.

His hands gripped onto my calves, forcing my knees to bend up, and then he spread me wide. Like earlier, I was too far gone to be embarrassed at his blatant staring, and it wasn't just staring, he was transfixed. His hands cupped underneath me, his middle finger testing a path from top to bottom, spreading my lips, releasing a gush of wetness into his palm.

The vibrations running through my entire nervous system turned into tremors that would have registered on the Richter Scale when his mouth lowered and his tongue took a long lap along my slit, flicking my clit to finish.

My juices coated his mouth as his eyes locked with mine; erotic and so fucking sexy. This was going to be over in seconds.

He slowly ran his tongue over his lips. "You taste incredible."

His tongue dipped for a second go-round, taking me to detonation. As predicted, the third time sent me freefalling into an abyss I'd never travelled to before, wave after wave crashing violently through my body until my brain was shaking in my skull, and I thought my heart would implode. When I finally managed to open my eyes, my breath didn't just catch, it suctioned into a vacuum of our making.

It was one of those situations you had to see to believe, except I didn't want anyone else seeing this. Murray had kicked off his shorts and was standing at the end of the bed; his cock was also standing at full attention, long, thick, and hard, the tip glistening with pre-cum as he stroked it lazily. It wasn't just impressive, it was remarkable. Beautiful. His cock was as beautiful as he was.

My body throbbed again, deep in my core, although it hadn't ever really stopped.

His eyes slowly scanned my body. "You're so fucking perfect. That was the most perfect thing I'd ever seen; you, coming on my tongue, bursting in my mouth. Jesus. I want to do it forever..."

I could only stare, stare as you would at a priceless piece of art in a museum. He said nothing more but his raised eyebrow spoke volumes.

"Murray, I need..." For an English major I was doing a terrible job at forming cohesive sentences, not that it was a priority for me right in this second.

"What do you need?" He was still lazily stroking his cock, doing nothing for my heartbeat, which didn't seem to have any plans to subside. "Tell me, Kit."

"More, I need more."

"Okay, darling. You can have more." He took hold of my legs and pulled me toward the end of the bed, where he was now kneeling. He picked up a foil packet I hadn't noticed before now, ripping it open with his teeth, wrapping himself. He ran the tip of his cock through my soaking wet center, jolts of electricity shooting through me as he flicked my hyper-sensitive clit.

"Fuck, I want you as close as I can get you. I want to be wrapped round you while you're riding my dick."

He scooped me into his arms in one swift movement, while maneuvering the pair of us so I was straddling him. His cock was banging against my stomach, both him and I having the same goal of being inside me.

He lifted me onto my knees. "Ease down on me."

I did as he asked; gingerly lowering onto him, inch by agonizingly slow inch. Even with how dripping wet I already was, I couldn't go faster. I hadn't taken into account the size of him and the length of time it had been since I'd last had sex. His teeth gritted as he filled me up and stretched me out, delicious and hot and so fucking amazing I knew I'd never felt anything like it before.

I tried to hold in my groans as my walls tightened around him, still recovering from the force of my orgasm. I swallowed him up to the hilt.

"Oh God… this… you… feel amazing."

Never in a million years would I have imagined this on my first day at work; that I'd be wrapped around the most beautiful man I'd ever seen in my life, sweat rolling down the hair's breadth of space between our bodies, my breasts pressed up against his solid chest as he ever so gently started moving inside me. It produced a groan as loudly from him, as the one he'd made sure I kept quiet.

"Jesus Christ, you feel incredible. Incredible." His palms held onto my back, his fingers curling around the nape of my neck. "Kit, fuck. Your pussy was made for me."

We moved together like we really *had* been made for each other; in perfect symmetry and rhythm. His lips met my throat as I rolled my hips forward, tipping myself enough so his cock pushed against my G-spot and grinding my clit.

His fist wrapped round my hair forcing me to lean back, granting himself access to my nipples, my chest, my neck, needing his mouth everywhere it could be until it wasn't enough.

"More."

My hands found their way into his hair, gripping it in my fingers as I pulled his lips to mine, the taste of me still on his tongue, devouring him as he'd devoured me. I was building up to something I knew would rip me to shreds, but I couldn't stop if I tried. Rocking against his lap, finding purchase in the soft mattress, he swelled another degree inside me.

His fingers moved to my hips, digging in as he drove into me, slamming me down hard. Rockets shot up my spine, the flames they left in their wake curling round me like a corkscrew pulling hard in my core, twisting for the release I desperately needed. They soon turned into a full-blown wildfire, spreading through my body as though my blood was laced with kerosene.

Our heartbeats merged as our bodies pulsed in sync. He placed my palm on his chest again. "You feel that, baby? You feel how we're made for each. Holy shit, you're perfect."

I felt it; I could feel nothing but him, filling me up, filling me everywhere until I couldn't see or hear anything but him either. He'd taken leave of all my senses. One final ferocious thrust sent us both into our own cyclones, destroying us from the inside out.

He came with a loud cry, drowning out my own as I collapsed against him, almost sliding down his chest from the sweat we were both slick with. The iron taste of pennies flushed my mouth and I realized I pierced the skin, biting down on my cheek trying to keep quiet; I sucked it away with a shiver.

Lifting my chin, he brought his lips to mine, kissing me with a tenderness that turned any bones I had left to marshmallow.

"That was definitely using fuck as a verb," he snickered before his tone became serious. "I never knew sex could be like that."

I craned my head back, almost drowning in the emotion filling his eyes. "Like what?"

He stroked my cheek. "Like so intense that I didn't think I'd ever get close enough to you. I still don't feel I am."

It had been the same for me, all consuming, not getting anywhere near enough as I wanted. There was no logic or reason to this intensity.

"I'm not letting you go."

I didn't answer. Instead, I curled up into his sweaty chest, forgetting anything I'd been worried about today, yesterday, all week. The constant niggling had been dulled with Murray flavored Valium.

I briefly wondered if I'd get in a small power nap before we started on round two, but that thought was quashed the moment his fingers began inching up my thigh.

18

MURRAY

I propped myself up on my elbow, admiring the view in front of me.

As usual, I'd woken up before her, my body filled with the same adrenaline that had been keeping me on high alert all week.

I carefully eased the sheet down her body, desperate to glimpse what had immediately become my favorite part of her; the soft curve of her back rising up into the ass I now knew was made for my hands. Perfectly heart shaped. I couldn't see her face, her hair a mass of golden waves filling the pillow as she breathed deep, but I didn't need to. I saw her face every time I closed my eyes, having studied it every waking second for the past week since we'd returned from the Hamptons.

It had been a week of firsts.

A week of new experiences for both of us.

A week where there had barely been any talking because talking wasted time, especially when we could be enjoying each other in a different way. A naked way. I hadn't been to the office once. I'd worked the bare minimum, usually confined to when she was napping, resting from the exertions of the night before, the morning, the afternoon, or evening. Our body clocks only kept in place by the tiny baby we were both looking after, because without her, our lives would have revolved around the clock of sex, eating, sleeping, and more sex.

It was amazing my dick hadn't fallen off, but it was still there, raring to go as it was every time I saw her. She was like a homing beacon, and the second Bell went to sleep, we never got further than a few rooms without launching ourselves at each other again. I'd devoured her, fucked her, made love to her in every single inch of my apartment. And at nearly seven thousand square feet, that was a lot of space.

I was fully consumed.

I had fallen hard.

I couldn't get enough.

The other woman I couldn't get enough of began gurgling over the baby monitor, and I grabbed it before she woke Kit up. I took one more glance at her before running to the bathroom to brush my teeth. The bathroom counter was now taken up with all Kit's products – hair products, moisturizer, facial oils – girls came with so many products, one of the myriad reasons I'd never wanted to share my space with any. But I would give her all the counter she needed, because now it was impossible to imagine my life before she was in it, or my life without her, now I knew we existed in the same world.

I opened Bell's door, lifted her out with a kiss as she happily gurgled away, smiling at me with her big baby smile - always the best part of my morning. Barclay's tail thudded from his bed in the corner, having now become a permanent resident of this room, which I wasn't sure had anything to do with Kit moving into the bed with me.

Heading downstairs, she kicked out in her bouncy chair as I placed it on the counter so I could watch her while I made us both a drink - me, coffee; her, milk. Barclay sat down, almost on top of my feet, reminding me he also wanted breakfast in case I dared to forget.

"Yes, yes. Come on." I took him into the pantry and poured his biscuits into a bowl, leaving him there to gobble up.

The terrace was already warm from the morning sun as I threw open the patio doors, carrying Bell's chair out, before fetching my coffee and her bottle. The unseasonal heatwave we'd had in the Hamptons had followed us back to the city, making it a perfect day for a picnic in the park, which, I decided, is what we would do today.

I pulled my phone out to call the deli, only then noticing the deluge of messages from Rafe banging on about the fucking contract. I still hadn't brought up the subject with Kit, the thought of it setting my teeth on edge. But after this past week, I knew I'd have to do it, and soon. She wasn't just my nanny. She wasn't my nanny at all. I wanted that to end.

I'd support her for as long as she needed, I'd support her forever, but not as an employer.

There was, however, something I needed from Penn.

Murray: *Pennington, is everything still good for tomorrow?*

Penn: *Yes all set, just arrive forty-five minutes early and you'll be met*

Murray: *You're a little treasure, aren't you? Thanks, matey, I owe you big time*

Penn: *I'll remember that*

Tomorrow night was the opening of the Picasso exhibit at The Met, which Penn's family was sponsoring. I was taking Kit as my date, but I'd also arranged a little pre-event surprise for her, one I hoped would win me points and lessen the blow around the conversation we needed to have. Although either way, this was something I wanted to give her. Something I hoped she'd enjoy.

I lifted Bell out of her chair, offering her the bottle, which she took as greedily as Barclay did, only stopping half way for a giant burp which luckily didn't produce anything which would have me smelling like an old farm until I managed to shower.

"Hey,"

I spun to find Kit in the doorway, a bashful smile tipping her lips. Even after a week of devouring each other's bodies, she still displayed initial shyness first thing in the morning, always baffling me and warming my heart in equal measure.

"Hey, darling." With my hands full, I could only tip my chin up to her, which she correctly read as me needing her lips on mine, obliging me with a kiss which I felt deep in my groin. "Come, sit. Bell's nearly done then I'll make you coffee."

"I can make it." Her fingers brushed through my hair, "I'll be right back."

By the time she returned, Bell had finished, adding another impressive burp to her morning's achievements. She sat down with her coffee, placing a second one for me on the table.

"Thank you."

"You're welcome."

"How did you sleep?"

"All three hours?" She chuckled. "Like the dead."

"Three hours?" I feigned. Though surely it was more than that, but I knew exactly what had kept her up.

"Yes, three."

"We'll have to squeeze a nap in later."

She sipped her coffee. "Nope, not we, me. Just me. The two of us won't nap and I'll turn into a zombie."

"Sexy zombie." I placed Bell in her chair and pulled Kit onto my lap, needing to touch her somewhere, anywhere. I settled for wrapping my arms around her, which was the place least likely to lead me into trouble or temptation, or both.

"Murray, is it normal to have this much sex?"

I chuckled into her shoulder. "It's normal for us."

She turned to me. "I'm serious. Is this normal? It's never been like this for me, like I can't go five minutes without needing you inside me."

I tried not to laugh at how grave her face was. I personally didn't see a problem, but if she wanted me to take her seriously, then I would.

"No," I answered truthfully. "No, I've never had anything like this."

"Do you think there's something wrong with us?"

"Not in the slightest." She relaxed against me a fraction. "But I have a great cure if you're feeling anxious about it..." I waggled my eyebrows suggestively, receiving a deep eye roll in response.

She nestled back into me. "Shall we do something today? Let's go out. It's a beautiful day."

"I'm already way ahead of you."

"You are?" Her eyebrows shot up in surprise.

"I am..." I grinned. "I've ordered a picnic from the deli, which we're going to collect on our way to the park."

Her eyes, which were milk chocolate today, sparkled as she clapped her hands together. "That sounds perfect, thank you."

"You're welcome. Now if you'd care to go to the front door and retrieve the paper, we can fill out the crossword while we have some playtime with Bell. Then when she's napping, you and I have a date in the shower."

My lips found her neck and I didn't miss her pulse kick at the base of her throat before she ran to collect it.

"Now We Are Six, author?"

"Milne."

I printed out the letters into the boxes, reaching for a

baby tomato and threw it in my mouth before moving onto the next clue.

"Greek philosopher who said, 'Man is the Measure of All Things'?"

This time there was at least thirty seconds of thought before she answered, and I used that time to fill in the boxes. "I don't know."

"Ah, not so easy, that one."

She sat up slightly, peering at me underneath her dark sunglasses. "Do you know it?"

"I do."

She raised her eyebrow in disbelief.

"I do, it's Protagoras. It was one of Rafe's favorite quotes during college. That and 'When Men are Pure, Laws are Useless'. Rafe always used to quote them when he was being particularly obnoxious. I guarantee they've made it into more than one closing argument." I grinned at her and she lay back down.

We'd found the quietest spot in the park we could, harder than it sounded given that everyone in New York seemed to have the same idea we had on a sunny Saturday. Partially shaded by the umbrella I'd brought for Bell, we were all laid out on the large picnic blankets we'd spread on the ground. The deli had packed us an array of mini *everything*, along with a chilled bottle of champagne which we were half-way through. Barclay lay on the edge, under Bell's shade, hot from his lengthy exertions of chasing the ball.

"Next question."

"The most versatile word in the English language,"

Her eyes shot open, making me laugh loudly, then even louder when she snatched the paper from my hands. "It does not say that."

Her eyes narrowed at me, then opened wide in shock as a soccer ball came out of nowhere, narrowly missing Bell, lying in between us, and hitting me. I spun round in the direction it came from, ready to launch hell on whoever had such shitty aim. My temper subsided slightly when I saw a frazzled mum running over, towing a smallish child by his hand.

"I'm so sorry, are you okay?" she cried, and then noticed Bell in Kit's arms. "Oh no, did we hit her? Brandon," she turned to her child, "apologize please. You need to be more careful."

"I'm sorry," his lip quivered, on the verge of tears.

"Don't worry about it, bud. It's fine. No harm done, though maybe soccer school wouldn't be such a bad place for you."

He stared at me unblinking.

"I'm so sorry, again." His mom picked up the ball, then peered at Bell and Kit. "You have a beautiful family, your daughter is gorgeous. She looks just like you."

"Thank you. I do." I could already feel the heat of Kit's glare. "Anyway, see you around. Watch where you're kicking that thing next time, kiddo."

I took a breath before I turned to her. It wasn't like I was doing it on purpose. I barely even thought about the answer I gave, and I certainly wasn't about to explain my private life to a nosy passerby who couldn't keep comments to themselves. Either that or they were genuinely being polite.

"Don't look at me like that."

"Murray!"

I sighed. I pulled the pair of them onto my lap. "If it makes you feel better, I do it when I'm out with the boys too. People have no idea whether the three of us are in a relationship, so I always say thank you when someone compliments us. Penn won't carry Bell any more from the amount of times people have assumed we are."

She rolled her eyes at my teasing, and then moved off me, sitting so she could see me face on. Once she'd placed Bell on her tummy, she looked up.

"It doesn't actually. Murray, you've not been to work all week. We've been naked more than we've been clothed." She ran her hands through her hair, and I could see she was frustrated. Now, now was the time to have the awkward conversation I didn't want to have. "I just, we..."

As always when she was flustered, she struggled with getting her sentences together.

"Okay, we need to talk. I'm sorry, I know we should have spoken before now, but I didn't want to ruin anything."

Her eyes immediately filled with horror and unshed tears. "Oh."

"Hey, hey." I pulled her back to my lap. "What's wrong? Why are you crying?"

"I'm not," she sniffed, rubbing her nose. "Are you about to end this, or break up with me? Or something?"

"What?" The idea of ending anything with her was utterly absurd. "No, of course I'm not!"

She sniffed again. "Okay. Why do I get the impression there's a 'but' coming?"

"There isn't a 'but'. However..."

She groaned. And not the type of groan I'd become accustomed to the last week.

"However," I continued, "do you remember the contract you signed when you came to work for me?"

She nodded over the words I'd come to hate. I swallowed away the anxiety creeping into my throat.

"In it there was a clause about us not sleeping together. Which we... well, I've broken. And Rafe's been on my case about it."

She turned in my lap. "What does that mean?"

"It means we shouldn't be together while you're working for me."

Fuck, this was coming out worse than it sounded in my head.

"So, you're firing me?"

"No. I want you here. I want you here with Bell and me."

She moved away again, her expression skeptical. "So you want me to work for you for free?"

I snapped, standing up, pacing as I thought. Not that I had anything to think about, I knew exactly what I wanted. "No, I don't want you to work for me. I want you to live with us. I want you to be my girlfriend. I don't want a fucking contract!"

She stared at me, her thick lashes almost brushing past her eyebrows with how wide her eyes had open.

"You're asking me to move in with you?"

"No, you already moved in. I'm asking you to stay, as my girlfriend."

"And my job?"

I knelt in front of her, brushing her hair out of her face. "I'll support you for as long as you need or want. You can take your time to find the job you love. I'll still pay you for the entire time; you won't lose out on anything."

Her single raised eyebrow told me I'd not exactly said the right thing.

I waited far too long for her to speak, but I was too scared of opening my mouth to say something else fucking stupid. But I'd done it now, I'd put it out there so I just had to wait and ride the wave.

"Okay, we can tear up the contract. Or change it, or whatever you want, whatever we have to do to it." She smiled softly.

I yanked her forward once more into my lap, crushing my lips to hers in victory. But she hadn't finished speaking, and slowly pushed me back with a hand on my sinking chest.

"The moving in, I need to think about. It's a lot."

I didn't really think it was a lot at all, we already lived together; the rest were semantics, and she was my girlfriend. But I wasn't going to say that, because she could have whatever she wanted and I would give it to her, as long as it meant we were together.

"Okay." I kissed her again, more gently this time, softening my mouth to hers as it molded round her lips, eager to lighten the mood which seemed to have appeared like an errant raincloud on an otherwise sunny day. "Hey, you know, I've been thinking…"

"Oh, yeah?"

"Yes, about the Columbia job."

"Oh?"

"Working there gives you access to the library. And I'll get us into Harvard. We could make it our mission to have sex in all the major libraries of the world." She gasped in shock, making me laugh so hard my ribs ached. "Shit, even thinking about it now is giving me a boner. Who knew dusty old books could be such a turn on?"

She snatched her hand back as I tried to place it on my dick so she could see the evidence.

"I'm not taking the Columbia job to hook up in the library."

"But still, a good reason to put on the pro list." I winked.

At some point over the last month, she'd mentioned the offer from Columbia. We'd been talking about what she wanted to do with her degree and I'd started a pros and cons list for her, to help her decide.

I was very firmly pro the Columbia job, and it had nothing to do with the library. She deserved that job, she'd earned it through hard work and being fucking smart, and I'd told her on more than one occasion it was stupid to wait until she found something else. I'd long decided that it was the smart move to make, she didn't need to hedge any bets with this one. The Columbia job would set her up for life, even if she didn't want to stay there, it would open up jobs that nothing else would. The only selfish part of me that wanted her to take it was the one that meant she'd be close to me, to us, to our home, something I was more in favor of daily. But I wasn't about to say that either.

"I'll consider adding it to the pro list."

I held my hands up. "That's all I'm asking for, darling."

She smiled, her eyes twinkling, and I knew I was on the way to being forgiven.

"Hey, you excited about tomorrow?"

"The Met party?"

I nodded, "Yeah, although it's not really a party. More a gathering of snooty rich people, but the boys will be there so it'll be fun."

Her head tilted slightly. "The invitation said gala. Or is that just the word snooty rich people use for party? Also, aren't you a snooty rich person?"

"No, I'm just rich," I poked her in the ribs, making her screech loudly. "But I do have an additional surprise for us."

"Oh yeah, what?"

"Hmmmm, that's odd." My brows creased as deeply as I could get them. "For someone who's so good at the crossword, I'm alarmed you don't know the meaning of the word 'surprise'."

Her lips pursed. "Don't be a smartass."

"I thought you liked my smart ass."

She reached round to pinch it. "No, I just like your ass."

"Speaking of, let's go home. Bell's due for a nap and then you can have as much of my ass as you'd like."

She jumped up, packing as quickly as possible while I did nothing but laugh at her.

"Careful what you wish for, Murray Williams."

The only thing I was wishing for was her. And I had no plans to be careful about that at all.

19

KIT

"This dress is really stunning. I can't believe you've never worn it before." Payton took the hanger, carrying my vintage Dior floor length dress over to the mirror and held it in front of herself.

Payton had come over to help me get ready for the gala. She was also lending her babysitting skills, sleeping over in my room. The room next to Bell's, my old room before Murray had moved me into his, although the majority of my stuff was still in here. In the reflection of my dressing table mirror, I could see her twirling around, the intricate beading along the neckline catching the light.

I'd seen it three years ago in a thrift store in Greenwich Village, although it had still cost me a month's rent. I'd needed to wait until the next month so I could have it tailored to my body. I'd never had an opportunity to wear it, given I didn't tend to go to parties where the dress code was a floor length gown, not that tonight's was either, but I knew Murray was wearing a tux, so I figured this would complement it nicely.

Thankfully, I hadn't changed size since then, which was a

miracle in itself given I'd survived on a diet of Krispy Kreme's and breadsticks during my finals.

"I know, but it's not exactly brunch then shopping attire. Or drinks at the bar."

"I dunno; you'd turn a few heads, that's for sure." She put the dress back on the closet door. "I've brought six pairs of shoes, so you can decide which ones you want."

"Thank you, you're a lifesaver." I was attempting to perfect my make-up to the *natural beauty* look, even though I'd spent two hours getting the eyeliner right. I'd also coaxed my hair into Hollywood curls, which would sit over one shoulder, leaving the other bare thanks to the asymmetrical neckline.

"Do you know what's going to happen tonight?"

I flicked the end of the liner along my lashes. "Murray said it's a bunch of snooty rich people standing around. But I'm sure we'll see the exhibit too."

"That sounds fun! And it's so cool that you get to see it before everyone else, without having to wait in line. It's like your dream come true," she laughed.

I tried not to laugh while I was applying mascara, because with my luck, I'd end up with the wand in my eye. "I know."

"How's life in the love bubble?"

I put the wand back in the tube. "It's good..."

She got up from the couch in the corner and perched on the edge of the dressing table. "Good?" She elongated the vowels almost like a sneer. "Good?"

"Yes. Good."

"Okay, what's wrong with him?"

"Nothing. Nothing's wrong with him. He's totally perfect, and sweet and kind. And hot."

God, so hot.

Her finger swirled in front of me. "Then what's with the face?"

I stopped what I was doing and looked up at her. I placed

the mascara down with a heavy sigh. "The chemistry, the sex, it's off the charts. I can't get enough of him and him of me. I'm so insanely attracted to him, but what if that's all this is? It's happened so quickly that I'm tied up in knots trying to figure it out. But I forget literally everything when he's around."

She looked at me like I was a little crazy, which was fair, because I'd been thinking that perhaps I was. "I started crying yesterday when I thought he was going to break up with me. I feel like I've lost my mind."

"What? He broke up with you?" She jumped up, outraged.

"No, he didn't. I just thought he was."

The crazy look came back. "What did he do instead?"

"He asked me to move in with him and be his girlfriend."

"But you already live here."

I shook my head. "Not as his girlfriend, as his nanny. That's the other thing; he doesn't want me to be his nanny, so technically he fired me but he's still giving me the money, or something, I dunno." I'd honestly tried not to think about it. The whole situation was giving me heartburn.

She frowned. "And what about Bell?"

"He said he'd get a new nanny, and I could figure out what I wanted to do."

She picked up my blusher brush and started running it over her face. "Whoa."

"I know. I'm not going crazy, right? It's a lot?"

"I mean…"

"Pay," I interrupted before she could disagree with me. "Even if I wasn't living here already, we've known each other less than three months. That's quick to move in together, isn't it? Everything is heightened and intense; it's been freaking me out."

"No, really? I couldn't tell." She crossed her arms over her chest. "Why do you care if the sex is so good?"

"What if it's only about sex?" I chewed down on my lip,

not wanting to spill what I really thought, but knowing it was going to come out anyway. "Sometimes, I feel like he's created this ready-made family. I'm working for him because Freddie and Wolf thought I'd make a good girlfriend, and now I am his girlfriend. It's all been mapped out and I haven't had a say in anything."

I thought she'd talk me down off my ledge, but like the best friend she was, she supported my craziness.

"It does sound a little full on. What d'you mean about the crazy girls?"

I groaned. "Basically, they set us up. They hired me because they wanted us to be together."

He jaw dropped open. "Wow, no wonder you're freaked out. It is kind of romantic though. Think about what you'll tell your grandchildren while you're counting all your money."

"Pay…" I whined.

She ignored me and continued her roll. "He's going to get a shock though, he only knows you to live with as a nanny. Once he stops paying you… I mean, does he know what you're like to live with really? Does he know how messy you are?" she grinned.

"I know you think you're funny, but this is my point."

She frowned. "Kit, do you want to be his girlfriend? Because the way you're talking sounds like you don't."

It was a question I knew the answer to without hesitation.

"Yes, I do."

"Then what's the issue?"

I stood up, dropping my towel as I did and picked my dress off the hanger. "I don't want to move in by default because I already live here. I want it to be on equal terms. I'm always going to be the nanny if I stay here."

"What are you saying?"

I stepped into my dress, zipping as much as I could. "I don't know. It's like he never stops to consider things, just takes what he wants and I feel like this is the same. I can't think when he's around, it's like he fogs my brain with his beauty and I can't say no."

"Hot, rich man, asks you to be his girlfriend, asks you to move in with him. Yeah, sucks to be you."

I pursed my lips. "Okay, why are you here?"

"To give you my unwavering support, and bring you shoes." She passed me a pair of dark green satin Manolos, which fastened with a jeweled buckle.

"Thank you." I hopped about on one foot as I tried to find the balance to put it on, followed by the other. "You can stay for the shoes but don't worry about the support."

"Great, I knew you'd see sense."

I turned my back to her. "Do the rest of my zipper please."

She obliged then spun me round by the shoulders, gasping as she got a proper look at me.

"Oh, Kit. You are so beautiful. No wonder he wants to whip you off the market." She hugged me tight with a lot of care not to crush my dress or ruin my hair.

"Thank you." I ran my hands down my dress, purposely snug against my curves and in a shade of peach which made my skin seem as golden as Murray's.

"Enjoy yourself tonight, don't stress about anything. You have loads of time to figure this out, and think of all the hot sex you'll have while you do."

I gave her a sly smile. "Yep."

"You're a lucky bitch, even if you are crazy. Good job I love you or I'd hate you."

"Come on, let's go."

I smelled him before we opened the door, the heady, woody scent coating my synapses so they were more finely tuned to him than usual. I found him with his hand raised ready to knock, and my core clenched so tight it was like I'd been punched. He was standing there, my very own James Bond, in the sharpest custom tux fitting his body like a second skin, emphasizing the muscles I knew so well. He was the best-looking man I'd ever seen.

Maybe I *was* crazy. How could I not want to be with him twenty-four seven?

"Whoa, holy fuck," Payton announced with absolutely no tact.

"My sentiments exactly," replied Murray, whose eyes hadn't left mine, the back of his hand brushing my cheek.

"Jesus, you two are sickeningly good looking."

"I know we are." Murray turned to her with the utmost seriousness before breaking into a wide, toothy grin which only added to his Hollywood looks.

Her head flicked to mine. "Seriously, just marry the guy."

Murray's laugh was loud and belly shaking, in total contrast to the murderous glare I shot her. He pulled me into him and kissed my head. "One step at a time, but I'm glad you approve."

She grinned at me, taking no notice of the daggers I was firing her way.

"Thanks for coming, Payton, we really appreciate it. I've put Bell down and left out her bottle in case she wakes up, but she should be fine. Barclay's been fed, and Graham on the front desk will be up to take him out. Help yourself to anything you want, or call down to Graham and he'll order something in."

That got her attention. She tried to act nonchalant, but her eyes still said *holy fuck*. "Thank you, I'll be fine. I'm just going to catch up on some Netflix and eat ice-cream in bed."

I smirked, because even a babysitting stint wouldn't break Payton's Sunday night ritual of her version of Netflix and chill. "Sounds good to me, but should we all leave and walk downstairs?"

Murray checked his watch, "Yes, we need to go or we'll be late."

"For the big surprise?"

"Exactly. Except…" He made a show of checking me over as though taking the role of an expert tailor, then reached into his inner pocket, pulling out a dark red box, and opened it. "You're missing something."

Payton's gasped echoed mine, both of which could have been heard across the Park, and followed with another *holy fuck*. I, myself, was speechless and partially blinded by the sparkle on the long, drop earrings, where tiny links of pavé held a diamond the size of a grape. I peered back up at Murray, his eyes eager and seeking approval.

"I don't know what to say."

He chuckled, removing one and, with the greatest care, fastened it in my lobe, followed by the other. I rolled my thumbs over the clasps, testing the security of them, not daring to move in case they fell from the weight. The true weight of them, however, felt significantly more than the considerable carats they actually were, in the heaviness and confusion sitting in the center of my heart. But as always, the confusion was blinded by his brilliance and maybe it didn't matter, maybe nothing mattered except him and me.

"They're beyond stunning. Thank you." Even in my heels I needed to reach on my tiptoes to kiss him.

"No, you're beyond stunning. These are merely shiny."

"Marry. Him." Payton hissed loudly in my newly shiny ear, killing any moment we were having.

My hand was still clutched in his and resting on his lap, where it had been the entire journey, as the Range Rover pulled up outside a door on the east side of The Met.

"This is the surprise? Aren't we supposed to be here anyway?" I winked at him.

"Stop being a smart arse." He leaned over for a quick

smack of my lips, but not so quick that it didn't leave a hint of the cherry red lipstick I was wearing.

I wiped it off with my thumb. "I learned from the best."

The driver opened his door and Murray hopped out, running around to open my door for me, extending his hand so I could step down without toppling.

"Thank you."

"No, thank you. I'm so fucking lucky to be here with you on my arm. These events are so dull usually. You look blindingly beautiful tonight, Miss Hawkes. It's really very unfair on all the other guests, not to mention the artwork. Everyone will be staring at you."

The familiar heat of a blush rose through me, warming me from my toes to the ends of my hair, which had miraculously stayed in place. I still hadn't gotten used to all the compliments he bestowed on me.

"Thank you. You don't look so bad yourself," which was the understatement of the century.

"I think Payton summed us up well then." He kissed my cheek as I noticed a man walking toward us. "I like her a lot. She seems fun."

Payton and Murray were actually very similar, which might have something to do with why I was so comfortable with him. Always joking, never taking life too seriously, not to mention their love of winding me up.

"She has her moments."

I turned to the man as he reached us. From a distance, it looked like he'd been dressed in suit, but up close, I could see it was the uniform of The Met officials.

"Mr. Williams, Miss Hawkes," the man greeted us, Murray shaking his outstretched hand. "I'm Todd Palmerson, the head curator of The Met. Welcome to the museum."

"Thank you, Todd. I'm Murray, this is Kit. We appreciate you accommodating us before the rest of the guests arrive. It's very kind."

"Not at all, we're always delighted to have fans of our work here."

Murray's hand pressed into the small of my back. "Kit's the fan; she comes to all the exhibits."

My head was moving back and forth between them. We were here to see the launch of the new exhibit, so I didn't quite understand what was going on.

"Let's go in, shall we?" Todd swept his arm out in front of us, guiding us to the open doorway.

We followed him through, walking up a sloped floor and into the massive atrium, where museum event staff were busying themselves, putting the finishing touches to the evening's festivities. Hundreds of champagne bottles were lined up along a table, alongside hundreds of fine stemmed flutes.

"How many people are coming tonight?" I whispered to Murray.

"Not sure. There's usually a few hundred at these things."

"Oh." I looked up at the enormous flags hanging from the ceiling, all adorned with images from the Picasso exhibit, and Penn's family name.

I'd been so busy watching what everyone else was doing that I hadn't noticed we'd continued walking or where we were as Todd stopped before the entrance to another huge room. Collecting two thick, glossy bound books, he handed one to each of us. It was a guide to the exhibit.

"These are for you. They detail every painting you'll see tonight, along with the history of Picasso and each period of his life, his influences, his loves, and his many varied achievements. This is the first time we've had a showing of this magnitude in the United States, so it's very exciting for us." His face became more animated with each sentence.

"Thank you." Murray took the guides.

"Murray, what's going on?"

He turned to me. "We're seeing it first, before everyone

else. I wanted you to be the first to see it, and Todd is going to show us round."

"Murray..." I blinked through the moisture rapidly filling my eyes, before they spilled over and smudged all my carefully applied eyeliner, and lashings of mascara. He was the sweetest, most thoughtful man I'd ever met.

I'd meant what I'd said to Payton earlier, I did want to be his girlfriend, more than anything.

He smiled his perfect smile, "Oh, tears. That means I did a good job, hopefully."

I laughed them away, "You did. I can't believe how much you're spoiling me. Thank you."

"You're welcome." He took my hand again and we followed Todd into the gallery.

The walls of the first room we entered were filled with enormous canvases depicting abstract shapes of women painted in bright, primary colors and blocks of shade. Todd walked ahead, talking about Picasso's expressiveness; his years experimenting with sculpture and pencils; his creation of Cubism, which we were viewing now; his mistresses. I listened intently as we moved from room to room, taking in as much as I could, while Murray held my hand tightly.

We were standing in front of what looked like a cartoon octopus when I remembered why we were here.

"Which ones are Penn's?" I leaned closer to Murray.

"I don't know actually." He retrieved his phone from his breast pocket and typed out a message. Before he had time to put it back, it chimed with a response.

"What did he say?"

"He doesn't know." His wry smile told me Penn had typed more than a simple 'no'.

I looked at him, my nose scrunched in confusion; Murray tilted the screen to me so I could see it.

Penn: *Some naked chick with massive tits, a blob, and something else I can't remember*

My hand flew up too late to stifle the laugh, interrupting Todd mid lecture and receiving a strange look in the process.

Moving into the final room, one single gargantuan canvas completed the tour. The blue, black, and white shapes depicted the Spanish Civil War, and we stood in silence staring at it while Todd told us about the cultural importance of Guernica.

I'd never been in a museum alone. I'd never experienced a museum without the bustle of tourists fighting over who could get closest to the exhibits. It was incredible and affecting and made so much more special because it had been arranged for me, by Murray.

I tilted my chin up to his, angling for a kiss, which he only too happily obliged. "Thank you. Thank you so much for this. It was amazing."

He kissed me again, his eyes shining like emeralds. "Anything for you, Columbia."

I'd almost forgotten we weren't alone when Todd cleared his throat. "That's the end, I'm afraid. I do hope you enjoyed it."

I spun round to his eager face, my hands clasping his. "It was wonderful. Thank you for taking us around. I feel so lucky to have seen it, especially as I didn't manage to get tickets before they sold out."

"You're very welcome." His cheeks glowed with a pale tint before he reached into his pocket and handed over a business card to me. "Please do call me if you ever want to come to anything again. We'll sort you out with tickets."

I took it silently.

"I think you've made her day," Murray added, given I was a little speechless, holding the card for *THE* head curator of The Met, the guy that oversaw every exhibit.

He guided us back out to where the first few guests were milling around in the atrium, glass of champagne in hand.

"Darling, unless you're desperate to walk the red carpet, let's stay in here and get drunk. The boys will be here soon."

I shook my head so hard the diamonds almost bruised my chin. "No, I'm not."

He grinned, leading me over to a nearby waiter with a full tray of drinks, who hadn't yet spotted us. "Good, didn't think so. Thank you for being here with me." His glass clinked against mine, before taking a sip.

Another influx of people walked into the swiftly filling room, but this cluster was different to everyone else, set apart by the way people reverentially moved for them to pass, parting as they might for Beyoncé or other celebrities who'd reached the same echelons of fame. As they neared, I realized at the center of the parting sea were Rafe and Penn, followed by several museum officials, almost running alongside them as they strode over to where we were standing.

They were as resplendent as Murray in his tux, tall and broad, looking like they'd been born to wear it; as they did with all clothes, but they were nowhere near as handsome, as beautiful, or as striking as Murray.

"Muzzer, looking fantastic as always." Rafe smacked him on the back, pulling him into a big hug, Penn going in next like it hadn't been mere hours since they'd last seen each other. "Kit, you're also looking very beautiful." They both kissed my cheek.

"Thank you," I grinned. One of the things I loved most about Murray was his friendship with these two.

Huh. Loved. *Loved.*

"You okay? You look like you've just remembered you left brownies in the oven or something."

I shook my head, with a broad smile. "No, no I'm all good. Didn't leave the oven on."

I scanned the room, which now seemed to be at capacity, volume levels rising along with the thick odor of immense wealth. Everyone in this room was somebody, although none of them seemed to be less interested yet most in demand for attention than the three men I was with, given that every thirty seconds someone interrupted us. And not once did Murray let go of my hand, or fail to introduce me as his girlfriend. Not once did he make me feel less than the most important person in the room.

As groups peeled off to tour the exhibit, two exceptionally beautiful and impossibly glamorous women joined us, making my spine stiffen almost as hard as it had when I'd opened the door to Satan's Mistress. Except these two didn't look like someone was wafting shit under their noses, and with the way the tall brunette pinched Penn's arm, hard, making him jump with a squeal, I'd hazard a guess that she didn't want to sleep with him either unless it was a new, very bizarre flirting technique I hadn't yet read about in Cosmo.

"Hello, troubles," she drawled in an international accent I couldn't place. Not quite as English as Murray's, but not as American as Penn or Rafe, who both greeted her with a kiss to the cheek, although Penn's not filled with quite as much warmth while he rubbed his arm.

"God, who allowed you entry?" Murray let go of me for the first time and pulled her into an enormous hug, which, to my relief, was the same as the hugs he gave to Freddie and Wolf. As soon as he released her, his hand took mine again. "Laurie, this is Kit, my girlfriend." He turned to me. "Darling, this is Lauren, Penn's youngest sister."

"I'm still older than him." She pinned him with a look. "Kit, it's amazing to meet you, finally. I've heard so much about you."

My head jolted back in surprise, which Murray noticed. "She's heard nothing."

She side-eyed him then grinned, kissing my cheek, her arms wrapping around me with a big squeeze as though we'd known each other years and I liked her immediately. "You're right, I haven't at all. But I can't believe Murray was the first of the Tuesday Club boys to fall. Hell must have frozen over." She waved her champagne glass around, before nudging Rafe. "Which one of you is next? Rafey boy, who do you think? Probably you, seeing as there is no one brave enough to take on my brother, right?"

Rafe merely raised an eyebrow, not willing to engage in this chat.

"Kit," Lauren grabbed the other girl's hand and pulled her over. Her hair was a shade of blonde so white and shiny there's no way it came from a bottle; she was either descended from angels or the Scandinavians. I also didn't miss the very thorough assessment Penn gave her. Granted, I'd never seen Penn around a woman before, but I was fairly sure that this look was not the usual look he gave to women. "This is my best friend in the world, Lowe Slater."

"Hello, it's so lovely to meet you." Like Lauren, she greeted me with a hug that almost realigned my spine. "Laurie told me you're the first to infiltrate this group. Congratulations, and about time, although I haven't seen the boys in a while."

Laurie halted a passing waiter in his tracks and relieved him of three full glasses of champagne, swapping out our empty ones.

"Thank you."

"God, these events are so boring. The best thing about them is getting drunk."

I was going to take her word for it, seeing as this was the first one I'd been to, but even then, it did seem like a lot of people just standing around telling each other how great they were, except the group I was in. If I've learned anything about Murray and his friends, it was how seriously they took their work, yet absolutely nothing else.

"Do you come to them a lot?"

"More than I'd like, that's for sure. But you know, it's family," she said with a shrug. "I always drag Lowe along though, one of the consequences of having been best friends since we were kids."

Lowe nudged her playfully. "Kit, tell us about yourself. How did you meet Murray?"

I shifted, slightly uncomfortably. It was the first time I'd been asked this question and it was the first time we'd been out as a couple, so I should have been more mentally prepared.

"I nanny for Bell, his daughter."

Lowe's face lit up, but it wasn't in judgment. "Oh! I didn't realize that was you. Have you two met already then?" She pointed between Laurie and me.

Laurie shook her head, "No, although I can't believe we haven't," She turned to me, "I'm her pediatrician, Doctor James. I met her when she first arrived with Murray, but I haven't seen her for a month. Bet she's grown."

My jaw dropped, because I had her on speed dial in my cell, even though I'd never needed to use it, and Murray had taken her for all check-ups. "You're Doctor James?"

She took in my confusion, "Not expecting that, were you?"

No, no I wasn't. Not because there was no reason why she wouldn't be a doctor, but I'd never seen such an effortlessly dazzling one, and I also knew Penn's surname. "Do you and Penn not have the same name?"

"We do, but I use James which is our grandmother's maiden name. It makes things easier when your surname is literally written across the tops of hospitals. I work for the medical arm of the company, so it stops immediate accusations of nepotism and people hating me." She winked. "I'd rather they hated me for a legitimate reason."

She was way too likable for anyone to hate, and I suddenly thought how much Payton would like her too. The phrase *house on fire* sprang to mind.

"Wow, that's really awesome. Now I'm sad we haven't met before."

"We'll rectify that immediately. Let's the three of us go out for cocktails this week."

"I'd love that. I have a friend I can bring too; you'll love her."

"And to think we almost skipped this one." She linked her arms through both mine and Lowe's. "Come on, let's have some fun tonight and leave the boys to their very boring conversation."

Murray glanced over from his current boring conversation with the boys, throwing me a wink as she dragged us away.

The rest of the evening flew by and then it was midnight; my new partners-in-crime including me in everything they did, which I appreciated more than they knew. I'd never wanted to be one of those girlfriends who needed babysitting, and even if they hadn't been here, I wouldn't have needed one, but Murray would have felt obliged.

His arm roped around my waist, and his lips found my temple. "Have you had fun tonight?"

I smiled up at him, relaxing into his embrace. "I have, a lot. Have you?"

His eyes warmed more than they already were. "Yes, but I'm ready to leave. I want you alone now. I've had enough of sharing you with the room."

If we didn't have to say goodbye to everyone I'd have hauled him to the waiting car there and then. "Let's go."

The driver got us home in record time and we burst through the doors of his apartment, lips glued together, clothing partially unzipped.

"Upstairs. I don't want to wake up Payton and have to chat for half an hour. I need inside you. Now," he growled in my ear, increasing the goosebumps already pebbling my skin, almost carrying me as he strode through the hallway. Clearly, I wasn't walking quickly enough.

He kicked his bedroom door shut, stopping in the middle of the room, confusion slashing through the lust in his eyes as I pushed him away when he tried to remove my dress.

"No. It's my turn."

His eyes followed the direction of my dress as it dropped, before they rose back to my exposed bolt-tight nipples. I left it where it landed, moving toward him with the same slow predatory gait he used on me, his pants tightening with every step I took. His breath hitched as I reached out, cupping him through the finely woven wool, rubbing him as he grew hard as the diamonds still glittering in my ears. On a loud groan I unzipped his pants, releasing his impressive cock, and sank to the floor.

I wanted him. I wanted to bring him to his knees in the way he brought me to mine every damn day.

I wanted to give him everything

A sharp hiss reverberated through his body as he sucked in air through his teeth when I licked off the glistening pearl drop from the tip of his dick, before swallowing him down in one, a steel rod encased in the softest satin. His fingers threaded through my hair, collecting it in his hand, the knuckles on his other hand stroking along my jaw.

"Fuck, Kit… baby I need you to stop."

I sucked harder and the groan he let out was dirty and raw, hitting my clit like an arrow to a bullseye. My tongue flickered along the underside and he gave me ten more seconds, his balls tightening with each one, until he forced me off with a pop and threw me on the bed. He took his time removing his clothes. I was already very familiar with the particular clench of the jaw he was exhibiting right now, the one that told me he was so close to the edge he needed to gather himself. But I didn't want him to gather himself; I wanted him to lose control, completely.

I rid myself of my panties. "Murray, come here please."

He crawled over me, holding his body inches from mine, his biceps straining under his stillness. The smell of his testosterone, rich, musky, and dark, seeped into my airways as I breathed him in, making me lightheaded.

"Lift up your knees." His nose was almost touching mine, his irises so dark with lust the fine line where they met his pupils was indiscernible.

I held my knees in place, crying out as he shifted slightly then drove into me with one smooth, purposeful thrust. His composure never wavered, but the throbbing at the vein in his temple matched the throbbing of my vagina, fluttering around him as I held onto my orgasm with all the strength I could gather.

His massive thighs spread my knees further, one of his hands gathering both of mine and holding them tight above my head, then moved back, sliding until I felt the cool breeze of too much space between us.

He stole my breath as he plunged forward, harder than before. "Do you know how many people were watching you tonight?"

He eased back, thrusting again, so forcefully I thought he might split me in half. "All of them, wanting what's mine."

I couldn't move, still pinned underneath him as he asserted total control. The control I wanted him to lose.

His jaw clenched firm. "I'm used to people wanting what I have, but I've never cared about it until I saw everyone wanting you."

He was shaking, so close to the edge but determined to hold on as long as he could.

I finally found my voice. "Tell me, baby. Show me."

I was desperately trying to stave off what I knew was about to ruin me forever. Who was I kidding? He'd ruined me for any other man the day I'd knocked on the door.

He reared up, finally releasing my hands; only to move

my thighs so far apart I could have qualified for the Olympic gymnastics team. His hair fell over his forehead, loosening from stroke after punishing stroke, each one leaving me more ragged than the last.

The blood in my veins was crashing hard against the dam wall, leaking through the tiny cracks which were growing bigger with every demanding thrust of his dick rubbing against my G-spot, hitting my cervix until I couldn't hold on any longer. I was ripped apart, destroyed by the force of him, the force of *us*, and I clenched him hard with each convulsion until he lost his own control, collapsing against me with a groan which tipped me into another orgasm.

"Mother fucker!" he roared into my neck, gently licking the sweat beading at the base of my throat, before he fell to the side pulling me to rest on top of him. "I don't think I have any dick left."

His fingers combed through my hair, detangling the mess of waves. My palm lay flat on his chest, his heart beat slowing under my touch as his breathing evened out.

"Thank you for tonight, for everything you did for me. I had so much fun."

He kissed the top of my head. "You're welcome."

My eyelids fluttered, trying to stay open as his soft breathing levelled out into his own sleep.

"Kit?"

My neck tipped back so I could look at him and I found his green eyes glowing and earnest. "Yes?"

"I love you."

My heart stalled mid pump, before kick-starting so hard I thought it was the early onset of a heart attack. I reminded myself to blink as I stared at him.

"I love you so much, and I can't stop it. There's an ache in my chest with your name on it that only disappears when we're together. I meant what I said - I would have killed everyone in that room tonight if they'd tried to take you from me."

I was all too familiar with that feeling, every single atom in me tuned to him and nothing else when he was around. I loved him. I had no doubt about it.

"I love you, too. I know I never answered, but yes, I'll be your girlfriend."

The smile he gave me lit up the darkened room better than if the sun had been shining her beams directly onto the bed. His hand fisted the back of my head, as he lifted up off the pillow and met my lips with a kiss which totally lacked any finesse, but made up for it a hundredfold with the passion sparking through it.

He loved me and I loved him.

The rest we'd figure out.

Hopefully.

20

MURRAY

Her delicious body curled into mine, lit by a single beam of light that had crept through a gap in the thick blinds. Her peachy ass fit perfectly into the curve of my thighs as I big spooned into her little spoon. The faint shadows of her rib cage darkened then lightened with every steady breath.

She was perfection.

Never in my life had I imagined I'd meet someone like her; so *lassez-faire*, so vibrant and calm, with the biggest heart and kindest soul. It never occurred to me that anyone else I'd been with previously hadn't been, but she'd upped the ante the second I'd laid eyes on her, and now it was perfectly clear why I'd never been in a relationship… I was waiting for her.

Her and Bell.

My life was complete without me even realizing it.

Last night, she'd outshone the diamonds hanging from her ears, and I'd seen every single pair of eyes follow her as she passed. All night, my blood had been charged with an overwhelming possessiveness which would have had me kill anyone who'd tried to take her away from me – or at least deliver a swift punch to the face - and knowing we'd be going home together? My heart had swollen so big I was amazed it hadn't broken through my rib cage.

A low hum escaped her lips as my dick thumped against her, because he was less patient about letting her sleep. She shifted against me and he took it as a sign to poke her, hard. As I began lightly tracing the soft dip of her waist with my fingertips, her leg moved back and hooked over mine twisting her body toward me, urging my dick forward.

The white noise of the baby monitor was broken with a shriek. I froze, to see if it was followed by another one, which it was. My daughter was cock blocking me for what was the first, and I guessed wouldn't be the last, time.

My lips brushed her shoulder. "I'll go."

"No, I will."

"No, you stay in bed. I'll have your overflowing coffee ready when you're down and we can pick this up later."

Then we both froze. It took a second for us to recognize the voice coming through the monitor app and remember that Payton was here.

Kit turned to me, eyes open wide. "Fuck, yes. What a genius idea it was to have her sleep over."

My phone clattered to the floor as I tried to switch the monitor off as quickly as I could, pulling her back into me, nibbling into her neck. "How long do you think I can get her to stay so we can remain right here?"

She answered with a gasp, my palm sliding over her stomach, down to the hot, smooth skin between her thighs, already slick, and waiting for me. Her head fell back against my shoulder when two of my fingers slipped over her hard, sensitive clit, and into her soft warm pussy, winning myself a groan so low and gravelly it would have stripped me bare if I hadn't already been naked. The noises I could get this woman to make almost had me coming before she'd even touched me.

I hooked her leg further over mine, my fingers slipping

free, but her maneuver now had my cock nudging her entrance, pushing just enough so she could feel my tip throbbing. But, I eased back, as she fluttered around me.

"Don't tease me," she moaned.

Gathering her hair in my free hand, I ignored her request and repeated the movement, as torturous for me as it was for her, but I needed to prolong it somehow, or I'd be coming in seconds.

I brushed so lightly over her pebbled nipples she'd have felt more of a breeze, until I rolled one between my fingers.

"Murray, please..."

I felt her begging deep in my balls, and holding her in place I lifted her leg up under my arm, thrusting into her in one swift movement, swallowing her cry as she slanted her mouth up to reach mine. The feeling of being inside her, of being owned by her hot, wet, velvety pussy was something else entirely; an experience I could happily have twenty-four hours a day and yet it wouldn't be nearly enough.

The lazy, sensual morning fuck I'd woken up wanting went up in the flames we always set our bed alight with as she pulled away and moved to her knees, her ass high in the air.

"I see I need to take things into my own hands," she sassed me, with a slow swipe of her tongue across my open, astounded mouth.

In less than a second, I gathered myself and slammed back inside her with such force the painting above the bed rattled against the wall, and I swear a few teeth loosened. I stilled us both until the pounding echoing between our already sweat soaked bodies lessened.

"Is this what you had in mind?" I clenched my jaw, trying to halt the adrenaline powering through me at a punishing speed. My body was not in sync with what my mind was trying to accomplish – a little savoring of this incredible sensation. Neither was hers; the soft clenching of her pussy already trying to milk me for every drop of cum I had to give her.

She nodded, unable to speak.

I slapped her ass, leaving a pink hand print which swelled my already very swollen dick. "What have I told you about fucking waiting?"

Her pussy squeezed me again, and I held back the groan I wanted to let out. Instead, I fisted a thick handful of her silky curls, tugging her back until I could breathe in every moan that escaped her luscious lips.

"You're coming when I say you are."

Keeping hold of her hair, I moved back, my fingers trailing along the ridges of her concave spine until they reached the tip of her crack. I palmed her ass cheeks, holding her as I watched my dick disappear inside her hot, tight walls, stretching her out with slow, measured thrusts which had her mewling loudly. Her juices soaked us both, slicking through her ass to her dusky pink asshole lubing her up perfectly, my thumb pressing firmly against it until it broke the barrier of puckered skin.

"All I wanted was a leisurely morning fuck..." I thrust into her, "to make love to my girlfriend…" thrust, "worship her body in my own time…" thrust, "and she thinks she can take control."

I slammed into her so hard it forced her forward, her scream muffled by the pillow. "But I own this pussy. I own your orgasms, and you're going to be coming so fucking hard you won't be able to see straight, let alone walk, but it'll be when I say you can."

Her legs trembled under my touch, her walls fluttering before an iron tight grip on my cock kicked up the pace. My balls strained to stay whole from the electricity zapping along my spine, and I began driving into her with purpose, my only goal to deliver on the promise that it wouldn't be stars she'd be seeing, I'd create fucking meteors.

"Murray!" she cried, trying to lift herself up, but I was driving her so hard she could only grip the sheets around her.

My thumb pulsed into her ass with every thrust of my cock, tightening her already exquisitely snug pussy. Her hips pushed back onto me, still needing more than I was giving her, until I let loose, frenzied, pummeling, wanting her to feel every single cell in my body, like I could feel hers pumping through my veins and jamming in my heart.

"Now, baby. Fucking now. Come on me." I couldn't hold on any longer, roaring through my orgasm as she ripped it from me with violent convulsions, renting the air as she cried my name.

We lay there, panting, as if we'd just run the New York City marathon in record breaking time, and I found myself tuning into the heavy beating of her heart as our breathlessness steadied. Her heart, part owner of mine.

"Holy shit!" Peals of her throaty laughter broke the silence. "That was some wake up call."

I eased myself out of her, my semi hard dick objecting to the sudden rush of cool air. "Are you saying I'm better than an alarm clock?"

She turned, her flushed cheeks glowing with a sheen which stuck tendrils of hair to her smooth forehead. I swept them away as she grinned at me. "I am, except I'm much sweatier than an alarm clock would have made me."

My dick took that as a checkered flag for the next round, and I went from semi hard to very hard with the speed of the MacLaren team at the Monaco Grand Prix. "I can clean you up real good. I have an excellent shower."

"Oh yeah?"

"Yeah." I scooped her up and threw her over my shoulder, only dropping to my knees once we were under hot jets of water.

Half an hour and three orgasms later, I scrolled through

the emails which had come in overnight, stopping on a Google alert which grabbed my attention. I clicked on it to open.

My heart juddered and I couldn't hold back my smile if I'd tried. Staring out from my phone was a picture from last night, my arm around Kit's waist as she chatted to Laurie. Underneath the picture, the caption read: *Financier Murray Williams and his fiancée.*

I was used to the papers making up stories about me, about my friends, about my family. This one was the first they'd invented I hoped would come true.

I'd make it come true.

I slipped my phone away as she walked into the bathroom, fully dressed.

"Hi, darling, Rafe's going to come by for the new contracts this morning. My mum's coming over so she'll take Bell and we can have a long lunch." I wrapped my arms around her until my hands rested on the top of her ass.

"Sounds good to me, especially the long lunch." Her face tipped up toward mine and I kissed her nose.

"Maybe I won't even go back to the office."

"Oh yeah? Lucky me."

"I'm the lucky one."

My reflection agreed with me.

"Morning, Joanie. How are you today?" I placed a purple box containing what I knew was her favorite chocolate brownie on the desk in front of her, and was met with a very arched eyebrow above a look dripping in suspicion.

"What do you want?"

"Nothing, it's Monday and I wanted to show you my appreciation for your dedication and hard work."

The arch disappeared but the suspicion didn't. "Hmmm.

The Milton paperwork is on your desk, you have a call with Briar Jepson at ten a.m. and PWC at eleven."

My grin was wide, mostly because it had been on my face since I'd woken up and I didn't seem to be able to get rid of it, which was probably why she was still staring at me like I'd escaped from somewhere. "Thanks, Joan. You're the best." I started to walk off, "Oh, Rafe will be by at some point this morning too."

I swear I heard her groan as I opened my office door.

The screens were already flickering away, and, as always, the day's papers were laid out on my desk. I had to force myself not to think about Kit; about her face as she squeezed the life out of my dick, as she kissed me with her soft, voluptuous mouth; in order to concentrate on what I needed to do.

I picked up the Wall Street Journal first, scanning the pages for anything which might affect the markets once the bell rang for the NYSE opening. Just as Bloomberg was reporting live on the screen in my office, all the papers were talking about a Global Technology Summit, attended by all the major tech firms; news coming out of there would be key for me over the next few days, especially as I tended to invest a lot in technology and crypto.

Joan walked in carrying coffee and what looked like a large, very green juice from Body by Luck, placing them in front of me. "Thank you. What's that?" I pointed to the container of what could have quite easily been radioactive materials given the color.

"The gym sent it over for you. The note said they're trying the new delivery service."

My nose wrinkled. "Oh, thanks."

She walked out without saying another word and closed the door. Pushing the juice to one side, I leaned back in my chair and watched the lines on my screens flicker aggressively as trading began.

I was three coffees in by the end of my second meeting. So far, the morning had been a resounding success; the markets had held strong, my predictions on tech and crypto accurate, and Jamie and I had signed a new client. The FTSE had closed up, paving the way for a good close on this side of the pond.

I had two private lines on my phone, which came straight through to me, bypassing Joan. Line One every member of my family, plus Kit, could dial; Line Two, which Penn had named The Bat Line, belonged only to him and Rafe. It was currently the latter which was flashing red and disturbing my daydream about what I'd be doing to Kit later.

I pressed the button down. "Happy Monday, sweetheart."

"Ugh, how has the relationship smugness not worn off yet? It's been a week. The pair of you were nauseating last night. I don't think you heard a single thing I said."

I snickered at Rafe's standard Monday grumpiness, although this was excessive even for him. "Get out of the wrong side of bed did you? Or was it that you got out of a bed that didn't have anyone else in it?"

He grunted and I knew I'd hit a sore point.

"Where's Pennington? Why isn't he on this call too? I feel like it shouldn't just be me enjoying your delightful mood this morning."

"He didn't answer, but I'm keeping the redial on."

"Keep dialing, he's really missing out," I chuckled.

"I just told you that's what I was doing!" he snapped.

"Okay…" If he'd been on video conference he'd have seen me roll my eyes. "Want to tell me why you're being extra delightful this morning? I thought you'd be happy Kit is coming to change the documents."

"I am. You're a walking law suit right now. I'd have preferred you'd kept your dick in your pants before anything happened, but I can't have everything can I?"

"Seriously, Raferty, what's the matter with you this morning?"

I reached for my juice, swirling the cup to mix up the sediment which had sunk to the bottom, resuming my position tipping in my chair, and I never heard his answer because the lid fell off, spilling it everywhere.

"FUCK!" I jumped up, dripping green on the floor until it looked like a Jackson Pollock knock off.

"What? What's happened? Murray?"

"Fucking hell!" I put the now empty container on my desk. "I spilled my juice everywhere and now it looks like Kermit the Frog exploded in here. Sorry, bud, can I call you back? I need to change."

He huffed. "Keep me on speaker phone. I actually do have a problem that I need to talk about."

I wiped a wet hand down my ruined pants.

"Okay, hang on." I opened my office door, "Joan, can you get some towels or something please? The juice spilled everywhere."

I didn't wait for her reply because I knew she'd be on it, and walked into my bathroom, stripping off my shirt as I went and threw it in the laundry, along with my pants.

"Okay, shoot. What's up?" I called out to him as I turned on the faucet to wash off the smell of spirulina.

"Fucking Beulah Holmes."

I stared at my confused face in the mirror. "Have we gone back twelve years?"

"What?"

I grabbed a towel from the rail. "It's been a while since we've had some Beulah bashing."

"Can you shut up? This is serious."

"I'm shutting up."

"Remember I told you about that divorce case my mom wanted help with?"

"Yes, the one that wasn't Chip."

"Right, her friend. I said I'd take it because, get this," he paused for dramatic effect, "she's divorcing Johnson Maynard."

The effect worked. I stopped what I was doing. "That crook? He belongs in jail, not a divorce court. Fuck, that must be worth billions."

"Yeah, you'd think, except he's hiding it somewhere, because the spreadsheets say he's only worth twenty mil. Plus they met in college when he had no money and there's no pre-nup. He's a vicious fuck, and I'm going to enjoy taking him down."

I whistled low.

"Wow." I opened my wardrobe, pulling out a fresh pair of pants and a cleanly pressed shirt. "What's this got to do with Beulah Holmes?"

He let out an exasperated sigh like I was already supposed to know what he was talking about, or at least guessed. "She's the opposing counsel. They've transferred her from the Mouths of Hell to the New York office."

It's a good job I'd already spilled my juice because if there was any left, I'd have spat it out instead. Fuck, I wish Penn was on this call. Where the fuck was he?

"Holy shit."

As if he'd telepathically understood the urgency of his presence, a beep sounded. "Hang on, his highness is here."

I pulled my pants on, extracting the belt from my green juice pair, pushing it through the loops.

"Pennington, wait until you hear this! There's a dart board we need to dust off!" I called loudly.

"Sounds exciting, which one?"

"Raf, tell him."

There was silence where there should have been a flurry of conversation and Penn pissing himself laughing.

"Penn?" I pulled the shirt off the hanger and pushed my arms through the sleeves. "Raf?"

Morons clearly couldn't use technology and cut themselves off instead. I walked out of the bathroom and halted, blinking hard at the view in front of me. A view that had my dick almost crawling back inside me.

I turned round to the bathroom again. Where the fuck had I just come from and how long had I been in there? My office door was shut, and how in the hell did she get past Joan?

In fact, where the fuck was Joan?

Green juice was still dripping off the desk, pooling onto the hardwood floor. It was difficult to believe she hadn't noticed she was sitting in a puddle of liquified vegetables, seeing as she was only wearing a bra and panties, her trenchcoat dropped on the floor.

"Your friends talk too much." Dasha's finger moved off the call end button.

It took me a couple of seconds, but I finally broke out of my shock. "What the fuck are you doing here? Not to mention, get the fuck out before I have you arrested for trespassing."

If she was concerned about any part of my threat, she didn't show it. "I've come to tell you I forgive you. I saw your picture last night, with that housekeeper you have…"

My fucking housekeeper? Last night I was at the gala with… the temperature of my blood shot up like mercury in a thermometer.

"And you've made your point, but now I'm reminding you what it's like to be with a real woman."

"Dasha, put your fucking clothes on and get the fuck out."

I started toward the door, both our heads whipping round as it opened. For the second time in almost as many months, my world imploded in slow motion. Kit was standing in the doorway, and if I hadn't already been in shock, I'd have been proud of the disgust painted all over her face, along with a snarl that would have impressed Barclay.

"What. A. Cliché," she addressed Dasha, but then the snarl turned on me, taking in my lack of suitable dress, my unbuttoned shirt and open pants. "I'd ask Joan to disinfect your desk along with whatever she's fetching cleaning products for."

"Kit…" I reached out, then realized I was still holding my pants up, and like a dagger to my heart, tears filled her anger laced eyes, but didn't spill over before she turned and left, not quite running but not walking either.

The slam of the door triggered the release on whatever was keeping me frozen in the bathroom doorway.

I stabbed my finger in Dasha's direction. "Put your fucking clothes on and stay the fuck away from my family."

"Family? Her and a kid that was dumped on you? We can start over and make a real family."

I ignored her and sprinted after the only woman I'd ever met who I did want a real family with.

Was already a real family with.

21

KIT

I backed out of the room, tears lodging firm in my throat, stinging my eyes until they overspilled, unsure, but also not surprised in the slightest by what I'd just seen. After Payton had slammed the door in her face, I'd had a feeling it wouldn't be the last I'd see of her.

I sat down heavily on the couch outside his office, ramming my hands between my thighs to stop the shaking. Joan appeared out of nowhere with cleaning equipment. She hadn't been at her desk which must have been how Dasha had gotten through.

Less than ten seconds later, Murray sprinted out, still doing up his pants, and ran straight into Joan.

"Where the fuck were you?" he growled. "Call the cops!"

"Don't speak to her like that," I snarled back with equal, if not more, vehemence.

He spun, his face painted with guilt and remorse, "Kit!" He almost slid along the floor as he dropped to his knees in front of me, our eyes level with how low the couch was, his glistening with sorrow, adding to the considerable weight already in my heart. "I'm so sorry! I know how it looked, but nothing happened… I walked out of the bathroom… green juice had spilled… I was changing. Fuck!" His hands ran through his hair before he gripped onto my thighs,

"It didn't look great." I swiped away another tear before it fell. "I don't think anything happened."

His shoulders dropped profoundly with relief. Quite frankly if he had the energy, not to mention time, to have sex with another woman after last night and again with the morning we'd had, then fair play to him. But I wasn't about to say that.

"Get up, Murray." He stood, helping me off the couch to stand too, cupping my cheeks and wiped away another tear. "I'm going to go to the coffee shop on the corner. Deal with whatever you need to do in there, then please come and meet me."

He took a step back, trying to assess my mood, but as though he couldn't bare the space between us he quickly pulled me back into his solid chest. His heart pounded in my ear as I pressed against him. Or maybe it was my heart pounding, my blood rushing like a raging torrent.

"Thank you," he murmured into my hair, breathing deeply, his body relaxing even though mine remained stiff. "I'll be there within thirty minutes."

I pulled away and collected my bag, which I'd dropped by the door. "Okay."

I didn't want to turn around as I knew he was watching me leave, instead I smiled weakly at Joan as I left, earning a wink as I passed and called the elevator, heading out of the building.

I sat down on the leather seats of the coffee shop, cooled from the unnecessary A/C. I sat there crossing and uncrossing my legs, lining up the sugar cubes from the bowl in front of me, piling up the packets of Sweet N Low… anything I could do to speed up the time or slow down the time or do anything to stop me thinking about what I'd just witnessed or the emotional battle taking place between my brain and my heart.

Last night he'd told me he loved me, and I loved him.

Both these things I knew to be true and uncontestable.

Except less than twelve hours later, I'd found a naked woman on his desk and my muscles had seized up as quickly as if I'd been thrown into an industrial deep freeze, my brain screaming at me, reminding me of everything I was trying to be cautious about. We needed to slow down, the pain lancing through my chest only confirmed that.

True to his word, it took him less than thirty minutes to get to me and I didn't envy anyone who'd been within the blast radius of his temper. He rushed into the coffee shop looking much less put together than he had when he'd left this morning, but still as devastatingly handsome. When he'd left this morning, I'd been certain in my decision. We loved each other, I was his girlfriend, I'd figure out my job, life, everything on the way... but now? Now I felt like I'd been slapped in the face with a heavy dose of reality.

We'd been moving too fast.

Lighting fast.

Warp speed.

Supersonic.

For the first time ever, I was thinking clearly in his presence, my brain not fogged by his nearness, his perfect bone structure or his green eyes – today's shade resembling the tops of the Douglas Firs during an Oregon summer.

"Hi, darling. Are you okay?" His lips pressed softly against mine, when he reached my table, taking my hands in his as he sat down next to me. "I'm so sorry, Kit."

I looked at the pain etched in his face.

I still wanted to be his girlfriend. I still loved him. I *had* fallen in love with him; I was on the way to falling so hard it would leave permanent scars. The only way to ensure our survival was to slow it down before we ended in a collision neither one of us would live through, which meant I couldn't move in with him yet.

I cupped his cheek, trying to give him reassurance by raising as much of a smile as I could muster.

"I know, it wasn't…" I was about to say it hadn't been his fault, but I actually didn't know that. I didn't know whether he'd done anything to discourage her further after she'd turned up at the apartment. I only trusted that he had. "I know nothing happened."

"She's gone. The cops just left with her, if you want to come back to the office." His expression was still marred with guilt. "Rafe is heading over too, so we can go through the contract business and draw a line under it. Start our lives fresh; you, me, Bell, and Barclay."

I wanted that, I wanted to start our lives fresh more than anything, but I didn't want to do it the way he wanted. I needed him to understand I wasn't saying no to us living together at any point, I was only saying no to right now.

I prayed he would see that.

I took a deep breath, pushing away the clogging that had built in my throat again, along with the pressure in my heart. "I'm not going to come back to your office."

His face fell. "Oh, okay, I understand. We can do it at home instead. Our home."

I bit down on my lip, hard, trying to quell the emotions bashing through me and bruising every one of my organs. "It's your home, Murray."

"What?" The worry lines which had been there since I'd burst into his office darkened. "What do you mean?"

"It's not my home, it's yours." I squeezed his hand that was still holding onto mine. "I've been staying there as part of my job, but it's your home."

His fingers flexed. "Kit, what are you talking about?"

"I want to start our lives fresh, like you said." I sucked in my cheek, chewing on it, but nothing was going to stop the anxiety flushing my body. "In order to do that, I need to move out."

He scoured my face, searching for any type of sign that I was joking, that I didn't mean what I was saying. "Kit, baby, I don't understand."

I took a deep breath, speaking aloud the words which had been going round my head on an endless loop. "We need some space from each other…"

"I don't need any space from you," he argued before I could continue, pulling his hand away.

"Murray, please…" I rubbed my clammy palms down my jeans, "let me finish."

He tried to hold back the annoyance that I was questioning the state of our relationship, but couldn't. I could tell by the way he ground his jaw, because I was now an expert in reading his expressions.

"We've done everything backwards. The last few months we've been in a bubble, thrown together under exceptional circumstances, living together, with your daughter. We've started a relationship and we've fallen in love. It's been intense."

He stared at me. "What are you saying?"

"I'm saying it's been a lot and we need to slow down. If we don't, I'm scared we're heading for a fall. This morning was…"

"Nothing happened, Kit. I told you."

"I know nothing happened, but there was still a naked woman on your desk when I was supposed to be meeting you for lunch," I hissed loudly, not wanting to broadcast our entire relationship to the rest of the coffee shop, although that only included an older lady in the corner feeding a croissant to a small dog. He reeled back like I'd slapped him, filling me with guilt, misplaced or not.

"If I stay living with you, I'm the nanny who never left. I want to be the girlfriend you fell in love with, who you then asked to move in because you couldn't live without. I don't want to be there by default."

"This is about labels?! I don't care what people think. You should know that."

I wasn't expecting this to be easy, but we'd be here all day if he had an argument for everything I said. My internal panic button started flashing red as the fear he might not agree with my thinking hit me like a sledgehammer, because Murray always got his own way and this wouldn't be one of those times.

"I don't either. This isn't about what people think."

"You're changing our story." His frown became more pronounced with every point he put forward, the anger at everything that had happened this morning, resurfacing.

"I'm not; I'm trying to make it stronger by giving us the time we need. I don't want to lose you."

"You've got a funny way of showing it. You're pushing me away."

"Murray, I'm not." My throat thickened again and I faltered on my words. "Please… I'm not pushing you away. I'm trying to build us a strong foundation where we start on equal footing. I don't want us to break up six months down the line when life becomes real and we realize we don't have anything in common besides sex and Bell."

He managed to master an expression that was a combination of incredulity and anger. "That's bullshit and you know it."

"No, that's the thing; I don't know, and neither do you."

"No one who has sex like us is going to break up in six months. We're made for each other."

"I want to be about more than sex, don't you?"

"Don't put words in my mouth," he snapped. "You know full well I think we're about more than sex. I love you, you love me. What more do you need?"

Wow. I was no relationship expert, but what the *ACTUAL* fuck?

"I want to date, I want to miss you, I want to build something. We've been swimming in the deep end."

"This is bullshit," he spat. Then his face softened, and he tried again. A different tack – and right there, I understood the reason he was so successful, beyond his incredible smarts - he never gave up. "I'm sorry about this morning, I'm so, *so* sorry. But please don't do this."

"Murray…"

"No!" His voice grew loud with frustration that I wasn't bending at his whim. Frustration I was also feeling, but for a different reason. "This *is* bullshit. We talked about this already, we talked it through on Saturday, and now you're running at the first hurdle. This is the first step to us breaking up."

We didn't talk about it, and I didn't want to break up. At no point had I said I wanted to break up. In fact, I'd told him the *exact* opposite, but he was only hearing what he wanted to hear, and I was having to work hard on keeping my own temper in check, even though he clearly couldn't.

I took a deep breath. "This isn't the first hurdle; it's not even a hurdle. I haven't just thought this through in the last thirty minutes while you were removing a naked woman from your desk. Are you even listening to anything I've said?"

"Yes, I've heard that you're scared, just like you're scared of taking the Columbia job. That you can't accept or recognize when something perfect comes along, because you're so fucking risk averse. Well, you know what? This is perfect, we're perfect, so open your fucking eyes and admit we're meant to be together, because you're being ridiculous right now," he snarled.

I craned my neck back to look at him, sliding away from him in my seat. "No, Murray, I'm not. If this is going to work, then we need to date and get to know each other in a more normal way. I want to date. I want to miss you. I want space to miss you, and to achieve that, I need to move out."

"Kit, please don't do this," he begged again, the tears filling his eyes were like acid to my heart, burning holes that would never repair in the same way.

"I love you, Murray. We'll be okay, this is a good thing."

"There's nothing good about this. You're running because you're scared."

The shred of control holding on my temper stretched too far, snapping like a taut rubber band. "And you're behaving like a petulant child who doesn't get his own way! Is this how our entire relationship's going to go? Every time I disagree with something you want, you throw a tantrum? Because I'm telling you right now, I am not on board if it is."

He glared at me in a way I hoped I'd never be on the receiving end of again. "Well, let's see shall we?"

I watched in open mouthed silence as he stood and stormed out of the coffee shop, opening the door so aggressively the glass clattered against the wall, but held firm. Unlike my resolve, which didn't, and I finally crumbled, the tears I'd been holding back for over an hour poured forth until I was a sobbing, blotchy red mess.

It had been so much worse than I thought it would have. I didn't think he'd take it well, but that hadn't just been a crash, that had been a twelve-car pile-up caused by a spectacularly backfiring jack-knifed truck. This guy who'd brought me to orgasm five time since last night, had stormed out and left me sitting by myself, leaving me with absolutely no idea about when I'd see him again.

If I'd see him again.

My chest heaved so hard at the thought I might not, that I almost couldn't breathe and the old lady stopped feeding her dog croissants and came over, putting her arm around me until I stopped sobbing enough to call Payton.

"What happened?" she cried loudly as she rushed through the doors of the coffee shop, opening them with significantly less violence than Murray had.

I managed to crack a smile at the shock on her face. "Is your couch still available?"

"Of course it is, but only if you tell me whose ass I need to kick."

"No one's. Mine. Take your pick."

She hugged me tight as I sobbed again at the idea I'd fucked it all up through my own cowardice, Murray's words ringing loud in my ears and my heart. I stayed there, soaking her shoulder as she rubbed my back until I'd calmed enough to tell her.

"This morning, you know how I was meeting Murray for lunch?"

She nodded. Before she'd left the apartment this morning, I'd filled her in on how my day was supposed to have gone.

"When I got there, that woman was on his desk, practically naked."

She pushed me back with such ferocity I almost had whiplash. "WHAT THE FUCK?"

"Nothing happened," I held her arm, desperately wanting to clarify that fact, omitting he was also half dressed. "Murray looked as shocked as I did, but..."

"Wait, what woman?" she interrupted.

"The one that came to the door, Dasha?"

"Holy fuck! Fucking hell, Kit. That bitch. Jesus, women like her give women like us a bad name. OHMYGOD, what did you do?"

I shrugged; maybe I was still in shock. "Not much. I turned and left. Murray ran after me."

"Good, then what happened?"

"I came here and I think he called the police and they took her. Then he came and met me here."

"Okay, good. I'm so sorry," she pulled me in for another hug, but I pushed her away.

"Wait, that's not why I'm upset."

"Oh, why are you upset then? What happened?"

"I told Murray that I wanted to move out so we could date properly and start a relationship that wasn't backward, and he didn't agree."

"What does that mean? What didn't he agree with?"

I sipped the glass of water which had been left for me during my sobbing fit. "Any of it. He was so angry. He said I was running away because I was scared, like I was scared of taking the Columbia job, and that it was all bullshit."

Her eyes spread wide. "Wow."

I started sobbing again, trying to catch my breath as I got to the bit that really hurt. "He kept saying I was being ridiculous and so I called him a petulant child who always got his own way, and he stormed out. I honestly don't know if he's ever coming back."

She scooped me back into her side, "Oh, honey, of course he will. It's just a first argument. That's all."

My shoulders heaved with each cry. "I don't know. I've never seen him so angry, or hurt."

"But you haven't known him that long though," she said softly. "Maybe this is just him. And it doesn't sound like he's challenged very often, so he's not used to it."

She handed me a paper napkin and I wiped my nose. "Maybe. But I don't want to be in a relationship with someone who always needs to have his own way. That's not how it's supposed to be."

She sighed, her expression sad, not as sad as mine was, but still sad enough that I knew it was upsetting her too. "I know, but it's always better to find these things out now rather than down the road, because then you're really fucked."

I nodded weakly.

She pulled her purse out, threw some dollars on the table and stood up. "Come on, let's get out of here. Do we need to get your things from the apartment?"

Ugh, I hadn't even thought of that. Or I had and forgotten.

"Yes, please."

"Okay, let's go. Then once we've done that, we're going to find a bar."

"Don't you have work to do?" I was so grateful she wanted to stay, but was very aware she had a busy job.

She waved her phone at me. "The beauty of technology means I can work anywhere. How long does his mom have Bell?"

"Diane is taking her tonight. Her and Freddie are taking her to the country to spend time with the girls."

I followed her out of the doors, into the Monday which had started so much better than it was going now.

"Have you spoken to Marcia?"

I shook my head. "The girls were talking to her today, as they hired me. It's why Diane has Bell; Murray wanted me to stop working immediately so I could spend the time finding a permanent job."

"Is that where his Columbia comment came from?"

My head hung, "Yeah." I glanced at her when she didn't say anything. "What?"

She chewed her thumbnail for second. "He has a point. That's an excellent job and you know it. I can't even believe they've kept the option open for you. That should tell you everything."

"It's not that I don't want the job, I just didn't want it by default. I wanted to earn it, just like I didn't want to move in by default."

"Why on earth do you think you wouldn't have earned it?" she scoffed.

"Because I was her favorite student. I wanted to see if I could get other jobs without preferential treatment."

Her eyes rolled dramatically. "You were her favorite student for a reason, because you were top of the class and you worked your ass off. If you think that old bat, Grady, would have offered you a job you didn't deserve, then you need your head checked. You earned that job, Kit. Take it."

I could feel her gaze on me while the next question whirred in my mind, unsure I wanted to hear her honest response. "Do you think he's also right to be pissed about me wanting to move out?"

"No," the firmness of her reply made me feel a little better, "I mean, he can be pissed, but I don't agree with what he did or said. He needs to respect your feelings, too."

A lone tear dropped down my cheek, grateful for her presence in my life. "Thank you, Pay. Thank you for coming to find me."

"Hey, you've saved my ass on too many occasions to count. I will always come and find you." She linked her arm through mine as she hailed a cab. "Don't worry, Murray will too. He probably just needs some time to cool off. I've seen the way he looks at you, that shit doesn't go away because of an argument."

I climbed into the back of the cab which had screeched to a halt by us, hoping, praying she was right. But she hadn't seen his face before he'd stormed out.

Hurt, anger, betrayal.

None of which was a recipe for a happy ever after.

22

MURRAY

My head throbbed. Banged. Pounded. Hammered. Like my brain was trying to escape from my skull.

If fatherhood had robbed me of anything, it was my ability to hold my alcohol. My hands flew to my temples as I attempted to sit up and reach for the water at the side of my bed, the pain almost unbearable.

Almost.

Because yesterday came flooding back to me in a tidal wave, wiping out any hope of even temporary alcohol amnesia, and nothing was worse than the crushing silence I'd come home to last night.

That *had* been unbearable.

Not even the wagging tail of Barclay had been there to greet me.

I'd taken three steps into the hallway, stopped, then promptly turned back around, called the boys, and proceeded to get very, *very* drunk.

I twisted the cap and downed the bottle in one, gagging slightly before making a sprint to the bathroom - avoiding the pillows I'd launched across my bedroom in rage because they smelled like her - getting there just in time to hurl a combination of whiskey and bile until my throat was scorched. Sliding to the floor, the ceramic toilet bowl cooled my burning skin as I hugged it for everything my life was worth.

Jesus. It wasn't even the weekend; it was a goddamn Tuesday morning, although fuck knows what the time was. My only prayer was the markets hadn't crashed overnight because I was fit for nothing today.

Nothing except wallowing in my own self-pity.

The only thing which could possibly pull me out was seeing my daughter, who thankfully wasn't coming back until after lunch. I sent out a second prayer that it wasn't already after lunch, then a third that it had all been a bad dream I was still in.

The room spun as I eased off the floor, only managing to move from there to the long, padded bench underneath the eight-foot-high picture windows overlooking Central Park, then lay down again. It can't have been that late because the sun hadn't fully risen above the trees; already the day was far sunnier and chirpier than I knew I'd be feeling for a while.

Without opening my eyes, I patted around the side table to my right, then the shelf behind me before finding the remote control to lower the blinds, shrouding myself in much needed darkness.

A darkness which perfectly suited my current mood.

By the time I felt more human and opened the blinds back up, the sun was fully risen, high in the sky. Moving off the bench to brush my teeth, I saw that I was in desperate need of a shave and a shower, but didn't have the energy to accomplish both. I compromised and spent the next forty minutes standing under the hot, powerful jets, trying to sweat out my hangover and contemplate my life choices.

Yesterday morning I'd been blissfully happy, happier than I'd possibly ever been. Now... I was propping myself up on the coarse slate tiles, nursing a most certainly bruised and cracked, if not broken, heart, along with my hangover, while ignoring the bare space on my bathroom countertops, which her products had filled this time yesterday. To say I'd felt better would be an understatement of momentous proportions.

Throwing on shorts and a t-shirt and slipping my phone in my pocket without looking at it, I made my way down to the kitchen; the disturbingly empty kitchen, in my disturbingly empty apartment. It even smelled different. Is this what I used to come home to every night? Kit was gone. Bell and Barclay were with my mom, and I was here alone.

Alone like I used to relish, but now it felt like punishment.

Last night I should have come home to Kit, to have a night alone together. We were going to order in, crack open a bottle of champagne, enjoy each other several times and celebrate the start of our new relationship. Instead, I could only hear the echoing of my own thoughts.

There was a pull in my chest so tight it felt like my circulation was being cut off.

She'd asked for space, but from what I'd heard, that meant the beginning of the end. We hadn't even had a beginning of a beginning.

She wanted to miss me, but I didn't know what that meant. Did it mean I couldn't call her? Couldn't text her? Couldn't see how she was? Did it mean I had to leave her alone until she'd decided she wanted to see me?

What the fuck was this situation? And what the fuck was I supposed to do?

Not to mention, it wasn't just me she'd left. She'd left Bell. And Barclay.

What the fuck was that about?

The mood which had eased slightly in the shower was now blackening quicker than the coffee dripping into my mug.

Another twist in my chest tightened it further and I tried

not to pay attention, instead focusing on the incessant buzzing of my phone as another message came through. I needed to sit down for this and pulled out a stool at the island, settling in before I dared to glance.

I scrolled through a few missed calls from Freddie; dozens of messages, mostly from Rafe and Penn, plus a couple from my mum. None from Kit.

Not a single one.

I guess space meant we didn't talk.

Well, that was just fucking fine.

The hefty amount of emails didn't report on anything alarming, giving me no good reason why I shouldn't go back to bed until I could wake up and everything had returned to the way it was. Or until someone had invented a functioning time machine. Either way, that's how long I wanted to go back to bed for.

The clock on the kitchen wall told me it had been twenty-three hours since I stormed back to my office to find Rafe waiting. Rafe with his stupid *it'll be okay* and *she'll be at home when you get there* advice. She hadn't been. And twenty-three hours in, it still wasn't okay, the buzzing of anxiety in my ears a clear reminder.

The faint click of the front door opening preceded Barclay bounding into the kitchen, running over to me for a woof and a bounce, followed by an enormous Freddie, and Cooper, both of them stopped in the doorway to stare. I didn't miss the hint of a smirk whetting Coop's lips. I was waiting for my mother to round to corner with Bell, but no one came.

I offered a biscuit to Barclay, which he eagerly gobbled up. "Where's Bell?"

Freddie ignored my question as she tried to wrap her arms around me. However, given I was on a stool and she was nearly nine months pregnant, it wasn't so much a hug as a pat. Her nose wrinkled up as she moved away. "Wow, this is worse than I thought it would be."

"What's that supposed to mean?" I grumbled at her.

She waddled to the fridge, grabbed a bottle of water and some painkillers from the cupboard, placing them both in front of me. "It's been a while since I've seen you this hungover."

I stared down at the rudimentary first-aid kit. "How did you know I was going to be hungover?"

I hadn't spoken to anyone except the boys since Coffeeshopgate, which is what Penn obviously named it, and now I couldn't un-name it.

"Beside the smell? I guessed."

I sniffed inside my shirt; I couldn't smell anything except the scent of clean laundry.

She smirked through her lie.

"Franks, can you just spit it out?" I snapped, "I don't have the energy to play games today, and tell me where my daughter is."

I'd been expecting Bell, desperate to see the smile on her little face; hold her in my arms as she drank her milk; make her laugh as I read her a story. The tightness in my chest wasn't only from Kit. This was the first morning since she'd arrived that she hadn't been the first - *or more recently second* - person I'd laid eyes on each morning, and my already aching chest was aching more deeply because of it.

She nodded to the Advil she'd placed on the counter. "Take those, and then I will."

Cooper was still leaning against the wall, his arms crossed over his chest, his eyes lambent with amusement. I shot him a scowl, which only amused him further.

"Why are you two here again?" I tried to knock back the painkillers, but as I was still having trouble swallowing it took more than one attempt.

"We brought Barclay back."

"Where is Bell?" I enunciated each word clearly, not caring that I was taking my mood out on her.

"Still with mum and dad."

I scowled. "Why exactly?"

"We thought you could use some time, and possibly a little reminder of what your life used to be like."

I'd already had a reminder of that, for thirty seconds, which is why I was in my current hungover predicament. I didn't want another, nor did I understand why Freddie seemed to think I did, eyeing me smugly as only those who haven't been hungover in a while, do.

"What's that supposed to mean?"

She pulled out a stool. I glanced over to Cooper who still hadn't said anything while Freddie was taking her sweet time to sit down. "I saw Kit yesterday."

My eyes flicked to hers so hard and fast, a severe piercing shot through my brain and I genuinely questioned whether I was having an aneurysm. "What? When? How?"

"Mum and I were still here when she came back from coffee with you. She was with her friend, Payton," her eyes widened, "whom I love by the way. She was so funny. Oh my God I want..."

I couldn't give a single fuck about Payton right now, and Freddie's pregnancy meant she tended to wander off topic more frequently than I currently had patience for.

"Jesus, get to the point!"

She tried to wither me with a look, but I was already fucking withered. "She was very upset, she hadn't expected us to still be here, but I'd needed to pee again and then I was hungry so made some lunch, then Bell fell asleep and everything took longer than expected."

I inhaled a deep, not very cleansing, breath, and concentrated on not snapping again, while waiting for her to focus.

"Babe..." Cooper interrupted her current detour from the only piece of information I was interested in. Kit.

"Sorry, she was really upset. Incredibly upset."

Guilt punched me hard in the gut, the visual of her tears once again gnawing my brain. I shouldn't have stormed out. I should have stayed to show her how much I loved her. I should have worked harder to prove we didn't need space, we just needed each other.

"She told us about what happened. What you said to her."

My head shot her way again, what I said to her?

"Wait, what d'you mean? What did I say?"

She tried to lean over the counter but couldn't, instead pinning me with a dirty, snarly, squinty look instead. "Jesus, Murray, are you serious? You don't remember?"

"I thought you were going to say she told you about Dasha."

Her eyebrows shot up. "Oh, we heard about that, too. And we can cover that later, but that's not what she was upset about."

"Freddie..." I hoped she took my tone as a warning. Cooper certainly did as he stepped forward to sit at the island with us, crossing his arms over his chest like I was some kind of imminent threat, and he was her security detail.

"She told you how she felt and you called her ridiculous and stormed out."

I slumped back down. I'd been expecting some big revelation. "Oh."

I had no rebuttal. I stood by what I'd said. She was being ridiculous.

"Murray, what the fuck is wrong with you?"

"What's wrong with *me*?!" I fumed.

"Yes, you." She pointed at me like I didn't know who she was referring to and needed a reminder. "This girl is perfect for you, she loves you and she's trying to make a proper go of it, and you storm out and call her ridiculous. Now you're sitting here, hungover and pathetic. So yes, what's wrong with you?"

I didn't want to hear any of this. I didn't want to hear that Kit was perfect for me, I already knew that. We *were* perfect for each other, and I didn't need my sister to rub it in my face that she now wasn't here with me, where she should be.

"You know what, Francesca? For once in your life, mind your own fucking business. Always with the fucking meddling! If you and Wolf hadn't meddled in the first place, then I wouldn't be in this position, would I?"

Her lips pursed as hard as her glare. "No, you'd still be fucking your way through New York's mind-numbingly dull, not to mention stupid, bitches, like the one who turned up in your office, instead of actually feeling something for the first time in your life."

The nerve she hit was already exposed down to the root.

"Oh, fuck off!" I yelled, startling Barclay.

"No, you fuck off!" she yelled back.

An ear-bleedingly shrill whistle pierced the air.

"Okay, enough. Pack it in, both of you!" Cooper yelled the loudest, his fingers still hovering by his lips in case he needed to burst our eardrums a second time. We both stopped yelling, but we didn't stop glowering at each other though.

He turned to Freddie, his voice much quieter. "Francesca, why don't you go and have a nap? I'll stay and keep an eye on Murray."

She saw right though his attempt to separate us. "Don't fight my battles, Cooper."

His hands rose up. "I wouldn't dream of it, but you're growing my baby and I'd rather they entered the world *before* realizing what a force of nature their mother is and decide to stay inside a little longer."

She slid off the stool, her temper now aimed firmly at Cooper, but didn't put up a fight because she lived for her naps. It's also hard to storm off when you're nearly nine months pregnant, and watching her waddle when I knew she wanted to stomp and slam made me feel so much happier than it should have. Thankfully, she didn't see the smile I cracked or she'd have probably thrown something at me.

He waited a minute, making sure she'd really gone, before turning to me. "She has a point you know."

"Who?"

"Your sister."

My bad mood returned. "You know, if you're going to stay here and slate me like she did, then save your breath."

"Stop being a dick, Murray." He got off his stool, fetching himself a beer and some more water for me. "I know you're hurting, but behaving like an asshole won't get her back."

"What's that supposed to mean?"

"Have you ever been dumped before?"

"She didn't dump me; she just said she needed space. Space! From me. And Bell. What the fuck's that about?" I slumped again, my face in my hands. "What the fuck does it even mean?"

"Christ, you're dramatic." He rolled his eyes with no empathy. "We all think Florence gets her drama from Wolfie, but it's more likely coming from you."

I ignored him, although in hindsight that was probably only fueling his argument.

"Look, I wasn't here yesterday, but Fred and your mom both told me what Kit said."

"Yes, she wants space."

"No, you fuckhead!" He slapped me round my ear, which didn't do anything to help my hangover. "She loves you. She wants to date and be in a relationship, *with you*. She wants it to be on equal terms, which is commendable in my eyes. She's not trying to sponge off you, unlike every other fucking woman you've been with. So stop behaving like a spoiled brat and throwing your toys out of the stroller like Sammy."

"I'm not," I huffed, because he clearly didn't understand.

"You are. You're exactly like Freddie when she doesn't get her own way either."

"Freddie who I helped you win back after you royally fucked up," I grumbled with my weakest argument yet.

"You did, and I'm returning the favor."

"She wants space, Coop."

"Bud..."

"What the fuck am I supposed to do? I don't understand why she couldn't have just come home. I love her, she loves me. Why doesn't she understand how important she is to me? We were supposed to be a proper family."

His jaw dropped open. "Fucking hell, listen to yourself. You've known her less than three months."

"Your point?"

He scratched through his beard and took a long draw of his beer before looking at me again. "My point is, take the fucking time she's asked for. Listen to her. Get to know each other without being in each other's space. Date, have fun. Stop being such as asshole. For fuck's sake, man, any woman worth having you need to fight for, every idiot knows that. If Kit is worth having, then you should be fighting balls to the wall to give her exactly what she wants."

She *was* worth fighting for, of course she was. I'd fight to the death for her, even though I already felt defeated.

I sighed through to my marrow. For the first time in my life, I was in a bind I couldn't seem to find my way out of.

"I don't know how to. My chest hurts like a motherfucker, and it's only been twenty-four hours. And that's only the part Kit owns, that's not counting Bell's half, which almost hurts more, because I miss her more than I've ever missed anything. You were supposed to be bringing her."

He got back up and I thought he was going to hug me, but he went to the fridge again, pulling out bread, tomatoes, mayo and chicken. He peeled the tomatoes and began slicing them. "I can speak to the Bell half, that shit never goes away, man. The half Kit owns, it feels like that because you've never had anything you cared enough about losing. This is what it's like when you have to work for something."

I took another sip of water. "I know how to fucking work for something! What I don't know is how to give her space. I don't want to give her space. I want her here with me. Why doesn't she want to be here?"

He rolled his eyes, cutting the fully loaded sandwich into two, putting half on a plate and pushed it over to me.

"How long is it supposed to last? Am I supposed to contact her or wait for her to contact me? I don't know the fucking rules."

He walked into the pantry, returning with chips. "Dude, there aren't any rules. It's not literal. Space doesn't mean you have to stay away from her, it means you're not around each other twenty-four-seven. You have your own lives, and the time you spend together means something. Put the fucking effort in." He threw his arms in the air, with much more drama than I ever had. "She fucking loves you, you moron. How am I having to explain this to you?"

"Because I've never been asked for space before!" I snapped, my hands running through my hair, practically pulling out the ends. "Doesn't sound like the sort of thing you say to someone you love. Everyone knows space means the end."

"Who the fuck is everyone?" He countered with a question I didn't actually know the answer to, but it was one of those things you just knew, right?

I shrugged. "I dunno, people, movies. It's always the end."

Cooper took a massive bite of his sandwich, chewing annoyingly slowly, and washed it all down with another long draw of beer. "Murray, what else do you remember her saying?"

I sat back. I didn't need to close my eyes to see her, picture her holding my hands as she said she was moving out, that she wanted us to have space. That everything had been happening too quickly.

"I dunno. She said things had been intense."

"And?"

I remembered her eyes flashing fire as she shouted at me. "She said she wanted to build us a strong foundation."

"Right, there you go. What else?" He waved his hands for me to continue.

I dug deep again. "She wanted us to get to know each other in a normal way."

He snapped his fingers. "Bingo. There's your answer. Nothing more normal than dating and you already had dates planned for her; you told us so at Easter."

The tightness in my chest eased up a little, and the pain in my heart felt less acute. "Yeah, I guess."

"Murray, Fred is right. Kit is perfect for you. You love her, everyone in the family loves her, and she fitted in so well at Easter. Make this right, or you'll regret it forever."

I already did regret it. I regretted everything that had caused her pain; everything that I'd done to totally fuck up one of the best things in my life.

"I will. But first, I want my daughter back." I stood up, moving to Cooper and wrapped him in the hug I thought he was going to give me earlier. "Thanks, mate. Thank you for coming over. You're much more effective than Franks, but don't tell her I said that.

He patted me on the back, laughing. "Don't worry, I value my life. Don't tell her I said she was right."

"Deal." I picked up the phone to dial my mom, requesting that she returned my child.

I fasten the poppers on Bell's sleepsuit as she smiled up at me. My mom had brought her back, and then left without an argument which I was grateful for. I wanted time alone with Bell, just the two of us and Barclay. I ordered pizza, drank my water, then I filled the bath with Bell's lavender bubbles and we both got ready for an early night. Or it was an early night for me; it was regular bedtime for her.

Tomorrow would be a new day, and first thing in the morning, I was going to come up with a plan to get Kit back while giving her the space she'd asked for, something which was too much for my hangover-addled brain to figure out.

I lifted Bell up and breathed her in as deeply as I could. I didn't know whether it was my baby specifically or something all babies came with, but she worked better than the bottle of Valium in my bathroom drawer at calming my racing mind and heart.

While her bottle was cooling, I carried her through the bathroom, to the open door of Kit's room. But even Bell couldn't keep my heart rate down as I stood in the doorway, scanning around the shell she'd left. Everything was gone except the flowers, now drooping, in the vase.

As if sensing Kit wasn't here, Bell started fussing

"I know, little one, I know." I kissed her head, rubbing her back as I returned to her room and sat down with her bottle. "But we're going to get her back. I'm going to get her back for us. I promise."

And I didn't break my promises.

23

KIT

"Sweetie, can you stop crying please? You really don't pull off the emo vibe, even with the mascara streaking down your face," Payton whispered, but loud enough for me and anyone else to hear over the noisy chatter and thumping music in the bar she'd dragged me to.

Dragged being the operative word because I hadn't wanted to come out, hadn't wanted to leave the apartment where I'd holed myself up for the last five days waiting for my phone to ring, or buzz, or something.

But you know what they say; a watched phone never makes a fucking sound unless it's from every single person *except* the one you're waiting for.

In the end, Payton had forced me to shower and get dressed, and even though I was trying to be happy and put on a brave face, less than an hour after we'd arrived, a man had walked past me who not only smelled like Murray, but looked like him – from the back anyway – and the pain in my heart had been so severe the tears burned within seconds, and now I couldn't seem to stop them even if I wanted to.

This bar also seemed to be exclusively full of couples enjoying themselves, only reminding me of how a week ago,

I'd been part of a couple, while now it was looking increasingly likely that relationship status was in the back of the ambulance on the way to the morgue, and probably wouldn't be resurrected any time soon.

Since I'd fucked everything up.

Instead of sitting here with my margarita, growing saltier with every tear that dropped into it, all I wanted to do was go home, crawl back under the comforter, and lick my wounded heart until it was better, while trying to convince myself that everything would still be okay. Because the flip side of the card I'd dealt myself, was that I wasn't about to cave to my belief of what we needed. I'd been right, and I stood by that.

"I'm trying, but..."

She peered round me. "Shhhh. Wipe your tears, there's a super-hot guy coming over."

I assumed she meant for her because I couldn't give a single shit about any other guy whose name didn't start with Murray and end with Williams. I also didn't give a shit what I looked like right now, although I would try to be a good friend so it didn't appear that she associated herself with unstable, weeping messes, such as me. I wiped my nose and attempted to blot my face, although given the look of horror on hers, I hadn't done a very good job.

"Hello ladies..."

The deep baritone spread over me like the cooling breeze at the end of a scorching hot summer's day, and I forgot about my appearance as my eyes snapped up into the emerald green pools I was so familiar with. For the second time since I'd arrived here, my heart nearly stopped. It had been five days since I'd seen him, and, somehow, he'd become even more handsome, even taller, even broader, his smile bigger and more beautiful.

"I'm sorry for interrupting your evening. I saw you from across the bar," I remained speechless as he nodded over, and we followed his line of sight to see Penn and Rafe sitting at the corner, both looking handsome, but less so in my opinion, waving emphatically, "and I wanted to come over and introduce myself. And, if I may be so bold, ask for your number."

I know I blinked because I made myself do it, although for the life of me I couldn't understand what was happening. He had my number. "Murray, what are you doing?"

His head tilted in confusion, although a ghost of a smirk coaxed his perfect lips. "How did you know my name? I don't think we've met before, because I would have definitely remembered someone as beautiful as you. I would never be stupid enough to forget, or stupid enough to let you get away from me if we had."

The tears pooled again, as I realized what he was saying.

His smile softened to the one I seen so many times when he held Bell, and he reached out, his thumb gently running under my eye to catch a tear before sweeping it away. "Is giving me your number really that terrible an idea?"

I felt fifty pounds lighter with the laugh I let out. "No, it isn't. My number is 914-555-7867.

He punched it into his phone with a wide toothy smile.

"Thank you. Count on me calling you very soon." He leaned down and kissed my cheek, his head resting on mine for the briefest of seconds before walking away and disappearing in the sea of people as quickly as he'd appeared.

I turned back to Payton, who was sitting opposite me with the type of grin that told me she'd known exactly what would happen tonight. "Looks like you've got yourself a game, young lady."

My brow furrowed. "A game?"

"You wanted to know him in a normal setting, you wanted space, you wanted to date. He's giving you what you asked for. And I have a feeling he's about to hit a home run."

If someone had cracked me open, a rainbow would have

burst forth from the settling storm inside. I'd seen Murray, and he'd asked for my number so he could date me.

Payton knocked back the rest of her cocktail. "Come on. Let's go home before you see what you look like."

I'd never realized how much of dating was spent waiting. If I'd thought waiting the five days since he stormed out of the coffee shop was hard, waiting to find out when our first date was going to be was even harder. He left it twelve hours before my phone pinged, as loudly as my heart was thumping in expectation for it. His message was simple and to the point.

Murray: *Are you free tomorrow? X*

Even if I'd had any plans, I would have cleared my entire schedule for the month. He arrived on the dot of eleven a.m., and I'd opened the door to an even bigger bouquet of pink roses than the ones he'd brought home the day of our first kiss. After Payton had shooed me out, with the promise of putting them in water, I'd taken his hand and we'd wandered through the busy New York streets into the park, our conversations about family bringing an overpowering sense of déjà vu. When it dawned on me that he was recreating our first walk, my heart skipped several beats while the butterflies emerged from their chrysalis and fluttered, newly energized, in my belly. We walked with our coffees back to Payton's, where he kissed me on the cheek and promised to make plans for our second date. And unlike every other first date I'd been on, there was zero shred of uncertainty that he wouldn't keep it. Also unlike every other first date I'd been on was the immediate need to dissect every minute detail with Payton, over wine and ice cream, quite simply because it was unlike every other first date I'd been on.

It was *the* first date.

The week between our first and second date, I floated around on the shiniest silver lined cloud, powered by bubbles nothing could burst. Every day I'd wake up to a message telling me to have a beautiful day, and every night, he'd send one wishing me sweet dreams. In between, my phone would light up with random cross-word clues or pictures of Bell and Barclay, because it wasn't just Murray I was missing. I filled my time looking for an apartment, viewing more than any other New Yorker had possibly viewed, before I found the perfect one bed, situated on the Upper East Side, a stone's throw from Columbia and ready for me to move in at the end of the month.

Just before my new job started.

After Payton and I had packed up my things and I'd had time to think about what he'd said, I'd decided that maybe he was right about Columbia. I was right about us needing space, but he was right about my job hunt, or lack thereof. I *was* scared. Scared of failing. Ironically though, the determination I had for *us* to survive by walking away ignited the fire I needed to see me through my visit to Professor Grady. The role she'd offered me as one of her research assistants across her portfolio of Shakespeare focused courses, was to start on June 1.

I called to tell him. He was waiting on the doorstep when I reached my apartment, announcing he'd brought forward our second date, and then swept me away for dinner and champagne telling me how proud he was. And just like the end of our first date, he walked me to the door and kissed me on the cheek.

I'd thought for our third date I might have received at least a kiss on the lips, but I was wrong. Even after I'd planned our day out - taking him to a spring fairground which had opened in Riverside Park where I'd succeeded in winning him a giant stuffed toy lion on the coconut shy – I'd still only received the briefest of kisses to my cheek as a goodbye.

It was a good job my vibrator was rechargeable, because by the time our fourth date arrived, it had been nineteen days since he'd touched me, since his lips had been on mine, since I'd tasted him on my tongue, and it felt like every single cell in my body had been soaked in gasoline and I needed to be kept away from any open flame or electronic device for fear I'd explode in a ball of fire.

The situation was becoming dire. Day twenty was rolling around and I'd decided to no longer play fair, making the only sensible decision I could under the circumstances. I bribed Payton into coming shopping with me, and that was why I was currently wearing a dress which made my previous Payton purchases seem positively nun-like.

"Pay, are you ready?"

For our fourth date, Murray announced he wanted me to meet his best friends, because except for any references to Bell and Barclay, we were still keeping up the pretense that we'd met in the bar. It was also a date I was particularly excited about because aside from the gala, I'd not spent much time with them as a trio, and as it was both our best friends, it meant Payton was coming along too.

"Two minutes!" she yelled from the bathroom.

I checked myself in the full length mirror she'd hung in her bedroom. It was Friday night and the dress I was wearing had been specifically chosen because it showed off the assets of mine which Murray had deemed his favorite – or the most favorite – tits, ass, and legs.

Thick gold shoulder straps hoisted up my boobs, creating a cleavage even I'd be envious of if I hadn't known they were mine, darker gold bands crisscrossing underneath and over my body, creating the illusion I was wrapped up, for Murray to undo. I'd left my hair to fall in the loose curls he liked to twirl his fingers around, and my lips were bare, except for a swipe of balm, because I'd planned on being kissed all night. Finally, another raid of Payton's shoe closet had me standing in a pair of strappy five inch heels, lengthening my legs which I'd painstakingly spent hours applying fake tan to.

"Jesus," Payton whistled, walking over to the mirror and looking her usual effortlessly glamourous self in ripped jeans and a bandage top. "He's going to come in his pants."

Which was exactly the effect I wanted to have on him. "Either him or me."

"Come on, you fiend, let's go," she smirked.

Twenty minutes later, our cab pulled up outside the bar Murray told us to meet him in, to find him waiting outside the door. He didn't come in his pants, but his reaction was almost as good.

His slow gaze draped over me, scorching me from the inside out. "Jesus Ker-ist."

He wrapped my hand in his, pulling me into the bar.

"Payton, the boys are over there," he pointed to somewhere across the room, though his eyes never left mine, "go and find them. They have drinks waiting, and we'll catch up."

Payton snorted loudly with an *I told you so* rise of her eyebrow, and took off to find Penn and Rafe.

My arm was nearly wrenched from the socket at the speed with which he hauled me away from the entrance, in the opposite direction Payton had headed, and I found myself pushed hard against a wall along a dark corridor, my body hidden by his massive one, his hands pinned by my head.

His nose brushed through my hair, tracing along my jaw. "Do you know how impossible it's been for me to keep my hands off you the past few weeks? And then you turn up wearing this?"

I groaned as his lips tickled under my ear, his breath as hot as my skin. "You've managed it though. You haven't touched me once."

He pulled back, his green eyes blazing with flecks of gold reflected off my dress.

"You haven't even kissed me," I sulked, the heavy beat between my legs louder than the music vibrating across my body.

"I wanted to respect your wishes. I wanted to give you what you asked for." His hands were still firmly planted on the wall, as if moving them would have been too much for his resolve to stay chaste.

I had no memory of asking him not to touch me. I must have been crazy, or maybe I was suffering from amnesia, or idiocy, because I couldn't imagine any scenario where I'd want that. My body yearned for it; practically buzzing in his presence, waiting to be reignited.

No, there's no way I would have denied myself his touch.

No. Way.

His chin tilted at my confusion, his lips still mere inches from my skin, sending the familiar hot shivers across my body. "You said you didn't want us to be only about sex."

My jaw dropped. "I didn't mean for it to be taken away completely."

"Tsk tsk. You should have been more specific then, shouldn't you?" His mouth curled with a smugness that told me he knew exactly what he was doing.

"Murray..." My fingertips ran along the outline of his chest under the soft cotton of his crisp black shirt. He was right, it was impossible not to touch. "I'm just trying to recreate the first time we went out, you know, like you've been recreating our dates."

The green sparkle in his eyes burned bright before they narrowed, his voice turned raw. "Are you asking me to make you come in this bar? Are you telling me that if I slip my fingers up the heat of your thigh, they'll discover how wet you are? That your hot, tight pussy will squeeze the life out of me?" His lips found the column of my neck, my legs nearly giving way, and I must have let out a moan because he pulled back with a smirk. "No, Kit, that's not happening."

My entire body would have deflated if it wasn't on the verge of orgasm. "You haven't even kissed me."

He rolled his shoulders back, making him seem twice his size, his muscles rippling under my touch. "Okay, I'll concede to that."

A strand of hair fell over my eyes, and he unstuck one hand from the wall to sweep it away, curling it round his finger. He tracked the movement, brushing his nose over it, inhaling deeply. "You can have one kiss now, and one later, so you better make it good."

It was a challenge, one I was all too happy to accept.

I'd make it a kiss he'd never forget.

I held his gaze as my palms slid up the outside of his shirt, up the solid plains of his chest, to the dips in his thick shoulders I knew so well. I leaned in a fraction, slipping my fingers through the soft blonde curls at the base of his neck and up until I needed to stand on my tiptoes to reach. His stance widened out of habit, bringing himself nearer to my level.

When I leaned in, his lips parted in expectation, but I wasn't ready or close enough to touch his lips yet. This was my kiss, and his quiet chuckle as I bypassed his mouth told me he knew it. Cupping his face as he so often did to me, his soft stubble tickled my skin and I grazed the tips of his cheek with my lips; first one then the other. He might have appeared cool and collected on the outside, but my finger over his pulse told me otherwise - a well-positioned lie detector – hammering hard and in rhythm with mine.

Mine.

He was mine. Mine to claim, and I did just that when my mouth finally found his, slanting over his lips, my tongue losing no time in hungrily rediscovering the taste of him or the feel of him stroking against me. Even in the very minimal clothing I was wearing, beads of sweat trickled between my breasts from the inferno level heat of his body.

He gave me all the control he could, until he couldn't, and I found myself forced further into the wall until I wasn't able to move. His body pressed into me, his need eclipsing mine, and the air which had been thick and hanging heavily around us, vanished in a vacuum as he removed the last remnants of space between us. A tug on my hair tipped my head back and he made my mouth his prisoner, his tongue feasting on me with a fervor that said he'd been starved as much as I had.

The sound of someone hollering nearby broke our spell, and he slowed before grudgingly let me go with a soft groan. Because that kiss was an incendiary device in my panties, and from the unmistakable feel of his thick, rigid cock against my hip, his pants by all accounts. His thumb pulled my lip as I caught it in my teeth, trying not to smirk at his predicament.

His forehead dropped to rest on mine, his eyes closing while he calmed his breathing.

"Did I make it a good one?" I didn't bother trying to keep the smugness out of my tone, because I knew the answer.

"You fucking did," he growled, his breath catching. "And I'm telling you now; I will be the last man you kiss like that."

Blood whooshed through my veins as I let his words settle.

He stepped back, readjusting himself as best he could.

"Come on. Let's go and find the others before I drag you out of here." His fingers laced through mine as he reluctantly led me away and back to his table.

"Fucking finally. There you are!" Penn lifted a bottle of champagne in the air and poured out two glasses for Murray and me as we sat down, his hand still firmly holding onto mine. "We were about to leave with Payton, show her how we actually party."

Payton didn't look like she'd object to that change of

plans in the slightest, and Murray seemed to come to the same conclusion. "Later. First I want to introduce you to Kit."

Penn looked around the table to check we were all as confused as he was. Everyone except me, because I'd expected this. "Dude, we've met her already."

Murray shook his head, his hand let go of mine but moved to my knee, the touch of his skin on my thigh sending a fresh shot of adrenalin between my legs. "No, this is Kit who I'm dating and who will soon be my girlfriend. Before, you met Kit, my nanny."

"Whom you were banging?" Rafe piped up with a grin, high fiving Penn.

"Exactly."

"It's lovely to meet you, Kit," Penn announced with his usual dramatic effect. "Do stick with Murray, he's a miserable fuck without you."

I giggled through a sip of champagne, Payton interrupting before I got the chance to retort.

"I'm not sure anyone has ever been more miserable than she's been." She thumbed at me casually, like Murray and I weren't sitting here at all.

But I didn't care, because Murray's long fingers were teasingly stroking minuscule circles down the inside of my thigh and I was struggling to concentrate on anything else. I couldn't even cross my legs because his vice like grip was preventing it and he knew it.

"How long's this dating thing going to go on for?" Rafe smirked, but Murray didn't rise to the bait. "What number are we on now?"

"Tonight is date four," Murray answered and squeezed my leg.

"Is four the same as fourth base?" asked Rafe. "Pennington, what is fourth base?"

"Home run, baby." His eyebrows waggled, his broad grin aimed at us, and my vagina clenched hard. I didn't think I'd get a home run tonight, but I wondered how far I could push my second kiss.

"I don't know why I hang out with you," Murray shook his head playfully.

"Because you love us, and we know where the bodies are buried."

"You mean I know where yours are," he shot back to Penn.

"Exactly. And we keep Rafe around to bail us out."

Payton laughed loudly, "That sounds like a valid reason if I've ever heard one."

"When's date five?"

"Actually," Murray leaned forward before turning to me, "it's tomorrow."

I startled slightly, excitement coursing through me at this breaking news. "Really?"

"Yes," he grinned, pecking me with a quick kiss which in no way counted as our second one for the evening.

"Where is it?"

"It's a surprise."

My eyes flared wide. "What is it?"

He replied with a tipped head and a lift of his brow, giving me a second until I remembered the conversation we had about the meaning of the word, and I smothered my smile with a roll of my lips.

"The only thing I will tell you is that I'll be picking you up at eight a.m. and you need to pack an overnight bag."

Holy shit. An overnight bag.

Payton put down her glass, her expression filled with horror. "Murray, you can't just drop an overnight bag situation on her at," she picked up her phone, "nearly nine p.m. What's she supposed to pack and what's she supposed to wear?"

"After fourth base, she's probably not going to be wearing much," Penn threw his head back laughing.

"Watch it," Murray growled, and then addressed Payton. "You can let your friend know that whatever she wants to wear is more than fine with me because she looks beautiful in anything."

My heart melted, Payton's didn't. "That's spectacularly unhelpful."

He laughed, picking up my hand and kissing it. "Jeans and sneakers. That's all you need."

Payton still wasn't impressed, handing me my glass. "You need to go home and pack. Finish your drink."

"Wait," Penn held his hands up to stop her. "They can go, but we're going out and you're coming."

She didn't put up a fight, nor had I expected her to.

"Looks like we're going," Murray whispered in my ear, and my breath caught. He knocked back his own drink and stood up, holding out his hand to me. He wrapped his arm around my waist, pulling me into his side when I stood, too.

The pair of us had matching grins as we turned to our three friends.

"You could at least pretend you're sad you're not coming out with us."

Murray patted Penn's cheek. "But I promised to never lie to you."

"Don't wait up," Payton called after me as Murray took my hand and pulled me away from them, back into the open air where his driver was already waiting for us.

We moved through the traffic, his hand never straying from my lap, and when we pulled up outside Payton's apartment, he jumped out his side, rounding the back before opening my door.

It had been less than two hours since he'd stopped kissing me, but during that time, I'd been waiting for the feel of his lips on mine again. Just like in the past month, I hadn't just missed it; I'd missed a part of him. He walked me up the steps to Payton's door, and I expected him to push me against it like he had in the bar, but he didn't, he merely shielded my body from the road.

He picked up the ends of my hair and began twisting them through his fingers. "You have one more kiss, Columbia, and then I'm leaving you until the morning."

My heart tightened at the use of his name for me, I hadn't heard it since before our new dating relationship had started. "Better make it another good one then, hadn't I?"

I reached up, standing on the very tips of my toes, my lips pressing lightly against his, inviting him to sink into me until he did. His mouth enveloped mine, open and warm, totally different to the hungry, desperate kiss we'd had in the bar. This one was sweet, brimming with love and need, and more emotion than I'd ever felt in my life.

It was over too quickly, slipping away from me while I was far from finished. I wanted more. I knew I would always want more.

His knuckles brushed my cheek. "I'll see you in the morning. I'll be outside at eight a.m. sharp."

I melted into his touch. "I'll be waiting. And I only need jeans and sneakers?"

I had no idea what he'd planned, but jeans and sneakers cancelled out all options for fancy restaurants and glamorous dinners, which was more than okay with me. I was hoping our night away involved room service, and nothing else.

"Jeans and sneakers," he confirmed.

He waited until I walked in the door before moving off the step and back down to his waiting car. When he'd vanished into the traffic, I closed it behind me and sunk down to the floor, trying to calm my racing heart.

If I thought I was in love with him before, I knew for certain now.

He owned my heart, my mind, my soul.

Me.

24

MURRAY

When I was in college training for the Ivy League Swimming Championships, which took place every year over a four month period of qualifiers and heats before the knockout stages leading into the finals, I would stop drinking. Not a drop of alcohol touched my lips. I didn't go out and party, my diet was strict and my training regimen brutal. I trained, swam, and studied for four months, until I was crowned champion.

With the exception of the day I broke my leg, I won every single race.

At the end of every championship, the team would go out. The celebrations were legendary on campus and everyone knew it; we weren't bigger than the football team, harder than the hockey team, or as crazy as the baseball team, but we had longevity. We partied until we collapsed.

That first glass of beer after the tournaments had finished was hands down *the* most incredible thing to ever pass my lips – that first sip was better than the champagne parties, better than any vintage whiskey or rarest wines. The crispness of the hops, the chilled bubbles hitting my tongue and bursting in my mouth, refreshed me like a cold shower after a day at the beach. The second the alcohol hit my bloodstream and rocketed to my brain, I was giddy and lightheaded.

Floating.

I didn't think that feeling could be beaten. I'd never found anything that had.

Until last night.

That feeling, euphoric and heady and exhilarating, had paled in comparison to what had flooded my veins as her lips touched mine after almost a month of holding back. The sweetness of her tongue hit me like a lightning storm on the ocean, her unique current surging through me, bringing me back to life, and to my senses.

If anyone had asked me a month ago whether I thought it was possible to fall more in love with Kit than I already was, I'd have answered with a resounding fuck, no. If anyone had asked me whether I'd manage a month without touching her, kissing her, tasting her, I'd have laughed all the way to the bank, having placed a very hefty bet against it.

But I had.

When Cooper and Freddie had pointed out the error of my ways, forcing me to listen to a few hard truths, I'd formulated the beginnings of a plan. Kit wanted us to meet under more normal circumstances, and what was more normal than Friday night cocktails at a busy New York bar?

The night was supposed to go on from there, a night of partying and fun and laughter. But seeing the tears roll down her creamy cheeks broke my bruised heart in half, and all I wanted to do was scoop her up, take her home, and kiss her until it was better. Instead, I did the opposite. She'd asked for space, to build our foundations on more than sex, to be able to miss each other.

I was renewed with determination to give Kit what she'd

wanted, more than anything. Anything to stop the tears I'd caused. I was determined to respect her wishes, determined to show her how seriously I was taking her, even though I disagreed. I didn't think we needed time apart, didn't think we needed space, didn't want to miss her… and no sex? What the fuck was that about? Especially when our sex was more explosive than C-4.

I'd planned each date to remind her of how much we'd already experienced, of what we already meant to each other, but in the course of doing so, I'd inadvertently taught myself how much more there was for us. For our relationship.

It turns out, before Kit, I'd known nothing. Before her, I'd known nothing of building foundations. I'd known nothing of actual love; the love between a man and a woman, the depths of which was so scarily powerful it had knocked me on my ass and slapped me round the face.

But she'd known.

And as she'd proved to me time and again, she was smarter than I was.

I wasn't the same person I'd been a month ago. Then, I'd been happy. But in the space of four weeks, I'd become one of those annoying as fuck people with a perma-grin and cartoon hearts floating around their heads. The ones you wanted to punch on sight.

She'd been right, and I'd been wrong.

The foundations she'd wanted to build were now encased in reinforced concrete and sealed in tungsten that even the strongest C-4 couldn't break. In four weeks, I'd fallen harder, faster, indelibly, and there was no doubt whatsoever that she was it for me.

The One.

My endgame, my future. Bell's future, our future.

And now, here I was, in the back of the car, en route to collect her for a night away. The penetrating ache which had been present in my chest since I'd dropped her home ten hours ago was lessening with each mile the car ate up, but wouldn't be totally gone until she was in my arms, where she'd be for at least the next thirty-six hours.

I'd booked a two-bedroom suite at our destination, though after last night, I doubted we'd be using more than one bedroom. Or maybe we would, but only on a quest to fuck on every single available surface. We had a month to make up for, and after *that* kiss, I didn't intend to waste any time.

There was one stop to make first.

It was a stop I'd been planning for weeks, and one I was more excited about her experiencing than the prospect of getting her naked. A very close second, anyway.

I hopped out as the car stopped by Payton's apartment, the front door opening before I'd had a chance to run up the steps. My heart pounded hard as she came into view, halting as she saw me. Her hair flowed in the huge waves I'd become addicted to, addicted to running my fingers through, addicted to wrapping my fists around.

The night of the gala, she'd looked fucking blindingly beautiful, so unbelievably stunning; but now, standing in front of me wearing a pair of skinny jeans, sneakers, and a pale grey t-shirt with the word *heartbreaker* embroidered in red across her left breast, she was like nothing else. My own heart was testament to that truth. She *was* goddamn heart-breaking.

She was perfection.

And she was mine.

"Good morning." Her smile was brighter than the sun.

I took the last two steps in one, standing in front of her, level with her warm, chocolate eye line. I greeted her with a kiss, taking her mouth, cushioning my lips to hers until she opened up for me and I took her tongue too; the faint taste of toothpaste on her breath.

I moved away before I got carried away. "We have more

time for that later." Easing her bag from her shoulder, I slung it over mine and held my hand out. "Come on."

I led her to the car, opening the door and she jumped in, me following after putting her bag in the trunk next to mine. The car swept us away as soon as the door slammed, heading for the first stage of our journey.

"Oh my God, where are we going?" Her excited face spun round to meet mine as we stopped in front of the jet-black Sikorsky S-92 helicopter Rafe, Penn, and I jointly owned – our logo outlined on the tail. "Are we going in that?"

I stole the quickest of kisses, although she was staring hard at the chopper. "We are. Come on, hurry up."

She scooted out when the door was opened for her, not bothering to wait for me before rushing forward. She was just about to step up into the cabin, when her hand paused on the rail. "You're not flying it are you?"

"Fuck no, that's Mike's job," I laughed loudly, nodding to our pilot, "so you can remove the look of abject horror and sit your ass down, young lady."

She took a place by the window and I took position opposite her. I could have sat next to her, but I didn't want to miss a second of her face as we flew away from the city. The sky was so blue and clear, I suddenly wished I'd added in time to give her an aerial tour of Manhattan, but we were under constraints.

After our bags were loaded, the twin engines started up, the rotors whirring loudly. I placed headphones over her ears before putting on my own.

"Speak to me though these. Can you hear me?"

She nodded but her eyes were glued to the view as we rose up from the heliport, huge concentric circles breaking the Hudson's calm water underneath us from the enormous blades slicing the air. She gripped the arm rest from the sharp left turn we made, taking us off to the west, for the next stop.

"Holy shit, the view is amazing! Are we doing a flyover?"

I shook my head, "No, but we'll come one evening and do a proper circuit."

Her face dropped slightly. "Oh, where are we going?"

I leaned forward, taking hold of her hands in mine, kissing each fingertip. "You'll see soon enough."

Twenty minutes later, we dropped onto the helipad at Teterboro, where a golf buggy was waiting to whisk us safely across the tarmac, pulling up in front of a black plane with the exact detailing the helicopter had, a more recent purchase of The Tuesday Club LLC.

I couldn't match the width of her grin. "Murray! Where are we going?"

"Kit Isobel Hawkes, you should know by now I don't ruin my surprises."

She shook her head, but her eyes glittered with amusement, and she ran to it as she had the helicopter.

"Good morning, ma'am, Mr. Williams." Bryan, our steward, was waiting as the bottom of the steps.

I shook his hand. "Hi, mate, how's everything looking?"

"Everything's good. Captain Niven says it'll be a quick and easy flight."

I winked at Kit. "That's good to hear."

Motioning for her to walk up the steps, I followed. She sat down silently and I knew from the light furrowing between her eyebrows she was trying to figure out where we were going. An hour and fifteen minutes later, she spied the globally recognizable landmarks of the Washington Monument, the glistening water of the Lincoln Memorial Reflecting Pool, The Capitol, and The White House.

"We're going to DC?"

I nodded. "We are."

"Oh cool. I haven't been here for ages!" Her eyes sparkled at me before she turned back to the view.

I chuckled so quietly she wouldn't hear. She still had no

idea what we were doing. She'd guessed incorrectly twenty seven times. She was none the wiser as our car drove through downtown DC, along Pennsylvania Avenue - where the blossoms were well past their peak but still in impressive bloom - down toward the Smithsonian, then round The Capitol and the Library of Congress, until we reached our destination.

The huge sign outside the white, mausoleum style building of The Folger Shakespeare Library stopped her guessing.

"Here?" Her head flicked between the sign and me. "Seriously? You've really brought me here?"

"I really have." Since she'd told me about the research role she'd accepted at Columbia, the one which focused on Shakespeare and his influences, I knew I'd be bringing her here as one of our dates because I'd been planning on bringing her here since our very first walk in the park.

She launched herself at me, flying into my lap, her lips landing with precision accuracy on mine as though we'd practiced it thousands of times, which I had no objection to.

Her excitement at getting inside meant I had less of a kiss than I wanted. "Thank you, thank you. This is an incredible surprise!"

Our driver opened the door and we were greeted by Quincy Philips, the rotund, studious looking gentleman curator and Shakespearean expert I'd been chatting to over the past few weeks.

He peered at us over the top of his thick rimmed bifocals. "Hello, Mr. Williams, Ms. Hawkes."

I shook his outstretched hand, the formality between us hadn't dropped once in the time we'd been conversing, and seeing him, I understood why.

"Mr. Philips, thank you so much for accommodating us this morning. It's much appreciated and very kind of you to arrange this for us."

I wasn't about to bring up the six figure donation I'd gifted in order to make this morning happen. Quincy Philips drove a harder bargain than I did, and more than once during negotiations I'd been tempted to offer him a job, although I doubted anything would part him from his beloved manuscripts.

"Please, please, do follow me."

If Christmas had come early for Kit, then Quincy Philips was her Santa Claus, and she trotted off after him, glancing back at me occasionally to check I was behind her, which I was, staring at her ass. I was still there as we entered the building, with a vast oak paneled entrance, and ceilings so high they could have stacked all the books on end and they probably wouldn't have reached.

Her neck craned as she read each Shakespeare inscription carved into the walls, and Quincy Philips began his detailed tour, holding her rapt attention. I doubted he'd ever had anyone on a tour who was as eager about Shakespeare as Kit was.

I tried to stick with them, tried to listen to what he was saying, but Shakespeare and I had never seen eye to eye, and at some point I fell far enough behind that I felt it was acceptable to sit down to make some calls, catch up on work, send some emails, and check in with my portfolios while the markets were closed for the weekend.

An hour later, I wandered off in the direction they'd gone. My sizeable contribution had bought a 'before hours' tour, which meant the only people in the building were employees of the Folger, and there were few enough around that my footsteps echoed as I walked. It also meant I could find them easier than I would have been able to, as I simply followed the sounds of Quincy Philips' exaggerated whispers.

I found them leaving an enormous cathedral style room, Kit waiting patiently as he opened a thick oak door marked

PRIVATE, with a bunch of keys that easily weighed a couple of pounds with how many there were on it.

"Hey," I kissed her head. "Enjoying yourself?"

"It's incredible. I've never experienced anything like it, nor met anyone who knows as much about Shakespeare as Quincy does. It's unbelievable."

Quincy, eh?

Quincy's cheeks turned a distinct shade of pink. Looks like I wasn't the only one smitten by Kit Isobel Hawkes.

Cool air rushed out as the door opened and he guided us down a narrow set of steps into a dark-ish room. Rows and rows of shelves lined the walls, reminding me of the wine cellar at Rafe's Hampton's house. Except instead of wine, the walls were filled with books. Along the far end were glass rooms, toward which we were walking.

Quincy Philips stopped outside one. "Mr. Williams, if you don't mind waiting here, there isn't enough space for three of us."

"Not at all." I was merely the spectator to Kit's show today, and all I cared about was making her happy, making sure she was having the best experience possible.

He held the door open for her and she stepped inside, closing the door behind both of them, and pushed a large green button on the wall I hadn't noticed before. A whoosh of air sounded around me. I rammed my hands into my pockets, tipping back on my heels as I watched him hand her a pair of white gloves then open a glass drawer containing a thick, ancient book which he lifted out and placed on the illuminated counter.

From the way her jaw dropped and her eyes widened, I hazarded a guess this was an original Shakespeare manuscript. The tightening in my chest coincided with the lump forming in my throat, one I was finding hard to swallow. The level of happiness I saw on her face matched the one I felt every day, and I'd been responsible for it.

I'd made her smile, I'd made her happy.

And fuck me, but if I hadn't been head over heels in love with her this morning, I was now. Cupid hit me with his arrow square between the eyes, and another one in the heart for good measure.

My stomach was rumbling by the time an alarm buzzed on the door, alerting them to get out of the room and marking the end of the tour. The three of us walked up to the daylight and outside, where the car was waiting for us.

"I can't thank you enough for this, Quincy. It was incredible." She wrapped him in a hug.

His cheeks flushed again. "You're welcome, Kit. Please do call me if you need anything for your course, or would like to come back and visit. It's open to you any time."

I was offered his hand. "Mr. Williams, thank you so much for contacting me."

"You're welcome. And thank you for organizing this morning. I can confidently say she's had a brilliant time."

He waved us off as we got into the car and she turned, her hands cupping my face and pulling me in for a kiss I had no objection to. Shifting her into my lap, my hands stilled at the base of her neck and I gave her the kiss she was asking for.

I dragged my lips away before she straddled me. Our driver might be paid a lot for discretion, but I had no intention of fucking her in the back of the car while he waited for instructions on where to go next.

"I take it you had fun," I laughed against her lips.

She reared back to answer me. "I can't believe you did that for me. It was the sweetest, most incredible gift I've ever had. I don't know how to thank you."

"You don't have to thank me; your happiness is all I need." I meant it. I didn't want or need thanks. Folding her in my arms, I kissed her nose. "Are you hungry?"

Her brown eyes flashed golden before darkening with

arousal, which had an immediate effect on my dick. "I am, but not for food."

"Sit there, and don't move." She giggled loudly as I shoved her off my lap and lowered the privacy screen to speak to the driver. "Can you take us to the hotel please?"

"Yes, sir. Mandarin Oriental?"

"Yes."

I raised the privacy screen but kept her on the other side of the car, allowing no contact. I was at the point where my dick was almost painful with how hard it was from the slightest touch from her. It was the longest ten minutes of my life before we eventually pulled up outside. The concierge swept us through the lobby to The Presidential Suite, our bags following closely behind on a porter guided trolley.

I peeled off a considerable number of notes, handing them to him before he insisted on giving us the guided tour of the suite. I'd spent enough time here that I already knew it, and from the look Kit was giving me, she definitely didn't care.

The door closed behind him and I turned to find her walking backward, shedding her clothes with every step she took. Her sneakers were kicked off one by one, landing... somewhere... I didn't see, my eyes glued to hers.

She hit the back of the long couch, using the arm to prop her up as she eased off her jeans. And then she was standing in front of me, only the sheerest underwear covering her; a sight I'd been dreaming about for a month. She reached behind her.

"Stop." My fists clenched. I wanted to savor this moment, and *I* wanted to unwrap the rest of her.

Her hands dropped down slowly, her expression glassy with equal amounts of arousal and goading, the rise and fall of her chest quickening as I stepped closer to her. Her soft skin was warm under my touch as my hands swept across her body, reminding me of everything I'd missed; every curve and sinew. They ran over the roundness of her perfect ass while my tongue rediscovered the depth of her belly button, my lips reliving the swell of her incredible breasts and the feel of her nipple tightening as I teased it between my teeth.

My arms wrapped round her. "Fuck, I've missed you. I missed you so much."

She fisted my hair, pulling me back, "I need you naked, now."

I didn't need asking twice. My dick almost sighed in relief as it was freed from the painful constraints of my jeans, surging toward Kit who was still perched on the arm of the couch.

"Fuck me, Murray. I need you to fuck me hard."

Jesus Christ. This was going to be over in seconds. The plans I had to take my time devouring her would have to wait.

I stood back; watching her watch me as I slowly stroked my cock, trying to regain a semblance of control. I wanted this to be good for her, but I was too jacked up from a month of not being near her to have any kind staying power.

And she could tell.

Slowly licking her lips, her fingers eased off her panties, touching herself where I wanted to touch, snapping my composure. In one swift movement, I hoisted her up and impaled her, both of us crying out loudly.

I was finally home.

Every second I'd been away from her was worth it to be here, in this moment, my heart on the brink of bursting.

"Jesus, fuck." Her walls were already clenching against me, her tits almost touching my lips as her back arched and I let my breathing relax. "Fuck. You feel incredible. You're incredible. Have you missed this like I've missed you?

Her eyes reached mine, dark and hooded, filled with lust and hunger, and love. "More. I've missed you more."

"Not possible." I wrapped her legs around my waist, rolling my hips to bury myself deeper. "It's not possible to miss anything as much as I've missed you."

A low moan rumbled through the air that might have come from her, but may have come from me. It was impossible to tell because we'd merged into one, joined in every possible way. She rocked against me, taking me deeper again and again, each movement adding to the pressure hardening my balls until I was on borrowed time before I exploded inside her.

She snared my lips with hers, her fingers threading through my hair, holding on like she never intended to let me go. Her thighs tightened, the quivering increasing which I knew signaled the beginning of the end. There was no space between us for me to reach her clit, instead I ground hard against her, swallowing a moan which shot straight down my spine and detonated in my balls.

Her orgasm hit as mine did, gripping me so hard I wasn't sure I'd stay conscious as she eked out every last drop of cum I had to give her. She collapsed onto my chest, both of us falling back onto the couch with a thud and a giggle, setting off a full blown belly laugh neither of us could stop, lightening the air and banishing any tension.

We lay there until a loud rumbling broke the silence. Her hand flew to her stomach.

"Sounds like someone needs feeding…" I kissed her head, easing out of her, immediately missing the warmth.

Half an hour later, the porter arrived with our order, leaving it on the dining room table. I signed the check and he left, Kit diving into a fully loaded burger that looked bigger than her head before the door closed behind him. Her bathrobe had loosened slightly, her cheeks were flushed, her hair mussed, and a dollop of mustard was sliding down her chin. She'd never looked more beautiful, and my chest swelled so big it was suddenly hard to breathe.

"I love you. I love you so fucking much," I blurted out, dropping to the floor by the side of her seat, demanding her attention. Her burger stopped midway to her mouth as I took a beat to gather my racing thoughts. "Thank you. Thank you for giving me this time. Thank you for believing in me, and in us. I didn't know what it meant or what you were asking of me when you said you wanted space, and you were right. We did need this time. I needed this time. I didn't know it, but you did, and I hope you realize what you've done, because I've fallen so in love with you I'll never find my way out."

She slowly put down the burger, her eyes brimming with emotion which soon spilled over. Picking up the napkin from her lap, she wiped her fingers then her nose, before she cupped my cheek with a shaking hand, the sensation sending a cascade of goosebumps over my skin.

But I wasn't done; I needed to say my piece before she could. I wanted her to hear my words, unprompted by anything she said.

"Do you remember what you said to me on our first walk together?" I waited, lacing my fingers with hers, but the words which were seared on my heart never came. "That I was chosen to be Bell's daddy?" She nodded slightly as her memory jogged. "I believe that. I loved my life, but until Bell came into it, I realized it didn't have meaning. I was flitting from girl to girl, adding more money onto my already obscene piles. But when you turned up, I knew the reason she came into my life was to help me find you, and with you came purpose. My purpose is to make you happy."

She sniffed loudly but it didn't stop the tears running down her cheeks.

"I know I come as a package deal, so I'm not going to ask you to move in with me again. When you're ready, you say the word and I'll have movers organized. I'll wait as long as you need because I know it'll happen. I *am* going to marry you and we *are* going to spend forever together, building our little family."

I sat back on my haunches, keeping hold of her hand with mine, waiting until she was ready to say something, anything.

She turned her body to face mine, squeezing her fingers around mine. "I've never not loved you, you know. I've never not wanted you. I just wanted to give us a chance at *more*, make us the strongest we could be."

I kissed her knuckles that were linked with mine. "I know."

"Murray, I love you so much. I think I've loved you since the first day I saw you. I know I've wanted you since that first day, and I know I'll always want you. Thank you for giving me this time, and for giving us a chance." She moved to the edge of her chair, her chin tipping down and meeting me for a kiss. "When you're ready to ask me to marry you, I'll say yes. And we'll add to our family of you, me, Bell, and Barc."

Fireworks went off; Catherine Wheels spinning in my chest, rockets and fountains and poppers exploding inside me until I thought I might burst.

She was the love of my life, and one day, she was going to be my wife, the mother of my children, the current one of which we had an overnight pass for.

We had a month to make up for.

She went back to her burger, side eyeing me as she read my mind, "Come on, eat up. We're going in for round two. We have one night to ourselves and then we need to get back to our girl. I've missed her too."

Our girl. I smirked, stealing a fry as I reached across the table for mine.

We'd need all the energy we could get.

I wasn't planning to sleep.

EPILOGUE

Murray

Nine months later.

I crept back into bed, making sure I didn't disturb the birthday girl sound asleep next to me. I'd been up for an hour getting everything ready, ensuring today would be perfect. Heart shaped balloons were floating all over the apartment for Valentine's Day, but our bedroom was decorated for a birthday. Two birthdays.

I silently placed the paper and coffee on her side of our bed, knowing she would be waking up very soon.

Our bed. Not my bed. *Our* bed.

Four months after we'd returned from DC, she'd moved in. During that time, we'd kept up our dates, each one different, each one including very active sleepovers. We hadn't seen each other every day, but the days we did we made the most of. Sometimes it included our family of four, and sometimes it was just the two of us. Gradually, the dates became more frequent, and the day we realized she had more stuff here than at her apartment was the day she stopped going back.

We hired a new nanny, but she only worked three days a week, and nights were ours where we cherished our routine of Bell's bath and bedtime, followed by a dinner she cooked or I ordered in.

"Mama Ma Ma Mama!" Our daughter's very vocal demands for her mother's attention echoed over the monitor, right on schedule.

I rolled over and kissed Kit's stirring form, "Happy Birthday, darling. I'll get her. There's coffee on the nightstand waiting for you."

I found Bell standing in her crib, smiling with her hands outstretched as I walked in and opened the blinds. "Happy Birthday, little girl. Let's get you dressed and give mummy enough time to find what we've left her shall we?"

"Dada!" she agreed.

I lifted her out, removing her sleepsuit and diaper, letting her wander around naked while I fixed her bottle and gathered up the birthday outfit Kit had picked out for her, the first of many. This afternoon we were having a little birthday party for Bell - if eight kids and thirteen adults, including my parents, Kit's parents, Payton and the boys, was little.

Everyone was due to arrive at three p.m. sharp, which gave us plenty of time for the rest of the morning, which I'd planned for a much more exclusive group; me, Kit, Bell, and Barclay.

I finished dressing Bell and handed her the cooling bottle of milk, which she carried through with both hands, waddling alongside Barclay who rarely left her side, propping her up when she toppled over. She'd only been walking a few weeks, and he'd been next to her for every step.

I stopped us all by the door for our bedroom, watching Kit as she stared down at the crossword, her entire body still.

"You started it without me," I said softly. "You want to read one out?"

She glanced up, tears streaming down her face. "Together forever. Fourteen letters."

I put Bell down and she toddled over to the side of the bed, arms outstretched for Kit.

"Hello, baby," she sniffed through her smile. "Happy Birthday, little girl."

I followed Bell's path, kneeling in front of them at her side.

"Together forever, huh. Fourteen letters?"

She nodded, silently, the tears starting up again.

I took her hand and slowly uncurled her fingers. One for each letter. "Will, four. You, three. Marry, five. Me, two."

She stared at me as I reached into my pocket, pulling out the black velvet box I'd kept locked in my vault since shortly after we'd returned from DC, and placed it on her knees, on top of the comforter. "Will you marry me? Fourteen letters."

She opened the box; the Table cut diamond catching the light as she did. It wasn't as sparkly as I'd wanted, but I'd spent weeks trying to find an antique from the Elizabethan era, and when I couldn't, I'd had a replica made. Five carats sitting in a thick gold band, twisted with intricate sapphire inlays, original, and perfectly her.

I swiped away another tear, amusement twitching the corner of my mouth "Is it really that terrible an idea?"

"No." She shook her head. "I mean, yes!" she cried. "Yes, of course I'll marry you!"

I leaned forward, my lips pressing hard against hers, tasting the salt of her tears and feeling like I could breathe again for the first time since I'd woken up.

I got to my feet, running to my dressing room to retrieve something just as precious.

"And now here's your birthday present." I handed over a large orange and black carrier bag.

She undid the ribbon from the handle, opening it and lifted out a box, easing another ribbon free and handing it to Bell to play with before opening the box and ripping through the tissue paper.

She gasped, her hands running over the smooth leather, the color of her eyes. Her fingers traced the embossed initials I'd added.

K.I.H.

"For your first day, Professor Hawkes."

Tomorrow, Kit would be holding her first official class – part of a series on classic literature and modern adolescence, or something – and the first lecture was focused on Shakespeare. In the course of pulling the material together, Quincy Philips had been more than helpful, giving her advice and access to anything she needed. She'd even visited him at the Folger a few times, occasions we always took advantage of with an overnight stay.

"Murray, this is beautiful." The diamond on her left hand caught the light as she stroked the leather and I wasn't sure which one she was referring to, or maybe it was both.

I didn't care. She'd agreed to be mine, forever, in a way that everyone would know.

There was just one more thing I wanted.

"You'll find something else inside if you open it."

She flicked the clasp, lifting out the thick cream envelope with her name on it. Easing her thumb under the tab, she ripped it and pulled out the contents, unfolding it. Her hand shot up to cover her mouth, the tears flowing once again as she looked up at me.

I stroked her cheek. "You've known her exactly five days less than me. She might not be your daughter biologically, but you're her mother in every way that counts, as much as

I'm her father, and you love her just the same, so we wanted to make it officially official."

She put down the adoption papers and scooped Bell up in a hug, throwing her in the air until she squealed with delight, Barclay jumping on the bed to join in.

"Yes, Arabella Grace Valentine Williams! I'd be delighted to officially be your mommy."

She pulled her in, the raspberries she blew on Bell's cheek making her squeal even louder, and then her hand found mine as our eyes met over our daughter's head.

"Thank you. Thank you for giving her to me, making her mine. I love you so much. Both of you."

I answered her with a kiss, because I didn't have the words to articulate what I wanted to.

But the kiss said everything I needed.

The kiss of our future, and we stayed like that until both Bell and Barclay reminded us loudly that they were there too.

The four of us.

Our perfect family.

THE END

ACKNOWLEDGMENTS

My readers and for those who've become book friends - you know who you are - this past year has been so immense and you've been with me every step and welcomed more along the way. THANK YOU! You guys are THE BEST. You honestly make my days, every day. I love love getting your DMs, emails and messages, please keep them coming and I'll keep giving these boys to you for as long as you want them.

For all my BFFs - seriously, you guys make parenting look easy and it's a testament to how incredible you are. I am in awe.

And for *my* Murray. Even though this is still a secret, this is for you 🤍.

ABOUT THE AUTHOR

Lulu is currently navigating her way around Romance Land one HEA at a time, and trying to figure out which social media platform she needs to post to.

She'd love to hear from you, hear your thoughts, your opinions and most of all how much you love the boys (or not…). So, please message her on any of the below (plus TikTok) at @lulumoorebooks

ALSO BY LULU MOORE

The New York Players

Jasper

Cooper

Drew

Felix

Huck will return soon

The Tuesday Club

The Secret

The Suit - released summer 2022

COMING SOON

THE SUIT

Have you ever met someone who makes your blood boil simply by existing?

Make your renowned icy cool demeanor flare up uncharacteristically?

Your body sense them like an errant nettle patch as soon as they come within a hundred feet?

Skin prickle? Teeth grind? Tension build?

Because that's exactly what happens when *she* walks into any room.

My name is Rafe Latham and that someone, that one with the berry red lips I want to throttle to within an inch of her life, is currently standing right in front of me, screaming at the top of her lungs.

The she-devil herself.

Beulah Holmes.

THE
TUESDAY
CLUB

Printed in Great Britain
by Amazon

37878746R00215